About the Authors

Kate Hardy has bee[...] [...] toddler. When she is [...] theatre, live music, ba[...] her husband, studen[...] Norwich, England. Y[...] www.katehardy.com

Christy Jeffries graduated from the University of California, Irvine and received her Juris Doctor from California Western School of Law. But drafting court documents and working in law enforcement was merely an apprenticeship for her current career in the relentless field of motherhood and romance writing. She lives in Southern California with her patient husband, two energetic sons, and one sassy grandmother. Follow her on Facebook or visit her website at www.christyjeffries.com

USA Today bestselling author **Teri Wilson** writes heartwarming romance with a touch of whimsy. Three of Teri's books have been adapted into Hallmark Channel Original Movies, including *Unleashing Mr Darcy, The Art Of Us* and *Northern Lights of Christmas*, based on her book *Sleigh Bell Sweethearts*. She is also a recipient of the prestigious *RITA*® Award for excellence in romantic fiction for her novel *The Bachelor's Baby Surprise*.

Affairs of the Heart

Affairs of the Heart:
An Affair of Consequence

KATE HARDY

CHRISTY JEFFRIES

TERI WILSON

MILLS & BOON

First Published in Great Britain 2021
By Mills & Boon, an imprint of HarperCollins*Publishers,* Ltd
1 London Bridge Street, London, SE1 9GF

www.harpercollins.co.uk

HarperCollins*Publishers*
1st Floor, Watermarque Building,
Ringsend Road, Dublin 4, Ireland

AFFAIRS OF THE HEART: AN AFFAIR OF CONSEQUENCE
© 2021 Harlequin Books S.A.

A Baby to Heal Their Hearts © 2015 Pamela Brooks
From Dare to Due Date © 2016 Christy Jeffries
The Bachelor's Baby Surprise © 2018 Teri Wilson

ISBN: 978-0-263-30056-7

MIX
Paper from
responsible sources
FSC™ C007454

This book is produced from independently certified FSC™ paper
to ensure responsible forest management.

For more information visit: www.harpercollins.co.uk/green

Printed and bound in Spain
by CPI, Barcelona

A BABY TO HEAL
THEIR HEARTS

KATE HARDY

**To C.C. Coburn and Cathleen Ross
—hope you enjoy Herod!**

CHAPTER ONE

'SHE'S A BONNY LASS, our Bailey,' Archie said.

Jared's heart sank at the expression on the coach's face. Clearly Archie had taken a fancy to the researcher. And Jared had a nasty feeling that this might be a case of the coach's libido taking over from his common sense.

Allegedly, this 'bonny lass' researcher had a system that could reduce soft-tissue injuries among the players. So far, so good—but the figures being bandied about were crazy. In Jared's experience, when something sounded too good to be true, it usually was. And he could really do without some pretty, flaky girl distracting the players and getting in the way when he needed to treat them. Especially when he'd only just started his new job as the doctor to the youth team of a premiership division football club.

He'd been here before, when a manager's or player's head had been turned by a pretty girl, and the outcome was always messy. Worse still, it tended to have an impact on the rest of the team. With a bunch of teenage lads, this could get very messy indeed.

But he kept his thoughts to himself and gave the coach a polite smile. 'That's nice.'

Hopefully this Bailey woman would get bored quickly, or her system would be debunked, and they could go back to a more sensible way of preventing soft-tissue injuries—like sport-specific training, after he'd assessed each of the players and taken a proper medical history.

In the meantime, he'd have to grit his teeth and be as polite and as neutral as possible.

'Bailey—oh, good, you're here. Come and meet Jared Fraser, the new team doctor,' Archie McLennan called over from the side of the football pitch as Bailey walked through the players' tunnel.

Bailey smiled at the youth team's coach, but she made sure that she stood just far enough away so that Archie couldn't put his arm round her shoulders. She liked him very much as a colleague—he was at least prepared to listen to new ideas and he'd been more than fair with her on the research project so far— but she really wasn't in the market for a relationship.

Particularly with someone who was recently divorced and with a lifestyle that really didn't work for her; that was just setting things up to fail. And Bailey had failed quite enough in her relationships, thank you very much. She wanted life to be simple in the future—full of her family, her friends and her work, and that was enough for her. She didn't need anything more.

'Jared, this is Bailey Randall—the doctor whose research project I was telling you about,' Archie said.

For a moment, Jared looked as if he'd seen a ghost. Then he seemed to pull himself together and gave her a brief nod of acknowledgement. 'Dr Randall.'

But he didn't smile at her. Did he not approve of women being involved with a football team? Was he not good at social skills? Or—given that his accent was quite distinctive—was he just living up to the stereotype of the slightly dour, strong-and-silent Scotsman?

It was a shame, because he had the most gorgeous eyes. A deep, intense blue—the colour of a bluebell carpet. If he smiled, she'd just bet his eyes would have an irresistible twinkle.

Which was crazy. Since when did she think so fancifully? Bluebells, indeed.

'Pleased to meet you,' she said, giving him her brightest smile, and held her hand out for him to shake.

He gave another brief inclination of his head and shook her hand. His grip was firm, brief and very businesslike. He still didn't smile, though. Or say any kind of social pleasantry.

Oh, well. It wasn't as if she'd need to have that much to do with him, was it? Her project—to test a monitoring system to see if it could help to reduce the number of soft-tissue injuries in the team—had been agreed by the football club's chair of directors. She'd been working with Archie, the youth team coach, at training sessions and on match days when they played at home, and so far the system's results were proving very interesting indeed.

'Hey, Bailey.' John, one of the players, came over to the side and high-fived her.

'Hey, John. How's the ankle?' she asked.

'It's holding up, thanks to you,' he said with a smile.

'And you're still wearing that support?'

He nodded. 'And I'm doing the wobble-board exercises, like you showed me last time,' he said.

'Good.'

'Bailey helped out on a couple of sessions when she was here and your predecessor called in sick,' Archie told Jared. 'John sprained his ankle a few weeks back.'

'Sprained ankles are the most common injury in football,' Bailey said, just so Jared Fraser would know that she did actually understand the situation—maybe he was the dinosaur kind of man who thought that women knew next to nothing about sport. 'He was running when he hit a bump in the field, the sole of his foot rolled under and the movement damaged the ligaments on the outside of his ankle.' She shrugged. 'The wobble-board training we've been doing reduces the risk of him damaging his ankle again.'

Jared gave her another of those brief nods, but otherwise he was completely impassive.

Oh, great. How on earth was he going to connect with the players? Or maybe he was better at communicating when he was in work mode, being a doctor. She certainly hoped so, because the boys were still young enough to need encouragement and support; they weren't likely to respond to dourness.

'I ought to give you each other's mobile phone numbers and email addresses and what have you— in case you need to discuss anything,' Archie said.

'I doubt we will,' Jared said, 'but fine.'

Oh, what was *the guy's problem?* She itched to shake him, but that wouldn't be professional. Particularly in front of the youth team. Doctors, coaches and managers were supposed to present a united front. OK, so strictly speaking she didn't work for the football club—she was here purely as a researcher—but she still needed to be professional. 'Give me your number,' she said, 'and I'll text you with my email address so you have all my details.'

Once that was sorted out, she took her laptop out of its case. 'OK, guys, you know the drill. Let's go.' As the players lined up, she switched on her laptop, then called each team member by name and handed him a monitor with a chest strap, checking each one in with the laptop as she went.

'So what exactly is this system?' Jared asked when the players had filed onto the field to warm up. 'Some kind of glorified pedometer, like those expensive wristband gadgets that tell people they woke up three times during the night, but don't actually tell them why they woke up or what they can do about it?'

He sounded downright hostile. *What was his problem?* she thought again. But she gritted her teeth and tried her best to be polite. 'It does measure the number of steps the players take, yes,' she said, 'but it also monitors their average speed, the average steps they take per game, their heart rate average and maximum, and their VO2.' VO2 measured the amount of oxygen used by the body to convert the energy from food into adenosine triphosphate; the higher the VO2 max, the higher the athlete's level of fitness.

He scoffed. 'How on earth can you measure VO2 properly without hooking someone up to a system with a mask?'

'It's an estimate,' she admitted, 'but this system is a lot more than just a "glorified pedometer".' She put exaggerated quotes round the phrase with her fingers, just to make the point that she wasn't impressed by his assessment. Sure, once he knew what the system did and how it worked, she'd be happy to listen to him and to any suggestions he might have for improving it. But right now he was speaking from a position of being totally uninformed, so how could his opinion be in the least bit valid?

'The point is,' she said, 'to look at reducing the number of soft-tissue injuries. That means the players get more time to train and play, and they spend less time recovering from injuries. This particular system has been tested with a rugby team and it reduced their soft-tissue injury rate by seventy per cent, and my boss thinks it's worth giving it a try on other sports.' She gave him a grim smile. 'Just so you know, I'm not trying to put you out of a job. If anything, I'm trying to make your life easier by taking out the small, time-consuming stuff.'

'And you're actually a qualified doctor?' he asked, sounding sceptical.

Give me strength, Bailey thought, but she gave him another polite smile. 'Remind me to bring my degree certificate in with me next time,' she said. 'Or you can look me up on the Internet, if you're that fussed. I run sports medicine clinics three days a week at the London Victoria, so you'll find me listed in the department there, and I spend the other two working days each week on a research project.'

'So you're using this system of yours with other teams as well?' he asked.

'No—this is the only team I'm working with, and I only do one research project at a time. My last one was preventative medicine,' she explained. 'Basically I worked with patients who had high blood pressure.

The aim was to help them to lose weight and maintain lean muscle mass, and that reduced both their blood pressure and their risk of cardiovascular incidents.' She couldn't resist adding, 'And by that I mean heart attacks and strokes.'

'Right.' Jared stared at Bailey. Archie had called her a 'bonny lass', but she was so much more than that. She was truly beautiful, with a heart-shaped face and huge brown eyes—emphasised by her elfin crop. She looked more like some glamorous Mediterranean princess than a doctor.

But, in Jared's experience, beautiful women spelled trouble and heartache. His ex, Sasha, had used her stunning looks to get her own way—and Jared had fallen for it hard enough to get very badly burned. Nowadays he was pretty much impervious to huge eyes and winsome smiles. But he'd already seen how Archie was following Bailey round like a lapdog; he had a nasty feeling that Bailey Randall had used her looks to get her own way with her ridiculous bit of computerised kit, the way Sasha always used her looks.

Still, at least this system of hers wasn't something that would actually hurt the players. It wouldn't be of much real use—like the pricey fitness wristbands he'd referred to earlier, it wouldn't give enough information about what was actually wrong or how to fix it—but it wouldn't do any real harm, either.

Jared spent the session on the side of the pitch, ready in case any of the players had an injury that needed treating. But there were no strains, sprains or anything more serious; and, at the other end of the scale, there wasn't even a bruise or a contusion.

Half a lifetime ago, he'd been one of them, he thought wryly. A young hopeful, planning a career in the sport and dreaming of playing for his country. He'd actually made it and played for the England under-nineteen squad, scoring several goals in international matches. But Bailey Randall's bit of kit wouldn't have done anything to save him from the knee injury in his final game—the tackle that had stopped his football career in its tracks. Jared had ended up pursuing his original plans instead, studying for his A-levels and following in the family tradition by taking a degree in medicine.

The lure of football had drawn Jared to work with a club as their team doctor, rather than working in a hospital or his parents' general practice. And he still enjoyed the highs and lows of the game, the camaraderie among the players and hearing the supporters roar their approval when a goal was scored.

At the end of the training session, Archie turned to Bailey. 'Over to you.'

Jared watched in sheer disbelief as Bailey proceeded to take the youth team through a series of yoga stretches and then breathing exercises.

What place did yoga have on a football pitch? In his experience, the players would do far better working on sport-specific training. As well as ball control, they needed to focus on muscular endurance and lower-body strength, and also work on explosive acceleration and short bursts of speed. If Archie wanted him to do it, Jared could design a training programme easily enough—either a warm-up routine that would work for the whole team, or some player-specific programmes to help deal with each player's weak spots—and it would do a lot more for the players' overall neuromuscular co-ordination than yoga would.

But having a go at Bailey Randall in front of the team wouldn't be professional, so Jared kept his mouth shut until the lads had gone for a shower and she was doing things on her laptop. Then he walked over to her and said, 'Can we have a quick word?'

She looked up from her laptop with an expression of surprise, but nodded. 'Sure.'

'What *exactly* does your box of tricks tell us?' he asked.

'It analyses each player's performance. For each player, I can show you a graph of his average performance over the last ten matches or training sessions, and how today's performance compares against that average.'

So far, so good. 'Which tells us what?'

'The system will pick up if a player is underperforming,' she said. 'Maybe he's coming down with a cold but isn't showing any symptoms yet—and if he's sick he's more at risk of sustaining injury and shouldn't be playing.'

He gave her a sceptical look. 'So you're telling me you can predict if a player's going to get a cough or a cold?'

'No, but I can predict the likelihood of the player sustaining an injury in his next match, based on his performance today and measured against an average of his last ten sessions.'

'Right.' Jared still wasn't totally convinced. And

then he tackled the subject that bothered him most about today's antics. 'And the yoga?'

'As a football team doctor—someone who's clearly specialised in sports medicine—you'd already know that dynamic stretches are more useful than static stretches.' She held his gaze. 'But if you want me to spell it out to prove that I know what I'm talking about, dynamic stretches means continuous movement. That promotes blood flow, strength and stability. It also means you can work on more than one muscle group at a time—so it's more functional, because it mimics what happens with everyday movements. And you only hold the stretch for a short period of time, so the muscle releases more effectively and you get a better range of movement with each repetition.' She raised her eyebrows, as if challenging him to call her on it. 'Happy?'

He nodded. She did at least know her stuff, then. Even if she was a bit misguided about the computer programme. 'So you're a qualified yoga teacher?'

'No. But a qualified teacher—the one who's taught me for the last five years—helped me put the routine together.'

'Right. And the breathing?'

She put her hands on her hips and gave him a hard stare. 'Oh, for goodness' sake! Are you going to quiz me on every aspect of this? Look, the project's already been approved by Mr Fincham.' The chairman of the club's board of directors. 'If you have a problem with it, then maybe you need to speak to him about it.'

'I just don't see what use yoga is going to be to a bunch of lads who need sport-specific training,' he said.

'"Lads" being the operative word,' she said. 'They're sixteen, seventeen—technically they're not quite adults, and most of their peers are either still in education or starting some kind of apprenticeship. I won't insult them by calling them children, because they're not, but they still have quite a lot of growing up to do. And, in the profession they've chosen, they're all very much in the public eye. The media hounds are just waiting to tear into the behaviour of overpaid footballers, whipping up a frenzy among their readers about how badly the boys behave.'

'That's true,' he said, 'but I still don't get what it has to do with yoga.'

'Discipline,' she said crisply.

'They already have the discipline of turning up for training and doing what Archie tells them to do.'

'Holding the yoga poses also takes discipline, and so does the breathing. So it's good practice and it helps to underline what Archie does with them. Plus it's good for helping to deal with stress,' she said.

That was the bit Jared really didn't buy into.

She clearly saw the scepticism in his expression, because she sighed. 'Look, if they get hassled by photographers or journalists or even just someone else in a club when they're out—someone who wants to prove himself as a big hero who can challenge a footballer and beat him up—then all they have to do is remember to breathe and it'll help them to take everything down a notch.'

'Hmm,' he said, still not convinced.

She threw her hands up in apparent disgust. 'You know what? You can think what you like, Dr Fraser. It's not going to make any difference to my research.

If you've got some good ideas for how the data can be used, or about different measurements that would be useful in analysing the team's performance, then I'd be very happy to listen. But if all you're going to do is moan and bitch, then please just go and find someone else to annoy, because I'm busy. Excuse me.'

Bailey Randall clearly didn't like it when someone actually questioned her. And she still hadn't convinced him of the benefits of her project. 'Of course you are,' he said, knowing how nasty it sounded but right at that moment not caring.

As he walked away, he was sure he heard her mutter, 'What an ass.'

She was entitled to her opinion. He wasn't very impressed by her, either. But they'd just have to make the best of it, for as long as it took for Archie and the team director to realise that her 'research' was all a load of hokum.

CHAPTER TWO

'HE'S IMPOSSIBLE. TALK about blinkered. And narrow-minded. And—and— Arrgh!' Bailey stabbed her fork into her cake in utter frustration.

To her dismay, Joni just laughed.

'You're my best friend,' Bailey reminded her. 'You're supposed to be supportive.'

'I am. Of course I am,' Joni soothed. 'But you're the queen of endorphins. You always see the best in people, and to see you having a hissy fit about someone—well, he's obviously made quite an impression on you.'

'And not a good one.' Bailey ate a forkful of cake and then rolled her eyes at the plate. 'Oh, come on. If I'm going to eat this stuff, it could at least reward me with a sugar rush.'

'Maybe it just makes you grumpy.'

Bailey narrowed her eyes at her best friend. 'Now you're laughing at me.'

Joni reached over the table and hugged her. 'I love you, and you're in an almighty strop. Which doesn't happen very often. This Jared Fraser guy has really rattled you.'

Bailey glowered. 'Honestly. He quizzed me on every single aspect of my project.'

'Which is better than just dismissing it.'

'He *did* dismiss it, actually. He thinks the players should be doing sport-specific training.'

Joni coughed. 'You're the sports medicine doctor, not me. And I seem to remember you saying something about sport-specific training being the most effective.'

'But it's not the only kind of training they should be doing,' Bailey said. 'Yoga means dynamic stretches, which are more effective than static ones. And there's the discipline of holding the pose and doing the breathing. It's really good for the boys, and it helps them to focus.'

'Maybe you should make Jared do the stuff with the boys,' Joni suggested. 'And you can make him do extra planks.'

'Don't tempt me.' Bailey ate more cake. 'Actually, Joni, that might be a good idea. He needs to chill out a bit. Downward dog and breathing—that would do the trick.'

'I'd love to be a fly on the wall when you suggest it to him,' Joni said.

'No, you wouldn't. You hate people fighting—and he really doesn't like me.'

'You don't like him, either,' Joni pointed out.

'Well, no. Because he's rude, arrogant and narrow-minded. With men like him around, I'm more than happy to stay single.'

They both knew that wasn't the real reason why Bailey was resolutely single. After her life had imploded two and a half years ago, her marriage had cracked beyond repair. And Bailey still wasn't ready to risk trying another relationship. She didn't know if she ever would be.

'I don't know what to say,' Joni said, giving her another hug, 'except I love you and I believe in you.'

'You, too,' Bailey said.

'And I worry about you. That you're lonely.'

'That's because you're all loved up. Which is just as it should be,' Bailey said, 'given that it's just under two months until you get married to Aaron. And he's a sweetie.'

'Even so, I worry about you, Bailey.'

'I'm fine,' Bailey said, forcing herself to smile. 'Just grumpy tonight. And don't breathe a word of this to my mum, or she'll say that I'm attracted to Jared Fraser and I'm in denial about it.'

'Are you?' Joni asked.

Bailey blew out a breath. 'You're about the only person who could get away with asking that. No. He might be nice looking if he smiled,' she said, 'and to be fair he does have nice eyes. The colour of bluebells. But even if he was as sweet as Aaron, I still wouldn't be interested. I'm fine exactly as I am. I don't need anyone to complicate my life.'

Her words were slightly hollow, and she was pretty sure that Joni would pick up on that. But to her relief Joni didn't push it any further, or comment on that stupid remark she'd made about bluebells.

She wasn't attracted to Jared Fraser. She wanted to give him a good shake and tell him to open his mind a bit.

And bluebells were out of the question.

* * *

Before the next match, Bailey had a meeting with Archie to discuss the latest results from her software. As she'd half expected, Jared was there. Still playing dour, strong and silent. Well, that was his problem. She had a job to do.

'Travis is underperforming,' she said, showing them the graph on her laptop screen. 'It might be that he's had too many late nights over the last week, or it might be that he's coming down with something—but I'd recommend that he doesn't play as part of the team today.'

'I've already assessed the squad this morning, and they're all perfectly fit,' Jared said.

'A player who's underperforming is at a greater risk of soft-tissue injury,' she reminded him.

'According to your theory. Which has yet to be proven, because if you pull a player off every time they do a few steps less per game, then of course he won't get a soft-tissue injury, because he won't actually be playing. And if you follow that through every time, you'll end up with a really tiny pool of players. And the rest of them won't have had enough practice to help them improve their skills.'

'If they're off for weeks with an injury, that's not going to help them improve their skills, either,' she pointed out.

'Travis is fine.' He folded his arms. 'You're making a fuss over nothing.'

'Travis *isn't* fine.' She mirrored his defensive stance. 'But it isn't our call. It's Archie's.'

'Fine,' Jared said.

Archie looked at them both and sighed. 'I'll have a word with the lad.'

Clearly Travis was desperate to play, because Archie came back to tell them that the boy was in the team.

If Jared said 'Told you so', she might just punch him.

He didn't. But it was written all over his face.

Cross, Bailey sat on the bench at the side of the pitch and texted her best friend: Jared Fraser has to be the most smug, self-satisfied man in the universe.

A few seconds later, her phone beeped. She glanced at the screen, expecting Joni to have sent her a chin-up-and-rise-above-it type of message, and was surprised to see that the message was from Jared Fraser. Why would he be texting her? He was sitting less than six feet away from her. He could lean across and talk to her. He didn't need to resort to texting.

Curious, she opened the message. Herod? What?

Don't understand, she texted back. Ridiculous man. What was he on about?

Her phone beeped a few seconds later. Your message: <<Herod Fraser has to be the most smug, self-satisfied man in the universe.>>

Then she realised exactly what had just happened. Oh, no.

She'd been typing so fast that she obviously hadn't noticed her phone autocorrecting 'Jared' to 'Herod'. And Jared's name was right next to Joni's in her phone book. When Bailey had tapped on the recipient box, she'd clearly pressed the wrong name on the screen.

So now Jared Fraser knew exactly what she thought about him.

Which could make life very awkward indeed.

Sorry, she typed back. Not that she was apologising for what she'd said. She stood by every word of that—well, bar the autocorrected name. She was only apologising for her mistake.

Didn't mean to send that to you.

I'd already worked that one out for myself.

She sneaked a glance at him to see if she could work out how much he was going to make her pay for that little error, and was shocked to realise that he was actually smiling. He wasn't angry or even irritated; he was amused.

There was a sudden rush of feeling in her stomach, as if champagne was fizzing through her veins instead of blood. Totally ridiculous. But when the man smiled, it changed him totally. Rather than being the dour, hard-faced, slightly intimidating man she'd instinctively disliked, he was beautiful.

Oh, help. She really couldn't afford to let her thoughts go in that direction. For all she knew, he could be married or at least involved with someone. She knew nothing about the man, other than that he was the new youth team doctor and he didn't believe in her research at all.

'Sir, are you *the* Jared Fraser?' Billy, one of the substitutes, asked, coming over to sit in the pointedly large gap on the bench between Bailey and Jared.

The Jared Fraser? Why would there be something special about a football team's doctor? Bailey wondered.

'How do you mean?' Jared asked.

'Me and the lads—we saw it on the Internet. We weren't sure if it was you. But if it is—you were one of the youngest players ever to score a goal in the England under-nineteen team. And on your debut match,' Billy added breathlessly. 'And you scored that goal in the championship, the one that won the match.'

'It was a long time ago now. I haven't played in years,' Jared said.

Bailey couldn't quite work this out. Jared had been a star football player as a teenager? Then how come he was a doctor now? He didn't look that much older than she was—five years at the most, she reckoned— so surely he could still play football. Or, if he'd retired from football, it was more likely that he would have become a coach or a manager. Footballer to medic was quite a career change. Especially given that you needed four years at university followed by two years' foundation training, and then you had to work your way up the ranks. To be experienced enough to have a job as a football team doctor, Jared must have been working in medicine for at least ten years. Maybe more. So why had he switched careers?

Feeling slightly guilty about being so nosy—but she could hardly ask the man himself, given how grumpy and impossible he was—she flicked onto the Internet on her phone and looked up 'Jared Fraser footballer England team' in a search engine.

The photograph was eighteen years old now, but the teenager was still recognisable as the man she knew. Jared Fraser had indeed been a footballer. One of the youngest players to score a goal for his country, at the age of seventeen. He'd played in several international matches and had scored the winning goal in a championship game. All the pundits had been tipping him to be one of the greatest players ever. But then, according to the online biography she was reading, he'd been involved in a bad tackle. One that had given him an anterior cruciate ligament injury that had ended his playing days.

So his dreams had been taken from him and he'd ended up in a totally different career. Poor guy. It would, perhaps, explain the dourness. She'd be pretty grumpy, too, if she was no longer able to do her dream job.

Maybe she'd give Jared Fraser just a little bit of slack in future.

Though not from pity. She remembered what it felt like, being an object of pity. It was one of the reasons why she'd moved departments. She might've been able to stick it out, had it not been for the guilt— the knowledge that people felt they had to be careful around her instead of beaming their heads off about a piece of personal good news, the kind of joy everyone else would celebrate with. Because how did you tell someone you were expecting a baby when you knew they'd lost theirs, and in such a difficult way?

Yeah. Bailey Randall knew all about broken dreams. And how you just had to pick yourself up, dust yourself down and pretend that everything was absolutely fine. Because, if you did that, hopefully one day it *would* be just fine.

Halfway through the match, she noticed Travis

lying on the ground, clutching his leg. Jared was already on his feet and running towards the boy; play had stopped and Jared was examining the player as she joined them.

'What's wrong?' she asked.

'Let me finish the SALTAPS stuff,' Jared said.

'SALTAPS?' It was obviously some kind of mnemonic, but not one she'd come across before.

'Stop play, analyse, look for injury, touch the site, active movement, passive movement, stand up,' he explained swiftly. 'Travis, what happened?'

'I don't know—there's just this pain down the back of my left leg,' the boy said, his face pale with pain.

Gently, Jared examined him. 'Did you hear a pop or a crack before the pain started?'

'I'm not sure,' Travis admitted. 'I was focusing on the ball.'

'OK. Does it hurt when you move?'

Travis nodded.

'I want you to bend your knee. If it hurts, stop moving straight away and tell me.'

The young player followed Jared's instructions and winced. 'It really hurts.'

'OK. I'm not even going to try the last bit—getting you up on your feet. I think you've got a hamstring injury, though I need to check a couple more things before I treat you. Archie's going to need to substitute you.'

'No, he can't!' Travis looked devastated. 'I'll be all right in a second or two. I'll be able to keep playing.'

Jared shook his head. 'Play on when you're injured and you'll do even more damage. You need treatment.'

Bailey had been pretty sure it was a hamstring

injury, too, given Travis's symptoms. Hopefully it would be a partial rupture and wouldn't affect the whole muscle. 'Dr Fraser, you need to be on the pitch in case there's another injury,' she said. 'I'll take Travis to the dressing room and finish off the assessments for you.'

He looked at her and, for a moment, she thought he was going to refuse. Then he gave a brief nod. 'Thank you, Dr Randall. That would be helpful.'

'I'll talk to you when I've assessed him,' she said. Even though she was pretty sure that they'd recommend the same course of treatment, strictly speaking, Jared was in charge and Travis was his patient, and she was only here for research purposes. She didn't have the right to make decisions for Jared.

She supported Travis back to the dressing room. There was a wide, flat bench that would do nicely for her purposes; she gestured to it. 'OK. I want you to lie down here on your back, Travis, so I can go through the assessments and see how much damage you've done.'

'There's no need, really. I'll be all right in a few minutes,' Travis said, but she could see that his mouth was tight with pain.

'I still have to assess you, or Dr Fraser will have my guts for garters,' she said with a smile. 'OK. I'm going to raise your legs one at a time, keeping your knees straight. Tell me as soon as it hurts, OK? And I'll stop immediately.' She took him through a range of tests, noting his reactions.

'I'll put a compression bandage on—that'll stop the pain and the bleeding inside your ligament, which causes the inflammation—and an ice pack,' she said when she'd finished. 'And now I'm going to make you a cup of tea, and I want you to sit there with your leg up and the ice pack on the back of your thigh for the next ten minutes or so, while I go and talk to Dr Fraser, OK?'

'Yes, Doc.' He sighed. 'Am I going to be out of the team for long?'

'For at least a couple of weeks,' she said. 'I know it's hard and I know you want to play, but it's better to let yourself recover fully now than to play on it too soon and do more damage.' She finished making the tea. 'Sugar?'

'No. You're all right.' He gave her a rueful smile. 'Thanks, Doc.'

'That's what I'm here for. And painkillers,' she said. 'Are you allergic to anything, or taking any medication for anything?'

'No.'

'OK. I'll give you a couple of paracetamol for now—you can take some more in another four hours—and I'll see what else Dr Fraser suggests.' She patted his shoulder. 'Chin up. It could be worse.'

'Could it?' Travis asked, looking miserable.

'Oh, yes. Imagine having an itch on your leg in the middle of a really hot summer day—except your leg's in a full cast and you can't reach the itchy bit.'

That earned her another wry smile. 'OK. That's worse. Because I'd be off even longer with an actual break, wouldn't I?'

'Yes. But you're young and fit, so you'll heal just fine—as long as you do what Dr Fraser says.'

'I guess.'

She left him miserably sipping his mug of tea while she went to find Jared.

Jared knew the very moment that Bailey stepped out of the tunnel onto the field, even though his back was to her. The fact that he was so aware of her was slightly unnerving. They didn't even like each other— he'd known that even before she'd accidentally sent him that text saying exactly how she felt about him, in very unflattering terms. Dressed in a hooded sweat- shirt, baggy tracksuit pants and flat training shoes, Bailey Randall should've looked slightly scruffy and absolutely unsexy—the complete opposite to his über- groomed ex-wife.

The problem was, Bailey was gorgeous. And those unflattering baggy clothes just made him want to peel them off and see exactly what was underneath them.

Not good. He didn't want to be attracted to her. He didn't want to be attracted to anyone.

Work, he reminded himself. This is work. You have an injured player, and she's helped you out. Be nice. Be polite. Be professional. And stay detached.

'How's young Travis?' he asked when she reached him.

'Pretty miserable,' she said.

Yeah. He knew how it felt, being taken off the pitch with an injury when you were desperate to keep play- ing. And, even though Travis's injury was relatively minor and he'd make a full recovery, Jared knew that the inactivity would make the boy utterly despon- dent. He'd been there himself. 'So what's your ver- dict?' he asked.

'I got him to do a straight leg raise and resisted

knee flexion, then did a slump test and palpation,' she
said. 'I'd say it's a grade two hamstring strain. I've put
an ice pack on and a compression bandage for now
and explained to him about standard RICE treatment.
He's having a cup of tea while I'm talking to you and
seeing what treatment you want him to have.'

'Thank you,' he said. He was impressed by the
quiet, no-fuss way she'd examined the boy and re-
ported back. There was no 'Told you so' or point-scor-
ing against him, even though he probably deserved it;
all her focus had been on making her patient comfortable. She'd also come to talk to him about a treatment
plan instead of telling him how to treat his patient,
despite the fact she was obviously more than capable
of doing her own treatment plan, so she'd respected
his position in the club, too. Maybe he'd been unfair
to her about her project, because she'd been spot on
about the actual medicine she'd discussed with him. If
she was that competent, she was unlikely to be working on a project that had no merit.

'The poor lad's going to be gutted about missing
training and matches, but he needs to do it properly
or he'll end up with another tear in the muscle on top
of this one, and it'll take even longer to heal,' she said.

Jared nodded. 'He needs cold therapy and compression every hour for the first day, and to keep his
leg elevated while he's sitting, to reduce the swelling.'

'I gave him some paracetamol—he said he's not
on any other medication and he's not allergic to anything.'

'Good. That'll help with the pain during the acute
stage, over the next couple of days,' he said.

'I told him that you'd come up with a rehab programme,' she said, 'but if he was my patient I'd suggest a sports massage at the end of the first week, and strengthening exercises in the meantime—standing knee flexion, bridge and seated hamstring curls with a resistance band. Nothing too strenuous, and he has to stop as soon as it hurts.'

'Good plan,' he said. Exactly what he would have suggested. They might not get on, but in medical terms they were definitely on the same page. 'He can also do some gentle walking and swimming, then introduce running gradually. Though it'll be several weeks before he's ready to come back to full training.'

She nodded. 'Look, I know you don't believe in the stuff I'm doing, and I'm not going to rub your nose in it and say "I told you so". But I do want some time to talk you through what I'm doing and—well, I suppose I really want to get you on board with the project,' she admitted. 'Can we have a meeting to talk about it—I mean *really* talk?'

If he'd listened to her and supported her argument that Travis was underperforming, the boy might not be sitting in the dressing room right now with a hamstring injury. Guilt made him sharp. 'The only free time I have is before breakfast.'

He knew he was being obnoxious, but he couldn't seem to stop himself. What was it about Bailey Randall that made him behave like this? Something about her just knocked him off balance, and he liked things to be in perfect equilibrium nowadays.

'Before breakfast,' she mused. 'I normally train at the gym then—but OK. I guess I can skip my session in the gym for once.'

'Or we could train in the gym together.' The words

were out of his mouth before he could stop them. What on earth was wrong with him? Panic flooded through him. This was *such* a bad idea.

'Train together, and then talk about my project over breakfast? That works for me. As long as your partner doesn't mind,' she added quickly.

'No partner.' Though he appreciated that she'd tried to be considerate. In the world of football, there was a lot of jealousy. Sasha definitely wouldn't have been happy about him having a breakfast meeting with a female colleague. Then again, Sasha had had meetings of her own with his male colleagues. In hotel rooms. He pushed the thought away. 'Will yours mind?' He tried to extend the same courtesy to Bailey.

'I'm single,' she said, 'and I like it that way.'

Which sounded to him as if she'd been hurt, too.

Not that it was any of his business. And he wouldn't dream of asking for details.

'One last thing to sort—my gym or yours?' she asked.

'So you don't go to a women-only gym?' Oh, great. And now he was insulting her.

She smiled. 'I'm not intimidated by anyone, regardless of their gender or their age or how pretty they are. I go to a place that has equipment I like and staff who can push me harder if I want a one-to-one training session. And it happens to be reasonably close to the London Victoria, so I can train before work.' She paused. 'There's a café there, too. The coffee's not brilliant, but they do a pretty good Eggs Florentine—which they don't serve in the hospital canteen, or I'd suggest breakfast there because their coffee's slightly better.'

There was no way he could back out of this now. 'OK. Your gym, tomorrow. Let me know the address and what time.'

'Seven,' she said. 'And I'll text you the address.' And there was a tiny, tiny hint of mischief in her eyes as she added, 'Herod.'

CHAPTER THREE

AT FIVE TO SEVEN the next morning, Jared walked down the street towards Bailey's gym. She was already waiting outside for him, wearing another of her hooded sweatshirts and baggy tracksuit pants, and she raised her hand to let him know she'd seen him. He acknowledged her with a nod.

'Good morning,' she said as he walked up to her. 'Are you ready for this?'

'Bring it on,' he said, responding to the challenge in her gaze and trying not to think about how gorgeous her mouth was. This was a challenge of sorts, not a date. They were supposed to be discussing business. And the fact that they were meeting here right now was his own fault—for being deliberately awkward and not trying to fit their meeting into normal working hours.

They walked into the reception, where she signed him in as her guest, and took him through to the changing rooms. 'I need to put my stuff in my locker. Meet you back outside here in five?'

'Sure.'

'Oh—and do you have a pound coin for your own locker? I have change if you need it.'

'Thanks, but I'm good.'

It didn't take him long to stow his things in the locker.

When Bailey came out from the women's changing rooms, Jared's jaw almost dropped. Clearly she'd been wearing the hoodie and the tracksuit pants just for warmth outside, because now she was wearing form-fitting black leggings and a bright cerise racer-back crop top. And he was horribly aware of just how gorgeous she was. Curvy, yet with fabulous muscle definition. Bailey Randall was a woman who looked after herself. She was utterly beautiful and could easily have held her own with any of the glamorous WAGs he'd known at the football clubs he'd worked at. And yet he didn't think she'd be the sort to go to endless spa days and nail parlours.

This was beginning to feel like the most enormous mistake. They were supposed to be training together and then discussing her project over breakfast, and all he wanted to do right now was to scoop her up and carry her to his bed. Even though it was actually a Tube ride away.

It was obvious that, like Sasha, Bailey was aware of her effect on men. She was gorgeous. So was Bailey like his ex-wife in using her physical attributes to get her own way? The idea made him pull himself together. Just. 'So what's your normal workout routine?' he asked.

'Today is a weights day,' she said, 'so that means a quick cardio warm-up and then a resistance routine. You?'

He shrugged. 'I'll join you and adjust the weights to suit me. Just tell me what we're doing and when.'

She nodded. 'Any injuries I should know about?'

Jared had no idea whether Archie had told her anything about his past, but it was irrelevant now. 'A very old knee problem,' he said. 'But I know my limits and I'm certainly not going to be stupid about it.'

'Good. Then let's do this. How about using the elliptical as a warm-up, then through into the back room with the free weights?'

'Fine by me.'

Why on earth had she agreed to train with him? Bailey asked herself. Jared was wearing baggy tracksuit pants and a loose sleeveless vest, like all the other men in the gym. She barely took any notice of them other than to smile hello, acknowledging the fellow athletes in her time slot. But Jared Fraser was different. She was horribly aware of the hard musculature of his body. Particularly his biceps.

He was an ex-footballer. A sports team doctor. He shouldn't have biceps that beautiful and that well defined.

Worst of all, she had a real thing about biceps. Bailey always dragged Joni off to the cinema whenever her favourite actor had a new movie out—and Joni still teased Bailey about the time she'd said, 'Ohhh, just look at his biceps,' really loudly, in the middle of the cinema. The actor was incredibly handsome, perfectly built, but so was Jared Fraser.

She sneaked a sideways look. He was concentrating on putting the time and intensity settings into the elliptical machine, and right at that moment he looked incredibly sexy. It made her wonder what it would be like to have that brooding concentration completely focused on her, and she went hot all over. This training thing was a very bad move. She wished now that she hadn't challenged him. How on earth was she going to be able to concentrate on talking to him over breakfast? Even if he changed into something with long sleeves after his shower, she knew now that he had gorgeous biceps and that could seriously distract her. Right at that moment, she really wanted to reach over and touch him.

Well, she was going to have to make a lot more of an effort, because no way was she acting on that pull of attraction. She liked her life exactly as it was, with no complications—and Jared Fraser could be a real complication. If she let him. Which she really didn't intend to do.

When they'd finished warming up, Bailey talked him through her planned routine, the large compound movements that worked several muscle groups at once. 'I thought I'd do a full-body workout today, if that's OK with you, rather than an upper or lower split.'

'It's a good balance,' he said. 'I notice you're doing hams and then quads.'

'You need to balance them out properly or you'll end up with a back injury,' she said, 'and you wouldn't believe how many patients I have to explain that to.'

Funny how easy it was to talk to him when they were both concentrating on doing the right number of reps and keeping their form correct.

'What made you specialise in sports medicine?' he asked.

'I started off in emergency medicine,' she said, 'but then I found myself doing more of the sporting injuries, especially at the weekends or on Monday

mornings. I did think about maybe working in ortho-
paedics, but then again I like the preventative stuff,
too—it's great being able to make a difference. Then
I had the chance of a secondment in the new sports
medicine department. I liked my colleagues and I
liked the work, so I stayed.'

That was the brief version. She had no intention of
telling Jared the rest of it—how that secondment had
saved her sanity, just over two years ago, and given
her something else to concentrate on when she'd desperately needed an escape. OK, so in sports medicine
there wasn't the speed and pressure that could take
her mind off things as there was in the emergency
department; but she also didn't have to walk into her
department again after first-hand experience of being
treated there, knowing that everyone in the department knew exactly what had happened to her and trying to avoid the concern that shaded too far into pity.

'What about you?' she asked. 'Why did you become the doctor of a football team?'

She wondered if he was going to tell her about
his past as a footballer, but he merely said, 'I enjoy
working in sports medicine, and this job means I get
to travel a bit.'

Surely he must've guessed that she'd looked him
up and knew what had happened to his knee? Then
again, it had been a life-changing accident, and he was
on a completely different path now. She didn't blame
him for not wanting to talk about the injury that had
wrecked his career—just as she didn't want to talk
about the ectopic pregnancy that had shattered her
dreams and then cracked her marriage beyond repair.

No doubt he, too, knew what it felt like to be sick and tired of pity. They didn't have to discuss it.

'How did you get involved in this research project, or have you always been a football fan?' he asked.

'I ought to admit that I'd much rather do sport than watch it, and football isn't really top of my list,' she said. 'My boss was asked if someone on his team would work on the project, and he thought I'd enjoy it because…' She felt her face heat. 'Well, I like techie stuff,' she confessed. 'A lot.'

'You mean gadgets?' He zeroed in on exactly the thing she knew he'd pick up on. 'And would I be right in guessing that you've got one of those expensive wristband things?'

'Um, yes,' she admitted. 'I use it all the time in the gym. I didn't wear it today simply because I knew you'd be really rude about it.'

He burst out laughing. It was the first time she'd actually heard him laugh and it was gorgeous, rich and deep. Sexy, even. *Oh, help.*

'Oh, come off it—are you trying to tell me that you don't like game consoles and whatever?' she asked. 'My brothers are total addicts and so are Joni's—my best friend,' she explained.

'I'm not so much into game consoles,' he said, 'but I do like music—and that's where my techie stuff comes in. I bought one of those systems where the sound follows you through the house.' Then he looked surprised, as if he hadn't meant to tell her something so personal.

'What kind of music?' she asked.

'What do you think?' he parried.

She looked at him as she put the barbell down. 'I'd say either dinosaur rock or very highbrow classical.'

'The first,' he said.

She almost—*almost*—told him about Joni's brother's band and invited him along to their next gig. But that would be too much like asking him out on a date. She and Jared Fraser most definitely weren't on dating terms.

'I'm assuming you like the stuff you can sing along to,' he said.

'Musicals,' she said. 'I'm pretty much word perfect on the soundtracks to *Grease*, *Cats* and *Evita*.'

'Uh-huh.'

But there was a tiny hint of superciliousness in his expression, so she added, 'And Dean Martin. Nonno's favourite. He taught me all the famous songs when I was tiny—"That's Amore", "Volare" and "Sway".' Just in case Jared had any intention of mocking *that*, she said, 'And, actually, it's great stuff to salsa to. It's not old-fashioned at all.'

'Nonno?' he asked, looking confused.

'My grandfather in Milan. My mum is Italian,' she said.

'That explains it.'

'Explains what?' She narrowed her eyes at him.

'Why I thought you were a bit like a pampered Mediterranean princess when I first met you.' Then he looked really horrified, as if he hadn't meant to say that.

'A pampered princess,' she said, and glowered at him. 'You think I'm *spoiled*?'

He stretched out a foot and prodded the floor next

to the mats. 'Ah. The floor's obviously not going to open up and swallow me.'

It amused her, though at the same time she was a bit annoyed at what he was implying. 'Princess,' she said again in disgust.

'Hey. You called me Herod,' he pointed out.

'That was an autocorrect thing on my phone, and it wasn't meant for you in any case. You know what they say about eavesdroppers hearing no good of themselves,' she said loftily.

'You didn't actually take it back, though,' he reminded her.

'No, I didn't—I do think you have tyrant tendencies,' she said, 'given how you wouldn't even listen to what Archie or I said about the project.' She paused. 'And the fact that you could dismiss me as princessy just now, when you barely even know me. That's definitely Herod-like behaviour.'

'I think,' he said, 'we just got back onto the wrong foot with each other—and this morning's meant to be about listening to each other's point of view and finding a bit of common ground.'

He had a point. Maybe she should cut him some slack. 'So you're actually going to listen to what I say? And you'll admit that you were wrong about Travis?'

'*Possibly* wrong,' he corrected. 'That injury might still have happened to one of the other players—one who was performing around his normal average on your charts.'

It was much less likely, she thought. But at least he was admitting the possibility that he was wrong. That was a start. 'What about the yoga?' she challenged.

'No. I'm not convinced. At all,' he said.

'So you think yoga is easy?'

'It's simple stretching.'

Remembering the conversation she'd had with Joni, Bailey smiled. 'Right. So we can finish this session with a bit of yoga, then.'

He rolled his eyes, but muttered, 'If you must.'

When they'd finished the weights routine, she said, 'Yoga will be the cool down and stretch. Have you ever done any before?'

He stared at her. 'Do I look as if I do yoga?'

'Actually, there are a couple of men in our class. They recognise the importance of flexibility training as part of a balanced exercise programme,' she pointed out. 'But OK. I'll talk you through the poses.' First, she talked him through the downward dog. She noticed that he seemed reasonably flexible, and she was impressed that he managed both the warrior pose and the tree without any difficulty. He had a strong core, then.

'So far, so easy?' she asked.

'I can tell which muscle groups each one works,' he said.

'Good. Now for the plank,' she said, and showed him the position. She moved so she could see the clock. 'And we'll start in five. Hold it for as long as you can.' She counted them down, then they both assumed the position.

Jared managed to hold it for a minute before he flopped.

Bailey took it to three—even though that was pushing it, for her—just to make the point.

It looked effortless, though Jared could see Bailey's arms just beginning to shake and he knew that her muscles were right on the verge of giving in. But, when she stopped the pose, he knew he was going to have to be gracious about it—especially given that her performance had been so much better than his.

'OK,' he said, 'I admit that was hard. And clearly you've done that particular one a lot.'

She grinned. 'I have. That one usually shuts people up when they say yoga's an easy option. Though, actually, you did well. A lot of people cave after twenty seconds, or even before that.'

He appreciated the compliment, particularly as it sounded genuine and as if she was trying to meet him halfway.

'So you do a lot of yoga?' he asked.

'Every Monday night with my best friend. Any decent training regime needs flexibility work as well as resistance and cardio.'

He agreed with that. 'So what do you do for cardio?'

She actually blushed.

And he started to have all kinds of seriously impure thoughts about her. He really wished he hadn't started this discussion. The fact that she'd blushed meant she must be thinking something similar. So the attraction was mutual, then? Heat zinged through him. If she felt the same pull, what did that mean?

Then again, he didn't want to get involved with anyone. Sasha had hurt him badly—not just with the affair, but the bit she'd really lied to him about—and Jared wasn't sure he was ready to trust again.

'Cardio. I like dance-based classes,' she said. 'Also there's a salsa night at a local club. I quite often go to that. I like the music, and the dancing's fun. I'm a great believer in endorphins.'

For a moment Jared thought she was going to challenge him to go with her—and he wasn't sure if he was more relieved or disappointed when she didn't. He'd hated clubbing with Sasha in any case; a salsa club was probably just as much of a meat market as any other kind of dance club, and that didn't really appeal to him. Though the idea of dancing with Bailey Randall, up close, hot and sweaty, with her body pressed against his...

Focus, he told himself. Work, not sex.

'I assume you run?' she asked.

'Intervals,' he said, 'and rowing—it's more effective than hamster-wheel cardio. No offence to your warm-up today, because that was fine—it's just that it would bore me stupid if it lasted for more than ten minutes, even with a decent playlist to keep me going.'

'Each to their own,' she said. 'I don't mind doing a whole session on the elliptical if I have a good playlist. There are programmes on the machine that change the resistance and make it a bit more interesting.'

He just grimaced.

'So, rowing, hmm? That would explain your biceps.'

And then she blushed again.

Now he was really intrigued. She liked his biceps?

Well, he liked the muscles in her back. They had beautiful definition. And he really, really wanted to touch them. No. More than that. He wanted to kiss his way down her spine.

'Would that be proper rowing on a river, or machine?' she asked.

'Machine,' he admitted.

'And I assume you're careful with your knee.'

'I'm wearing a knee support under my tracksuit pants,' he said. 'I'm hardly going to nag my players about looking after themselves properly and then not take my own advice.'

'I guess.' She held out her hand to shake his, and his palm tingled where their skin touched. How long had it been since he'd been so aware of someone? 'That was a good session. I enjoyed working with you, Jared.'

'I enjoyed working with you,' he said, meaning it; he was surprised to realise just how much he'd enjoyed it.

'Let's hit the shower and have breakfast.'

He went hot all over again at the thought of sharing a shower with her. He knew perfectly well that wasn't what she'd meant, but now the idea was stuck in his head. And he was glad they had temperature settings on the showers in the male changing rooms, because he needed a blast of cold water to get his common sense back and the fantasies out of his mind.

When he met Bailey outside the changing rooms, he noticed that she was wearing a black tailored suit for work. This was yet another side of her; he'd seen the slightly scruffy scientist on the football pitch and the sculpted goddess in the gym, and now she was the calm, confident medical professional.

He wished that he was wearing something a bit more tailored, too—but then again he was off to work himself after this and that meant dressing appropriately. A sharp suit wasn't what you needed when you were working on a football pitch.

Clearly the staff knew Bailey well here, because the waitress didn't bat an eyelid when Bailey ordered Eggs Florentine without the hollandaise sauce. 'And a rich roast latte?' the waitress asked.

It was obviously Bailey's usual, because she smiled. 'That'd be lovely, thanks.'

He ordered porridge with blueberries and cinnamon, paired with a protein shake.

'Not a coffee fiend?' she asked.

'I had mine before my workout. It gets the best use out of the caffeine,' he said. 'I'm balancing my protein and my carbs now, post-workout.'

She nodded. 'Good point.'

'So, are you going to take me through this system of yours while we wait for breakfast to arrive?'

'Sure. The idea behind it is that you're more likely to end up with a soft-tissue injury if you play while you're under par. You'll be slower and your reactions won't be as fast. So if you look at your performance during training or a game and your VO2 is down, you're doing fewer steps, your resting heart rate is up and your average speed is down, either you've had a slow game—and that's where Archie comes in, to tell me if playing conditions on the field have been different and affected anyone's performance— or you're under par and you're more likely to be injured in your next game.'

He asked her various questions about the measurements she used, and he was impressed that she didn't have to look up a single answer. Bailey Randall wasn't the glib salesman type, able to put a spin on her answers; she really knew her stuff. And she clearly believed in her research project. He liked her enthusiasm; it was one of the reasons why he'd chosen to look after the youth team, because he loved the enthusiasm that young players brought to the job, unjaded by internal politics.

And he also liked the way Bailey talked with her hands, completely animated when she was caught up in the subject. Now he knew she was half-Italian, he could really see it. Everything from her classic bone structure, to the slightly olive colour of her skin, to the rich depths of her eyes. Naturally stylish, she was like an Italian Audrey Hepburn, with that gamine haircut and those huge eyes.

'OK,' he said. 'I still think those wristband things are ploys to extort money out of the gullible with too much disposable income and too little common sense, but the stuff you're doing has a point.'

'Thank you,' she said. 'So do you take it back about my system being a glorified pedometer?'

'I'll reserve judgement until I've seen a month of results,' he said, 'but I will agree that it's better than the wristband things. Especially because you do at least use a proper heart-rate monitor strap with your system.'

'And the yoga?'

He shook his head. 'Even though the plank was hard, I'm not convinced that yoga's going to do what you think it will. Not for a bunch of seventeen-year-old boys.'

'It's still worth a try.'

'Do you make them do the plank?'

She laughed. 'No. That was just to prove a point to you.'

He liked the fact that she'd admitted it.

And it worried him that he liked it. Now that he was getting to know her, he quite liked Bailey Randall. Which was a very dangerous position. He couldn't afford to think of her in terms of anything other than a colleague, but she seriously tempted him. To the point where he could actually imagine asking her out on a date.

Bad, bad move.

He had a feeling that he was going to have to resort to a lot of cold showers to keep his common sense in place. Dating Bailey Randall was absolutely not on the cards. He'd only just finished gluing the pieces of his heart back together, and he had no intention of putting himself back in a position where it could shatter again.

CHAPTER FOUR

OVER THE NEXT couple of weeks, working at the football club was easier, Bailey thought. Jared was at least showing some interest in her research project rather than being an insurmountable bulwark, and he'd even come up with a couple of suggestions that she was trying to incorporate into her data.

Then she noticed that he was favouring his right knee when he went onto the pitch to treat one of the players. She waited until he'd come back to sit next to her on the bench, and then asked, 'What did you do?'

'For Mitch?' He shrugged. 'It was just a flesh wound—some studs scraped against his shin, so I cleaned it and dressed it. He shouldn't have too much trouble with it.'

'No, I meant what did you do to your knee?'

He looked away. 'Nothing.'

'Jared, I'm a doctor, so don't try to flannel me. I could see you were favouring your right knee,' she said.

He sighed. 'It's an old injury. I guess I might have overdone the running a tad at the weekend.'

'Tsk. And you're a sports medicine doctor,' she said.

He gave her a crooked grin that made her libido sit up and beg. 'It'll be fine. It's strapped up.'

'So you didn't actually see anyone about it?'

'I didn't need to.'

She tutted. 'What a fine example to set the team—*not*. Let me have a look when they've gone, so they don't know what an idiot you are.'

He shook his head. 'It's fine. You don't have to do that.'

'You're my colleague. You'd do the same for me.'

Jared thought about it. Would he? Yes, probably. And he'd nag her if she was being stubborn about it, just as he'd nag Archie. Just as she was nagging him. 'I guess,' he admitted.

'Are you icing it? Because obviously you're not resting it or elevating it.'

'No. I'm taking painkillers,' he said. 'And not strong ones, either. Just normal ibuprofen to deal with the inflammation.'

'Hmm,' she said.

After the training session, Jared said to Archie, 'I'll lock up if you need to go. I want to discuss a couple of things with Dr Randall.'

'Cheers,' Archie said. 'It'll give me a few extra minutes to make myself beautiful for my date.'

'What, another one?' Bailey teased. 'I'm sure she'll think you look beautiful.' She blew him a kiss.

Archie grinned and sketched a bow.

'Why didn't you just tell him that your knee hurts?' Bailey asked quietly when Archie and the players had gone, and she and Jared were alone in the dressing room.

'Because it isn't relevant.'

'Of course it's relevant. If you have to kneel on the pitch to treat one of the players, it's going to hurt you.' She rolled her eyes. 'Men.'

'Women,' he sniped back.

'Just shut up and lose the tracksuit bottoms.'

Oh, help. The pictures that put into his head. To clear them, he drawled, 'Fabulous bedside manner, Dr Randall.'

Except that made it worse. Bed. Bailey. Two words he really shouldn't have put together inside his head, because now he could imagine her lying against his pillows and giving him a come-hither smile...

She just gave him a dry look. He shut up and removed his tracksuit bottoms. He knew she wasn't thinking of him in terms of a man right now, but in terms of a patient. What she saw wasn't six foot two of man; she saw a sore knee. An old injury playing up that needed to be looked at and soothed.

Gently she examined his knee. 'Tell me where it hurts, and don't be stubborn about it—because I can't help you if you're not honest with me.'

'Do you talk to all your patients like this?' he asked.

'Just the awkward ones.'

He guessed he deserved that. 'OK. It hurts there. And there.' He gave a sharp intake of breath. 'And there.'

'All righty.' She grabbed a towel and spread it across her lap. 'Leg. Here. Now.'

His bare leg astride her body.

Uh-oh. How on earth was he meant to stop his thoughts doing a happy dance?

'Yes, ma'am,' he drawled, hoping she didn't have a clue what was going through his head right now.

Her hands had been gentle when she'd examined his knee. Now they were firm. There wasn't anything remotely sexual about the way she touched him, and he had to grit his teeth on more than one occasion.

But when she'd finished the deep-tissue massage, he could move an awful lot more easily.

'You're very good at that,' he said when she'd finished and he'd put his tracksuit bottoms back on. 'Thank you.'

'Better?' she asked.

He nodded. 'Sorry for being snippy with you.'

She shrugged. 'You were in pain. Of course you were going to be snippy. It's forgotten.'

'Thanks. I owe you one,' he said lightly, expecting her to brush it aside.

To his surprise, she looked thoughtful. 'I wonder.'

'Wonder what?'

'I do need a favour, actually, and you'd be perfect.'

He still wasn't following this. 'For what?'

She took a deep breath. 'My best friend's getting married in three weeks' time. And I'm under a bit of pressure to take someone to the wedding with me. My family's convinced that I need someone in my life, and I can't get them to see that I'm perfectly happy just concentrating on my career.'

'You want me to go to a wedding with you?'

'Yes.'

'As your partner?'

She grimaced. 'I'm not asking you on a date, Jared. I'm asking you to do me a favour.'

'To be your pretend boyfriend.'

'For one day. And an evening,' she added.

Go with her to a wedding.

She'd just made his knee feel a lot better. And this would be payback.

But…a *wedding*.

Where people promised to love, honour and cherish, until death did them part.

Vows he'd taken himself, and had meant every single word—although it turned out that Sasha hadn't. For all he knew, Tom hadn't even been her first affair. He'd been so clueless, thinking that his wife was happy, when all the time she'd been looking for something else.

Sasha had broken every single one of her vows.

She'd lied, she'd cheated—and then she'd made a crucial decision without talking it over with him. A decision that had cut Jared to the quick because he really couldn't understand her reasoning and it was totally the opposite of what he'd wanted. Even *if* the baby hadn't been his, it would still have been hers. They could've worked something out.

Except she hadn't wanted to. The only person she'd thought about had been herself. Not him, not the baby, not the other man who also might've been the baby's father—as she'd been sleeping with them both, she'd had no idea who the father of her baby was.

To go and celebrate someone else making those same vows when he'd lost his faith in marriage…that would be hard.

'If it's a problem…' her voice was very cool '…then forget I asked.'

He didn't want to tell Bailey about the mess of his divorce, Sasha's betrayal and the termination. He didn't want her to pity him. Besides, he owed her for helping him with his knee. 'OK. I'll do it.'

He knew it sounded grudging, and her raised eyebrow confirmed it. He sighed. 'Sorry. I didn't mean to sound quite so—well—Herod-ish.'

That netted him the glimmer of a smile. 'Knee still hurting?' she asked.

It would be an easy excuse. But he thought she deserved the truth. 'Let's just say I've seen a lot of divorces.' He'd been through a messy one, too. Not that she needed to know that bit. 'So I guess my view of weddings is a bit dark.'

'This one,' Bailey said, 'is definitely going to work. My best friend used to be engaged to a total jerk, but thankfully she realised how miserable her life was going to be with him, and she called it off.'

Interesting. So Bailey was a realist rather than seeing things through rose-tinted glasses? 'I take it you like the guy she's marrying?'

She nodded. 'Aaron's a genuinely nice guy. And he loves Joni as much as she loves him. It's equal.'

Did that mean Bailey had been in a relationship that hadn't been equal, or was he reading too much into this?

'Plus,' she said, 'I happen to know the food's going to be good—and the music. Joni's brother has a band, and they're playing at the evening do.' She paused. 'Dinosaur rock. They're seriously good. So I think you'll enjoy that.'

'You don't need to sell it to me. I've already said I'll go with you, and I keep my word.'

Funny how brown eyes could suddenly seem so piercing. And then she nodded. 'Yes. You have integrity. It's better to be grumpy with integrity than to be charming and unreliable.'

That *definitely* sounded personal. And it intrigued him. But if he asked her any more, then she'd be able to ask him things he'd rather not answer. 'Let me know when and where the plus-one thing is, then,' he said instead.

'Thanks. I will.'

Bailey couldn't stop thinking about Jared on the way home. The world of football was pretty high profile—as much as the worlds of music and Hollywood were—and the gossip magazines were forever reporting divorces and affairs among sporting stars. But something in Jared's expression had made her think that it was a bit more personal than that. Was Jared divorced? Not that she'd pry and ask him. But it made her feel a bit as if she'd railroaded him into agreeing to be her partner at the wedding. And that wasn't fair.

When she got home, she texted him: You really *don't* have to go to the wedding.

The answer came back promptly: I said I'd do it. I'll keep my word.

Typical Jared. Stubborn.

Well, she'd given him the chance to back out. But hopefully he wouldn't hate it as much as he seemed to think he would. OK, thanks, she texted back, and added all the details of the wedding.

The next day was one of Bailey's clinic days at the London Victoria. Her first patient was a teenager who'd been injured playing tennis.

'Viv landed awkwardly in training,' Mr Kaine said.

'She said she felt her knee give and heard a popping sound. And her knee's started to swell really badly.' He indicated his daughter's knee. 'It hurts to walk.'

'It's just a sprain, Dad. It'll be fine,' Vivienne said. 'Let's stop wasting the doctor's time and go home.'

'No,' he said firmly. 'You're going to get this checked out *properly.*'

It sounded as if Mr Kaine was putting his daughter's welfare first and would support her through any treatment programme—which was a good thing, Bailey thought, because what he'd just described sounded very like the injury that had finished Jared's career. Damage to the anterior cruciate ligament.

She pushed Jared to the back of her mind. Not here, not now. Her patient came first.

'Thank you for giving me the background, Mr Kaine. That's very useful,' she said cheerfully. 'Vivienne, would you mind if I examine your knee?' she asked.

The girl rolled her eyes, as if she thought this was a total waste of time, but nodded. She flinched when Bailey touched her knee, so clearly it hurt to the touch and Bailey was very, very gentle as she finished examining the girl's knee.

'I'm going to send you for an MRI scan to confirm it,' she said, 'but I'm fairly sure you've torn your anterior cruciate ligament. I'm afraid you're going to be out of play for a little while.'

Again, she thought of Jared. He must have had a similar consultation with a doctor at a very similar age.

'What? But I *have* to play! I've got an important

tournament next week,' Vivienne said, looking horrified. 'I've been training for months. I can't miss it!'

However bad the girl felt about it, she had to face up to the severity of her injury. She wouldn't even be able to have a casual knockabout on the court for a while, let alone play an important match on the junior tennis circuit. Not even if her knee was strapped up.

'Viv, you have to listen to the doctor. She knows what she's talking about,' Mr Kaine said. 'I'm sorry, Dr Randall. You were explaining to us what Vivienne's done to her knee.'

Bailey drew a couple of diagrams to show Vivienne how the ligaments worked and what had happened to her knee. 'You have a complete tear of the ligament—it's the most common type, and I'm afraid it also means you've damaged the other ligaments and your cartilage.'

'Will it take long to fix?' Vivienne asked. 'If I miss this tournament, can I play in the next one?'

'I'm afraid that's unlikely,' Bailey said. 'You're going to need surgery.'

'Surgery?' The girl looked totally shocked. 'But—but—that means I'll be out for ages!'

'The injury won't heal on its own and unfortunately you can't just stitch a ligament back together. Vivienne, I'll need to send you to a specialist surgeon. I know Dr Martyn here quite well, and he's really good at his job, so I promise you'll be in the best hands.' She looked up at Vivienne's father and gave him a reassuring smile, too. 'He'll replace your torn ligament with a tissue graft, which will act as a kind of scaffolding for the new ligament to grow on. You'll be on crutches for a while afterwards.'

'Crutches. I can't play tennis with *crutches*.' Vivienne shook her head. 'This can't be happening. It just can't.'

'Crutches will stop you putting weight on your leg and damaging the structure of your knee further,' Bailey said. 'I can also give you a brace to protect your knee and make it more stable. But I'm afraid it's going to be at least six months until you can play sports again. After the surgery, you'll need a rehab physiotherapy programme—that means exercises tailored to strengthen your leg muscles and make your knee functional again.'

'Six months.' Vivienne closed her eyes. 'Oh, my God. My life's over.'

'Viv, it's going to take six months for you to get better. I know it feels bad, but it's not the end of the world. You'll come back stronger,' Mr Kaine said.

It was good that her dad was so supportive, Bailey thought. But Vivienne was clearly finding it hard to adjust.

'If you go back to playing too soon, you might do more damage to your knee and you'll be out of action for a lot longer,' Bailey said. 'The good news is that the way they do surgery today is a lot less invasive. It's keyhole surgery, so that means you'll have less pain, you'll spend less time in hospital and you'll recover more quickly.'

'When will the surgeon do it?' Mr Kaine asked. 'Today? Tomorrow?'

'Not straight away,' Bailey said. 'We need the inflammation to go down a bit first, or there's a risk of scar tissue forming inside the joint and you'll lose part of your range of motion.'

'And that means I won't be able to play tennis the way I do now.' Vivienne bit her lip. 'Not ever.'

'Exactly,' Bailey said. 'What you do next is going to make the biggest difference. For the next seventy-two hours you need to remember RICE—rest, ice, compression and elevation.' She talked Vivienne through the treatment protocols.

'What about a hot-water bottle to help with the pain?' Mr Kaine asked.

Bailey shook her head. 'Not for the first three days—and no alcohol, either.'

Vivienne rolled her eyes. 'Fat chance of that. Dad's part of the food police. We were told in sixth form that as soon as you're sixteen you're allowed a glass of wine with your meal in a restaurant. But Dad won't let me.'

'Alcohol slows your reactions and you can't play tennis with a hangover,' he said. 'At least, not well—and I should know because I've tried it.'

Bailey smiled at him. He was definitely going to need a sense of humour to help coax Vivienne through the next few months of a total ban from tennis. 'No running or massage, either,' she said. 'But I can give you painkillers—ones that will help reduce the inflammation as well as the pain.' She looked at Mr Kaine. 'Are there any allergies I need to know about?'

'No,' he confirmed.

'Good.'

'Six months,' Vivienne said again, making it sound like a life sentence.

'Better to make up a bit of ground in a couple of months,' Bailey said softly, 'than to go back too soon, do more damage and then have to spend even more time recovering.'

'She's right, love.' Mr Kaine rested his hand briefly on his daughter's shoulder. 'So what happens after the operation?'

'For the first three weeks the physio will concentrate on increasing the range of motion in the joint but without ripping the graft,' Bailey said. 'By week six Vivienne should be able to use a stair-climber or a stationary bike to maintain the range of motion and start strengthening her muscles, and then the plan will be to work to full rehab over the next few months. You need a balance between doing enough to rehabilitate the knee,' she said gently to Vivienne, 'but not so much that you damage the surgical repair and make the ligament fail again.'

'Six months,' Vivienne said again, looking totally miserable.

'There are other things you can work on that won't involve your knee,' Mr Kaine said cheerfully. 'Chin up.'

Vivenne just sighed.

Once Bailey had sorted out a compression bandage and painkillers, she said, 'I'll see you again in a couple of days and then we'll see the surgeon. Reception will make an appointment for you. Call me if you're worried about anything. But we'll get your knee fixed and you'll be back to playing tennis again.'

And, some time before their next appointment, there was someone she needed to talk to who might just be able to give her some really, really good advice to help Vivienne cope with the next few months.

She hoped.

CHAPTER FIVE

THERE WAS NEVER going to be a perfect time to ask Jared, Bailey knew, and she certainly wasn't going to ring him outside office hours to talk it through with him. But once the next training session with the team was under way and she was seated on the bench next to him, she turned to him.

'Can I ask you for some professional advice—something that's a bit personal?'

He looked completely taken aback. 'Why?'

She'd known before she asked that this was going to be difficult; Jared had never talked to her about his injury. But he was the only one who might be able to help. 'I have a patient, a teenage female tennis player. She landed awkwardly from hitting a ball.'

'And?'

'She, um, has a complete tear to her ACL.'

He went very, very still and guilt flooded through her.

'I know I'm being intrusive,' she said, 'and I apologise for that. I really don't mean to dredge up bad memories for you about your own injury. And, yes, I did look you up, so I know what happened. I could hardly ask you, could I?'

'I guess not.'

Talk about inscrutable. Jared's voice and his face were completely expressionless, so she had absolutely no idea how he was feeling right now. Worrying that she was risking their newfound truce, but wanting to get some real help for her patient, she said, 'The reason I'm asking you is because when it happened you were about the same age as she is now, so you know how it feels. Her dad's really supportive and he's trying to get her to rest her knee sensibly so she'll recover well from the operation, but she's distraught at the idea that she's going to lose a lot of ground over the next year. So I guess what I'm asking you is if there's anything I can tell her to help her deal with it a bit better.'

For a moment she thought Jared was going to blank her, but then he blew out a breath. 'That really depends on whether she's going to recover fully or not.'

Clearly he hadn't recovered fully enough to be able to resume his sports career. But she knew that if she tried to give him a hug—out of empathy rather than pity—he'd push her away, both literally and figuratively. So she kept the topic to a discussion about her patient. 'I think there's a very good chance she'll recover fully. The surgeon's brilliant,' Bailey said.

'Good.'

A complete tear to the anterior cruciate ligament. Jared knew exactly how that felt. Like the end of the world. When all your dreams had suddenly exploded and there wasn't any meaning in your life any more. You couldn't do the one thing you knew you were really good at—the thing you were born to do. In a few moments it was all gone.

At seventeen, it had destroyed him. Knowing that his knee wouldn't hold up in the future—that if he played again he was likely to do more damage to his knee and eventually he'd be left with a permanent limp. Knowing that he'd never play for his country again. He'd been so sure that nothing would ever be that good for the rest of his life.

Although it hadn't actually turned out that way. He enjoyed his job, and he was still involved with the game he loved.

He blew out a breath. 'It's a lot to deal with. Especially at that age. Tell her to take it one day at a time, and to find someone she can talk to. Someone who won't let her wallow in self-pity and will talk her into being sensible.' He'd been so, so lucky that the team's deputy coach had been brilliant with him. He'd let Jared rant and rave, and then told him to look at his options, because there most definitely *would* be something he could do.

What goes around comes around. It was time to pass on that same advice now. 'Tell her there will be something else. At first it'll feel like second best, but she'll find something else she loves as much. Even if it doesn't look like it right now.'

'Thank you,' Bailey said quietly. 'I appreciate it—and I'm sorry I brought back bad memories. That really wasn't my intention.'

He shrugged again. 'It was a long time ago.'

She said nothing, simply waited, and he was surprised to find himself filling in the gap. 'At the time, it was bad,' he admitted. 'I wanted someone to blame for the end of my dreams—but I always knew that the tackle wasn't deliberate. It was just something that went wrong and it could've happened to anyone. The guy who tackled me felt as guilty as hell about it, but it wasn't his fault. It wasn't anyone's fault. It was just an accident. Wrong time, wrong place.' He paused. 'And I found something else to do.'

'Did you think about coaching?' She put a hand across her mouth. 'Sorry. You don't have to answer that.'

He liked the fact that she wasn't pressuring him. There was no malice in Bailey Randall. She just wanted to help her patient, and he'd had first-hand experience of what her patient was going through right now. Of course she'd want to know how he'd coped. 'I thought about it,' he said. 'Though I knew I was too young to be taken seriously when my knee was wrecked. At seventeen, you don't really have enough experience to coach a team.'

'So why did you choose medicine? That's—well, a huge change of direction.'

'My family are all GPs,' he said. 'I'd always thought I'd join them. I guess it was a surprise to everyone when I was spotted on the playing field at school and the local team took me on for training.' He shrugged. 'Then I had to make a choice. Risk trying for a career in football, or do my A-levels. My parents said to give it a go—I could always take my A-levels later if it didn't work out. And when I was picked for the England squad…they threw one hell of a party.'

He smiled at the memory. 'When my knee went, it hit me pretty hard. But I was lucky in a way, in that I could fall back on my original plans—I just took my A-levels two years later than I would've done if I hadn't tried for a career in sport.'

'So you trained as a GP?' she asked.

'No. I ended up training in emergency medicine,' he said. 'I liked the buzz. Then, like you, I had a secondment to a sports medicine department. And then it occurred to me that I could have the best of both worlds—I could be a doctor in the sport I'd always loved.'

'That's a good compromise,' she said.

Again, to his surprise, he found himself asking questions and actually wanting to know the answers rather than being polite. 'What about you? Is your family in medicine?'

'No—my family has a restaurant. Mum's the head chef, Dad's front of house and my brothers are both kitchen serfs.' At Jared's raised eyebrows, she added swiftly, 'Joke. Gio is Mum's deputy—he's going to take over when she retires. And Rob's probably the best pastry chef in the universe and he makes the most amazing wedding cakes. They're planning to expand the business that way, too.'

'Didn't your parents expect you to join the family firm?'

She shook her head. 'Mum and Dad always said that we should follow our hearts and do what we love, and that they'd back us whatever we decided. Rob and Gio were always in the kitchen making stuff, so it was obvious what they wanted to do. And I was always bandaging my teddies when I was a toddler.' She grinned. 'And the dog, if I could get him to sit still.'

He could just imagine that. He'd bet she'd been

the most determined and stubborn toddler ever. 'A born doctor, then?'

'I've no idea where it came from. It was just what I always wanted to do,' she said. 'And I guess I was lucky because my family's always supported me. Even when I nag them about healthy eating and saturated fat.' She laughed. 'Though the nagging has at least made them put some super-healthy options on the menu—that's gone down really well with the customers, so I feel I've made some kind of contribution to the family business, apart from volunteering to taste-test any new stuff.'

Clearly Bailey was very close to her family and Jared had a feeling that they adored her as much as she obviously adored them. And she cared enough about her patients to do something outside her comfort zone; he knew that it must've been daunting to ask him about the injury he didn't talk about, but she'd asked him to see if he could help her patient rather than because she wanted to pry into his life.

'Your patient,' he said. 'When are you seeing her next?'

'Friday morning.'

'I could,' he suggested, 'come and have a word with her, if you like.'

'Really?' The way she smiled at him made him feel as if the sun had just come out at midnight.

'It might help her to talk to someone who's been there and come out just fine on the other side,' he said.

'I think it would help her a lot. If you're sure.' She bit her lip. 'I mean, I don't want to rip open any old scars.'

He smiled. 'It was a long time ago now. And I was

lucky—I had someone who helped me. It's my chance to pay it forward.'

She rested a hand on his arm; even through his sleeve, her touch made his skin tingle. 'Thank you, Jared. I really appreciate it.'

'No worries,' he said.

On Friday, Bailey saw Vivienne in her clinic at the London Victoria and examined her knee. 'Obviously you've followed my advice about rest, ice, compression and elevation,' she said.

Vivienne nodded. 'I want to play again as soon as possible. That means doing what you say.'

Bailey smiled. 'Well, you'll be pleased to know you're good to go for surgery and you can see the surgeon this afternoon.'

'That's great news,' Mr Kaine said, patting his daughter's shoulder. 'Thank you.'

'Actually, there is something else,' Bailey said. 'Obviously I wouldn't dream of breaking patient confidentiality, but I happen to know someone who had an ACL injury at your age, and I asked him for some advice for someone in your position.'

'Was he a tennis player?' Vivienne asked, looking interested.

'No, he was in a different sport,' Bailey said, 'but the injury and the rehab are the same. Actually, he offered to come and have a chat with you. He's waiting outside, if you'd like a word.'

Vivienne turned to her father, who nodded. 'That'd be great. Thanks.'

Bailey opened her office door and looked out;

Jared glanced up, caught her eye and came to the door. 'She'd like to talk to me?' he asked.

'Yes. And thank you. I owe you,' she said.

'No. I'm just paying it forward,' he reminded her. 'Just as your patient will pay it forward, one day.'

It was a nice way of looking at it, Bailey thought. She brought him into the room and introduced him to Vivienne and Mr Kaine.

'Well, I never. Jared Fraser—the England footballer. I remember watching you play years ago. You were amazing.' Mr Kaine shook Jared's hand. 'It's very good of you to come in and talk to us.'

'My pleasure,' Jared said.

'So do you still play for England?' Vivienne asked.

'No. Unfortunately, they couldn't fix my knee. Though that's *not* likely to be the case for you,' he emphasised, 'because Dr Randall tells me that you're a really good candidate for surgery. If you follow the rehab programme to the letter you'll be fine. Dr Randall asked me for my advice, and I thought it might be better for you to have it in person, just in case you have any questions.'

Vivienne nodded. 'Thank you very much, Mr Fraser.'

'Right now,' he said gently, 'it probably feels like the end of the world and you're worrying that you're going to lose so much ground against everyone else.'

She bit her lip. 'That's exactly how it feels.'

'So you need to take it one day at a time, and find someone you can talk to—someone who won't let you pity yourself, but will make you be sensible and get the right balance between doing enough work to strengthen your knee, but not so much that you damage it again and end up back at square one,' Jared said.

'That's good advice,' Mr Kaine agreed. 'I'll always listen, Vivi, but he's right—you do need someone else to talk to.'

'I was lucky,' Jared said. 'I had a great coach. And he made me see that although my knee wouldn't hold up enough for me to play at international level again, I had other options. I could learn to coach, or I could do what I ended up doing—I trained as a doctor, and I'm still part of the sport because nowadays I work with the youth team of a premiership division club. So even if there are complications in the future and you don't end up playing at this level again, you'll still have options—you can still be part of tennis.'

'I don't mean to be rude,' Vivienne said, 'but I don't want to be a coach or a doctor. I just want to play tennis. It's all I've ever wanted to do.'

'And you will play again,' Bailey said. 'But, as Dr Fraser said, you need to follow your rehab programme.'

'Waiting is the worst bit,' Jared said. 'You'll want to push yourself too hard. But don't. Use that time to study instead. Look at different techniques, look at the way your opponents play and use that to hone your strategy. To really succeed at a top level in sport you need just as much up here...' he tapped his head '...as you need the physical skills.'

'Vivi picked up a racket practically as soon as she could walk,' Mr Kaine said. 'I used to play—nothing like at her level—just at a club on Sunday afternoons, and her mum would bring her to watch. And she ended up joining in.' He ruffled her hair. 'When she started beating us hollow and she wasn't even ten years old, we knew we were seeing something special in the making. And you'll get that back, love. We just have to make sure we do everything the doctors tell us, OK?'

'OK,' Vivienne said.

Bailey smiled at them both. 'And I'll do my very best to help you get that knee back to how it was, so you can go and get those grand slams.'

'Can I be rude and ask, Mr Fraser, do you miss playing?' Vivienne asked.

'Sometimes,' Jared said. 'But I'm thirty-five now, so I'd be near the end of my professional playing career in any case. And I'm lucky because I really enjoy my job. It means I get the chance to help players fulfil their potential. If someone had told me that when I was your age, I would have laughed at them—but I really do feel I've achieved something when I see them grow and improve. So don't rule it out as something you might do when you're ready to retire from playing.'

Vivienne looked thoughtful, and Bailey could see that Jared's words had given her a different perspective—something that would make all the waiting during her rehab a lot easier. 'Thank you, Mr F—*Dr* Fraser,' she amended.

When the Kaines had left, Jared was about to follow them out when Bailey stopped him. 'Thanks for doing that, Jared—you've made a real difference to her.'

'No worries.'

'If I wasn't up to my eyes in paperwork and appointments,' she said, 'I'd offer to take you for lunch to thank you properly. Or dinner—but I'm doing bridesmaid stuff for Joni tonight. So please consider this a kind of rain check.' She took a plain white patisserie box from her desk drawer and handed it to him.

'What's this?' he asked.

She smiled. 'A little slice of heaven. Don't open it now. Tell me what you think later.'

'OK.' He looked intrigued. 'I'll text you. Good luck for tonight.'

'Thanks.'

Later that evening, she had a text that made her laugh.

Best chocolate cake in the universe. Would very much like to help with more patients. Quite happy to be paid in cake.

I'll see what I can do, she texted back.

Funny, when she'd first met Jared, she'd thought him grumpy and surly and a pain in the neck. Now she rather liked his dry sense of humour and the quiet, sensible way he went about things.

But she'd better not let herself get too close. After the way her marriage to Ed had splintered, she just didn't trust herself to get it right next time. It was best to stick to being colleagues. Friends, too, maybe; but she'd have to dampen down the attraction that sparkled through her veins every time she saw him. To keep her heart safe.

CHAPTER SIX

'JONI, YOU LOOK BEAUTIFUL,' Bailey said, surveying her best friend.

'So do you.' But Joni also looked worried. 'Bailey, are you sure you're OK?'

'Of course I am—why wouldn't I be?'

'Because I remember the last time that one of us was in a bridesmaid's dress and the other was the bride,' Joni said softly.

Bailey's wedding day. A day so full of promise. A day when she'd thought she couldn't be happier... And then, two short years later, she'd discovered that she couldn't be any more unhappy when her whole world crashed down around her. 'I'm fine. More than fine. Don't give it another moment's thought,' she said brightly. Even if she hadn't been fine, no way would Bailey rain on her best friend's parade on her wedding day.

'I can't believe you're actually bringing Herod as your plus-one.'

Bailey groaned. 'Please don't call him that when you meet him—he'll be mortified.'

'You've been very cagey about him. So you're getting on OK together now?'

'We've reached an understanding.'

Joni raised an eyebrow. '*That* sort of understanding?'

'Absolutely not. Even if I was looking for someone, Jared Fraser wouldn't make my list of potentials.' That was a big fat lie—Jared Fraser was one of the most attractive men she'd met, particularly when he smiled—but hopefully Joni would be too distracted by all the bridal stuff going on to call her on it. Bailey hoped. 'No, he's just doing me a favour and taking a bit of heat off me where my family's concerned.'

'As long as you're OK.'

'Of course I'm OK,' Bailey reassured her. 'I'm thrilled that my best friend's getting married to the love of her life, and I get to follow her down the aisle in the most gorgeous bridesmaid's dress ever. Now, the car's going to be here at any second, so we need to get moving.'

Jared took a deep breath and walked down the path to the church. He hadn't been to a wedding since his own marriage to Sasha. And, despite Bailey's assurances that the bride and groom were right for each other, Jared still felt awkward. A cynic who'd lost his belief in marriage really shouldn't be here to celebrate a wedding. He half wished Bailey was going to be there with him to take his mind off it, but as she was Joni's bridesmaid he knew that she would be the very last person walking into the church, and she wouldn't be sitting with him, either.

He really should have asked if he could at least meet the bride and groom before the wedding, so he would know someone there. Right at that moment he was really regretting the impulse that had made him offer to be Bailey's 'plus-one'.

His only consolation had been the text she'd sent him that morning: See you at the church. And thank you. I appreciate it.

And being appreciated was nice. It had been a while since he'd last felt appreciated.

The usher greeted him with a smile. 'Bride's side or groom's?'

'Bride's,' Jared said, feeling a total fake.

'Sit anywhere on the left except the front two pews,' the usher said with a smile, handing him an order of service booklet.

Jared remembered the drill: anywhere except the front two pews, where the bride's and groom's immediate family would be sitting.

Over the next few minutes the church filled up. Two men walked down to the front of the church; one of them was obviously the groom and the other the best man, Jared thought.

A wedding.

A room full of hope, with everyone wishing the bride and groom happiness until the end of their days. But how often did that hope turn sour? How many people did he know who'd actually stayed together, apart from his parents and two of his siblings? Not that many.

The organist started to play the wedding march, and the bride walked in on her father's arm, looking gorgeous and deliriously happy. Behind her, carrying the long train and a bouquet of deep red roses—to match her knee-length dress and incredibly high-heeled shoes—was Bailey.

Jared had never seen her wearing make-up before, not even on that morning when they'd trained together and she'd come to breakfast in a suit. It was barely there—mainly mascara and a hint of lipstick, from what he could tell—but it served to show him that she was jaw-droppingly beautiful and didn't need anything to enhance her looks. Right now, she looked incredibly glamorous, a million miles away from the slightly scruffy doctor he was used to—the one who walked around the football pitch in tracksuit pants and a hoodie.

He caught her eye as she walked by and she actually winked at him.

And all the blood in his body rushed south.

Oh, help. They hadn't set any ground rules, so this might just be one of his biggest mistakes ever. God. He really should've agreed it with her beforehand. At the very least they should've agreed on no touching and no holding hands. And yet he was supposed to be her fake boyfriend. Everyone would expect him to hold her hand, put his arm round her, gaze at her adoringly, maybe even kiss her...

The idea of kissing her sent him into such a flat spin that he was barely aware of the marriage ceremony. But then the registers were signed and the bride and groom walked down the aisle, all smiles.

The usher handed him a box of bird-friendly confetti on the way out. Jared lined up on the side of the path to the church with everyone else and waited until the photographer directed them all to throw confetti over the happy couple.

He took a couple of photos on his phone and managed to catch one of Bailey with her head tipped back, laughing. The kind of picture that would make a rainy morning feel full of sunshine.

She came over to him while the bride and groom were being photographed on their own. 'Hey. Thanks for coming.'

'Pleasure.' And, actually, it was now. 'You, um, look very nice.'

'Thank you. So do you. I've never seen you in a proper suit before.' She grinned. 'I would say a suit "suits" you, but I need to find a better way of saying it.'

Funny, her easy manner put him at his ease, too. It suddenly didn't matter that this was a wedding, and all the darkness associated with the end of his own marriage just faded away—because Bailey was there and she *sparkled*.

'I'll introduce you properly to everyone at the reception,' she promised. 'Sorry, I should have organised this a lot better so I was travelling with you or something.'

'It's fine. You're the bridesmaid and you have things to do. I'll see you at the reception.'

She gave him another of those incredibly sexy winks. *'Ciao, bello.'*

The Italian side of her was really coming out today. He'd never really seen this before; but then again she'd never flirted with him before, either.

Oddly, he found himself looking forward to the reception—and what he really wanted to do was dance with her. Which was crazy, because he didn't even like dancing very much; but he had a feeling that Bailey did and that she'd be good at it.

He made his way to the hotel where the reception was being held, and joined the line-up of people waiting to kiss the bride and shake the groom's hand. Bailey came and found him in the line. 'Hey, there.'

'Hey.' How ridiculous was it that he should feel suddenly intimidated?

But Bailey took charge, making small talk until she could introduce him to the bride and groom. 'Jared, this is Joni and Aaron. Joni and Aaron, this is Jared Fraser.'

'Very pleased to meet you, Jared,' Joni said with a smile. Jared caught the meaningful look she gave Bailey, and wondered just what Bailey had told her best friend about him. 'Thanks for coming.'

'Thanks for inviting me. It was a lovely service, and you look gorgeous,' he said.

She kissed his cheek. 'You're too sweet. I knew Bailey was lying when she said you were grumpy.'

He laughed. 'I can be.' He gave Bailey a pointed look. 'Though so can she.'

'No way—she's the endorphin queen,' Joni said. 'Bailey believes endorphins are the answer to absolutely everything.'

Jared went hot all over, thinking just how endorphins could be released and how much he'd like to do that with her. He really hoped nobody could read his thoughts. But he managed to pull himself together and shook Aaron's hand. 'Congratulations, both of you, and I hope you'll be very happy together.'

They exchanged a glance, and he could see just how much they adored each other. So maybe Bailey was right and this would have a happy ending. Maybe he should start to believe in love again.

'Righty.' Bailey tucked her arm into his. 'Let's get

this over with. Come and meet my lot. They're the nicest family in the world, but I'm going to apologise in advance because they're a bit—well—full on.'

'Italian,' he said.

She nodded. 'Even though Dad's English, living with my mum and the rest of us has kind of made him Italian.'

'That's nice,' Jared said, and let her lead him over to her family.

'Jared, this is my mother, Lucia, my brothers, Roberto and Giorgio—Rob and Gio for short—and my dad, Paul.'

Jared shook hands and kissed cheeks as expected, and then turned to Bailey. 'How come you don't have an Italian first name?' he asked.

'Because I was born on Christmas Eve, and in my family it's tradition to watch *It's a Wonderful Life* every single Christmas Eve—including the year I was born, because Mum had me at home. So she really had to call me Bailey, after George's family.'

'It could be worse,' Lucia said with a grin. 'I could have called you Clarence.'

'Clarrie. Yes. That's *so* me.' Bailey flapped her hands in imitation of an angel's wings and laughed.

'She's kept you very quiet, Jared,' Lucia said.

'Because we haven't known each other very long, and I know what you're like, Mamma,' Bailey said. She switched into rapid Italian; clearly she was asking her mother not to interrogate him or embarrass her, Jared thought. Mischief prompted him to ask her if she realised that he spoke Italian, just to tease her; but, knowing Bailey, she'd call his bluff and speak in

Italian for the rest of the evening, so he resisted the temptation. Just.

'Sì, sì, bambina mia.' Lucia pinched Bailey's cheeks, and then continued her interrogation. 'So where did you meet, Jared?'

'At work,' he said carefully.

'So you're a doctor?'

'For a football team, yes.'

Bailey's dad smiled at him. 'Which one?'

Jared named the premier division club. 'I work with the youth team—and they've got real potential.'

'Oh, the team Bailey's testing her box of tricks on?' Paul asked. 'I thought you said the team doctor was about to retire, Bailey?'

'He did. Jared took over from him,' Bailey said. 'Are you going to grill the poor man all night, or can we talk about something else—like how gorgeous my best friend looks in her lovely floaty dress?'

'She does indeed.' Paul gave her a hug. 'And so do you, darling. We don't see you dressed up like this very often.'

'If you came to see me with a sports injury and I looked like this when I treated you, you'd be worried that I didn't have a clue what I was talking about and think that you were going to be injured and in pain for the rest of your life,' she said with a grin. 'That's why I don't dress like this very often.'

It turned out that they were at a table with Bailey's family for the wedding breakfast, and Jared was surprised by how easily they included him in the conversation, as if they'd known him for ever. In turn, he got them to talk about the restaurant—and learned a lot about Bailey as a child. Her family was merciless in telling tales; but they clearly adored her, because she was laughing along with the rest of them and giving just as good as she got by telling tales about them, too.

He discovered that Bailey, when she was with her family, was incredibly tactile, so it was just as well they hadn't agreed a no-touching rule, because she would've broken it several times a minute. He already knew that she talked with her hands, but this was something else. She touched his arm, his shoulder, his face, his hair. He wasn't used to that at all, but he was surprised to discover that he liked it. That he wanted more.

Though that wasn't part of the deal. He was her fake partner for tonight, not her real one, he reminded himself.

The food was excellent, but best of all was the cake. 'This has to be the best cake I've ever had in my life,' he said.

Rob looked pleased. 'I'm glad you like it. Actually, it's one of mine,' he said diffidently.

'Bailey said you were good—but she didn't say you were *this* good. And I'm going to beg for seconds.'

'You weren't listening properly,' she said, cuffing his arm. 'I told you Rob was the best pastry chef in the universe. And who do you think made that chocolate cake I gave you?'

'Oh, now, with those two pieces of evidence, I agree completely,' Jared said with a smile.

Funny, he'd been faintly dreading the reception. But it was all easy, from chatting at the tables to listening to the speeches. And then finally the band started playing and the dancing began. The bride and groom danced together first, followed by Bailey and the best man. Jared couldn't take his eyes off her. The way she moved was so graceful, so elegant. This was yet another side to the clever, slightly acerbic doctor he was used to. She'd turned out to be full of surprises.

And then she came over to him. 'Dance with me?'

How could he say no? Especially when he'd been wanting to hold her close all day, and this was the perfect excuse.

When he danced with her, it was the first time he'd ever noticed her perfume; it reminded him of an orange grove in full bloom, yet with a sweet undertone. Sparkly and warm, just like her personality. And he could feel the warmth of her body against his.

To keep his mind off that fact, he asked, 'Why do I recognise the guy playing guitar with the band?'

'That's Olly, Joni's brother—he was one of the ushers, so you would've met him at the church,' she explained.

'Oh.'

'Sorry about my family earlier. As I said, they're a little intense.'

'Don't apologise—I like them. They love you,' he said, 'and it's pretty clear they worry about you.'

She rolled her eyes. 'I'm thirty years old. I can look after myself.'

'Families are supposed to worry about you,' he reminded her.

'Does yours worry about you?' she challenged.

He smiled. 'When I let them, yes.'

'So you're as bad as I am—except I bet you keep yours at bay by being grumpy.'

'And you keep yours at bay by sparkling,' he fenced.

'Sparkling?'

'Like vintage champagne in candlelight,' he said.

Oh, for goodness' sake. Anyone would think he'd been drinking way too much of the vintage champagne. He simply didn't wax poetic like that. But something about Bailey made the words flow and he couldn't stop them.

She smiled. 'You think I'm sparkly?'

'Very,' he admitted.

'Thank you—that's a really lovely thing to say. Especially as I've pretty much neglected you today, and you're doing me a huge favour by being here in the first place.'

'You haven't neglected me.' And he was suddenly really glad that he'd agreed to do this. Because he was seeing a new side to Bailey Randall—a side he really liked. Sweet and playful and totally charming; yet it was totally genuine.

He held her closer. Somehow they were dancing cheek to cheek, and his hand was splayed at the top of her dress. He could feel the warmth of her skin against his fingertips and it sent a thrill right through him. Right at that moment it felt as if it was just the two of them on the dance floor, with nobody else around for miles and miles and miles.

'Your back is perfect,' he murmured.

'Why, thank you, Dr Fraser.'

'Sorry.' He sighed. 'I didn't mean to say that. Ignore me.'

She pulled back slightly to look him straight in the eye. 'I wasn't being sarcastic—and I wasn't offended. Seriously, Jared, thank you for the compliment.'

Her mouth was beautiful; her lower lip was full and he itched to catch it between his.

Oh, this was bad.

Why was he thinking about kissing her?

'I noticed how perfect your back was when we trained together,' he said. And now he was making things much worse. He really needed to shut up.

She ran one finger down his sleeve. 'And I noticed your biceps when we trained together.' Her voice had grown husky. 'I like your biceps. They're perfect, too.'

He knew that he was supposed to be just playing the part of her partner, but right now he wanted to make it reality. So he dipped his head. Just a little bit. Just enough that his mouth could brush against hers.

She tasted of champagne and wedding cake—and he liked it. A lot.

He pulled back so he could look her in the eye and take his cue from her. If she wanted him to back off, he'd do it.

But her lips were ever so slightly parted and there was a sparkle in her eyes that he'd never seen before.

'Bailey, I really want to kiss you,' he whispered.

'I want you to kiss me, too,' she whispered back.

That was all the encouragement he needed. He dipped his head again and took his sweet time kissing her. Every brush of his mouth against hers, every nibble, made him more and more aware of her. And she was kissing him back, her arms wrapped as tightly round him as his were round her.

He wanted this to last for ever.

But then he became aware that the music had changed and become more uptempo, and he and Bailey were still swaying together as if the band was playing a slow song. He broke the kiss, and he could see the exact moment that she realised what was going on, too. Those gorgeous dark eyes were absolutely huge. And she looked as shocked as he felt. Panicked, almost.

This wasn't supposed to be happening.

'I, um…' she said, and tailed off.

'Yeah.' He didn't know what to say, either. What he really wanted to do was kiss her again—but they were in a public place. With her best friend and her family in attendance. And doing what he really wanted to do would cause all kinds of complications. He didn't want to get involved with anyone. Apart from that one awful evening when his best friend had persuaded him to try speed dating—an experience he never wanted to repeat—Jared hadn't dated since his divorce. No way was he setting himself up to get hurt again, the way he he'd been with Sasha—even though he knew that Bailey wasn't a bit like Sasha.

'I guess I ought to do some chief bridesmaid stuff and get the kids dancing,' she said.

And he ought to offer to help her. Except there was just a hint of fear in her eyes. He didn't think she was scared of him; maybe, he thought, she was just as scared of getting involved as he was. Especially given that she'd asked him to be her fake partner to keep her family happy. Bailey had obviously been hurt at some point, too, and they clearly worried about her.

'I guess,' he said. 'Do you, um, want a hand?'

'Do you like kids?'

That was an easy one. 'Yes, I do.' And he'd always thought he'd have children of his own one day. Sasha had taken the choice of keeping the baby away from him, and at that point he'd realised just how much he wanted to be a dad. But unless he took the risk of giving someone his heart—the right woman, someone he could really trust—that wasn't going to happen.

He pushed the thought away and concentrated on helping Bailey organise the children. She was a natural with them—they responded to her warmth. Just like him.

'If you could dance with some of the wallflowers,' she said quietly to him, 'that would be kind.'

Kind wasn't what he was feeling right now, but kind would be a hell of a lot safer. 'Sure,' he said.

Even though he was polite and made conversation with the women he danced with, he was totally aware of Bailey throughout the entire evening. Her smile, her sparkle, her warmth. And she made him ache.

He wanted her. Really wanted her. But he knew she'd panicked as much as he had when they'd kissed, so it was a bad idea. They needed to go back to being strictly colleagues. Somehow.

At the end of the evening he said his goodbyes to Bailey's family, trusting that she'd manage to get him out of a promise to see them soon.

'I guess this is it, then,' she said as she walked him to the door of the ballroom.

'I'll call a taxi and see you home first,' he said.

She shook her head. 'You don't have to do that.'

He smiled. 'Yes, I do. I'm old-fashioned. So let's not argue about it—just humour me on this one, OK?'

She didn't argue and let him organise a taxi. She didn't say much on the journey back to her place; although Jared desperately wanted to reach for her hand, he kept a tight rein on himself and simply joined her in sitting quietly.

When the taxi stopped, he paid the cabbie.

'Isn't he taking you home now?' Bailey asked, and he could see the panic in her eyes. Did she really think that he expected her to invite him in for a nightcap— or more?

'No. I'm seeing you to your doorstep and waiting until you're safely inside, then I'm taking the Tube home,' Jared said. 'And, yes, I know you can look after yourself, but it's been a long day and you're wearing incredibly high heels.'

'Point taken.' Her expression softened. 'Thank you.'

She let him escort her to her doorstep.

'Thank you for today,' she said. 'I really appreciate it.'

'No worries.' He leaned forward, intending to give her a reassuring—and strictly platonic—kiss on the cheek. But somewhere along the way one or both of them moved their head, and the next thing he knew his lips were skimming against hers.

What started out as a soft, sweet, gentle kiss quickly turned to something else entirely, and he was kissing her as if he was starving. She was kissing him right back, opening her mouth to let him deepen the kiss. And this felt so right, so perfect.

When she pulled away, his head was swimming.

'No,' she said. 'We can't do this.'

The panic was back in her face.

Her ex, whoever he was, must have really hurt her badly, Jared thought.

And he had no intention of making her feel worse.

'It's OK.' He took her hand and squeezed it. Just once. The way she'd squeezed his hand when he'd talked about his knee injury. Sympathy, not pity. 'You're right. We're colleagues, and *just* colleagues.'

And he needed to keep that in mind. He didn't want the complication of falling for someone, either. The risk of everything going wrong. Been there, done that and learned from his mistakes.

The fear in her eyes faded—just a fraction, but she'd clearly heard what he'd said.

'I'll see you at work,' he said.

'Yeah. I'll see you.' She swallowed. 'And I'm sorry.'

'There's nothing to be sorry for,' he said.

He waited until she'd unlocked her front door and closed it again behind her, and then he left to find the Tube station. It was better this way. Being sensible.

Wasn't it?

CHAPTER SEVEN

BAILEY SLEPT REALLY badly that night. Every time she closed her eyes, all she could see was Jared in that wretched suit, looking totally edible. Worse, her mouth tingled in memory of the way he'd kissed her.

OK, she'd admit it. She was attracted to Jared Fraser. Big time.

But, after the way her marriage had imploded, she wasn't sure she could risk getting involved with anyone again. Letting herself be vulnerable. Risking the same thing happening all over again. After the ectopic pregnancy she'd ended up pushing Ed away—physically as well as emotionally—because she'd been so scared of getting pregnant again.

So, as much as she would like to date Jared—and to take things a lot further than they had at the wedding—she was going to be sensible and keep things between them just as colleagues. Because she didn't want to hurt him, the way she'd hurt Ed.

Do you like kids?

And he'd said yes. She could imagine him as a father, especially after she'd seen him with the children at the wedding. And that was another sticking point. She wanted children, too. But the ectopic pregnancy had shredded her confidence. What if it happened again and her other tube ruptured, leaving her infertile?

She'd been terrified of getting pregnant again, and that had made her scared of sex—a vicious circle she hadn't been able to break. Technically, Ed had been unfaithful to her; but Bailey blamed herself for it, because he'd only done it after she'd pushed him away and refused to let him touch her. She knew that the break-up of her marriage was all her fault.

Since her divorce, until Jared, she hadn't met anyone she'd wanted to date. But how could she expect him to deal with all her baggage? It wouldn't be fair.

So, the next morning, she sent Jared a text to clear the air—and also to make it very clear to him how she felt. And hopefully it would ease any potential awkwardness at work.

Sorry. Too much champagne yesterday. Hope I haven't wrecked our professional relationship.

Jared read the message for the fourth time.

Too much champagne? Hardly. He'd been watching Bailey. She'd had one glass, maybe two. With a meal. Most of the time she'd been drinking sparkling water—as had he.

It was an excuse, and he knew it. She'd looked so scared. As panicky as he'd felt. But why?

Next time he saw her, he decided, he'd get her to talk to him. For now, he'd try to keep things easy between them.

Medicinal recommendation of a fry-up for the hangover, he texted back. See you on the pitch later in the week.

* * *

Facing Jared for the first time since the wedding made Bailey squirm inside. In the end, she decided to brazen it out. Hadn't he said she was sparkly? Then she'd go into super-sparkly mode. So she chatted to all the players, gave Archie a smacking kiss hello on the cheek—while making quite sure she was out of grabbing reach half a second later—and gave Jared a lot of backchat about being too old and too stuck in his ways to do yoga with the boys in the team.

To her relief, he responded the same way, and things were back to the way they used to be. Before he'd kissed her.

Almost.

Because during the training session she looked up from her laptop and caught him looking at her; those amazing blue eyes were filled with wistfulness.

Yeah.

She'd like to repeat that kiss, too. Take things further. But she just couldn't take the risk. She knew he'd end up being just as hurt as she was. She couldn't destroy him, the way she'd destroyed Ed.

'Can we have a word?' Jared asked at the end of the training session.

'Um—sure.' Bailey looked spooked.

He waited until the players and Archie had gone into the dressing room. 'Are you OK?' he asked gently.

'Of course. Why wouldn't I be?'

'You and me. Saturday night,' he pointed out.

'Too much champagne,' she said swiftly.

'I don't think so.' He kept his voice soft. 'I think you're running scared.'

She lifted her chin and gave him a look that was clearly supposed to be haughty, but instead he saw the vulnerability there. 'I'm not scared.'

'That,' he said, 'is pure bravado. And I know that, because this thing between us scares me, too.'

The fight went out of her. 'Oh.'

'So what are we going to do about it?' he asked.

'I'm not looking for a relationship. I'm fine being single.'

'That's what I've been telling myself, too.' He paused. 'Maybe we could be brave. Together.'

'I...' She shook her head. 'I'm not ready for this.'

'Fair enough.' He held her gaze. 'But when you are...'

She swallowed hard. 'Yeah. I, um, ought to let you get on.'

He let her go. For now. And he could be patient, because Bailey Randall was definitely worth waiting for.

Everything was fine for the next week, until Bailey's system picked up a marked problem. Maybe it was a glitch in the system, she thought, and decided to keep it to herself for the time being. But when the same result showed after the next session, and after she'd caught the tail end of the lads gossiping outside the dressing room, she knew that she was going to have to do something.

'Jared, can we have a quick word?' she asked quietly.

He frowned. 'Is something wrong?'

'I think so.' She gestured to her laptop, so he'd know that it was to do with the monitoring system and one of the players.

'Hadn't we better talk to Archie if you want to pull someone from the team?' he asked.

She shook her head and kept her voice low. 'This is a tricky one, and you're the only person I can talk to about it.'

'OK,' he said. 'I assume you mean somewhere quiet, away from the club.'

'Definitely away from the club,' she said. 'Yes, please.'

'Are you free straight after training?'

She nodded.

'We'll talk then.'

'Thank you.' And just knowing that she could share this with him and he'd help her work out what to do made some of the sick feeling go away.

After the session, Jared took Bailey to a café not far from the football club. 'Sit down, and I'll get us some coffee.' He remembered what she'd drunk at the gym. 'I take it you'd like a latte?'

She smiled. 'I'm half-Italian. You only drink lattes at breakfast. Espresso for me, please.'

He smiled back. 'Sure.'

'And can I be greedy and ask for some cake, too?' she asked. 'I don't care what sort, as long as it's cake.'

'It's not going to be up to your brother's standards,' he warned.

'Right now, I don't care—I need the sugar rush.'

Worry flickered down Jared's spine. Whatever she wanted to discuss with him was clearly something serious if she needed a sugar rush. And he'd noticed that she'd been much quieter than normal during the training session.

He came back with two coffees, a blueberry muffin and a double chocolate muffin. 'You can have first pick.'

'Thank you.' She took the blueberry one.

He sat down opposite her. 'Spit it out. What's worrying you?'

'You know how my system picks up if someone's underperforming?'

'Yes.'

'I'm worried about one of the players. I've heard the rumours that he's in danger of losing his place on the team because he hasn't been playing well for a while.'

'Darren,' Jared said immediately.

She nodded. 'And I heard the boys talking. He's not coping with the pressure.' She sighed. 'It's hearsay and I don't want to accuse him of something when he might be perfectly innocent, but...' Her eyes were huge with concern. 'I think he's drinking. Apart from it making his performance worse, he's not even eighteen yet—he's underage.'

Jared blew out a breath. 'I've known a few players over the years who started drinking to handle the pressure, and it finished their careers.'

She looked miserable. 'I don't know what to do. If I tell Archie, then Darren will definitely lose his place. He'll be kicked out.'

'For breaking his contract,' Jared agreed.

'But if he *is* drinking, then it needs to stop right now, Jared. He's going to damage himself.'

'Agreed.'

'Maybe I'm being a bit paranoid and overthinking it. Have a look and see what you reckon.' She opened her laptop and drew up the graphs. Darren's performance had been very near his average in every session apart from the last two, where there was a marked difference.

'So you suspected it last time as well?' he asked.

She nodded. 'I wanted to monitor a second performance, just in case the first one was a one-off—a glitch in the programme or something.'

'No, I think your analysis is spot on. We need to tell Archie and Lyle Fincham.'

'But they'll kick him out.'

'Not necessarily. We can both put in a good word for him. He's not a bad kid—he's just made a mistake and he needs some help.' Jared shrugged. 'Extra coaching might make things easier for him, and I can design a workout programme tailored to his needs.'

'You'd do that for him?' She sounded surprised.

'Everyone makes mistakes. And everyone deserves a second chance,' he said. 'A chance to put it right.'

He hoped she'd think about it. And that she'd give them a second chance, too.

Mr Fincham wasn't available, so Jared and Bailey tackled Archie.

'So there's a problem with one of the players?' Archie asked.

Bailey nodded and talked the team coach through the computer evidence.

Archie frowned. 'So you think he's drinking?'

'You know as well as I do, some players do when they can't cope with the pressure,' Jared said.

'And it only makes things worse. Plus he's underage. If he can't cope, then he'll have to leave the team,'

Archie said with a sigh. 'I can't have him being a bad influence on the rest of the lads.'

'Or,' Bailey said, 'you could give him another chance. We could talk to him and tell him what damage he's doing to himself—in graphic enough terms to make him stop.'

'And I can give him an extra training programme to help him brush up his skills and make him feel that some of the pressure's off,' Jared said.

'If the papers get hold of this, the muck will really hit the fan,' Archie said, and shook his head. 'No. He'll have to go.'

'Archie. It's happened *twice*. That's not so bad—he'll be able to stop. Give the boy a chance to come good,' Bailey urged.

'And what message does that give the others? That I'm soft on the kind of behaviour that destroys a team?'

'No. It tells them that you understand they're still very young and some of them need a bit more guidance than others,' Jared said.

'Lyle won't be happy about it,' Archie warned.

'But you can talk him round. You're the team coach. He'll listen to you,' Bailey said.

Archie didn't look totally convinced. 'And what if Darren does it again?'

'Then there are all kinds of disciplinary options,' Jared said.

'But if we all give him the right support,' Bailey added, 'he won't do it again.'

Archie went silent, clearly thinking about it. 'All right,' he said. 'I'll square it with Lyle. But I'm going to read young Darren the Riot Act and make sure he knows that if he puts a single toe out of line from now on, he'll be out.'

'Thank you,' Bailey said.

'Everyone deserves a second chance,' Jared added. 'I think he'll make the most of it.'

Everyone deserves a second chance.

Could that be true for them, too? Bailey wondered.

Jared had clearly been thinking about it, too, because later that evening he called her. 'Are you busy?'

'I'm studying,' she said.

'Have you eaten yet?'

'Yes.' A sandwich at her desk. But it counted.

'Oh.' He paused. 'I wondered if you'd like to have dinner with me.'

Was he asking her on a date? Adrenalin fizzed through her veins. Strange how Jared made her feel like a teenager. 'As colleagues?' she asked carefully.

'No.'

So he *did* mean a date. Excitement was replaced by skittering panic. 'I'll think about it.'

'Is my company really that bad?' he asked.

'No—no, it's not that, Jared. Not at all.' She sighed. 'It's complicated.'

'I can take a hint.'

She *would* like to have dinner with him; it was just that the whole idea of dating again scared her. How could she tell him, without dumping all that baggage on him? Telling him what had happened to her, and why her marriage had ended? She couldn't. She just couldn't. 'I, um, haven't dated in a while,' she said.

'Me, neither,' he said, surprising her. 'I'm seriously out of practice, too.'

Something else they had in common. Who, she wondered, had hurt him?

'I was thinking,' he said, 'we were a good team, this afternoon.'

'Yes.'

'And I was thinking,' he said, 'maybe we should give ourselves a chance to see if we could be a good team outside work.'

'Maybe,' she said.

'I could,' he suggested, 'cook dinner for you.'

'You can cook?'

He coughed. 'Don't be sexist. Especially as your brothers are both chefs.'

She smiled wryly. 'Yeah, I guess.'

'So—how about it?'

'If I say yes,' she said, 'then it's just between us?'

'You want to keep it a secret?' He sounded slightly hurt.

'I want to keep life simple,' she said. 'Can I think about it?'

'It's just as well I'm a sports doctor. My ego could really use some liniment right now,' he said dryly.

And now he'd made her laugh. He was the first man to do that in a long while. Maybe, just maybe, she should give this a try. Maybe everyone was right and it was time she learned to live again. And Jared might just be the man to help her do that.

'All right. Thank you, Jared. I'd like to have dinner with you. I don't have any food allergies and I'm not fussy about what I eat.'

'That was a quick decision.'

And she still wasn't sure it was the right one. Part of her really, really wanted to do it; and part of her wanted to run. 'When do you want to do it?' Oh, and that sounded bad. She felt her face heat. Worse still, that was a definite Freudian slip. Because any woman with red blood in her veins would want to go to bed with someone as sexy as Jared Fraser. 'Have dinner, I mean,' she added hastily.

'Tomorrow night?' he suggested.

'That's fine.' Big, fat lie. Now they'd actually set a date, the panic was back. In triplicate. 'I'll need your address.'

'Got a pen?'

'Give me two seconds.' She grabbed a pen. 'OK, tell me.' She scribbled down his address as he dictated it. 'What time?'

'Seven?'

'Seven,' she confirmed. 'Can I bring anything? Pudding, maybe?' She could get Rob to make something special. Then again, Rob would tell their mother, and Lucia would go straight into interrogation mode. OK. She'd cheat and buy it from a top-end supermarket instead.

'No, that's fine. Just bring yourself,' he said.

And how scary that sounded.

Bailey was feeling antsy the next morning, and she was really glad that she was busy all day in clinic. There were the usual sprains and strains, although she did feel a bit sorry for the middle-aged woman who'd managed to give herself tennis elbow from taking her weightlifting training too hard and was horrified to learn it could take several months of rest before the tear in her ligament healed.

'Rest, ice it every couple of hours, take painkillers and use a support bandage when you exercise and whenever it's really sore,' Bailey said. 'And when you do go back to using weights, you'll need to drop the weights right down and take it very steadily. And don't do anything above your head before it's healed fully, or your rotator cuff in your shoulder will over-compensate for your elbow and you'll have to get over the damage to that, too.'

Mrs Curtis grimaced. 'I knew I shouldn't have done that last set. I just wanted to finish the last few reps, but I should've just admitted that I was tired and stopped there.'

'You'll know next time,' Bailey said. 'Come back and see me if it's not any better within a couple of weeks. It should heal on its own, but if it doesn't then a corticosteroid injection could help.'

'Thank you.' Mrs Curtis smiled wryly. 'That'll teach me to remember how old I am, not how old I feel.'

Bailey patted her shoulder. 'We all do it. Don't beat yourself up about it.'

She bought wine and chocolates on the way home, and changed her outfit three times before deciding that smart casual was the way forward—a little black dress would be way too much. Black trousers and a silky long-sleeved teal top would be better. She added her nice jet earrings to give her courage, put on a slightly brighter shade of lipstick than she would nor-mally and then stared at herself in the mirror.

How long had it been since she'd gone on a first date? Or since someone had cooked for her? How did you even behave in these sorts of situations? She thought about calling Joni and asking for help—but, then again, it would make Joni think she was really serious about Jared, and… No, it was all too complicated. She had no idea how he made her feel, other than that he put her in a flat spin.

'It's dinner. Just dinner,' she told her reflection. 'Treat him as a friend. A colleague. And then everything will be fine.'

Except she knew she was lying. Because since that kiss, she hadn't thought of Jared as a colleague—or as a friend. And he hadn't asked her to dinner as a colleague or friend, either.

Would he kiss her again tonight?

And she wasn't sure if the shiver down her spine was anticipation or fear.

CHAPTER EIGHT

BAILEY'S PANIC GREW as she walked up the path to Jared's door. She almost didn't ring the bell and scuttled home to safety instead, but she knew that would be unkind and unfair. He'd gone to the effort of cooking her a meal, so the least she could do was turn up to eat it—even if she did feel way more jumpy than the proverbial cat on a hot tin roof.

She took a deep breath and rang the bell.

When he answered the door, she was glad she'd opted for smart casual, because he'd done the same. He was wearing black trousers and a dark blue shirt that brought out the colour of his eyes. She could feel herself practically dissolving into a puddle of hormones, and her social skills had all suddenly deserted her.

How had she forgotten just how gorgeous the man was?

And his biceps.

Don't think about his biceps, she told herself. Concentrate. Friends and colleagues.

She handed him the wine and chocolates. 'I forgot to ask you if I should bring red or white, so I played it safe—and I should've asked you if you like milk, white or dark chocolate.' Oh, help. Now she was gabbling and she sounded like a fool.

'These are just fine, and you really didn't need to bring them—but I appreciate it,' he said.

And, oh, that smile was to die for. The butterflies in her tummy went into stampede mode.

'Come in.' He stood aside and gestured for her to enter.

How come he didn't look anywhere near as nervous as she felt? How could he be so cool and relaxed when she was a gibbering wreck?

She followed him inside, her tension and anticipation growing with every step.

'We're eating in the kitchen. I hope that's OK,' he said, obviously trying to put her at ease.

'That's very OK, thanks.' His kitchen was gorgeous: a deep terracotta tiled floor teamed with glossy cream cabinets, dark worktops and duck-egg-blue walls. There was a small square maple table at one end with two places set. 'I really like the way you've done your kitchen,' she said.

'I'm afraid it's all my sister's idea rather than mine,' he confessed. 'When I bought this place and did it up, she offered to paint for two hours a day until it was done if I would let her choose the kitchen.'

It sounded as if he was as close to his family as she was to hers. 'So you're not really a cook, then?'

'Given that you come from a family of restaurateurs and chefs, I wouldn't dare claim to be a cook,' he said.

She smiled. 'I promise I won't go into food critic mode.'

He pretended to mop his brow in relief, making her smile. 'Can I get you a drink?'

'Yes, please—whatever you're having.'

He took a bottle of Pinot Grigio from the fridge and poured them both a glass. Bailey noted that all his appliances were built-in and hidden behind doors to match the rest of the cabinets. Efficient and stylish at the same time. She liked that. It was how she organised her own kitchen.

'Have a seat,' he said, indicating the table.

'Thanks.' She bit her lip. 'Sorry. As I said, it's been a while since I dated.'

'Me, too. And it's hard to know what to say. We could make small talk about the team and work—but then it wouldn't be like a date.'

'And if we ask each other about ourselves, it'll feel like—well—we're grilling each other,' she said.

'Or speed dating.' He grimaced. 'I let my best friend talk me into that one six months ago. Never, *ever* again.'

Speed dating was something she'd never done—along with signing up to an online dating agency or letting anyone set her up on a blind date. She'd made it clear to everyone that she was just fine as she was. 'Was it really that bad?'

'Probably slightly worse,' he said. 'But how do you meet someone when you get to our age?'

'You make us sound middle-aged.' She laughed, even though she knew what he meant. By their age, most people had already settled into a relationship or had a lot of baggage that made starting a new relationship difficult. It wasn't like when you were just out of university and there were parties every week-end where most of the people there were still single.

'I'm thirty-five—and sometimes I feel really middle-aged,' he said wryly, 'especially when I hear the seventeen-year-olds talking in the changing room about their girlfriends.'

She raised an eyebrow. 'They don't do that in front of me. Probably because they think I'll tell them off.' Then she groaned, 'Which means they think I'm old enough to be their mother, and at thirty I'm not *quite* that old.'

'Or maybe they've got a secret crush on you and don't want to sound stupid in front of you,' Jared suggested.

'I think,' she said, 'that might be a slightly worse thought. They're still practically babies!'

He laughed and raised his glass. 'To us,' he said, 'and finding some way to talk to each other.'

'To us,' she echoed, feeling ridiculously shy.

'I forgot to ask you if you like fish,' he said.

'I do.'

'Good. Though I'm afraid I cheated on the starter,' he admitted. 'Which is ready right now.'

He took two plates from the fridge: baby crabs served in their shell with a salad garnish, and served with thin slices of rye bread and proper butter.

'I don't care if you cheated. This is lovely,' she said.

The main course was sea bass baked in foil with slices of lemon, rosemary potatoes, fine green beans and baby carrots. 'This is fabulous,' she said. 'Super-healthy and super-scrumptious.'

He inclined his head in acknowledgement of the compliment. 'Thank you.'

Pudding was a rich dark chocolate mousse served in a tiny pot with raspberries.

'Now, this,' Bailey said after the first mouthful, 'is what you'd use to make any woman say yes.'

And then she realised what she'd said.

She put one hand to her face in horror. 'Please tell me I didn't say that out loud.'

'I'm afraid you did.' His voice had grown slightly husky, and his pupils were huge, making his eyes look dark.

She blew out a breath. 'Um. I don't know what to say.'

'If it helps, I didn't actually make it with the intention of using it to seduce you,' he said. 'Only...you've put an image in my head now.'

'An image?'

He nodded. 'Of me feeding you this, one spoonful at a time.'

So much for telling herself to treat this as just dinner with a friend. Right now, he'd put exactly the same image in her own head and she could hardly breathe. Especially as she could vividly remember what it had felt like when he'd kissed her.

What would happen if she held out her spoon to him? Would he let her feed the rich chocolate mousse to him? Or would he lean forward and kiss her?

Time hung, suspended.

Which of them would make the first move?

Dark colour was slashed across his cheekbones. And she could feel the heat in her own face. The beat of desire.

Would he kiss her again?

'I think,' he said, his voice even huskier now, 'we probably need coffee.'

And some distance between them so they could both calm down again. 'Yes,' she whispered.

Though she couldn't help watching him while he moved round the kitchen. For someone who was over six feet tall and so muscular, he was very light on his feet. He'd moved lightly when he'd danced with her, too. What would it be like if he…?

No.

Do not think of Jared Fraser naked, she told herself.

Except she couldn't get the idea out of her head.

What would it be like, making love with Jared?

Her face heating even more, she tried to push the thought to the back of her mind and concentrated on her pudding. He did likewise when he'd finished making them both an espresso.

Silence stretched between them like wires, tighter and tighter.

They needed to break the tension now. Right now. Before they did something stupid. Like kissing each other until they were both dizzy. Right at that moment it was what she really wanted him to do. And she didn't dare look at him in case he didn't feel the same—or, worse, in case he did. She wasn't sure which scared her more.

She sipped the coffee. 'This is good,' she murmured. Oh, for pity's sake. Where was her stock of small talk when she needed it? Why couldn't she talk to him about books and films and theatre?

Probably because her tastes were on the girly side and his would be decidedly masculine.

'I'm glad you like the coffee.' He paused. 'Would you like to sit in the living room?'

'Can I help you wash up first?'

'No. That's what a dishwasher is for,' he said.

Actually, it probably wouldn't be a good idea to work with him in the kitchen. It would be way too easy to brush against each other. Turn to each other. *Touch each other...*

She followed him into his living room. Everything was in neutral tones and comfortable. There were several framed photographs on the mantelpiece and she couldn't resist putting her coffee down so she could look at them more closely. His graduation, three more graduation photographs of what had to be his brothers and his sister as they looked so like him, wedding photographs of his brothers and sister, and various family portraits—including one of him with a small child.

His daughter? Or maybe she was his niece or his godchild. If he'd had a daughter, he would've mentioned it when they talked about kids at Joni's wedding, surely?

'Your family?' she asked.

'Yes. Also known as the doctors at Lavender Lane Surgery.' He smiled. 'They try to poach me onto the team every so often, but I like what I'm doing now.'

Then she came to a picture of a football team. Judging by the haircuts, she'd say the picture was nearly twenty years old. So it was pretty obvious what that represented. His first ever international match. But something had puzzled her for ages. 'So how come, given that you have a Scots accent and a Scots surname, you played for England?'

'I was born in London,' he said, 'and my mum's English—so technically I could have played for either team, but as I lived in London I guess it made more sense to play for England.' He smiled. 'Dad said if my team ever played the under-twenty-one Scotland team, his loyalties would've been really divided.'

'Like in our house. Whenever England plays Italy in the World Cup the boys end up cheering both sides.'

She picked him out immediately in the middle of the photograph. Mainly because that was the one she'd seen when she'd snooped on the Internet—not that she was going to tell him that. 'That's you at seventeen?'

'Yes—the first time I played for England.' He smiled. 'It was an amazing feeling. And when I scored that goal, it felt like all my birthdays and Christmases at once.'

'I bet.' On impulse, she turned round and hugged him.

Big mistake, because then his arms came round her, and he dipped his head to kiss her. His mouth was warm and sweet and tempting, and she found herself responding, letting him deepen the kiss.

He picked her up and carried her over to the sofa, still kissing her, then settled down with her on his lap.

Right at that moment she really wanted him to carry her to his bed. To take her clothes off, bit by bit, and kiss every inch of skin as he uncovered it. And then to touch her again, make her forget about everything in the universe except him...

But then reality rushed back in. She wasn't on the Pill. She hadn't needed to be, because she'd steered clear of relationships, let alone sex. Condoms weren't always effective. If they made love, what if she got pregnant, and what if…? She swallowed hard. She could still remember being rushed into the emergency department, the crippling pain in her abdomen followed by an even worse pain in her soul. And it froze her.

Jared was aware that Bailey had stopped kissing him back. He pulled away slightly and he saw she looked incredibly panicky. Something had clearly happened in her past, something that had put absolute devastation in her eyes.

He stroked her face. 'Bailey, it's all right. We can stop right now and I'm not going to push you.'

But the fear didn't seem to go away. She remained where she was, looking haunted.

'If you want to talk to me,' he said, 'I'll listen, and whatever you tell me won't go any further than me.'

'I don't want to talk about it,' she muttered.

'That's OK, too.' He kept holding her close. He had a few trust issues, too, thanks to Sasha cheating on him and then not giving him any say in keeping the baby. But he really liked what he'd seen of Bailey. It would be worth the effort of learning to trust and teaching her to trust him. They just needed some time.

Maybe it would help if he opened up a little first.

'I used to be married,' he said.

Bailey still looked wary, but at least she hadn't pulled away.

'I loved her. A lot. Sasha.' Funny, saying her name didn't make him feel as if he'd been put through the shredder any more. 'We were married for three years. I thought we were happy, but I guess she wanted more of a WAG lifestyle than I could give her—so that meant seeing a footballer rather than the team doctor.'

Bailey looked surprised. 'She left you for a footballer?'

Sasha had done a lot more than that, but Jared wasn't quite ready to talk about that bit. About how she'd totally shattered his world. How she'd had an affair, got pregnant, decided she didn't actually know who the father of her baby was as she'd been sleeping with them both, and had a termination without even telling him. 'Yes,' he said. 'She'd been seeing him for a while.'

'That's hard,' Bailey said.

He shrugged. 'It was at the time. But it was a couple of years ago now and I'm over it. We could probably just about be civil to each other if we were in the same room.'

'It's easier when you can be civil to each other,' she said.

'You're on civil terms with your ex now?'

It was her own fault, Bailey thought. She'd practically invited the question.

And she had to be honest with Jared. 'It wasn't Ed's fault that we broke up.' She'd shut her husband out and pushed him away. Sex had been out of the question because the fear of getting pregnant and having another ectopic pregnancy had frozen her. Ed had tried to get through to her, but her barriers had been too strong. And so he'd given up and turned elsewhere for comfort. She couldn't blame him for that. She hadn't been in love with him any more, but the way her marriage had ended still made her sad. 'Jared, I don't want to talk about it. Not right now.' She wriggled off his lap. 'And I think I ought to go home.'

'I'll drive you. I only had one glass of wine so I'm under the limit.'

'I'll be fine on the Tube,' she said. 'To be honest, I could do with a bit of a walk to clear my head.'

'Would you at least let me walk you to the Tube station?'

She shook her head. 'I'll be fine. But thank you—that was a really nice meal, and I appreciate it.'

And she needed to get out of here now, before she did something really stupid—like resting her head on his shoulder and crying all over him. It wouldn't be fair to dump her baggage on him, and it really wasn't fair to lead him on and let him think that this thing between them was going anywhere, because it couldn't happen. She wasn't sure she was ready to get that involved with someone again—especially someone who'd been hurt in the past and had his own baggage to deal with. She was attracted to Jared, seriously attracted, but that just wasn't enough to let her take that risk. She didn't want it all to go wrong and for him to get hurt because of her.

When Bailey still hadn't texted him by lunchtime the next day, Jared knew that he'd have to make the first move.

But what had spooked her?

She'd flatly refused to talk about it, so it had to be something huge. He wasn't sure how to get her to talk to him without making her put even more barriers up.

In the end, he called her. He half expected her to

let the call go through to voicemail, but she answered. 'Hi, Jared.'

'How are you doing?' he asked softly.

'OK. Thanks for asking.'

'Want to go and get an ice cream or something?'

'Thanks, but I have a pile of work to do.'

It was an excuse, and he knew it. He could hear the panic in her voice, so he kept his tone calm and sensible. 'So if you have a lot of work to do, a short break will help refresh you.'

She sighed. 'You're not going to let this go, are you?'

'Nope,' he agreed.

'OK. What time?'

'Now?' he suggested. 'It's a nice afternoon.'

'Are you standing outside my flat or something?' she asked.

He laughed. 'No. I'm sitting in my kitchen, drinking coffee. Which is the alternative offer if you don't want ice cream.'

'You're pushy.'

'No. I'm not letting you push me away, and it's a subtle but important difference. I like you, Bailey,' he said. 'I think you and I could make a good team.'

There was a pause, and for a moment he thought he'd gone too far. But then she said, 'I like you, too.'

It was progress. Of sorts.

'I'll see you here in, what, an hour?' she asked.

'An hour's fine,' he said.

Jared turned up with flowers. Nothing hugely showy, nothing that made a statement or made Bailey feel under pressure; just a simple bunch of pretty yellow gerbera. 'They made me think of you,' he said.

Funny how that made her feel warm all over. 'Thank you. They're lovely.' She kissed his cheek, very quickly, and her mouth tingled at the touch of his skin. 'I'll put these in water.' Which was the perfect excuse for her to back away, and she was pretty sure he knew it, too.

They ended up going for a walk in the nearby park. And when Jared's fingers brushed against hers for the third time Bailey gave in and let him hold her hand. He didn't say a word about it, just chatted easily to her, and Bailey knew they'd turned another corner. That she was letting him closer, bit by bit.

Everything was fine until they walked past the children's play area.

'I used to take my niece to the park when she was small. Before she grew into a teen who's surgically attached to her mobile phone,' Jared said. 'The swings were her favourite. That and feeding the ducks.'

So that picture back at his place was of his niece. Even though Bailey's mouth felt as if it was full of sawdust, she had to ask the question. She needed to know the answer. Clearly he loved being an uncle— but would that be enough for him? 'Do you want children of your own?'

'Yes,' he said. 'I'd love to have kids—someone to kick a ball round with and read bedtime stories to. One day.'

Was it her imagination, or did he sound wistful? She didn't quite dare look at him. Besides, panic was flooding through her again.

He wanted children.

OK. So this thing between them was new. Fragile. There were no guarantees that things would work out. But it wouldn't be fair of her to let things go forward without at least telling him about her ectopic pregnancy. If he wanted kids, he needed to know that might not be an option for her. Yet, at the same time it felt too soon to raise the subject. As if she were presuming things.

She'd have to work out how to tell him. And when.

'What about you?' he asked.

How did she even begin answering that?

It was true. She did want children. But that would mean getting pregnant, and the whole idea of that terrified her. It was a vicious circle, and she didn't know how to break it. 'One day,' she said. Wanting to head him off the subject, she added, 'The café's just over there. The ice cream's on me.'

To her relief, he didn't argue or push the subject further. But he didn't let her hand go, either. He was just *there*. Warm and solid and dependable, not putting any pressure on her.

So maybe, she thought, they might have a chance. She just had to learn to stop being scared.

CHAPTER NINE

EVERYTHING WAS FINE until the following Monday, when Bailey was having her usual chicken salad with Joni after the yoga class.

Joni had been a bit quiet all evening, looking worried.

'Is everything OK?' Bailey asked.

'Ye-es.'

But she didn't sound too sure. Bailey reached across the table and squeezed her hand. 'What? You've had a fight with Aaron? It happens. One or both of you is being an idiot, one or both of you will apologise and it'll be fine.'

'It's not that.' Joni bit her lip and there were tears in her eyes. 'Bailey, I don't know how to say this—I mean, it's good news, but I also know that...'

At that moment Bailey knew exactly what her best friend was going to tell her. And, even though it was ripping the top off her scars, no way in this world was she ever going to do anything other than smile—and she was going to try and make this easy for Joni, because she knew exactly why her best friend was worried about telling her. 'Joni, are you about to tell me something really, really fantastic—that you and Aaron are going to be...?'

The sheer relief in Joni's eyes nearly broke her.

'I've been dying to tell you since before the wedding, but...'

Yeah. Bailey could remember how it felt. The moment she'd suspected she was pregnant, the moment she'd done the test and seen the positive result, the way Ed had scooped her up and swung her round when she'd shown him the test stick. The sheer joy and happiness of knowing that they were going to have a baby, start their own family... She'd managed to keep the news to herself for four whole days before it had been too much to keep it in any more; she'd sworn both her mum and her best friend to total secrecy and had burst into happy tears when she'd told them. And whilst Ed had been worried about her jinxing it by telling everyone too early and not waiting until the twelve-week point was up, she'd been so happy that she just couldn't contain her news any longer.

Maybe Ed was right—maybe she *had* jinxed it by telling everyone too soon.

She pushed the thought away. Not now. This was about her best friend's future, not the wreck of her own past.

'Oh, Joni, I'm so pleased for you.' And she was, she really was. Just because it had gone bad for her, it didn't mean that she couldn't appreciate anyone else's joy. 'That's fantastic news. How far are you?'

'Ten weeks. I went for the dating scan today,' Joni said almost shyly.

'Good.' So Joni definitely wasn't going to go

through the pain and fear of an ectopic pregnancy. Bailey almost sagged back in her chair in relief. 'So do I get to see a photograph, then?'

'Are you sure you want to see it?'

At that, Bailey got up, walked round to the other side of the table and hugged her friend. 'Don't be so daft! Of course I want to see the scan picture—I'd be really upset if you didn't show me.'

Joni blinked away tears. 'Sorry. I just didn't want to bring back...you know. And I'm being so wet.'

'Hormones,' Bailey said with a grin. 'You'll be crying at ads with puppies and kittens in them next.'

She sat down again as Joni reached into her bag for a little white folder and handed it to her. She studied the ultrasound photograph. 'You can see the baby's head, the feet, the spine—this is incredible, Joni.'

'And the heart—it was amazing to see the baby's heart beating.'

Bailey hadn't even got to do that bit, so it wasn't as if this was bringing back memories; it was more the shadow of what might have been. And she wasn't going to let any shadows get in the way of her best friend's joy. She was fiercely determined to share that joy with her.

'Bailey, there's something else I wanted to ask you,' Joni said. 'Will you be godmother?'

'Of course I will! I'd be utterly thrilled.' Bailey blanked out the fact that she'd wanted Joni to be god-mother to her baby, too. 'So that means I get to do all the fun things, all the cuddles and the smiles and the messy toys, and then I hand the baby back to you for nappy changes and the night feeds. Excellent.'

She could see in Joni's eyes that her best friend

knew exactly how much effort this was costing her and how much she was holding back, but to her relief Joni didn't say it. She simply smiled and said, 'Bailey Randall, you're going to be the best godmother in the history of the universe.'

'You can count on that,' Bailey said. 'And you can still do yoga during pregnancy, though maybe…' She took a deep breath. 'Maybe you need to switch to a water-aerobics class, one of the special antenatal ones. And I'll do it with you for moral support.'

She meant it, she really did—even though it would be hard seeing all those women with their bellies getting bigger each week and trying not to think about how that hadn't happened for her.

Joni reached across the table and squeezed her hand. 'I know you would. This is yet another reason why I love you. But I'm not going to make you do that. I'll stick to yoga—I'll talk to Jenna before the next class and ask her where I need to take it down a notch.'

Bailey kept it together at the restaurant, but all the way home she could feel the pressure behind her eyes, the sobs starting down low in her gut and forcing themselves upwards. Once her front door was closed behind her, she leaned against the wall and slowly slid down until she was sitting with her knees up to her chin and her arms wrapped round her legs. Then and only then did she let the tears flow—racking sobs of loss and loneliness, regrets for what might have been.

She didn't hear the doorbell at first. She was dimly aware of a noise then recognised the sound. Who was it? She wasn't expecting anyone. She scrubbed at her face with her sleeve and took a deep breath. Right at that moment she wished she hadn't cut her hair short, because then at least she could've hidden her face a bit. As it was, she'd have to brazen it out. She opened the door just a crack. 'Yes?'

'Bailey, are you all right?'

'Jared?' She frowned. 'What are you doing here?'

'We have a meeting to discuss Darren, remember?'

She remembered now. Joni's news had knocked the meeting completely out of her head.

She couldn't let Jared see her in this state. 'Can we do it tomorrow?'

'Are you all right?' he asked again, and this time he pushed the door open. He took one look at her and said, 'No, you're not all right.' Very gently, he manoeuvred her backwards, closed the door behind them and cupped her face between his hands. 'You've been crying.'

'Give the monkey a peanut,' she muttered, knowing that she was being rude and unfair to him but hating the fact that he'd caught her at a weak, vulnerable moment.

But he didn't pay any attention to her words. 'Come on. I'll get you a drink of water.' He put one arm round her. 'Your kitchen's at the end of the corridor, yes?'

'Yes.'

She let him lead her into the kitchen and sit her down at the bistro table. He opened several cupboard doors before he found where she kept her glasses, then poured her a glass of water; she accepted it gratefully.

Jared waited until Bailey had composed herself for a bit before he made her talk. He knew she'd been to yoga with Joni and then out for dinner; it was their regular Monday night catch-up. But he'd wanted to have a quick chat with Bailey about Darren, their problem player, so she'd agreed to be home for nine o'clock and meet him at her place. Jared had been caught up in a delay on the Tube after a signal had broken down, so he'd been all ready to apologise for being twenty minutes late for their meeting, but that didn't matter any more. Clearly something bad had just happened.

'What's happened? Is Joni all right?'

'She's fine.' Bailey dragged in a breath. 'It was good news.'

'Good news doesn't normally make you cry or look as if you've been put through the wringer,' he pointed out.

'I'm fine.'

They both knew she was lying.

'It's better out than in,' he said softly. And he should know. He'd bottled it up for a while after Sasha, until his oldest brother had read him the Riot Act and made him go to counselling. And that had made all the difference.

'I can't break a confidence.'

'Under the circumstances, I think,' he said softly, 'that Joni would forgive you. Or maybe I can guess. Good news, from someone who's just got married—it doesn't take a huge leap of the imagination to know what that's likely to be.'

And it didn't take a huge leap of the imagination to put the rest of it together, either. What would make someone bawl their eyes out when they learned that their best friend was going to have a baby? Either Bailey couldn't have children or she'd had a baby and lost it. Miscarriage, stillbirth, cot death…a loss so heartbreaking that she'd never really recovered from it. And neither had her marriage.

Was that why she'd been so adamant that the break-up hadn't been her ex's fault? And was that why she'd suddenly been so antsy at the park, when she'd asked him if he wanted children?

The way she looked at him, those beautiful dark eyes so tortured, was too much for him. He came round to her side of the table, scooped her out of her chair, sat in her place and settled her on his lap, his arms tightly wrapped round her. 'I'm not going anywhere until you talk to me. And whatever you say isn't going any further than me, I promise you.'

She didn't really know him well enough to be completely sure that he wouldn't break his promise, but he hoped that she'd got to know him enough over the time they'd worked together to work out that he had integrity.

'What happened, Bailey?' What had broken her heart?

'I was pregnant once,' she whispered.

He stroked her face. 'When?'

'Two and a half years ago. I was so thrilled. We both were. We wanted that baby so much.'

He said nothing, just holding her close and waiting for her to tell him the rest.

'And then I started getting pains. In my lower abdomen. It hurt so much, Jared. I was worried that I might be having a miscarriage. And my shoulder hurt—but I assumed that was because I was worried.'

Jared knew that when you were stressed and tense you tended to hold yourself more rigidly and the muscles of your shoulder and neck would go into spasm, causing shoulder pain. Clearly that hadn't been the reason for the pain in this case.

'I went to the toilet,' she said, 'and there was spotting.' She closed her eyes. 'I felt sick. Light-headed.' She dragged in a breath. 'Then I collapsed. Luckily one of my colleagues found me and they got me in to the department. I told them I was pregnant, but I knew what was happening. I *knew.*'

A miscarriage? Heartbreaking for her.

'They gave me a scan. I was six weeks and three days. The pregnancy was ectopic.'

Even harder than he'd guessed. The fertilised egg hadn't implanted into the uterus, the way it should've done. Instead, it had embedded in the Fallopian tube and stretched the tube as it had grown, causing Bailey's lower abdominal pain.

'My Fallopian tube had ruptured. They took me straight into Theatre,' she said, 'but they couldn't save the tube.' Her voice wobbled, and then a shudder ran through her. 'I wanted that baby so much. And I—I...'

'Shh, I know.' He stroked her hair. 'And it wasn't your fault.' It happened in something like one out of eighty pregnancies. Often it sorted itself out and the woman hadn't even known she was pregnant in the first place. But Bailey had been unlucky, caught up in one of the worst-case scenarios.

And clearly the fact her best friend had just shared the news of her pregnancy had brought it all back. Joni had doubtless been one of the first people that Bailey had told about her own pregnancy, and Jared would just bet that Joni had agonised over telling her best friend the news, knowing that it would bring all these excruciating memories back. And he was equally sure that Bailey had gone into super-sparkly mode to reassure her that it was fine, all the while her heart breaking into tiny pieces again.

'The ectopic pregnancy wasn't my fault,' Bailey said, 'but the rest of it was.'

The rest of it? He'd obviously spoken aloud without meaning to, or maybe the question was just obvious, because she started talking again.

'I pushed Ed away afterwards. I—I just couldn't cope with the idea of it happening all over again.'

Jared knew that a second ectopic pregnancy was more likely if you'd had a first. He'd never worked in obstetrics, but he was pretty sure that the statistics weren't shockingly high. Bailey's fears had obviously got the better of her.

'I was so scared of getting pregnant again. So scared of losing another baby. So scared of losing my other Fallopian tube, so I'd never be able to have a baby without medical intervention. I wouldn't let Ed touch me. I knew he was hurting and he needed me, but I just *couldn't* let him touch me. I couldn't give him the physical comfort he wanted.' She leaned her head against his shoulder. 'I was such a selfish bitch.'

'You were hurting, too, Bailey,' he reminded her softly. 'You weren't being selfish. You were hurting and you didn't know how to fix it—for yourself or for your husband.'

'In the end, Ed found comfort elsewhere. But he—he wasn't like your ex,' she whispered. 'He wasn't out there looking for someone else. He would never have done it if I hadn't pushed him away and made him feel as if I didn't care. It was all my fault.'

And now he understood why her family worried

about her so much and were so keen for her to meet someone. Not because she was 'on the shelf', but because they knew how much she'd been through and they wanted her to find someone to share her life with and to cherish her, someone who'd stop her being lonely and sad.

If she'd let him, maybe he could do that. Maybe they could both help each other heal.

But Bailey had pushed her husband away, terrified of getting pregnant again. She'd ended her marriage rather than risk another pregnancy going wrong.

And that explained why she'd responded to him and then backed off again so swiftly. She'd felt the pull of attraction between them just as much as he had, but she was too scared to act on it. Too scared to date, to grow intimate with him, to make love with him—in case she became pregnant and she ended up having another ectopic pregnancy.

'It takes two to break a marriage,' he said. 'Your ex gave up on you.'

'You gave up on your marriage,' she pointed out.

He knew she'd only said it because she was hurting. Clearly she thought that sniping at him would make him walk away and leave her to it. Maybe that was one of the tactics she'd used to push her husband away, but it wasn't going to work on him. 'Yes, I did,' he said. 'I'll take my share of the blame. Just as long as you accept that not all the blame of your break-up is yours.'

'It feels like it is,' she said, sounding totally broken.

If only he had a magic wand. But this wasn't something he could fix. The only one who could let her trust again, let her take the risk of sharing her life with someone, was Bailey herself. Until she was ready to try, it just wouldn't work.

So he said nothing, just held her. If necessary, he'd stay here all night, just cradling her on his lap and hoping she'd be able to draw some strength from the feel of her arms around him.

Eventually, she stroked his face. 'Thank you, Jared. For listening. And for not judging.'

Unable to help himself, he twisted his face round so he could drop a kiss into her palm. 'No worries.'

'I'm sorry I cried all over you.'

'It probably did you good,' he said.

'And we were supposed to be talking about Darren,' she said.

He smiled. 'Don't worry about it. Darren can wait. We'll talk about him tomorrow, maybe. Right now, this is a bit more important.'

'I don't normally cry over people.'

No. He'd guess that normally she sparkled that little bit more brightly, pretending everything was fine and waiting until she was on her own before letting her true feelings show. 'It's fine. Really.'

'I, um, ought to let you go. It's getting late.'

'I'm not going anywhere,' he said softly.

'But…'

'Bailey, do you really think I can walk away and just leave you here alone, upset and hurting?' he asked.

She just looked at him, those huge, huge eyes full of pain.

'It's your choice,' he said. 'I can sleep on your sofa tonight—just so I know you're not alone, and I'm here if you need anything. Or…' He paused.

'Or?' she whispered.

'Or I can hold you until you fall asleep. Sleep with you.'

Even though she tried to hide it, he could see the panic flood into her face. 'I said *sleep*, Bailey,' he reminded her quietly. 'Which isn't the same as having sex.'

'I—I'm sorry.'

He kissed the corner of her mouth. 'You're upset, you're trying to be brave and all your nightmares have come back to haunt you. Some people might use sex as a way of escaping it all, but you're not one of them. And I would never push you into anything you're not happy with.'

'I know.' She swallowed hard. 'I'm a mess, Jared. And you've been hurt in the past, too. I'm the last person you need to get involved with.'

'Let me be the judge of that,' he said gently. 'And let me be here for you tonight.'

Bailey knew it was a genuine offer. It would be, oh, so easy to take him up on it. To lean on him. To take comfort from the warmth of his body curled round hers.

But it would also make things really complicated.

'You're going to be stubborn about this, aren't you?' he asked wryly.

She nodded. 'And you said I had a choice.'

'Sofa?' he asked.

'Go home,' she said. 'Really. I'll be fine.'

'How about we compromise?' Jared suggested. 'You let me hold you—on the sofa—until you're asleep. Then I'll tuck you in and I'll leave—though if you wake at stupid o'clock and you need to talk, then you call me.'

So, so generous. She stroked his face. 'I'm sorry I called you Herod.'

He smiled. 'That was the autocorrect on your phone.'

'But I never took it back. And you're not a tyrant at all. You're more like Sir Galahad. A knight on a white charger coming to the rescue.'

He laughed. 'Hardly. I'm just a man, Bailey.'

'There's no "just". You're a good man, Jared Fraser. Kind. You do all that gruff, dour Scotsman stuff—but that's the opposite of who you really are.'

'Thank you,' he said. 'Now lead me to your sofa.'

'Don't you want a drink or anything? I've been horribly rude and haven't even offered you a coffee.'

He kissed the tip of her nose. 'In the circumstances, that's not so surprising. And I don't want a coffee. I just want to hold you until you fall asleep.'

'Yes,' she said softly, and led him through to the sofa in her living room.

CHAPTER TEN

THE NEXT MORNING, Bailey woke to find herself still fully clothed on the sofa, with her duvet tucked round her.

Falling asleep in Jared's arms last night had felt risky—but it had also felt so, so good.

She grabbed her phone, but a wave of unexpected shyness stopped her calling him. What would she even say?

Instead, she sent him a text: Thank you for last night.

Her phone pinged almost immediately with his reply: No worries. Sleep well?

Yes. Thank you.

Good. See you at work. And this time he'd signed his text with a kiss.

Maybe this was going to work out after all. Jared made her feel brave. And his ex, Bailey thought, really needed her head examined. Why would you throw away the love of a kind, decent, thoughtful man for a shallow, publicity-obsessed lifestyle?

Then again, unhappiness made you do stupid

things. Cruel things. Bailey knew she was just as guilty when it came to the way she'd pushed Ed away. And didn't they say you shouldn't judge someone until you'd walked a mile in their shoes?

She showered, changed and headed for the football pitch. But when she got there she was surprised to find that the players weren't warming up as usual on the field. Instead, they were sitting in the dressing room, and the mood was extremely subdued.

'What's the matter, lads?' she asked.

'You need to go in and see Mr Fincham in his office,' Billy said. 'Archie and Jared are already there.'

Mr Fincham? Why would the football club's chairman of directors want to see her? 'Why?' she asked.

'I can't say.' He bit his lip. 'But there's trouble, Bailey.'

Worried, Bailey hurried along to the office. Mandy, Lyle Fincham's PA, was typing furiously on her keyboard. 'Mandy, what's going on?' Bailey asked.

Mandy shook her head. 'That's for Mr Fincham to say, not me.' She inclined her head towards the door. 'They're in there, waiting. You'd better go in.'

Bailey knocked on the door out of courtesy and walked in. 'Sorry I'm a bit late. There was a delay on the Tube.'

Then she saw Darren sitting between Archie and Jared. And Jared was looking every inch the dour, unsmiling Scotsman.

'It's in all the papers this morning,' Lyle said, indicating the stack of newspapers on his desk. 'And all over the Internet.'

'What is?' she asked.

'The video of laddo here.' Lyle jerked his head towards Darren. 'In a club, getting drunk. Underage.'

She looked at Darren, who was white-faced and
looked utterly guilty. So much for making the most of
his second chance. Or maybe they just hadn't given
him enough support. After all, Jared had originally
wanted to talk to her last night about the boy; they
hadn't got round to discussing the situation, because
she'd been in meltdown.

And yet…something didn't quite stack up. The
last couple of weeks, since she'd picked up Darren's
underperformance and she and Jared had persuaded
Archie to give the boy another chance, his stats had
all been back to normal. 'When did all this happen?'
she asked.

'Last night,' Archie said grimly.

Darren shook his head. 'I wasn't out last night. You
can ask my mum. She'll tell you.'

'Actually, my stats show that Darren's performance
has been normal ever since we talked to you, Archie,'
Bailey said. 'If he'd still been drinking, it would've
shown up on my graphs.'

'Graphs, schmaphs,' Lyle Fincham said, flapping
a dismissive hand. 'Archie should never have let that
box of tricks of yours cloud his judgement. This is a
total mess, and I can't afford to let this affect the club.
As from today, you're out, Dr Randall. I don't care
how much of your research project's wasted. It's over.'

'Actually, I agree with Bailey,' Jared cut in. 'It
would show on the graphs. And if she goes, I go.'

No. No way was she letting Jared risk his career.
For her, this was a research project. Yes, there would
be repercussions about the way it had ended, but it

would eventually blow over. For Jared, it would be his whole career on the line. This wasn't fair.

'I was the one who talked Archie into giving Darren another chance, so don't take this out on Jared,' she said swiftly. 'Don't make him leave because of me.'

'And that video's from weeks back, I swear. I haven't touched a drop since you said I could stay, Mr McLennan,' Darren added desperately, giving Archie a beseeching look. 'I know I was stupid to do it before.'

'But you've still dragged the club's name into disrepute.' Lyle shook his head. 'No. You're out, boy, so go and pack your things.'

'That's not fair—he's owned up to his mistakes, and this is just bad timing,' Bailey said. 'Nobody's perfect. Can you honestly put your hand on your heart and say that you've never, ever made a decision you haven't later regretted?'

Lyle gave her a speaking look.

'We all have the potential to make the wrong choice somewhere along the way. It's hard to own up to it. But Darren admitted his mistake and he's doing something about it.' Bailey grimaced. 'Look, can Darren just go and wait in another room while we talk about this like the professionals we are? It's horrible, all of us standing round like vultures pecking at the poor lad.'

'I agree,' Jared chipped in. 'And I also think we can turn this around so the club can make this a positive. We'll need your PR manager to help us, but we can do it.'

For a moment, she thought Lyle Fincham was going

to refuse, but then he tightened his mouth and nodded. 'Darren, go and wait next door with Mandy. You don't move a muscle, you don't phone anyone or talk to anyone and you don't go anywhere near the Internet, do you hear? Leave your phone with us.'

Looking hunted, the boy handed over his phone and went to wait with Lyle's PA next door.

Lyle picked up his phone. 'Max? My office. Now. There's a situation that needs handling.' He put the phone down again. 'Right. So we'll sort this out between us.'

'Darren's only seventeen. He's still just a kid, really. He's not going to think things through properly, the way someone more mature would do. Instead of coming to you to ask about extra training, Archie, he got drunk to blot out how he felt. You agreed to give him a second chance. He's stayed clean since then—and I bet if you ask any of the other lads they'll be able to tell you that, too,' Bailey said.

'I let you persuade me into giving him another chance, yes,' Archie said. 'But if one player goes wrong, then all the players get tarred with the same brush. You know what the press is like about how much money is in football. They'll have a field day with the kid—and with the club. This isn't fair to the rest of the players, or to the fans.'

'Or the shareholders,' Lyle added. 'His behaviour's put everything at risk.'

'But we can turn this round,' Jared said. 'Really.'

There was a rap on the door and Max Porter, the PR manager, came in. 'So what's this situation?'

'Darren. There's a video of him drunk and underage.' Lyle's colour was dangerously high again, and

Bailey was really beginning to worry that the chairman of directors was about to have a heart attack or a stroke.

'Right,' Max said calmly. 'Talk me through it.'

'We picked it up on Bailey's system,' Jared said. 'He admitted he'd been drinking. Archie agreed to give him another chance.'

'And he hasn't touched anything since,' Bailey said. 'All his stats since we talked to him about it match his average. And it would show up if he was still drinking.'

'I've analysed the way he plays and designed a training programme to help him improve his weak spots,' Jared added.

'So you both obviously think he should stay,' Max said. Then he looked at Archie and Lyle. 'And I take it you both think he should go?'

'And not just him,' Lyle said with a pointed look at Jared and Bailey.

'We can turn this around,' Jared said again. 'This is a classic example of what the pressures of professional football can do to young players. We brought Darren into the club. We set the bar high. And what do we do with the players who can't handle the pressure? Do we just abandon them, in a cold-hearted business decision? Or do we treat them like a family member—knowing he has flaws, knowing he's human and helping him to get over the problem?'

'That's a good spin,' Max said. 'I do hope you're not planning to change career and go after my job, Jared.'

The joke was just enough to dissipate some of the tension in the room. *Just.*

'We don't just need to teach our young players ball skills,' Jared said. 'We need to teach them life skills, because this is a kind of apprenticeship and we're responsible for the way our players develop as people, not just as players. We need to show them how to own up to their mistakes and how to start to make things right.' He paused. 'When my knee was wrecked by that tackle, I was the same age as Darren and it felt like the end of the world, knowing I was never going to be able to play professional football again.'

Knowing how rarely he spoke about this, Bailey held her breath for a moment.

'I could so easily have gone off the rails,' Jared continued. 'But my family and my coach were brilliantly supportive. They stopped me doing anything stupid. And we need to do that for Darren.'

'Actually, Darren could be a good ambassador for the club,' Max said thoughtfully. 'We could get him to talk about his mistakes to kids at school, how he's overcome them and how he managed to get back on the right path with our help. They can learn from his mistakes rather than making those mistakes themselves.'

'So he gets away with it?' Lyle asked, his nostrils flaring in disgust.

'No. Because you could always fine him,' Bailey suggested. 'Donate the fine to a charity specialising in alcohol abuse among kids. Then his mistake will help people who also made mistakes.'

'Making the punishment fit the crime,' Archie said. 'I like that. And he's not a bad lad, Lyle. He's not wild. We need to give him a bit more pride in himself.'

'And what's the press going to think? That I condone all sorts of nonsense at the club?' Lyle demanded.

'No. They'll think that you expect the best from people, but you don't just throw them to the wolves if they get it wrong. You help them be the best they can be,' Max said. 'You're going to get all the mums on your side.'

'Mums don't buy season tickets,' Lyle grumbled.

'Maybe, but they can talk their partners into buying a season ticket for a club that gives a damn about the kids and doesn't just see them as future cash cows,' Jared said.

Lyle threw his hands up. 'I give up. All right. The boy gets a second chance. But you make sure everyone knows we fined him for doing wrong, and that we donated that money to help kids who made the same mistake.'

'Thank you,' Bailey said. 'And I'm sorry I didn't talk it over with you and Archie. I understand why you don't want me here again after today.'

'You know, it would be a shame to lose all that PR—it shows that we care so much about our players' well-being, we've worked with them using the latest technology to help reduce soft-tissue injuries,' Jared said, looking at Max and then Lyle.

'He's right,' Max said. 'It's a brilliant story and it would be a real pity to lose it.'

This time, Jared looked straight at Bailey. 'Everyone deserves a second chance,' he said softly.

She knew he didn't just mean Darren, or their work on the team. He meant them. A second chance to get it right. And it made her go hot all over.

'All right, all right,' Lyle grumbled. 'You can finish your research, Dr Randall. But one foot out of line from you in future…or you,' he warned, gesturing to Jared, 'and that's it.'

'I promise,' Bailey said.

'Me, too,' Jared said. 'Should we send Darren back in to learn his fate?'

'Do that,' Archie said, clapping them both on the back. 'And we'll postpone training until this afternoon. Two-thirty, sharp. Tell them for me, will you?'

Bailey and Jared went next door into Mandy's office. 'Darren, you can go back in now,' Jared said.

'What did Mr Fincham say?' Darren asked, looking anxious.

'He'll listen to you and be fair about it. Just go in, tell the truth and you'll be fine,' Bailey advised him.

Then they went into the dressing room to see the rest of the players. They were full of questions, all talking together and not giving anyone a chance to answer them.

'Has Darren been sacked?'

'Is the boss mad because of all the stuff that happened in that nightclub?'

'Are the rest of us going to be sacked?'

'Shh—calm down,' Bailey said. 'Archie will be in to see you later and he'll explain everything. In the meantime, training today has been postponed until two-thirty. I'm sure you lot have stuff you can get on with in the meantime—and stay out of trouble, OK?'

'Nicely done,' Jared said when they left the dressing room.

'I've got everyone into quite enough trouble as it is,' she said ruefully. 'And I'm sorry, Jared. I really thought you were going to lose your job because of me back there.'

'Lyle always blows up. He'll calm down again.' Jared gave her a wry smile. 'Though I was worrying about him back there. I didn't like his colour.'

'Me, neither,' she agreed.

'Maybe you could teach him some of your yoga stuff to help him relax and reduce his blood pressure.'

'Suggesting that,' she said, 'is probably more than my life's worth right now—and yours.'

'Well, it looks as if we have some unexpected free time.' He paused. 'Want some cake?'

'I think that's a really good idea,' she said.

'My place isn't far. And there's a good patisserie on the corner.'

'That sounds good to me,' she said. 'Though I insist on buying, considering I nearly got you the sack.'

'No, you didn't—but I'm not going to turn down the offer of cake,' he said with a smile. 'Let's go.'

CHAPTER ELEVEN

THEY BOUGHT CAKE at the café and walked back to Jared's place in comfortable silence. Jared made them both a mug of coffee; Bailey was relieved that they sat in his kitchen, given how they'd ended up kissing on his sofa. She didn't quite trust herself not to repeat that, especially as the more time she spent with Jared, the more attractive she found him.

He'd hinted at a second chance. Did she dare take it?

'I was wondering,' he said, 'if you were doing anything at the weekend.'

'Nothing out of the ordinary,' she said. What did he have in mind? Adrenalin fizzed through her at the possibilities.

'I know it's ridiculously short notice, but there's this football function on Saturday night—a charity ball thing. I, um, have two tickets.'

'And you've been let down at the last minute?'

He frowned. 'Bailey, I'm not the kind of man who asks someone to go to a dinner with me and then kisses someone else stupid.'

'No, of course not.' But he was obviously remembering those kisses, too. Had he been planning to ask her to the ball all along? Or had he just bought the tickets to do his bit to support the charity, not actually intending to be there on the night?

She blew out a breath. 'Sorry. I didn't mean to insult you. Honestly. First I nearly lose you your job, and then I practically accuse you of being a philanderer... I'm not doing very well today.'

'The job thing was just as much my fault,' he said. 'And I think you and I...' He blew out a breath. 'It's complicated.'

'Just a tad.' She paused. 'So is this an official date? In public?'

He held her gaze. 'It could be. Or it could be the same deal as you had with me at Joni and Aaron's wedding.'

A fake date, to take the heat off him?

'Sasha's going to be there?' she guessed.

'Possibly.' He shrugged. 'I have no idea.'

There was something she needed to know. 'Are you still in love with her?'

'No. Actually, I don't care whether she's there or not. That isn't the reason I asked you. I only bought the tickets to support the charity,' he admitted. 'I wasn't actually going to go.'

Just as she'd half suspected.

'But I've been thinking about it. And I'd like to go.' He paused. 'With you.'

It was tempting. So very tempting. And maybe the sugar rush of the cake was to blame for her opening her mouth and saying, 'Yes.'

His smile made her feel warm all over.

'So where do I meet you, and what time?' she asked.

'I could pick you up from your place at seven?' he suggested.

'That works for me.'

And how crazy it was that this made her feel like a teenager all over again.

A second chance. If you counted the wedding, this would be their third attempt at a date. At the wedding, and when they'd had dinner together, she'd ended up panicking and backing away. Would this be third time lucky? Would she be able to get over the fear this time?

Jared was a good man. He'd stuck up for her. He'd been there for her when she'd needed a shoulder. He ticked all her boxes. All she had to do was get rid of the fears inside her head.

All.

The training session that afternoon was pretty much as usual. The lads were a little subdued but did their best, including Darren. She was busy at clinic the rest of the week.

And all too soon Saturday night arrived.

Rather than going all out for a ballgown, Bailey had chosen a black lacy dress and patent black leather high heels. Simple yet sophisticated enough for the function, she hoped. And as soon as she opened the door to Jared, she knew from the flare of heat in his gaze that she'd made the right decision. He definitely liked what she was wearing.

'Hello,' she said, feeling ridiculously shy.

'You look fabulous,' he said softly.

'So do you.' She'd seen him in a suit before, but not a dinner jacket. How crazy that something as simple

as a dark red bow tie should look so incredibly sexy
on him. Just to stop herself doing something stupid—
like grabbing him and kissing him and dragging him
off to her bed instead of going to the ball—she said,
'Though I was half expecting you to wear a kilt.'

He laughed. 'That would be a wee bit clichéd.'

But, to her relief, laughter broke the tension just
enough to get her common sense back.

Jared had seen Bailey dressed up before, but it did
nothing to stop the shock of how attractive he found
her. Right at that moment he didn't want to go to the
charity ball and share her; he wanted her all to himself. He wanted to kiss her until they were both dizzy,
and then take her to bed and spend the whole night
finding out what gave her the most pleasure. But he
held himself in check. Just.

He ushered her to the taxi. When he reached for
her hand on the way to the dinner-dance, she curled
her fingers round his.

Maybe, just maybe, this thing between them was
going to go right.

At the dinner, Bailey went into sparkle mode. She
chatted to absolutely everyone, not in the slightest
bit fazed by the incredibly glamorous WAGs there
or how famous some of the players were. But Jared
noticed that she didn't only talk to the famous ones;
she talked to everyone and drew them out.

Bailey Randall had a gift for making people feel
special.

He watched her sparkle and thought, *I could really lose my heart to this woman.* He knew she was
as special as she made people feel, but he also knew

that she had a protective shell round her. He wasn't sure if he'd be able to persuade her to let him past it.

He turned round to see Sasha there with her third husband in tow. Jared had expected to feel some kind of reaction at seeing her again—but he was surprised and relieved to discover he didn't. What had happened was in the past. It couldn't be changed. And it didn't matter any more—it didn't *hurt* any more.

And he knew why: because Bailey was in his life. Being with Bailey made his world a much brighter place.

After he'd introduced Bailey to Sasha and her husband, Jared made his excuses and drew Bailey towards the dance floor.

'Are you OK?' Bailey asked.

'Sure. Why wouldn't I be?'

She coughed. 'Sasha's not exactly a common name. I take it she's *the* Sasha.'

'Yes. Actually, I thought I'd find it difficult to see her,' he admitted, 'but there's just nothing there any more. It's fine,' he reassured her. But he also noticed that Bailey didn't look fine. 'What's wrong?' he asked softly.

'Well—she's incredibly beautiful.'

'And?' He didn't get it.

She shook her head. 'Nothing.'

Then he got it. And it surprised him that Bailey was feeling vulnerable. The Bailey Randall he'd got to know was incredibly together and was comfortable in her own skin, and he really liked that. 'I know you're not fishing for compliments,' he said, 'but, just for the record, you can more than hold your own with her. You're just as beautiful, except yours is a natural beauty.' He paused. 'And I'm so glad you're nothing like her as a person.'

'Hmm,' she said.

'Just to make it clear,' he said softly, 'right now I'm dating a woman I really, really like. A woman I respect for who she is.' He held her gaze. 'And whom I happen to find very, very attractive.'

Had he gone too far?

Panicking that he might make her back off, he added, 'Anyway, your hair's shorter than Sasha's.'

'I used to wear it long.'

He held her closer. He could guess when she'd cut it. After she'd lost the baby. 'No shadows tonight,' he said softly. 'This is just you and me.' He pulled back slightly so she could see his eyes and know that he was telling the truth. 'I've put the past to rest.'

'Good.'

For a moment he wondered if she was going to say that she'd put her past to rest, too.

But she didn't. And he knew he was going to have to take this at her pace.

When he'd been younger he wouldn't have had the patience to do that. But Bailey Randall was going to be more than worth his patience, he thought. So he wasn't going to push her until she was ready.

During the evening, Bailey danced with both Lyle Fincham and Archie.

Archie tipped his head towards Jared. 'Are you and Jared…you know?'

She smiled. 'I'm taking the Fifth Amendment on that one.'

He laughed. 'You can't. You're not American.'

'I'm still doing it. Anyway, under English law you have the right to remain silent, too,' she pointed out.

'I guess.' He smiled. 'He's a good man. I know you two didn't exactly hit it off at first.'

'Jared's not the grumpy Scotsman he likes everyone to think he is,' she said with a grin.

'Exactly. And I think you'll be good together.'

'It's early days, Archie,' she said softly. She wasn't quite ready to believe this was all going to work out. But she really was going to try and put the past behind her.

Eventually Jared claimed Bailey back. Perfect timing, too, because the music changed to soft and slow, which meant that she was right where he wanted her—up close and personal. And she was holding him just as tightly. He wasn't going to embarrass her by kissing her stupid in public, but maybe…

'Shall we get out of here?' he murmured into her ear. 'Go and have a glass of wine back at my place?'

He didn't realise he was holding his breath until she said yes.

He held her hand in the taxi all the way back to his place.

And once the front door was closed behind him, he was able to do what he'd wanted to do all evening and kiss her.

He could drown in her warmth and sweetness.

He broke this kiss before he did something stupid, like carrying her upstairs to his bed. Too fast, too soon. 'I promised you a glass of wine,' he said hoarsely.

'I don't really want a drink,' she said softly.

Then what did she want?

Anticipation thrummed through him. Did she want the same thing that he did? Did she want to lose herself in him, the way he wanted to lose himself in her?

'Last time I was here, you put pictures in my head,' she said. 'Do you happen to have any more of that fabulous chocolate pudding?'

'No, but I can improvise,' he said. Then he went very still as he took in what she'd just said. Not quite sure he'd got this right, he asked, 'Bailey, are you saying we can...?'

'Yes. Provided,' she said, 'we're really careful and you use protection. I'm not on the Pill. I never thought I'd...' She tailed off, wrinkling her nose and looking awkward.

He knew what she meant. When she'd told him about her ectopic pregnancy, she'd also told him how scared she was of getting pregnant again and how she'd pushed her husband away physically. And so what she was offering him now was *hugely* brave. So generous it made him catch his breath. She was going to trust him. To let him prove to her that having sex again wasn't going to make her life implode. 'I'll take care of you,' he said softly, 'and I want you so badly it hurts—but I know this is really scary for you. If you change your mind at any point tonight and say you want to stop, that's also fine. We can take this as slowly as you like.'

Tears glittered in her eyes. 'Thank you, Jared.'

He needed to ask. 'Do you want me to stop now?'

She took a deep breath. 'Yes. And no. Both at the same time. I'm scared, Jared,' she admitted.

'I know. And I understand.' He held her close for

a moment. 'But maybe, just maybe, you can be brave with me. Maybe we can be brave with each other,' he said, and drew her hand to his mouth. He kissed each fingertip in turn, then her palm, folding her fingers over his kiss.

She stood on tiptoe and kissed the end of his nose. And then the corner of his mouth. And then she caught his lower lip between hers, in silent demand that they deepen the kiss.

He was more than happy to comply. And happier still when she kissed him back, matching him touch for touch and nibble for nibble.

'I want you,' he whispered. 'So very, very badly.'

'I want you, too,' she said, her voice low and husky and sensual.

He didn't need a second invitation. He scooped her up and carried her up the stairs to his bedroom. He'd already closed the curtains before he'd left that evening, so all he had to deal with was the light, once he'd set her back down on her feet.

In the soft light of the table lamp he could see the strain on her face. The fear.

'It's OK,' he said. 'We can stop.'

She shook her head. 'Not now.'

'Are you sure?'

She took a deep breath. 'I'm sure.'

He knew she wasn't yet she was clearly trying to push herself past the fear. So he'd do what he could to help. He kissed her lightly, then slid the zip at the back of her dress all the way down. He pushed the lacy material off her shoulders and the dress slid to the floor. She stepped out of it, and he hung it over the back of a chair, not wanting the dress to be spoiled.

And then he held her at arm's length. 'You take my breath away, Bailey,' he said huskily.

'Right now,' she said, with the tiniest wobble in her voice that told him she was still panicking inside, 'I think I'd feel a bit better if you weren't wearing quite so much.'

He smiled. 'I'm all yours. Do what you will with me.'

She slid his jacket off and placed it over her dress on the chair. Then she checked his bow tie. He could see the moment that she realised it was a proper one. 'Very flash,' she said, rolling her eyes, and pulled both ends. The knot came apart in her hands, and she draped the tie over his jacket.

Next was his shirt, and he noticed that her hands were slightly unsteady as she undid the buttons. She pushed the material off his shoulders. 'Oh, your biceps,' she breathed, and stroked the muscles. 'I've wanted to do this since we trained together. They're so beautiful.'

And so was she. He needed to see her. Properly. All of her. 'Can I play caveman now?' he asked. Stupid, because he'd already done that by carrying her up the stairs.

'I was thinking superhero,' she said. 'One with really, really sexy biceps. Though I can live with the fact you're not wearing a cape.'

'That works for me.' At her nod, he unclipped her bra and turned her round. 'Oh, my God, Bailey. You're glorious.' He kissed his way down her spine. 'If I could paint, I'd want you to model for me.' He stroked her back. 'You're perfect.' He drew her back against him so she could feel his erection pressing against her and would know that he meant every word of what he said. He cupped her breasts and kissed the curve of her shoulder. 'Right now, I want you so badly. You make me ache, Bailey. In a good way.'

She turned round in his arms. 'Then take me to bed, Jared.'

He didn't need her to ask again. He picked her up and carried her to the bed, then laid her gently against the covers.

Time seemed to stop. Bailey wasn't sure which of them had removed the rest of his clothes and her underwear, but finally they were skin to skin.

Then she froze as she realised what was just about to happen. She wanted this—she really, really did—but supposing this all went wrong?

'Stop thinking, Bailey,' he whispered. 'Let yourself go. Let yourself *feel*.'

He kissed her again; she tipped her head back against the pillows, and he kissed the curve of her throat, lingering in the hollows of her collarbones.

She could feel her nipples tightening; he nuzzled his way down her sternum and then took one nipple into his mouth, sucking hard. Bailey pushed her hands through his hair, urging him on, and his mouth moved lower, lower.

She almost forgot how to breathe when she felt the long, slow stroke of his tongue along her sex. And it was like a starburst in her head when he teased her clitoris with the tip of his tongue. Her climax was shockingly fast. Oh, God. She'd forgotten what this was like. Forgotten how it felt. Forgotten how good it could be. And it had been so long…

He waited until the aftershocks had died away, then came up to lie beside her and drew her into his arms. 'OK?'

'I think so,' she said. 'Which planet am I on again?'

He chuckled softly. 'I wanted that first time to be all for you.'

He cared that much? She felt a single tear leak out of the corner of her eye.

He kissed it away. 'Bailey, I think we're going to be good together.'

The panic threatened to spill over again, but she pushed it away. She'd said that she'd be brave with him. She wasn't going to back out now.

'Show me,' she whispered.

He took a condom from his drawer and handed her the packet. 'You're in control.'

She knew exactly why he'd done that—so she could be quite, quite sure that there was no chance of getting pregnant, because she'd know they'd used the condom properly—and had to blink back the tears, but she ripped open the packet and rolled the condom over his shaft. And then finally, finally, he was inside her. He held himself very still so her body could adjust to the feel of him, then began to move.

He was a concentrated lover, she discovered. One who didn't talk and who focused on his goals. And, oh, having that focus entirely on her... She was aware of every touch, every kiss, and she knew that he was exploring her and paying very, very close attention to what she liked, and what she liked even more.

It shouldn't be this good. Not their first time. It should be awkward and embarrassing and faintly ridiculous.

But then she stopped thinking as she felt a climax spiralling through her again. She clung onto him for dear life and knew the very second that he'd fallen over the edge, too.

When they'd both floated back to earth, he moved. 'I'd better deal with the condom,' he said softly, and kissed her shoulder. 'Stay there. You look comfortable.' She *was* comfortable. And even though there was a slow burn of panic deep inside her, knowing that Jared was there—that he was solid and dependable and real—helped her to ignore that panic. It was time she stopped letting what had happened to her dictate her life. Time she stopped letting it scare her away from what she wanted. With Jared by her side, supportive and compassionate, she could have everything.

That night, she fell asleep in his arms, just as she had on her sofa. But this time when she woke she was still in his arms. In his bed. Skin to skin. Warm and comfortable. She kept her eyes closed for a little while longer, just luxuriating in the feeling of being held. Of being cherished. She'd forgotten how good this could be.

'Good morning,' he said softly when she opened her eyes at last.

'Yes. It is,' she said with a smile. 'Because you're here.'

'It's the same for me. I don't care if it's raining outside, because it feels like the brightest summer day.' He stroked her face. 'So will you stay for breakfast?'

She kissed him lightly. 'Thank you. I'd love to.'

He made her pancakes with maple syrup and some truly excellent coffee. They went back to her flat so she could change from her lacy cocktail dress into something casual, and spent the rest of the day wandering hand in hand along the South Bank, enjoying the market stalls and the art installations and the street performers.

'No regrets?' he said on her doorstep when he finally saw her home.

'None,' she said. 'Today's been fantastic. Actually, it's the first time in a long while that I've felt this happy.'

'Me, too,' he said.

'So I was wondering,' she said. 'I'm not promising pancakes, but I make a mean bacon sandwich.'

His eyes widened. 'Are you asking me to stay for breakfast, Bailey?'

She took a deep breath. 'Yes.'

'Sure?' he checked.

'It still scares me a bit, the idea of having another relationship,' she admitted. 'But yes. You make me feel brave. I can do this, with you.'

In answer, he kissed her. And she opened her front door and ushered him inside.

CHAPTER TWELVE

FOR THE NEXT three weeks Bailey was really happy. She and Jared were so in tune—and she really liked the funny, kind, gentle man beneath his dour exterior. She also enjoyed the occasional sarcastic text he sent her, signed 'Herod'. He was never going to let her forget that, was he?

This was all still so new that she wasn't quite ready to share it with her family or her best friend, but she found herself looking forward to every evening that she spent with Jared, every night that she slept in his arms and every morning that she woke and he was the first one she saw.

Work was fantastic. She'd always enjoyed her clinic work, and she'd been accepted as one of the team at the football club, so both strands of her job suited her perfectly.

Life didn't get any better than this, she thought.

Until the middle of the day when she suddenly realised that her period was late. She calculated mentally. Not just late—*a whole week late*, and she was never late.

For a moment she couldn't breathe. *What if she was pregnant?* And why, why, *why* hadn't she waited to go on the Pill and insisted on using condoms as well, before she'd made love with Jared?

She took a deep breath, knowing that she was being ridiculous. OK, so the only form of contraception that was one hundred per cent effective was total abstinence, but condoms still had a pretty good success rate. She and Jared had been really, really careful. And she was thirty years old, so her fertility level was lower than when she'd fallen pregnant last time. She only had one Fallopian tube working, making the chances of falling pregnant even lower. This was probably just a stupid glitch.

But how many other women had been caught out that way? How many teenage girls had fallen pregnant after just one time? How many women, nearing menopause and thinking that their fertility was practically zero, had taken a risk and discovered they were having a 'happy accident'? She knew of several colleagues who hadn't planned their last babies.

And what if history repeated itself? What if she was pregnant and it was another ectopic pregnancy? What if, this time, she lost absolutely everything?

There was only one way to find out. And she was going to have to be brave and face it.

At lunchtime she went out and bought a pregnancy test kit. With every step back towards the hospital her legs felt as if they were turning into lead, heavy and dragging.

The last time she'd bought a pregnancy test she'd been so excited, so hopeful. She had actually run to the bathroom, because she'd so desperately wanted it to be positive—she'd wanted to know the result that very second.

This time, taking a pregnancy test felt more like a sentence of doom. Something she had to nerve herself to do. Panic made her hands shake as she opened the box. It took her three goes to open the test kit itself.

Oh, God. Oh, God. Oh, God.

Please don't let her be pregnant.

Please don't let the nightmare happen all over again.

Please don't let that low, dragging pain start as a nag and then flare into agony.

Please don't let her lose her last chance.

Time felt as if it was wading through treacle as she washed her hands and kept an eye on the test stick. One line in the window to let her know that the test had worked.

She felt sick. The line in the next window would tell her yes or no.

'Please let it be no. Please let it be no. Please let it be no.' The words were ripped from her, low and guttural.

But she knew that begging wasn't going to change a thing. The test stick was measuring the level of a hormone in her urine: human chorionic gonadotropin, which was produced by the placenta after fertilisation.

Then again, a negative result could be just as bad because it might mean that the embryo hadn't implanted yet—or that it had implanted in the wrong place. Just as it had before.

She stared at the next window. One line formed, and then a second.

Positive.

Her knees went weak and she sat down heavily.

And then there was the window to tell her how many weeks since conception…

She stared at the window until the words finally penetrated her brain. *Three weeks plus.* She and Jared had first made love three weeks and two days ago. Now she thought about it, it had been smack in the middle of her cycle. The most fertile stage. Which would make her five weeks and two days pregnant now.

No, no, no, no, no.

Nearly three years ago, at this stage, that meant that in one week and one day's time…

Her stomach heaved, she dropped the test stick and was promptly sick in the sink.

Bailey washed her face afterwards while she tried to think about what to do.

She was going to have to tell Jared; but she had absolutely no idea what she was going to say. Or what was going to happen next. He'd said he wanted kids one day. But they hadn't been together that long. This was way too soon. She didn't think Jared was the kind of man who'd walk away, or who paid towards a child's upbringing but had no emotional involvement with the baby whatsoever—yet something else worried her. Would he want the baby more than he wanted *her*?

Panic really had turned her into a gibbering, raving idiot. She was always so together, so organised. Not knowing what to do next just wasn't in her make-up. And it freaked her out even more that she was reacting like this. That all her common sense had vanished into thin air. That she couldn't think rationally.

What the hell was she going to do?

Right now, her parents were in Italy. She knew that all she had to do was pick up the phone and her mother would get on the next plane to London to be with her but that wasn't fair; her parents deserved a chance to enjoy having a holiday around their wedding anniversary. Her brothers were up to their eyeballs running the restaurant, so it wouldn't be fair to talk to them about it, either.

Then there was Joni. But how could Bailey dump something like this on her best friend, when Joni should have the chance to enjoy her own pregnancy without any shadows?

Besides, Jared was the one she *really* needed to talk to.

Today was one of her clinic days, so she wouldn't see him during working hours. She knew she could call him—but she didn't trust herself to make any sense on the phone. She had a nasty feeling that she'd start crying as soon as she heard his voice. The last thing she wanted to do was to panic him by sobbing uncontrollably and mumbling incoherent fragments at him. This conversation needed to be face-to-face. Rational. Together.

But her brain was so fried that she couldn't even remember what they'd arranged to do this evening. Was she meeting him at his place? At hers? Somewhere else?

'For pity's sake, Bailey Randall, get a *grip*,' she told herself sharply.

But she couldn't. She felt as if she was scrabbling around in the dark, wearing oversized boxing gloves.

She grabbed her phone and texted Jared. Can you meet me at my place after work?

* * *

Jared looked at Bailey's message on the screen of his phone: Can you meet me at my place after work?

Odd. They'd planned to go out for a pizza after work and then to the cinema. He was meeting her at the Tube station. Had she forgotten? Or had something happened that meant they had to change their plans?

Sure. Is everything OK? he texted back.

OK, she replied.

That was very un-Bailey-like. She was normally much chattier than this. Or maybe she was having a rough day in clinic and she was up to her eyes in work. Being busy might explain her forgetting their plans.

He was busy that afternoon, too, and didn't think anything more of it until she answered the door to him. Then he saw that her face was pale—paler than he'd ever seen it before—and her eyes were puffy, as if she'd been crying. 'Bailey? What's happened?' he asked.

She backed away before he could put his arms round her. 'You'd better come in and sit down.'

And now he was really worried. This definitely wasn't normal for her. The woman he'd been dating was warm and tactile. She liked being hugged, and he really enjoyed the physical side of being close to her. The fact that she'd just backed away... What was happening?

He followed her into the kitchen and she indicated the chair opposite hers.

'Do you want a drink?' she asked.

'No. I want to know what's wrong,' he said, sitting down. And his worry increased exponentially when he reached across the table to hold her hand and she pulled away.

'I'm, um…' She dragged in a breath. 'Well, the only way I can tell you is straight out. I'm pregnant.'

Jared wasn't sure what he'd been expecting, but it sure as hell hadn't been this.

Pregnant?

'But—how?' He knew the question was stupid as soon as the words left his mouth. They'd had sex. Which meant the risk of pregnancy. He shook his head in exasperation at his own ridiculousness. 'I mean, we were careful.'

'I know.'

'How far along are you?'

'Just over three weeks, according to the test.' She dragged in a breath. 'Five weeks since the start of my LMP.'

'OK.' He blinked, trying to clear his head.

Bailey was pregnant.

With his baby.

He'd been here before—sort of. When Sasha had told him that she'd had a termination. Saying that she didn't know whether the baby was his or not. Saying that she didn't want a baby anyway. Saying that she didn't want to be married to him any more.

This wasn't the same thing. At all.

But it was a hell of a lot more complicated. The last time Bailey had been pregnant it had been ectopic. She'd gone through enormous physical pain—and she'd lost part of her fertility as well as the baby. And the fear of it happening again had led to the breakdown of her marriage.

Right now, she was clearly panicking, worrying

that history was about to repeat itself. Would that panic make her consider having a termination even before the embryo had implanted—and would she make that decision without him?

He pushed the fears away. Bailey wasn't Sasha. And Bailey needed his full support. He had to put his own concerns and feelings aside and put her first. And he needed her to know that he'd be there. Given how she'd pushed Ed away, she was likely to do the same thing with him—he was learning that this was the way Bailey coped. She'd already begun pushing him away by not letting him hold her and comfort her when she was clearly so upset.

Well, Jared wasn't Ed, either. He wasn't going to let her push him away. The future might be tricky, but they had a lot more chance of surviving it if they faced it together.

He didn't think she'd listen to him right now—panic would've stopped up her ears. Which left him only one course of action. He stood up, walked round to her side of the table, scooped her out of her chair and sat down in her place. Once he'd settled her on his lap, he wrapped his arms tightly round her. Now she'd know for sure that he wasn't going to let her go.

She wriggled against him. 'Jared, what are you doing?'

'Showing you,' he said simply. 'That I'm here. That we're in this together. That I'm not going to let you push me away.'

She looked utterly confused. 'But—'

'But nothing,' he cut in gently. 'Oh, and just so you know—Bailey Randall, I love you.'

CHAPTER THIRTEEN

HE LOVED HER?

Bailey couldn't quite take this in. 'But…we've hardly…'

'It's too soon. I know. We haven't been dating long, we've both got baggage and we should both be taking this a hell of a lot more slowly.' Jared shrugged. 'But there it is. I don't know when it happened or how. It just *is*. I love you, Bailey. You make everything sparkle. My world's a better place with you in it. I know the very second you walk onto the football pitch at work, even if my back's to you and I haven't heard you speak, because the world immediately feels brighter.'

It was the nicest thing anyone had ever said to her.

But still the worry gnawed at her. He'd told her he wanted children. And she'd just told him she was pregnant. Why else would he say that he loved her? 'Are you saying this because of the baby?' she asked.

'No. The baby doesn't change anything about the way I feel about you.' He blew out a breath. 'But I guess there's something I ought to tell you. It's the wrong time to tell you, but if I don't tell you now then you'll be hurt that I didn't tell you when you eventually find out, and… Oh, hell, you'll be hurt if I do tell you.' He rested his forehead against her hair. 'I don't know how to say this.'

'You and Sasha had a baby?' she guessed.

'Not exactly,' he said.

She frowned. 'I don't understand.'

'She was pregnant,' he explained, 'but she didn't know whether the baby was mine or someone else's, because she'd been sleeping with another man, too. Until she told me, I didn't have a clue that she'd been having an affair, much less anything else.'

Bailey was too shocked to say anything. So Jared had been here before. Been hurt. And she'd just brought back all the bad memories for him, too.

'She, um, had a termination,' Jared said quietly. 'When I thought she was going on a girly weekend with her mates.'

'She didn't tell you until afterwards?'

'She didn't tell me,' he corrected softly, 'until the bank statement came through and it turned out she'd accidentally used the wrong debit card to pay for it.'

'How do you mean, the wrong debit card?'

'Sasha didn't work,' Jared explained. 'I used to put money into her account every month, because I didn't want her to feel that she had to check with me or ask me for money before she went out to lunch with her mates or had her hair done. That might've been the way our grandparents did things, but I thought it was important she should feel that she had money of her own.'

So Jared had done what he'd thought was the right thing, and it had come back to bite him.

He sighed. 'When I saw the payment to a private medical clinic, I realised something was wrong.' He gave a wry smile. 'I know I'm a sports medicine doctor, but I was a bit hurt that she hadn't talked to me about whatever medical thing was worrying her. I could've reassured her and maybe helped her get the right treatment. When she came home that night I asked her about it, and that's when she told me about the affair.' He swallowed hard. 'And the reason she'd been to the clinic was because she'd had a termination. She'd got rid of the baby without telling anyone what she was doing—without telling anyone at all. Not me, and not the other guy whose baby it might have been.'

Clearly the double betrayal had cut him to the bone.

'Don't get me wrong,' he said. 'I believe there are circumstances where a termination is the right choice. But I do think you should at least talk over all the options with your partner before you make a decision as life-changing as that.'

'And it wasn't the decision you would've made?' Bailey asked.

He shook his head. 'As I said, even if the baby hadn't been mine, we could've worked it out. Or at least tried to work it out. But then she came out with all this other stuff and I realised that even if the baby had definitely been mine, she would've done exactly the same thing. She didn't want a baby at all. She didn't want the changes it would make to her body.'

'That's... I don't know what to say,' Bailey admitted. 'That was hard on you.'

'On both of us,' Jared said ruefully.

'It wasn't your fault she had an affair, Jared.'

'Maybe, maybe not. My work took me away a lot, and that wasn't fair on her.'

Sasha had taken the choice away from Jared. Did he think Bailey would do the same? Was that why he was telling her this? Or was he telling her that he definitely wanted the baby? She swallowed hard. 'You said in the park, that time, that you wanted kids.'

'I do.' He paused. 'But that's not the be-all and end-all of a relationship, Bailey. You're pregnant with my baby, but that's not why I want to be with you. I want to be with you for *you*.' He took a deep breath. 'And right now I'm guessing that you're in a flat spin, worrying that history's going to repeat itself. This must be your worst nightmare. Your biggest fear come true.'

Her breath hitched. 'Yes.'

His arms tightened round her. 'I know you've had one ectopic pregnancy, but it doesn't mean that this one's definitely going to be ectopic as well.'

Brave, she thought, but misguided. 'We both know the risks of having another ectopic are higher in subsequent pregnancies.'

'It's a *risk*, not a guarantee,' he said. 'Let's start this again. You've just told me that you're pregnant. I know you're scared. I think I am, too. It's a huge thing. But this is amazing, Bailey. Really *amazing*. We're going to be parents.'

'What if...?' Again, she couldn't breathe. Couldn't say the words that haunted her.

'If it's another ectopic pregnancy or you have a miscarriage? Then we'll deal with it if and when that happens,' he said. *'Together.'*

And then she realised that he wasn't going to let her push him away. Even if she tried. He wasn't going to repeat his mistakes, and he wasn't going to let her repeat hers, either.

The bleakness and fear ever since she'd taken the pregnancy test suddenly started to recede. Only a little bit, but it was a start. 'You reckon?'

'I reckon.' He didn't sound as if he had any doubts. 'And I'll be brave and lay it on the line. I want you, Bailey. Yes, I'd like us to have children together—whether they're our natural children, whether we need IVF to help us or whether we adopt. But the non-negotiable bit is you. I love you, Bailey, and I want to be with you.'

He meant it. She could see that in his eyes. He'd been honest with her, and she owed him that same honesty. 'I want to be with you, too,' she said. 'But I'm scared that I'm going to make the same mistakes again. My marriage collapsed because I pushed Ed away, and I know I hurt him. I feel bad about that.' She blew out a breath. 'I don't want to hurt you like that, Jared. Especially as I know you've already been through a rough time.'

'Then maybe we both need to do something different this time,' he said softly. 'Maybe we need to take that leap and trust each other—and ourselves.'

She nodded. 'This is a start.'

He took a deep breath. 'If you decide that you can't go ahead with the baby, then I'll support you. I'll be right by your side.'

Even though a termination was clearly a hot button for him, he'd support her if that was what she wanted.

But that was only one option. What about the really scary one? 'And what if—what if I *do* want to go ahead?' she asked.

'Then I'll still be right by your side. Nothing changes.'

He'd be there for her. Whatever. Regardless. Because he loved her.

'I'm not going to wrap you up in cotton wool—even though part of me wants to—because I know it will drive you insane. So I'll be whatever you need me to be. Though, to be fair, I'm not a mind reader,' he added, 'so you'll have to tell me if I get it wrong, instead of expecting me to work it out for myself. Because I'm telling you now that I probably won't be able to work it out.'

Trust him.

Take the risk.

Could she?

She thought about it. When she'd told him about her ectopic pregnancy, he'd been brilliant. He hadn't pushed her, he hadn't told her what to feel—he'd just held her and listened. He'd backed her in front of Lyle Fincham; he'd even said that if she left the club, so would he. And he'd just opened his heart to her, been totally honest with her.

She knew he'd be by her side all the way through her pregnancy. Not smothering her, not making the decisions for her—but he'd be there to discuss things, to help her see a way forward through all the worries. Just as he was here for her now—holding her, letting her know that he was there, supporting her.

So, yes, she could take the risk.

But there was something else she needed to tell him. Something important.

'I love you, too,' she said softly. 'Even when you're being stubborn and awkward and I want to shake you.'

'I'm glad we cleared that up,' he said dryly.

'And here I am, insulting you again when I'm trying to tell you something really important.' She leaned forward to kiss him. 'I didn't date anyone after my divorce. I never wanted to be with anyone again. I didn't want to take the risk of loving and losing. But I noticed *you*. Even though you annoyed me the very first time I met you, at the same time I noticed your eyes were the colour of bluebells.'

'Bluebells…' He looked amused.

She cuffed him. 'Stop laughing at me. I'm trying to be romantic.'

'Are you, now?'

She loved that sarcastic Scottish drawl. 'And then you trained with me.' She went hot at the memory and her breath caught. 'Your biceps,' she whispered.

He nuzzled her earlobe. 'Yeah. Your back. I hope you know you gave me some seriously hot dreams.'

Just as she'd dreamed about him. 'You danced with me at my best friend's wedding. You kissed me.'

'I wanted to do a lot more than dance with you. And kiss you. Except you got spooked.'

'I know. It scared me that I wanted you so much, Jared. I didn't want to be attracted to anyone. I didn't want to love anyone again. But then,' she said simply, 'there you were. And it happened. I fell for you. As you said, I don't know how or where or when. I just *did*.' She paused. 'I love you.'

'Good.'

She kissed him again. 'So what are we going to do about this?'

'Given that you're expecting my baby and we haven't had a proper courtship?' he asked. 'I guess we're just going to have to take each day as it comes. But one thing I promise you is that I'll always have your back,' he said. 'Just as I know you have mine—I haven't forgotten the way you stood up to Lyle Fincham on my behalf.'

'You stood up for me, too,' she pointed out. And then suddenly it was clear as the panic ebbed further and further away. 'You make me feel safe, Jared. And you make me feel as if I can do everything I'm too scared to do.'

'And you make me want to be a better man,' he said.

'You're already enough for me, just as you are,' she said.

He held her closer. 'So I'm going to ask you properly. I don't have a ring, but that's something we'd choose together later in any case.' He kissed her, then gently moved her off his lap and dropped to one knee in front of her. 'Bailey Randall, will you do me the honour of being my wife?'

'Yes. Absolutely yes,' she said, drawing him to his feet and kissing him. 'I think I'd like a quiet wedding, though.' Particularly as it would be second time round for both of them. Their second chance.

'We can do whatever we want,' Jared said. 'Whether you want a tiny church or a deserted island or a remote castle—whatever you want, that's fine by me. I don't care where we get married or how, just as long as you marry me.'

'I'd like just our family and closest friends there—the people who mean most to us,' she said. 'And then maybe a meal afterwards.'

'Maybe a little dancing. I quite like the idea of dancing with my bride,' he mused. 'And a wedding cake made by Rob.'

'White chocolate and raspberry,' she suggested.

He grinned and kissed her. 'Good choice. I agree.'

'When did you have in mind?'

'I would say as soon as we can, which means a fortnight, but that might be rushing it a tad,' he said. 'So how about…say…six weeks from now?'

Around the time of the twelve-week scan. *If* the baby was even viable. If she wasn't in the middle of another ectopic pregnancy.

'What if it goes wrong?' she whispered.

Luckily he seemed to realise that she was talking about the baby and not them. 'It's not going to stop me loving you and wanting to be married to you,' he said.

'But what if everything goes wrong and I can't have children?' She dragged in a breath. 'You said you wanted children.'

'There are other ways,' he said. 'Adoption. Fostering. Or even if it's just the two of us and a dog and a cat, and we just get to spoil our nieces, nephews and godchildren. We'll still be a family. We'll be together.'

He really, really believed in them.

And the strength of that belief nearly made her cry.

'Agreed. Six weeks,' she said. 'On a weekend?'

'Or a weekday. Whenever they can fit us in.' He paused. 'I need to buy you an engagement ring. Maybe we can go shopping at the weekend.'

She smiled. 'That's not important. It's not about the jewellery. It's about how we feel.'

'I know. But I still want to buy you an engagement ring.' He hammed up his accent. 'I'm traditional, you know.'

'And you're going to marry me in a kilt?'

That made him laugh. 'No.'

She rolled her eyes. 'Spoilsport.'

'It might clash with your dress. Anyway, we need a ring first. We're going to do this properly, Dr Randall.'

She laughed and kissed him. 'OK. An engagement ring it is.'

He paused. 'Though maybe you should meet my family before I give you the ring.'

'And we need to tell mine,' she said. 'Be warned, there will be a party. And nobody parties like Italians.'

'No? Try the Scots,' he said. 'Now, we can party all night.'

She smiled. 'So your family likes partying as much as mine? We might have a bit of trouble talking them into a quiet wedding.'

'No. They love us. They'll back us in having exactly what we want,' Jared said. 'My family's going to love you.'

'Mine already likes you.'

'Then we're going to be just fine.' He sat down on the chair again and pulled her back onto his lap. 'I love you, Bailey.'

'I love you, too.'

'And I know you're still scared—so am I,' he admitted. 'But we can talk to the experts and make sure we know what all our options are.'

'They did tell me last time,' she said, 'but I didn't really take any of it in. I guess I was a bit too shell-shocked.'

'Then we'll ask again,' he said. 'We'll get the first appointment we can and ask for an early scan—maybe even more than one, until we're sure this pregnancy definitely isn't ectopic—and the one thing I promise you is that your other tube isn't going to rupture. Because if it *is* another ectopic, we'll do something before that happens.'

She swallowed hard. 'Have a termination, you mean.'

He nodded. 'But it won't be because we don't want the baby. It'll be because the baby doesn't have a chance of survival and it's a risk to your health, which isn't the same thing at all. And I will be right by your side, holding your hand, all the way.'

Giving her courage when she faltered. And letting her give him courage in the bits he found difficult. A true partnership. The same team. That worked for her. 'That,' she said, 'is a deal.'

The next morning, Bailey booked an appointment with her GP. She texted Jared to let him know the time and where to meet her, just in case he could make it.

He made it. She was pretty sure he'd had to call in some favours to do it, but she was glad that he'd kept his promise to her: he was right by her side, all the way.

He held her hand while she told the GP about her previous pregnancy and the GP rang through to the hospital to book her in for an urgent scan.

And he was right by her side as they walked through the corridors towards the ultrasound department at the hospital later that afternoon.

'I'm scared,' she whispered.

'I know you are, but I've got a good feeling about this.' His fingers tightened round hers. 'And, whatever happens, I'm here and I'm not going away.'

No matter what she did or said, he wasn't going to let her push him away. He wouldn't let her repeat her mistakes. Funny how that made everything feel so much safer.

Jared held her hand while the trans-vaginal scan was done, and he didn't say a word about the fact that her fingers were so tightly wrapped round his that she must've been close to cutting off his circulation. He was just there. Solid. Immovable. Her personal rock.

'Dr Randall, I'm absolutely delighted to say,' the ultrasonographer said with a broad smile, 'that you have an embryo attached very firmly to the wall of your placenta.'

The picture on the screen was just a fuzzy blob to both of them; they couldn't really make anything out at all.

But it was their baby.

In her womb, not in her Fallopian tube.

And the nightmare that had happened last time definitely wasn't going to happen again. *It wasn't an ectopic pregnancy.*

Bailey felt the tears spilling out of her eyes as she looked over at Jared; and she could see that his eyes were shiny with tears, too. 'Are you crying?' she whispered. Her big, tough, dour Scotsman, in tears?

'Yes, and I'm not ashamed of it. We're seeing our own little miracle,' he whispered back. 'I'm so happy. I want to climb on top of the hospital roof and yell it out to the whole world.'

The picture that put in her head made her smile but then the panic came crashing back in to spoil it. 'Not yet. We don't say a word to anyone, not until twelve weeks,' she said. Just in case she lost the baby. There were still no guarantees that everything would be all right. But at least they'd passed the first hurdle.

CHAPTER FOURTEEN

JARED'S PREDICTION ABOUT his family turned out to be spot on. Bailey adored Jared's family—particularly when Aileen, Jared's sister, took her quietly to one side and confided in her. 'We've all been so worried about him.'

'After Sasha, you mean?'

Aileen nodded. 'But he's seemed a lot happier lately. Now I've met you, I can see exactly why. And I'm so pleased you're joining our family.'

'Me, too,' Bailey said, and hugged her impulsively.

And her family was just as ecstatic when Jared and Bailey dropped in to announce the news of their wedding. And they insisted on having a small party with cake and champagne—including Jared's family—when Jared bought Bailey a very pretty sapphire-and-diamond knot.

To Bailey's relief, Jared didn't wrap her in cotton wool. Instead, he insisted that her life should be pretty much as it always was—only just not quite so intense on the exercise front. But he did move into her place, and he insisted on bringing her breakfast in bed every morning.

Bailey couldn't ever remember being this happy before.

It was hard not to share the news about the baby with her mum and Joni, especially as Joni was blooming with her own pregnancy, but Bailey was completely superstitious about it. She wasn't going to do anything the same this time. She wasn't even going to start looking at baby clothes, or nursery furniture, or baby name books, until they'd reached the twenty-week mark.

But she was glad that Jared had suggested getting married in six weeks' time, because planning everything would keep them both occupied. He'd already booked the register office and asked his oldest brother to be his best man. Her family had immediately offered to sort out the wedding breakfast and the wedding cake—raspberry and white chocolate, as she'd suggested. So all she had to do was sort out her bridesmaid, the dresses, the invitations and the flowers.

On Monday evening, after the yoga class—and luckily Joni had told Bailey exactly which bits Jenna had suggested to tone down during pregnancy, so she was able to do the same without having to ask—she and Joni had their usual catch-up over a chicken salad.

'There was something I wanted to ask you, Joni,' she said. 'How do you fancy being a bridesmaid again?'

Joni stared at her in shock. 'You and Jared, you mean? But...you stopped talking about him. I thought it had gone wrong. And, um—well, I thought you'd tell me about the break-up when you were ready.'

Bailey grinned. 'In answer to your questions—

yes, yes, yes, and we've sorted it out so there's nothing to talk about.'

'You and Jared,' Joni repeated.

'Me and Jared,' Bailey confirmed.

Joni hugged her. 'That's the best news ever.'

'Don't cry, or you'll start me off,' Bailey warned, seeing the telltale glitter in her best friend's eyes.

'Sorry. It's hormones making me so wet and crying over everything,' Joni said.

Me, too, Bailey thought, but hugged the secret to herself.

'So when is it all happening?'

'Um, that would be…a little under six weeks.'

Joni looked shell-shocked. 'That soon?'

Bailey shrugged. 'We couldn't see any reason to wait. The reception's going to be at the restaurant, Rob's doing the cake, the register office is booked… so all I need to do is sort out flowers, dresses, and ask you if Olly's band would come and play during the meal.'

'I'm sure they will—in fact, I'll ring him now.' A couple of minutes later she hung up. 'Deal. Olly says he needs to know what the "our song" is.'

'I have no idea.' Bailey spread her hands. 'I guess I'll have to ask my fiancé what he thinks.'

'And I'll go dress-shopping with you any time.'

'Good. That means this Saturday,' Bailey said.

And by the end of Saturday she had the perfect dress—a skater-style strapless dress in deep red velvet that wouldn't let her pregnancy show, even in another five weeks' time, with matching shoes. Joni had a similar dress in ivory with red shoes and a red sash, and her mother found a champagne-coloured suit.

'Look at us. We rock,' Bailey said, when they were dressed up and standing in front of the mirror.

'Jared's going to be totally bowled over. You look so beautiful,' Lucia said. 'You both do.'

They agreed on simple flowers—ivory roses for Bailey and red roses for Joni. The invitations were written and posted. And all they had to do then was hope for a sunny day.

Finally it was the Thursday of Bailey and Jared's wedding day. Bailey had spent the previous night at her parents' house, to preserve the tradition of not seeing the groom until the actual wedding. Jared had sent her a single red rose, first thing, with the message, 'I love you and I can't wait to marry you'—in his own handwriting, she noticed, rather than the florist's.

Joni and Aaron came over to help them get ready, and finally they were ready to go to the register office. As Bailey had been expecting, she and Jared were both interviewed by the registrar—in separate rooms so they wouldn't see each other until the wedding—and then finally the guests were all seated and it was time to walk into the room itself.

They'd arranged for Olly to play a song on acoustic guitar as she walked down the aisle on her father's arm—a love song from Jared's favourite rock band, with the mushiest words in the world, and she'd nearly cried the first time Jared had played it to her.

And her dour Scotsman—wearing morning dress rather than a kilt, but with a velvet bow tie to match her dress—lit up in smiles as he turned to watch her walk up the aisle.

'You look amazing,' he said. 'I love that dress. But, most of all, I love you.'

'I love you, too,' she whispered.

Every moment of the ceremony felt as if it had been engraved on her heart—from the registrar welcoming everyone to declaring all the legal wording.

'I do solemnly declare that I know not of any lawful impediment why I, Jared Lachlan Fraser, may not be joined in matrimony to Bailey Lucia Randall,' he said, and she echoed the declaration.

He took her hand. 'I call upon these persons here present to witness that I, Jared Lachlan Fraser, do take thee, Bailey Lucia Randall, to be my lawful wedded wife.'

And then, once they were legally married, the registrar smiled. 'You may kiss the bride,' she said, and Jared took Bailey into his arms, kissing her lingeringly to the applause of their family and friends.

Once the registration was complete and they'd checked the entry was correct before signing it, there was time to take photographs on the marble staircase. And then, outside the register office, everyone threw dried white rose petals over them.

She smiled at Jared. 'This is even better than snow,' she said.

'Especially as it won't result in broken bones on the football pitch,' he said.

She grinned. 'Indeed, Dr Fraser.'

'Absolutely, Dr Fraser.' His eyes were full of love.

He helped her into the wedding car. There were some last photographs, and then the chauffeur drove them off. It was only when Jared stopped kissing her that she realised they weren't heading in the right direction for her family's restaurant.

'Um, excuse me, please?' she said to the driver. 'I think we're going in the wrong direction.'

'No, we're fine, ma'am,' he said with a smile.

'But we're going the opposite way to the restaurant. Would you mind turning round, please?'

'Sorry, ma'am, I have my orders,' he said.

'Orders?' She frowned. What orders? 'Jared, do you know anything about this?'

He looked blank. 'We already made the arrangements. We're going to your family's restaurant—aren't we?'

She frowned. 'Can I borrow your phone?'

'Sure.'

She rang her mother. Lucia made some completely unsubtle noises that were clearly meant to be static and didn't sound remotely like it. 'Sorry. This mobile phone signal is breaking up,' she said, and hung up.

'I'll try Joni,' Bailey said, but her bridesmaid did exactly the same as the mother of the bride.

'Let me try my mother,' Jared said. Bailey handed the phone back to him, but the result was the same.

'This is obviously their idea of a surprise,' he said. 'Whatever they've planned, they're all in it together.'

'I'm not very keen on surprises,' Bailey said.

'Me, neither, but right now I don't think there's anything we can do but go with it.' Jared smiled at her. 'Their hearts are in the right place.'

'I know,' she said ruefully. 'Sorry. It's hormones making me grumpy. I love you.'

He kissed her. 'I love you, too, Dr Fraser.'

Then she realised they'd pulled up outside the football club. 'What are we doing here?' she asked.

'I have no idea,' Jared said.

Bailey's father opened the door with a beaming smile. 'Dr and Dr Fraser, this way, if you please.' He helped Bailey out of the car.

There was a red carpet unrolled outside, and Jared and Bailey exchanged a glance; both of them had a glimmer of an idea now of what was happening.

They followed the red carpet into the room that the club used for functions. As soon as they walked in, there was a massive cheer from everyone in the room and a flurry of confetti in the air. The walls had been decorated with hearts, balloons and a huge banner saying 'Congratulations, Bailey and Jared'.

She could see everyone there—their families and friends, everyone from the football club, and all her colleagues at the sports medicine unit.

Archie and Darren came up to them. 'We know you wanted to keep it quiet—but we wanted to throw a party for you because you're both so special,' Darren said, and hugged them both.

Bailey had to blink back tears. 'Did you arrange all this, Darren?'

The boy nodded shyly.

'It was all his idea,' Archie said. 'He went to see Lyle about it, and Lyle got Mandy to help him with the details. He's been talking to both sets of parents and to your best friend, Bailey.'

'I don't know what to say,' Bailey said, 'except this is fantastic—thank you so much!'

The food was fabulous, and the centrepiece was an amazing wedding cake made by her brother. No wonder he'd refused to let her see it, as it was a lot bigger than the one she'd planned—it was the same raspberry and white chocolate cake, but scaled up for many more guests.

'I can't believe you kept it all a secret,' she said to Rob. 'And that cake is just stunning.'

'Anything for my little sister,' he said, 'and the man who made her smile again.'

Finally it was time for the speeches. Jared stood up. 'This wasn't quite what we'd planned for the reception, so I don't have a huge speech. I'd just planned to thank my bride for making me the happiest man alive and I'm going to stick with my plan—well, almost.' He smiled. 'Some of you know that something quite special happened to me when I was seventeen. I thought when I scored the winning goal in the championship that it was the happiest moment of my life, but I was wrong—because today is even better than that. Today, the love of my life married me. So I'd like to make a toast to her. To Bailey.'

'To Bailey,' everyone echoed.

'And I'd also like to thank our family and friends, who managed to surprise us this afternoon as much as we surprised them with the announcement of our wedding,' he said. 'You're all fantastic and we love you.'

Jared's oldest brother gave a short, witty best-man's speech. And then it was the turn of the father of the bride; Paul was almost in tears. 'There's so much I could say—but I want to keep it short and sweet. Bailey's the apple of my eye, and I couldn't find a better son-in-law than Jared. So I want to wish Bailey and Jared a long, fabulous life together.'

Darren stood up next. 'I know I don't really have the right to do this, because I'm not family, but I wanted to make a tiny speech, too.'

'You organised our reception, so I think you earned the right,' Jared said with a smile. 'Go for it.'

Darren took a deep breath. 'I think most of you know that I got into a bit of trouble a few months back, when I wasn't doing very well and I started drinking. Between them, Bailey and Jared straightened me out and gave me a second chance, and I owe them everything. Jared's been a brilliant father figure to me and I just wanted to say thank you. To Jared.'

A brilliant father figure. Yes, Bailey thought, he's going to be a brilliant dad. She squeezed her husband's hand under the table. He caught her eye and at her raised eyebrow he gave a small nod.

'In that case, I think I need to make a speech, too,' Bailey said, standing up. 'Doing this research into soft-tissue injuries at the football club has turned out to be the best decision I ever made, because it's how I met Jared. But what Darren just said really struck a chord with me. Jared's a brilliant father figure. And we've been keeping things under wraps a bit because—well, some of you know it's been a bit tricky for me in the past. But we'd like the world to know officially that Jared's going to be a dad in about six months' time.'

And the room erupted in a froth of cheering and champagne.

EPILOGUE

Six months later

JARED SAT ON the edge of the hospital bed, one arm round his wife and the other resting on the pink-swathed sleeping bundle in her arms.

'She has eyes the colour of bluebells—just like yours,' Bailey said dreamily.

'All babies have blue eyes,' Jared pointed out. 'She'll have brown eyes like you when she's older.'

'Not necessarily—my dad's eyes are blue,' she reminded him.

Jared stroked his daughter's cheek. 'She has your mouth.'

'And your nose.'

'She's beautiful. Our Ailsa.' He leaned over to kiss his new daughter. 'I thought on our wedding day I could never be happier than at that moment, but seeing her safely here in your arms and knowing you're both OK—life doesn't get any better than this.'

She smiled at him. 'Oh, I rather think it will. We have the first smile, the first word, the first step, the first "I love you, Daddy"—there's all that to come.'

'We're lucky. We got our second chance,' he said softly. 'And I love you, Bailey Fraser.'

'I love you, too,' she said. 'Always.'

* * * * *

FROM DARE TO
DUE DATE

CHRISTY JEFFRIES

To my handsome, hard-working and tolerant husband. When I finally figured out what I was looking for, you ended up being there all along. I was beyond lucky when you called me back.

You are my heart.

Chapter One

The melting ice cubes in Mia Palinski's vodka and tonic were symbolic of the way her future was dissolving before her eyes.

She'd just turned thirty, yet no matter how many times she'd told herself that it was time to come to terms with her new life, she still couldn't shake the lingering wish that tonight it should've been her up on the stage of the Egyptian Theatre, pirouetting across the dance floor.

Watching the piano player on the opposite end of the bar, she wondered if the balding man once had bigger aspirations than playing old standards in the lounge of some swanky hotel in downtown Boise. Most performers did. At least she could take comfort in the thought that she wasn't the only one not living her dream.

And while she didn't begrudge her darling students

their chance to shine in their roles as the fairy-tale wedding guests in the Idaho Youth Performing Arts' rendition of Tchaikovsky's *Sleeping Beauty*, Mia would have
been more comfortable if she hadn't been stuck back-
stage with Mrs. Rosellino, who thought her six-year-
old daughter was going to be the next Martha Graham.

Along with most of the other dance instructors who
had students performing in tonight's ballet, Mia referred
to the delusional stage moms as idealists. Because unless sweet Madison Rosellino miraculously developed
a decent amount of rhythm and learned to keep her finger out of her nose during performances, the sweet and
quiet girl would probably never make it to Juilliard.

Her eye gave an involuntary twitch at the memory of
her own mother, who was so similar to the Mrs. Rosellinos of the world. Mia took a sip of her now diluted
drink, trying to wash away the reminder of the well-
meaning but overbearing woman who had pushed her
only child into competitive cheer rather than classical
dance. Rhonda Palinski had wanted all eyes on Mia
and had forcefully maneuvered her daughter onto the
football fields, where the stages were bigger, the lights
were brighter and the crowds were rowdier.

Her phone vibrated on the smooth-finished walnut
bar beside her glass. She saw a group text message from
her friends Maxine Cooper and Kylie Gregson. She
loved them and knew they wanted an update on how
the Labor Day performance had gone, but she couldn't
bear to put on the brave face and pretend she wasn't
hosting a pity party for one in an empty hotel bar. She
grabbed a handful of fancy nuts out of a silver bowl.
At least she gave in to her self-commiserations only in
first-class establishments.

Mia loved and hated nights like tonight. She loved the music and she loved the dancing and she loved watching her young students and their contemporaries get to display the talents that they had worked so hard on during summer rehearsals. She truly didn't even mind the overbearing parents who expected their first-graders to be ballet prodigies and became annoyed when Mia didn't push the kids harder.

But the thing she hated was the fact that *she* could no longer be the one on stage dancing. Thinking such a miserable thought made her feel like a jealous old has-been, an emotion she despised even more.

She rubbed her sore knee through the black satin fabric of her slim-fitting pants, and then took another sip, willing the throbbing to go away. One of her pre-scribed pills might help with the physical pain, but nothing could diminish the emotional trauma of having her dancing career cut short by a golf club–wielding stalker who couldn't take no for an answer.

Nope. She wouldn't go there. It was one thing to wish things had worked out differently. It was quite another to sit here and relive the scariest moment of her life. She pushed her drink away and decided to go upstairs to her suite, order several desserts from room service and scroll through the pay-per-view channel looking for an interesting movie that could take her mind off what could have been.

Keeping a low profile meant she didn't get to travel the country as much as she once had as an NFL cheer-leader, so Mia normally took advantage of these quick forays into what her neighbors termed the "Big City" and made the most of the plush hotel accommodations. She'd grown up as middle class as they came, with most of her single mom's child support checks going toward cheer camps and extra lessons. And while Mia was careful with her income as the owner of the Snowflake Dance Academy in the small town of Sugar Falls, Idaho, she wasn't opposed to little splurges a couple of times a year—especially if they provided a quick, but safe, escape from the boring reality of her quiet existence.

And that was why she tried to ignore the text message that just flashed on her screen.

You're a great dance teacher. We're sure everything went perfectly. Don't go back to your room and sulk. Go out and live it up. We dare you!

Yep. Her best friends knew her, all right. Which meant they also knew she had no intention of accepting their ridiculous dare.

As she lifted a hand to signal the bartender to bring her check, a man walked into the lounge, his quick steps purposeful. Mia instinctively turned in the opposite direction, away from the stranger, and hoped that the guy was simply meeting someone in the nearly vacant bar. Ever since that incident with Nick Galveston, she had been careful not to draw any unwanted attention to herself and normally didn't hang out in cocktail lounges where traveling businessmen or lonely males might take any sort of interest in a young woman sitting alone at the bar.

She pulled her handbag closer to her. Why had she even stopped off here on her way back to her room? It wasn't as if she was a big drinker or looking for companionship. But after seeing the girl who played Aurora receive a huge bouquet of flowers right before the curtain closed and knowing that she would never experience that thrill again, Mia wanted something stronger than chocolate lava cake with peanut butter ganache to drown out her sorrows.

Unfortunately, the newcomer bypassed several of the empty tables and headed directly toward the small bar, near where she was sitting. He was handsome in that clean-cut all-American-boy way. However, in her experience, most men who looked like that were anything but pure and innocent.

She tried to keep her gaze averted, not wanting to risk making eye contact with him. But the large mirror across the room allowed her to take in his appearance. He wasn't overly large—just under six feet—and his suit was well tailored, but his silk designer tie was undone and hanging loosely around his neck. He didn't even look in her direction as he pulled out the leather upholstered bar stool a couple of feet away. His brown hair was close cropped and his face was set in a serious scowl. If he hadn't been dressed so well, she would've assumed he was in the military.

"I'll take a Glenlivet, neat, please," he said to the bartender. When the man still didn't acknowledge her in any way, she relaxed her shoulders and attempted a covert glance down at his shoes.

She was no expert, but her friend Kylie had just ordered those same handcrafted Italian leather shoes online for her new husband. So Mia knew they cost more than the monthly rent on her small dance studio. Nope. The guy definitely wasn't military because there was no way he would be able to afford to dress or drink that well on an enlisted man's salary.

Her ears picked up the tinny sound of Harry Chapin

singing about cats in cradles. The noise was in direct contrast to the piano and it took her a second to realize the song was a ringtone. His ringtone.

Whoa. This guy must have some serious daddy issues.

He fumbled, pulling his phone out of his pocket before silencing it and setting it on the bar. It immediately rang again and he whispered a curse before jabbing his finger at the screen. He had nice hands. Strong and capable-looking hands. Hands that would feel wonderful on…

"GP? Hello?" The hearty male voice coming out of the small speaker interrupted her wayward thoughts and caused the man next to her to practically jump off his leather stool in surprise. "Are you there, GP? Can you hear me?"

The skilled-looking fingers she'd just been lusting over must have pushed the wrong button, accepting rather than ignoring the call.

"Stupid damn phone," he said as he lifted the offending gadget off the bar and put it to his ear.

"No, Dad," he continued. "I don't want to talk about it anymore."

Mia took a sip of the drink she'd pushed away merely minutes ago, finding herself fascinated by the father-son drama unfolding right next to her. "You can't change my mind," she heard. Pause. "No, do not have them call me." Pause. "Listen, we will just have to agree to disagree. Have a safe flight home."

GP, or whatever his name was, looked as if he wanted to throw his now disconnected phone through the large window facing the quiet downtown street. The bartender brought the man's drink and Mia signaled for her own check. Damn it. She should've left when he was on his call. She didn't do angry confrontations.

"Sorry," he said, as he slipped his cell back into his sport coat pocket. "I hate people who take personal calls in public places."

He hadn't looked in her direction at all, so it took her a moment to realize he was speaking to her. She lifted her eyes to his and had to grip the bar's counter to steady herself when his hazel gaze met hers. A little pop exploded in her tummy and she suddenly felt like she was a fizzy bottle of champagne whose cork had just been released.

He was handsome. More than handsome. His clenched jaw was chiseled, yet serious, and his sad eyes didn't look the least apologetic. Nor did they seem very predatory.

Her eyes were drawn to his hands again and she noticed something funny about the way his suit jacket hit his wrists. She realized the man was wearing cuff-links—and expensive-looking ones at that. They were small gold-plated squares that had some type of an insignia embossed on them—an anchor maybe, but she couldn't tell for sure without getting too close.

And Mia knew better than to get too close.

Whoever this GP guy was, he seemed more upset with his father than intent on hitting on her. She kept her purse clenched tightly next to her side, but exhaled enough to loosen some of the tension in her body.

"Don't worry about it," she said, as the bartender set a small leather folder in front of her. "I was just getting ready to go anyway."

"Please, don't leave on my account. I didn't mean to disturb you. In fact—" he reached for her bill "—let me pay for your drink."

"No," she said a bit too loudly. "I'm not leaving."

He looked at the bill she had scooped up before he could grab it.

"I mean, I *was* leaving. But not because of you."

He smiled and his even white teeth softened his expression, making him appear more boyish, rather than hawkish. Swiftly, that fizzy sensation bubbled throughout her entire bloodstream. Wow. How strong had her vodka and tonic been? She would've stood up and ran out of the lounge, but she now couldn't trust her normally well-muscled legs to hold her petite frame.

Harry Chapin began singing from GP's pocket again. "Crap. I'm sorry, I have this new phone and I can't figure out how to turn it off."

He held up the ringing device with the contact name of "Dad" lighting up the screen. It was the same model as hers, and she was an expert at screening calls.

"Here," she said, taking it from him. "You just tap on this red dot and then, once the call goes to voice mail, you go to Settings…" He leaned in toward her and she could smell his musky citrus cologne. She didn't dare make eye contact with him again—not when they were this close. Instead, she stared intently at the screen as her fingers keyed in all the appropriate commands to effectively silence his phone.

"Then how do I turn it back on? You know, like next week when my dad calms down a little and finally accepts the fact that I want to live my own life and not follow in his footsteps?"

Yep, this guy definitely had daddy issues. But really, who was she to judge?

"Well, if he's anything like my mom—" she couldn't

stop the shudder that raised bumps on her bare arms "—I doubt it will only take a week."

"You don't know the half of it. But I *do* need this phone for work, so as tempting as it might be, I can't stay off the grid forever."

She nodded at his true statement. As much as Mia had tried to hide out these past couple of years, it was impossible to disappear completely. At least not without losing a part of herself. And if she lost any more of herself, she wondered what would be left.

"In that case, you can just block his number like this, but still get calls from everyone else." She tapped away at his screen. "Of course, this will only work until he catches on and tries calling from an unblocked number."

"Hmm. Sneaky. But my father's pretty resourceful, so I wouldn't put it past him."

"My mother learned to call me from my great-aunt Nonnie's rest home, knowing I couldn't *not* answer. I'm sure your dad will figure out a way eventually. I find it's best to just take the call, let them lecture you for exactly two and half minutes and then pretend you have a UPS delivery at the door that you need to sign for and disconnect the call."

The man who'd been called GP laughed loudly enough to draw the attention of the piano player and the bartender. If she thought his smile made her insides all bubbly, his laughter made her want to melt.

Seriously, what kind of person made jokes about wacky family members with someone she'd never even met? Apparently, the same person who was still sitting here grinning like a giddy schoolgirl at the good-looking man.

He slipped his phone back inside his inner jacket

pocket and when he did so, his hand rooted around before pulling out something else. He tossed a velvet-covered box on the bar and then looked up to the ceiling before running his hand over his forehead. The case looked like something that would hold jewelry—an engagement ring perhaps. The thought that this man was walking around with such an item, yet appeared to be so frustrated and let down, made her wonder what exactly had happened to him earlier this evening.

"That's a pretty swanky-looking box," Mia said.

"My father thought so when he gave them to me." The man opened the case to reveal a set of black onyx cuff links, the initials GPM embossed in gold over each one.

"They're very nice." Mia forced a polite smile, wondering why the man had such a wry look on his face.

"He said they're to remind me of who I am and where I came from." GP, whose last name must begin with an *M*, took another drink of his scotch. "The irony of the gift is that my father detests cuff links. In fact, he hates the way I dress altogether."

Mia leaned back so she could get a better look at his suit. As far as she could see, the man was dressed impeccably. Sure, maybe it was a little too tailored, a bit too metropolitan chic for Idaho standards. After all, this was Boise. Who wore such luxurious accessories in this part of the country?

Bolo ties, yes, but cuff links, no.

Maybe his father was some potato farmer who thought his son had gotten a little too fancy for his britches. Her own mother was the exact opposite. Every time she saw Mia, she chastised her for wearing her workout clothes around town and told her she had the potential of landing the coveted position of trophy wife, if only she'd put in some effort with her appearance.

"I take it your father isn't a suit man?"

"You could say that. Dad likes to describe himself as anti-establishment. He's what you'd call a free spirit and prefers to dress like he's just been eighty-sixed from a Beach Boys concert. Which never made sense to me, considering his education and what he does for a living. He calls me his rebel child."

"You don't look like much of a rebel," she said. He looked like an international businessman about to close a multibillion-dollar deal.

"I'll tell him you said so next time he calls." He gave the jewelry case a slight tap and it slid down the smooth bar a couple of inches. "So two and a half minutes, huh?"

He took another sip of the single malt scotch that was the exact shade of his eyes. Sheesh. Why did she have to look at those eyes of his again?

"Yep. I've got it down to a science. Anything less and they'll feel like they were short-changed and will only call back later. Anything more and it becomes the snowball effect, picking up speed and intensity and then there's no interrupting them once the full sermon gets going about all the sacrifices they made for you and how you're throwing away opportunities."

"I feel like I should be taking notes. Please, let me buy you a drink. You can tell me the top five best excuses for getting out of Thanksgiving family dinners."

She should've politely refused, grabbed her jacket and purse, and walked as quickly to the elevator bank as she could. But she thought of her own prospects for the holiday that was only a couple of months around the corner, and the hard, familiar lump of loneliness wedged in her throat. When was the last time she'd talked with a man who wasn't a well-known neighbor or hadn't been vetted by her two closest friends?

He must have sensed her vacillating because he shot her that boyish smile. "What are you having?"

Her nerve endings fizzled again and, before she could stop herself, she blurted out, "Champagne."

He looked doubtfully at the glass sitting in front of her—the one containing clear liquid and the remnants of a lime—and then raised his perfectly arched brown brows at her before asking the bartender to bring a bottle of Veuve Clicquot.

A whole bottle? What had she been thinking?

Maxine and Kylie would've told her she'd been thinking with her lady parts. Then they'd have high-fived her for double downing on their dare and told her it was about time she tested the waters of the romance pond. It had been so long, it wouldn't hurt to just dip her toe in.

Hopefully, she wasn't already in way over her head.

Garrett McCormick had been having the most frustrating evening of his life when he'd aimlessly wandered into the deserted lounge at the upper-class hotel. And that was saying something considering he'd been a battlefield surgeon in some of the hottest combat zones in the world. When he'd stormed out of the five-star restaurant down the street, leaving his argumentative and overbearing father at the table, he'd wanted a stiff drink and the kind of solitude he knew he couldn't get from the downtown college bar scene or from the officer's club near the Shadowview Military Hospital, where he was on staff.

He'd been so angry and so intent on downing something that would steady his nerves, he hadn't even noticed the petite raven-haired beauty sitting at the bar. If he had, his internal warning bells would've gone off and he'd have found another place to sit.

When his cell phone rang, he'd been startled and his embarrassment had forced him to take in his surroundings. What he'd told her was true—he hated people who were so self-important they answered their phones in public places, forcing strangers to have to listen to their private calls.

Yet, he wasn't sorry if his obnoxious telephone etiquette was the reason he now sat talking with her. She was wearing a strapless sequined top, and a black satin jacket hung off the back of her high leather chair. The shiny material matched her form-fitting black pants, making him think she was wearing some sort of feminine tuxedo. But softer. Sexier.

Considering it was almost eleven o'clock on a weeknight, she must've been at some fancy party before stopping into the hotel lounge for a nightcap. Either that or she was just all dressed up and on the hunt for some lonely traveling businessman.

He knew the types well. The gold diggers, the celebrity seekers, even the bored soccer moms who got their kicks by meeting random strangers at bars for one-night stands. But there was something about her shimmering blue eyes that made her look more like a scared rabbit than a prowling sex kitten. Besides, she was beautiful, but not in that surgically enhanced "tries too hard" way.

That was the first thing he shied away from when it came to women. His father was a plastic surgeon turned television producer who specialized in shows about surgical enhancements and makeovers. If there was one thing Garrett knew, it was artificial beauty. And he'd spent the past fifteen or so years of his life trying to get away from Med TV and the people who perpetuated that false and pretentious ideal.

He swallowed back his scotch just as the ice bucket and champagne showed up. The bartender set two glasses in front of them and, while Garrett had been intent on keeping company with only a bottle of Glenlivet Eighteen, his plans for tonight had suddenly taken a different turn.

"Here's to parents who don't know when to let go," he said as he tipped his champagne flute toward hers.

"Here's to a lot of people who don't know when to let go."

Garrett didn't know if her added comment was in reference to someone else she knew or if it was a premonition that they were both too uptight and needed to cut loose. He chose to focus on the latter because, after all, once he was discharged from the navy next week, he would be letting go of everything and starting his life all over again.

"So how far away did you have to move to get away from your parents?" he asked, wanting to get to know her better. She took a sip and tilted her head, as if pondering how much personal information she wanted to share with him. After all, they were two random people sitting in a bar. Who opened up to a complete stranger?

"My mom lives in Florida."

"Is that where you're from?"

"Not originally. We moved a lot when I was a kid. My mom was a bit of a flake when it came to herself, but as her only child, she was always seeking greater opportunities for me. She'd hear about some new dance troupe or a hyped-up instructor and she'd pack up all of my tights and leotards and off we'd go."

"So you're a dancer?"

"I was," she murmured before finishing off her glass. "What about you? Did you have to go far to get away from your parents?"

He took the hint that she didn't want to expand on what might be a personal subject and refilled her glass. "I moved away from home the day after my high school graduation, much to the chagrin of my dad and step-mothers."

"Stepmothers plural?"

"Well, Dad has gone through his share of wives. Not at the same time, mind you," he clarified when it looked as if she was going to choke on her cham-pagne. "But most of them kept in touch with me, even if it was only for the length of time they received their alimony checks."

"My mom always hoped for an alimony check. But she and my father never got married so she had to make do with lowly child support. I never got it, you know?"

"The child support? She didn't use it for you?"

"No, she did. I meant that I never got that whole de-pending-on-a-man-for-money mentality. I guess, sure, men should pay for their kids and stuff, but I always thought it would just be easier to make a clean break from the loser and start fresh. Support yourself."

Wow, some guy must've really done a number on this lady. While it was refreshing to hear that there was a woman out there who wasn't looking to get rich off some unsuspecting meal ticket, Garrett couldn't help thinking of all the fake blondes back home who'd made it more than clear that they would love nothing more than to gain access to his large trust fund or the rolling cameras that constantly surrounded his family.

"I couldn't agree more," he said, raising his glass in an acknowledging salute. After all, cutting ties was exactly what he'd done when he'd left home at eighteen. He'd had access to everything his family's money could buy. But it came with the heavy cost of bowing down to his father's will and his father's lifestyle. "In fact, that's why my dad and I were arguing tonight. He doesn't understand why I want to support myself and make my own decisions—live my own life."

"My mother and I have had that same conversation multiple times. My girlfriend says that when I become a mom myself, I'll understand." Garrett made a mental note of the fact that she didn't have kids. She wasn't wearing a wedding ring, but that didn't mean much to some women. "She said to think how sad I'd be if my mom stayed out of my life because she didn't care about me at all. But you know what? I think I could live with that kind of sadness."

He nodded his head in earnest. "I've been told the same thing. Yet, most of the time it doesn't feel like caring. It feels like an ego trip. Like he doesn't necessarily want the best for me, he just wants my life to be a reflection of *his* accomplishments and his success."

"Yes!" she agreed and they clinked glasses again.

Here was someone who got it—who understood what his unorthodox childhood had been like. His head was lighter and his smile was freer. He must be feeling the effects of the scotch. Or the champagne. Or maybe a combo of both. "I don't think it matters what we tell our parents, though. It never seems to sink in."

"It probably never will," she said. "Ten years from now, you and I could meet up in this same bar and we'll be voicing the same complaints."

"Promise me that in ten years, we will," he said more seriously than he intended. But here was a kindred spirit. A woman who knew exactly where he was coming from.

"Oh, I don't know. That sounds a bit pathetic."

"Meeting up with me again?"

"No. That we'll still be so stuck in our issues that we'll need to travel back to Boise just to commiserate in our overbearing parents support group."

She was right. They did sound a little pathetic. And that was the last thing he wanted a charming and genuine woman to think about him. "So Boise isn't home for you?"

She darted her eyes to the left before reaching for the chilled bottle and refilling their glasses. "I'm in town for a ballet performance. I'm going home tomorrow."

That explained the fancy outfit—and allayed his fears that she was a local groupie or some suburban wife out looking for an anonymous fling.

God, she was beautiful. Her high cheekbones, her pale blue eyes, her creamy skin. She was turned facing him, her legs crossed with one of her kitten heels hooked into a lower rung of the bar stool.

"You have a gorgeous collarbone," he finally said, unable to look away from her.

"Did you say *collarbone*?"

"Yes." He reached out a finger, tracing the ridge between her neck and her shoulders. He heard her sharp intake of breath, but he was well and truly buzzed and unless she moved away or told him to stop, he planned to touch her smooth, velvety skin for as long as she'd let him. "I've always had a thing for clavicles."

Yep, he was definitely on his way to being intoxicated. Any more booze and he'd be calling things by their biological Latin terms.

She held herself completely still, but her tongue darted out and licked her full lips. "Why is that?"

"I just find them incredibly sexy. And real. It's one of the few parts on a woman's body that can't be surgically enhanced." He looked up into her eyes and saw her dilated pupils. Tonight, he didn't want to worry about his father, or the new practice he was opening next month. He just wanted to think about the incredible woman in front of him. His hand trailed down her arm and settled onto her waist, and still she didn't move away.

"I also find you incredibly sexy and real," he said right before dipping his head and placing his mouth on hers.

She made a slight sound that could have been a moan or a protest, but she didn't pull back. He tilted his head and opened his lips, coaxing her mouth to accept more of him. When she finally opened up, she welcomed his tongue wholeheartedly and responded by wrapping her bare arms around his shoulders.

He tasted the champagne on her tongue and wanted to drink her up. He wanted to feel all of her, but these damn bar stools were making things awkward. Without breaking contact, he rose to his feet, bringing their heads to the same height. He groaned when she allowed him to deepen the kiss, and he brought his other hand up to her waist to pull her closer.

A discreet cough, followed by the bartender's voice announcing last call, finally cut through the fog of passion that had overtaken him. He pulled back his head but didn't release his grip, wanting to maintain as much physical contact as he possibly could without drawing any more attention.

"I've never kissed anyone like that in a public place," she said, her voice much huskier than it had been earlier. The pink flush creeping up her cheeks could have been from embarrassment or could have been from desire. He was hoping it was the latter.

"Would you like to try it again in private place?"

"Like where?"

"Well... I could get a room..." What in the hell was he thinking? He didn't go around propositioning women in hotels. But it wasn't as if he could take her back to the officers' barracks. And he definitely wasn't ready to let her go.

His emotions were storming at top speed, and the alcohol he didn't normally consume wasn't helping him think straight. Yet for once in his life, he didn't want to think straight. He ran his fingers along the satiny waistband of her pants and wondered what kind of undergarments she could possibly be wearing underneath.

She looked around at the mostly empty bar and again lightly licked her lips, which had remained mere inches from his own. "I already have a room."

Garrett didn't bother to ask her for clarification. Pulling his wallet out of his pocket, he peeled out two one-hundred-dollar bills and threw them on the bar before grabbing the half-full bottle of champagne with one hand and reaching for her fingers with the other.

Chapter Two

The shrill ringing of the phone startled Garrett awake. He quickly reached out to answer it, fumbling with the receiver. "H'lo," he said when he finally got the right side to his ear.

"Who's this?" a woman's voice on the other end of the line demanded.

Opening his eyes, he squinted and looked around the dark hotel room. Old habits kicked in and he stayed silent until his hazy brain could register where he was and whom he was with. The memories from last night came flooding back and even though he sensed he was alone, he looked around, confirming his disappointment.

She was gone.

The caller must've been impatient because he heard the dial tone instead of more questions. He'd just hung up when the phone let out another shrill ring.

"Hello," he said, this time more clearly but with some added annoyance.

"You again?" the same person demanded. "Is this room eight oh four?"

"I have no idea," Garrett replied before thinking better of it. He sat up and flipped on the light switch by the bed, but it took a second for his eyes to adjust enough to focus on the numbers typed into the printed directory on the telephone. "Uh, yeah, it is. Can I help you?"

He heard mumbled voices on the other end, then the caller told a person in the background, "It's her room, but some guy answered."

Wait, did they know the woman from last night? "Excuse me. Hello? Do you know the woman who was staying in this room?"

"Oh, my gosh! Is there a problem?" The caller's voice became frantic. "Did something happen to her?"

Heck, he wasn't trying to scare anyone or cause an alarm. "What? No. I…uh…met her last night, but I didn't catch her name."

"If you don't know her name then why are you in her room?"

That was a damn good question. And one he didn't have an answer for.

"Is anyone there?" After a few seconds, the caller said, "Maybe we should call hotel security."

"No." Garrett stood up. "No need to call security. I think she left. She invited me up here and…" He let his voice trail off, not wanting to get the woman he'd slept with in trouble.

"No way. She would never invite some guy up to her hotel room."

Clearly, this person wasn't going to give him any answers and he couldn't very well defend himself without incriminating someone else. "Oh, did you say you were calling room eight oh four? Sorry, this is room four oh eight. Apparently, there's been a mix-up. Have a nice day."

He quickly slammed the receiver down and tried to think about what to do next. But his brain wasn't adapting as quickly as it used to when he'd get startled out of a deep slumber. Garrett had been a heavy sleeper ever since med school. When he was a resident at the Naval Medical Center in San Diego, he'd learned to crash whenever he got the chance. If there was an emergency, then an on-duty corpsman would be there to wake him up.

That must be why he'd never even heard the woman leave.

He stood in the hotel room, wearing nothing but a confused expression, looking at the tangled four-hundred-thread-count sheets and the empty bottle of champagne near the bed. He studied his bare torso in the mirror over the dresser and noticed the faint purple hue of a love bite on the left side of his neck. He ran a hand through his still-short military haircut, which made his already tender head ache even more. What could he possibly have been thinking to come back to a hotel room with a woman he'd just met?

Being raised with video cameras always hovering nearby, Garrett had learned to be especially cautious not to let anyone get too close to him for fear that they were after something bigger—like a shot at television stardom. Growing up under the harsh lights of studio sets back when his dad had been the star of his own television talk show, then later a producer of a string of other reality series, Garrett had suffered the spillover effects of being followed by the Hollywood paparazzi who constantly linked him to his dad's notoriety.

He was thirty-six years old and still had a difficult time discerning women who were genuinely interested in him from those who were on the hunt for their fifteen minutes of fame.

And judging by the way the beautiful woman had sneaked out this morning without a trace, it was obvious she hadn't been looking for much more than a good time. Or a notch in her D-list celebrity belt.

How could he have been so stupid?

Had his father set this up? Had she been sent by the show's assistants? Was the caller standing outside right now with a camera, hoping to catch them in the act? He hadn't watched any of his dad's shows in several years, but at dinner last night, his old man had confided that ratings were down and if they couldn't breathe some new life into the series, he could be facing cancellation.

God, he hoped this wasn't some sort of last-ditch publicity stunt.

No. He was pretty sure his gut reaction last night had been on target. The caller sounded surprised that the woman would take a man up to her room. So hopefully she had simply been a lonely traveler looking for a little excitement and companionship.

His official discharge from the military was right around the corner and he didn't want to worry about any risqué photos or incriminating evidence ruining his career.

Still. He'd hate for any news about him to leak to the press. He'd spent his whole adult life avoiding the cameras, and the only place he'd been able to feel comfortable in his own skin was in the navy. Garrett had purposely volunteered for the most remote assignments whenever possible just to escape the constant media attention that came from being Dr. Gerald McCormick's son.

He damn well wasn't going to blow his cover now, which was exactly what he'd told his father at dinner yesterday evening when they'd gotten into their heated argument about the career path he'd just taken.

Garrett sat down on the edge of the bed and looked at the abandoned luggage stand in the open closet. He remembered the woman had an open suitcase there last night. And she'd already had a key to this room when they'd come upstairs. He let out a breath and eased back onto the bed. So she had obviously been a registered hotel guest, and since even he had no idea that he'd end up at some hotel bar when he'd stormed out of the restaurant a few blocks away, then nobody would've had the foresight to set him up.

That was one crisis averted. There was also the fact that he'd been the one who'd approached her. Fragments of conversation were slowly coming back to him. She'd said she was a dancer—well, she'd definitely had the lithe and graceful body to prove it. She'd also mentioned not being from Boise. Maybe she was just some bored housewife who had to fly home before her husband and kids woke up.

Wait, she'd said she didn't have kids. He couldn't remember anything about a husband, but would she have been honest if she'd had one?

He pulled a pillow over his head, wishing he could bury his shame along with his guilt. He took a deep breath, hoping he wasn't the cause of some poor cuckold's broken heart. But inhaling was a big mistake because when he did, the lingering aroma of jasmine tickled his nose, reminding him of her intoxicating fragrance and of how he hadn't been able to get enough of her heady scent. Of how he'd smelled, kissed and tasted every square inch of the woman's perfect, flexible body last night.

Crap. *The woman?* He still didn't even know her name.

This wasn't like him. Lieutenant Commander Garrett McCormick was a trained battlefield surgeon and an orthopedic specialist. He was cool under pressure and never got rattled. He for sure never let his guard down and didn't do anything unbecoming an officer. So then why had he allowed some sad-eyed, incredibly stunning woman get to him? What had come over him?

He took one last sniff and then threw the pillow to the floor. *Lust,* he thought before standing up and striding toward the bathroom. That's what had gotten into him. Pure, old-fashioned lust combined with frustration at his old man and a need to establish his autonomy with a woman who'd actually taken the time to listen to him and could relate to having an overbearing and egotistical parent.

He wasn't his dad. He didn't sleep with every beautiful woman who fluttered her eyelashes at him. But Garrett deserved to have a little companionship in his life, didn't he?

He stepped into the shower and turned the water on as hot as he could stand it before trying to unscrew the cap off the miniscule shampoo bottle. He'd wash all trace of the woman from his body and then try to banish all indications of last night's events from his mind.

The problem was, he didn't think he could forget how perfect she'd felt in his arms. How warm and willing she'd been when he'd eased himself inside her. Or how her breath came in short gasps when she'd reached her peak and begged him not to stop.

Man. He needed to get over it. To get over *her*.

He dried off and wrapped the towel around his waist before going out into the room to look for his clothes. He spotted his smartphone on the bedside table, and his heart flipped over when he recalled her slim fingers running along his screen in the bar, showing him how to block his incoming calls.

Maybe she had programmed her telephone number in his list of contacts.

His pulse picked up speed as he scrolled through his phone, only to slow down until it was a disappointing lump in his throat. Nope, there was nothing but four missed calls from his father and one from his dad's assistant, Marty. Well, Dad and Marty would have to wait until hell froze over.

Control yourself, McCormick. He hated getting worked up like this. But he was angry with himself for falling for the beautiful woman in the first place and coming upstairs with her. And he was angry with her for disappearing into thin air.

He got dressed and took one last look around the room, maybe so that he could memorize this moment or maybe because he was searching for one last clue about the woman's identity. A knock sounded and his stomach flipped over.

Was that her? Had she come back after all? Or was it security?

He opened the heavy door and frowned when he saw

a tall, older lady in a maid's uniform. "Sorry." She spoke in halting English. "I thought you checked out already."

She picked up the clipboard hanging off her service cart, as though to make sure she hadn't made a mistake. Likely, she hadn't, and the woman who'd spent the evening with him had in fact checked out of the hotel. Garrett took a step closer, thinking he might be able to find out the woman's name by looking at the guest info sheet.

But the motion forced him to accidentally release the room door, and it whooshed closed with a heavy thunk. The sound caused the maid to look up at him sharply, and she pulled the clipboard to her gray uniform. She stared at him and he glanced at the locked knob and realized he couldn't get back in.

If he stood here much longer, this employee would also realize that he didn't have a key and he had no way to prove that he was a guest of the hotel. The walkie-talkie on her cart crackled to life and Garrett decided the last thing he needed was to have security made aware of his presence.

"Yes, my wife already checked us out," Garrett finally said, thankful he'd at least gotten dressed and that his wallet and keys were still in his pants pocket. "I'm supposed to meet her at the bar."

What in the world had made a confirmed bachelor like him refer to the woman from last night as his wife? Or mention that they were meeting at a bar. Who met at a bar at oh eight hundred?

The maid lifted an eyebrow at him and he couldn't blame her for being suspicious. Then again, this was a hotel and he was sure the employees had seen more scandalous behavior than his. But just to be on the safe side, he pulled out a twenty-dollar bill and handed it to her. "Here. We forgot to leave a tip for the turndown service last night," he mumbled before making his way to the elevator and down to the lobby.

The bar was deserted except for the lone bartender reading a newspaper and a busboy wiping down the tables from the night before. He flashed back to a memory of entering the lounge last night, hell-bent on drinking his anger away. The nerve of his dad trying to talk him into moving back to California to film a new show. Those cuff links had been the icing on the smug cake his father had served after dinner over a nice cold glass of familial guilt.

Garrett patted his coat pocket and pulled out the velvet case. He snapped it open, a visual reminder of what had brought him storming in here last night.

Then he frowned when he realized one of the cuff links was missing. Had he left it in the room? He looked back at the bank of elevators and wondered if it was worth the risk of having the maid call security on him. He remembered taking them out of his pocket last night as he and the woman had been drinking. But before they'd left, he clearly recalled her handing the box back to him. She must have known that he wasn't the kind of guy who would throw away something so personal and expensive, even if he didn't understand his father's purpose in presenting him with such a questionable gift.

He also remembered picking up both his jacket and the cuff link case off the elevator floor last night, then smiled at the memory of how those items had gotten there in the first place. He walked back over to the elevators and wasted several minutes looking into each one for the missing cuff link. But like the woman from last night, it was long gone.

So then what happened to it?

And what had happened to her?

The front desk was busy and Garrett quickly dismissed the thought of asking the clerk for a guest's information. The cleaning lady upstairs had eyeballed him as if he was a criminal. So what was he supposed to ask the college-age-looking kid behind the desk? *Excuse me, but can you tell me the name of the woman who was staying in room eight oh four? I spent the night with her, but I never thought to ask her myself.*

Please. Maybe if this was some no-tell motel, he could bribe the employee. But he doubted that a high-quality establishment, which had most likely already been put on notice by his mystery caller this morning, would be willing to bend the rules.

And did he really want it leaked to the press who was asking? He'd be lucky if he didn't appear on some sleazy tabloid show for this stunt.

His thoughts were circling around like the whirling blades of a Huey helicopter, and he couldn't decide on a course of action.

Or inaction for that matter. Maybe he'd just dodged a bullet. It wasn't as though he was in the market for a relationship anyway, so he really didn't need the extra chaos that this situation might cause. Especially during this transitional time in his life. It was best to get the woman and this whole experience out of his mind.

Leaving the hotel, he walked down the busy Boise street to where he'd left his car, doing a double take at any woman with long dark hair to see if it was her. His cell phone vibrated in his pocket and when he pulled it out, he saw Matt Cooper's name on the screen. A year ago, the chief of police for Sugar Falls had been one of

Garrett's more stubborn patients. But the former marine had also become a friend and had been instrumental in talking him into opening a specialized clinic in the small Idaho town.

Cooper had sold him on the concept that where there was a tourist trade that catered to extreme sports such as downhill skiing, river rafting and hiking, there was a need for orthopedic surgeons. It wasn't a hard sell since not only was the town unpretentious and as far removed from the limelight as Garrett could get, it also desperately needed a physician who could actually serve the local community for the better.

"What's happening, Coop?" Garrett said by way of greeting.

"I just got off the phone with Mayor Johnston and the city approved the zoning for converting that old lumber mill you bought into medical offices. My wife's friend has a brother who is doing some contracting and thinks he can have a crew start construction tomorrow."

"Is he any good?"

"As far as I can tell. But now that you're going to be living in a small town, it's best to realize that's how they do things here." Cooper was a transplant himself, first from Detroit and then the military, and during a previous conversation he'd confided that he was still adapting to the slower-paced life. "Everyone knows somebody who is related to someone else who can get things done for you. It took me a while to get used to it, but the system can be beneficial."

"Okay. Have him email me an estimate and a contract. As long as people up there know how to mind their own business, then I'll hire whoever they want."

Coop laughed. "Now, I didn't say they know how to

mind their own business. But the community as a whole is a tight-knit group, and if they like you well enough, they wouldn't sell you out to some big-city paparazzi. How did that talk with your old man go, by the way?"

Cooper was one of the few people who knew Garrett was related to the famous television producer. But that's because the guy would investigate the depth lines on a ship's anchor if he felt like it. And when he'd been hospitalized with two consecutive knee surgeries and nothing else to look forward to, the marine had been bored enough to investigate his surgeon.

"It went as expected. He wanted what he always wants, which is for me to return to California and start filming alongside him. I told him about my new plans. He said there's no reason for me to go into private practice in some—no offense—Podunk town where my patients will only be able to pay for my services in taxidermy animals and squirrel meat casserole."

"Ouch. Although, that's what I expected, too, before I actually visited Sugar Falls."

"Well, let's hope for everyone's sake that my dad and his entourage of cameras never decide to visit." Garrett thought about his former patient's family history and realized he might sound like a spoiled, ungrateful child. "Don't get me wrong, I love the man. But I should've known better than to meet him last night. If it weren't for that stupid dinner, I never would've gotten so pissed off and..."

What? He never would've walked to the hotel bar and experienced the most magical evening in his life?

Of course, he couldn't say any of that to Cooper. Even though the two men's relationship was moving into friendship territory, Garrett wasn't ready to confess to anyone that his unsinkable heart had nearly been caught in a rip current.

He climbed into his late-model truck and dropped his head to the leather-covered steering wheel. He was too embarrassed to say anything to anyone and didn't need a bored police chief to start asking too many questions.

Wait a second. Having Cooper asking questions on Garrett's behalf might be another thing altogether. The idea of having his friend assist him in finding the mystery lady was ridiculous, but that wouldn't stop him from exploring the possibility of it later. When he didn't already have eight hundred things to do before the big move.

"Anyway." Garrett started his engine. "Speaking of expectations, tell me more about some of these small-town neighbors I'm going to be meeting in Sugar Falls."

Chapter Three

Eight weeks later, while her two best friends sat in her living room for their regular Thursday night dinner together, Mia came out of the bathroom holding the small plastic stick in her hand.

"That was quick," Kylie Gregson said, looking down at the empty box. "It says that you needed to wait three minutes for the results."

"I know. But I didn't want to wait in there alone to find out. Here." Mia set the pregnancy test on a paper towel on the kitchen counter then rushed back to the couch and pulled her favorite throw blanket up to her chin. "It probably needs about two more minutes. I can't look. You guys tell me what it says."

Maxine Cooper walked over to the counter and looked at the stick. "Well, I don't think we need to wait that long. The second blue line is pretty clear already."

"What do two blue lines mean again?"

"It means positive," Kylie said, checking the instructions.

"Let's give it a little more time," Mia whispered. "Maybe the other blue line will go away." But she was a smart woman with a bachelor's degree in fine arts. She knew none of this was going away.

She was pregnant. Single and pregnant.

A flood of emotion overcame her and she didn't know how to feel at first. Even though she'd thought about this possibility well before she'd sent her friend around the corner to Lester's Pharmacy to pick up the test, she knew she wasn't upset.

She was terrified, but she'd dealt with scarier things in her life. She was in denial, but then, she'd lived as a shell of herself for the past few years, so the feeling wasn't too uncommon. She was ashamed, but there was something else pushing her guilt aside and giving her a glimpse at a happiness she hadn't experienced in a long time.

"Aw, sweetie," Kylie said. "I know this is overwhelming, but you're a strong woman. And you have us to help you."

"I know," she said, tears threatening to spill from her eyes. "I promised myself I would forget about that night in Boise. And it was almost getting easier until I realized my cycle had never been this late. I guess in my determination to forget everything, I didn't think about the consequences, either."

"Do you want to talk about your plans?" Maxine asked.

"I'm scared. Obviously. I don't know how I'll do it." As soon as she realized she was late, a fear set in. But so did another emotion—excitement. "Like a tiny part of me is kind of looking forward to having this baby. I know this sounds selfish because I hated growing up without a father and I always swore that if I had kids of my own I wouldn't make the same mistakes that my mom made with me. But I'm actually a little bit excited." She rubbed her knee, which was getting sorer with each passing day. "That bastard Nick took so much from me—and not just physically. I thought I'd never recover after he attacked me, that my life was ruined. Yet, the thought of having a baby—having someone who is only mine and who needs me—is unreal, but in a positive way. This pregnancy might make me feel like I have a purpose again."

Both of her friends looked at each other before turning back toward her. Then Kylie asked, "What about the baby's father?"

"What about him? It's not like I know him or would even know where to find him."

Maxine hesitated before saying, "Cooper has some connections with the Boise PD and he can talk to the hotel security, maybe ask some questions on the down low—"

"No," Mia interrupted. "What if the guy is married? Or a psychopath? I don't need him. *We* don't need him," she corrected, as she put her hands protectively over the not yet visible bump of her tummy.

Her friends looked at each other again and Maxine shrugged. "Nobody has to make any decisions right this second. How about you let everything sink in and then, if you change your mind, we'll help you find him."

Mia nodded, but knew she wouldn't ever change her mind. She was about to take control of her own life, of her own destiny, and she wasn't going to invite some strange man into her world to start calling the shots or vetoing her decisions—even if she knew where to find him.

The women turned their conversation to pregnancy symptoms and childbirth and their doubts about ancient Dr. Suarez, who was the town's only general practitioner and should have retired twenty years prior.

"I think I might look for an obstetrician in Boise," Mia said.

"Thank goodness I'm covered under Drew's insurance," said Kylie. She was married to a lieutenant commander in the navy and twenty weeks pregnant. "I only have to drive as far as Shadowview Hospital when it's my time to deliver. Don't you think going all the way to Boise might be a bit far?"

Mia flexed her knee, trying to stretch out the pain that had only increased over these past weeks. Her friend was right, but going to the town doctor would be tantamount to hanging a huge banner outside her dance studio announcing to the world that she was pregnant and unmarried. Some of her students' parents might think she wasn't a fit role model for their precious offspring. She also helped coach the high school cheerleading team and knew the PTA would surely call her morals into question. Sugar Falls was a small town, and her career didn't need that kind of negative publicity.

"What about that new medical center out at the old lumber mill?" Maxine asked.

"Oh, yeah." Kylie was nodding her head. "My brother, Kane, has been doing the construction on the building and said the first offices are unofficially opening next week."

"What kind of doctors will they have?" Mia was skeptical but any physician who was new to town would still be considered an outsider and wouldn't be so quick to divulge patient information to the rest of his cronies in the Kiwanis Club, as Doc Suarez was known to do.

"Cooper's surgeon from the base hospital is opening up an orthopedic clinic there now that he's out of the military. And I heard there was a new dentist moving in next month. But no OBs, as far as I know."

"Actually," Max added, "it would probably be a good idea to talk to Dr. McCormick about your knee, Mia."

"I know. It's been killing me lately. But now that I'm pregnant, I probably shouldn't have surgery or anything." Besides, a retired navy doctor sounded just as old and cantankerous as Dr. Suarez.

"That's true." Kylie patted her own stomach. "But trust me, when you start packing on the pounds, it's only going to get worse. Maybe he could give you a cortisone shot or something to get you through the next several months."

"Yep, the last thing you want is a bum knee when you have a newborn to take care of," Maxine said. "Trying to run the dance studio on top of everything else is going to be taxing on you."

These women knew Mia better than anyone. They were her former teammates on the Boise State cheer team and her lifesavers when she'd later fled Miami to start over in Sugar Falls. And now Mia was turning to them again.

Maxine was the owner of the Sugar Falls Cookie Company, the star attraction of the downtown Sugar Falls tourist industry and a famous bakery specializing in flavored cookies. She'd opened her shop when her eleven-year-old son had been a toddler and had first-hand experience on raising a child alone while managing a growing business. Kylie was a CPA and had spent last summer raising her husband's twin nephews while singlehandedly maintaining the financial records for half the town. Mia was glad she had friends who had already gone through something similar and could help her navigate the unfamiliar terrain.

"Okay," she said with a sigh. "Give me his number and I'll make an appointment."

Her friends left and, as much as she adored the two women, she was glad to finally be alone to come to terms with her new reality.

After securing the dead bolt, she grabbed the paper towel off the counter, sat down on her comfy old sofa and stared at the little test stick with the two blue lines. She was going to be a mother. Mia could hardly believe it. Growing up, whenever she'd complain about not wanting to audition for a certain play that had nothing to do with dancing or not wanting to move to an entirely different state because her mother had it in her head that Mia could land a talent agent if she would only take up acting classes, Rhonda Palinski would tell her daughter that she didn't even know *what* she wanted.

And for the past few years, Mia had allowed herself to believe that maybe her mom was right and she didn't know what she wanted out of life.

Putting the stick down, she stroked her still-flat belly. She knew with a certainty she hadn't felt in years that she wanted this child more than she had ever wanted anything. She'd always lived her life for others, having her dreams diminished or jerked out from under her feet. But this baby was hers. And nobody, not even GP What's-his-name, could take this away from her.

She reached into her sweater pocket and pulled out the gold and onyx cuff link, looking at the initials.

GPM.

The morning following their lovemaking she'd almost made it down to the lobby when she'd spotted a small bit of gold winking at her from the corner of the elevator. When she'd picked it up, she remembered the way he'd had her body pressed up against the mirrored walls, her hands pulling him in closer and slipping under his suit jacket—which had gotten in her way. She'd heard a thunk right before the ping of the elevator alerted them that they'd reached her floor. But he'd scooped up the fallen case along with his discarded coat before they exited and fatefully made their way to her room.

Mia didn't wear much jewelry and had no idea what the cuff link was worth, but its potential monetary value wasn't what made her slip it into her satiny pocket that morning. She should've turned it in at the front desk lost and found. And if she hadn't been completely embarrassed by her lack of inhibitions and the threat of discovery, maybe she would've.

She thought about the careless way he'd left them at the bar and his annoyance at his father's idea of a gift, telling herself that GPM probably didn't care about the things anyway. Sneaking away from the elevator, she decided that having such a small memento would help her remember that she was still a woman with passion and life left in her.

Even Prince Charming had kept a glass slipper. Of course, unlike the smitten royal, Mia had no intention of traipsing around the countryside trying to find its owner.

She traced her finger over the gold-embossed letters.

If she thought about the man she'd left naked and asleep in her hotel bed, or the way he'd made her body come alive, responding to his skillful touch and his adoring mouth, she would lose all rational thought and make a pathetic attempt to take Maxine up on her offer to have Chief Cooper perform some miracle and attempt to track him down.

No. Things would be better if she just forgot about him and their night of sensual lovemaking. She reached for the little wooden treasure chest Maxine's son had given her for her birthday three years ago. She put the cuff link inside then snapped the box closed, along with her heart.

She doubted that a man like GPM would even want to be found. He'd seemed to have his own share of problems he'd been trying to escape from and probably wouldn't appreciate having any long-lasting reminders of that night, let alone an unexpected paternal responsibility. In fact, he'd most likely been more than relieved to have found Mia long gone the morning after.

Really, she'd saved them both from an awkward situation.

She'd never been the type of woman who had casual sex with strangers she'd met in bars. Heck, she wasn't even the kind of woman who went to bars, or slept with many men, for that matter. Her actions that night had been so out of character for her that her first instinct the next morning was to run and hide before pretending that it had never happened.

From the moment she'd driven her five-year-old Prius

away from the hotel, she'd forbidden herself from ever thinking about GP again.

Yet she couldn't help remembering how, as they'd walked down the deserted hallway, her plastic key card quivering in her hand, she'd known that she was making a conscious choice.

When they'd stood at her door she lifted her face toward his and saw the passion in his eyes, dimmed only slightly by a furrowed brow, as if his own set of second thoughts was playing out in his mind. Then and there she decided that maybe he needed her just as much as she needed him.

It had taken her two tries to get the key card inserted and she remembered letting out a breath when the little green light signaled that the lock had finally released, because for once in Mia's life, she had followed her physical urges—and her heart.

But now it was time to return to reality.

Getting off her sofa, she walked across her tiny apartment and opened her patio doors looking out onto Snowflake Boulevard, the main street leading through Sugar Falls. *This* was her reality. This town was her safe haven and home now. She took a deep breath of the cool mountain air, wanting to inhale the familiar sights and scents as if she could absorb enough of the environment into her brain so that she could push aside all thought of her carefree and careless night in the anonymous big city.

Because that was the key. Anonymity. She'd thought about leaving her telephone number for him, or staying a couple more hours to share breakfast and possibly something more.

But no matter how much she might want to see her

mystery lover again, or how guilty she might feel for keeping this baby a secret, she knew she wasn't ready for that kind of intimacy. She was just now allowing herself to put down roots and come out of her shell. All it would take was one bad relationship to put her right back to square one.

And that was a chance she just wasn't willing to take.

Garrett wasn't quite sure what to make of Cessy Walker. The older socialite had kindly volunteered to fill in at the front desk until he hired a nursing staff, but she didn't seem like the best fit for a small-town physician's office. After all, she was dressed in a designer wool knit pantsuit—Garrett recognized it as a staple brand from his last stepmother's closet—and enough pearls to sink a life raft.

"Have you ever worked in a doctor's office before, Ms. Walker?"

"Please, call me Cessy. Not in an office per se, but I did chair the Boise Children's Hospital black-tie gala back in eighty-nine and we raised over fifty thousand dollars for a new sports medicine wing."

"And tell me again why you want to work here?"

"I figure I needed to be doing something a bit more stimulating with my time. I tried to do that volunteer patrol program with the police department, but Cooper got all bent out of shape when I played my Barry Manilow CD on the squad car's loudspeaker."

Garrett bit the inside of his cheek, all too familiar with the eccentric personalities of the bored elite. Apparently, even small towns such as Sugar Falls had their share of overprivileged do-gooders looking for something to spice up their daily routines. The woman was sincere enough and probably had good intentions, but he really didn't need her help. If his first patient wasn't coming this afternoon, he would've politely declined her offer to act as a quasi-receptionist. But before he could make a decision one way or the other, she continued talking.

"I can see by your expression that you're a bit shocked at my resourcefulness when it comes to entertaining. My third husband used to look at me the same way. But just between the two of us, it didn't take a party-planning whiz to realize that the Labor Day parade was going to be a major snoozefest with that Mae Johnston running the show. Personally, I think the townspeople enjoyed me adding some festive music and pepping things up. But afterward, the chief was concerned other townspeople might follow suit and utilize public resources in an *un*authorized manner." Ms. Walker made it sound as if *her* Fanilow utilization was completely authorized. "Anyhoo, Cooper suggested that you might need some temp help, and since I know everyone who's anyone in town, I figured I would be an asset to you setting up shop and establishing yourself with the crème de la crème of our town."

Hmm. It sounded to Garrett as if Cooper wanted his wife's former mother-in-law out of his hair and had dumped her into his lap. He'd met her a couple of times when she'd brought her grandson to visit Cooper at Shadowview and had an idea that she was used to getting what she wanted. But he was new in Sugar Falls and, as much as he prided himself on his independence, it couldn't hurt to have an established and well-connected member of the community give him her bedazzled seal of approval.

Plus, he was about to ask for a favor himself, so keeping Cessy Walker busy would make the chief of police indebted to him.

It had been over eight weeks since that night in the hotel, and he hadn't been able to get the woman from the bar out of his mind. He'd tried everything he could think of to look for her—everything from calling the hotel the following day to try to find the guest who'd been staying in room 804 to researching dance performances in Boise hoping to come across her picture. He'd even spent a few evenings sitting in the hotel bar the following week, closely watching every brunette that walked through the door—but always ended up at a dead end. The more time that went by, the colder her trail would get. It was time to call in the big guns.

"All right, well I appreciate your helping me out just for the next couple of *days*." He purposely paused to emphasize that her receptionist skills—or lack thereof— would only be temporary. "My first patient is a referral from a friend and she's coming in an hour. Have her fill out these forms and get copies of her insurance card. Technically we're not open for business yet, and I don't expect many calls in the next few days, but if you could answer the phone and take down messages for me, that'd be great."

"No problem, Doc. And keep in mind that I can only volunteer for the next two weeks. I go on my sabbatical after that."

He couldn't imagine what a woman like Cessy Walker needed a sabbatical from. But he wasn't going to ask because he had a feeling she'd tell him.

He took a seat behind the battered desk he'd found online. Garrett wasn't in the habit of using money he hadn't earned himself, and he'd already dipped into his trust fund account to finance the building and splurge on his top-of-the-line medical equipment. While he wanted to make his patients comfortable, he didn't really see the need for wasting money on decorations or frivolous extras when it was surgical equipment and state-of-the-art radiology machines that he needed most. But hiring a full-time professional staff just jumped to the top of his to-do list.

He probably should've made a telephone call, but he didn't want his new "receptionist" to overhear his very personal conversation. So he fired off an email to Cooper, listing as much information as he could think of about the mystery woman from the hotel. He told himself that if she wanted to be found, she would've left her contact information. But the more time he spent recalling every little detail about that night, the more obsessed he became with locating her and seeing her again.

Maybe he was romanticizing it. Or maybe he didn't like the lingering feeling of rejection. Although he'd grown up a pampered rich kid, it wasn't as if he was some spoiled brat who only wanted things he couldn't have. Most likely, it had been a one-time experience and, if he met her again in person, none of that sizzling spark would be there anymore.

But what if it was?

He clicked Send and then slammed his laptop closed. This whole search was probably the most futile endeavor he'd ever embarked upon. And it would probably only give Cooper extra ammunition for busting his chops. Garrett needed to focus and get back to work.

He was putting away supplies and arranging one of his exam rooms when he heard his first patient arrive. She was early and he wasn't quite ready. Besides, he didn't want to look too eager—as if he had nothing more important or doctoral to do with his time.

Cessy Walker's voice carried back to him as she greeted the patient. "Mia, you're going to just *adore* Dr. McCormick. He's a family friend and is known to be the best orthopedic specialist in the state. He'll have your knee all fixed up in no time."

Okay, that might be a bit of an exaggeration, but his suddenly fragile ego could use the boost. Also, technically, he was a friend of the new husband to Cessy's former daughter-in-law, but in a small town such as this, he figured everyone had some kind of connection with everyone else. The woman might not be experienced as a receptionist, but perhaps she'd been right in declaring herself an asset to his growing practice.

He looked at his stainless steel watch. It would probably take a few more minutes for the patient to complete the insurance paperwork, so he went back to puttering.

After about ten minutes, he heard murmuring, and then Ms. Walker's voice again. "Great. Follow me on back to the exam room."

Garrett was shoving his left arm into the sleeve of his white lab coat when his receptionist walked in and handed the file to him.

"Doctor, Mia Palinski is here to see you," Cessy said then walked out, leaving Garrett face-to-face with his first patient.

But instead of sticking out his hand to introduce himself, he froze when he recognized the midnight-black hair, the pale blue eyes and the graceful body he could never forget.

Chapter Four

No, Mia thought. *No, no, no.*

GPM was here in Sugar Falls? And he was her doctor? How had this happened?

"It's you," was all he said. She stood there, stiff and numb, drinking in the sight of him, at a complete loss of what to say without looking foolish.

"You live here in Sugar Falls?" he asked when she remained silent. His eyes hadn't stopped their constant perusal of her. "How could this have happened?"

His words mirrored her own thoughts so exactly that the nervous giggle she'd been trying to swallow almost bubbled out. But then he smiled as though Santa had just delivered a long-sought-after Christmas gift to him and a familiar cold panic spread through her. Mia reached for the file, the one containing all her personal information, including the fact that she was now carrying this stranger's child, and tried to yank it from his hands. The hands that had so skillfully brought her body to life just two months ago.

Judging by the way he was gripping the manila folder, she probably would've had better luck ripping a present away from a child. She dropped her arms instead, the instinctive response of flight winning over her urge to fight.

She inched backward, calculating an escape route in her mind. The exam room was in the farthest corner of the building and if her knee was in better shape, she could probably make it out of his office in less than three seconds.

But then she recalled that the self-appointed socialite of Sugar Falls was sitting right outside and had a penchant for spreading her unsolicited opinions around town. Of course, it wasn't as if Mia was going to be able to hide her pregnancy much longer, but she would've at least liked to keep the baby's paternity somewhat secret.

Which brought her back to the question: How had this happened? What in the world was he doing here? And how was she going to deal with the consequences of her actions?

"Miss," he paused and looked down at the file still in his hands. "Palinski? It is miss, right? Not missus?"

His eyes seemed to be pleading with her to assure him that she wasn't married. Was he hoping that if she was single, she'd be up for a repeat performance? She didn't respond only because she didn't want to feed his unrealistic expectations.

Of course, he'd find out the answer soon enough since he was still holding on to her medical history, which clearly listed her full name, insurance information and, unfortunately, her address. But that didn't mean Mia had to show her hand just yet.

"Why don't you step inside so we can talk—" he looked pointedly at her feet, which were now completely backed into in the hallway "—more privately."

Being alone with this guy was the last thing she wanted. But it wasn't as if she could hide from him if he was truly setting up shop in Sugar Falls.

At least, not yet. Plus, Mrs. Walker would be right outside the room, probably with a stethoscope pressed against the door, and could hopefully intervene if things took a bad turn.

Mia took a deep breath. Really, she knew better than to project her one bad experience onto other men. She needed to think logically. GP or Dr. McCormick or whatever his name was a reputable surgeon. Her best friend's husband—the chief of police, for crying out loud—had been one of his patients. Chances were he wasn't some obsessed sociopath who, several weeks after meeting her, decided to uproot his whole life and move his medical practice to Sugar Falls, Idaho, in order to stalk her.

Besides, she'd already let down way more than her guard with him before.

Maybe that was what she was really afraid of. She'd already proved that she couldn't trust herself alone in a room with him.

He put his hand on her elbow and Mia immediately flinched and pulled her arm away. He looked surprised and a bit offended by her response, and she felt so stupid for being there in the first place. She swallowed a gulp of air and entered the room, turning around quickly so

that she wouldn't have her back to him or be susceptible to a surprise attack.

*Calm down. He isn't Nick. He's not going to hurt
you.* Even as Mia tried to reassure herself, she couldn't
help but take inventory of her surroundings. Old habits died hard when she was thrown into an uncomfortable environment. Plus, she had more than just herself
to protect now.

There was an exam table, which she had absolutely
no intention of lying down on, a stool and a hard plastic
chair that looked like the kind her elementary school
would've thrown out a couple of decades ago.

For a guy with impeccable taste in shoes and scotch,
he really could benefit from hiring Cessy Walker as a
decorator rather than a receptionist.

"Do you mind if I close this?" He was holding the
heavy birch wood door and Mia was grateful he was
at least giving her the option of escaping. She nodded
after checking to ensure there were no internal locks
on the knob.

The room was small and they stood inches away
from each other. The only way to put some distance between them would be if one of them sat down, but she
didn't want to put herself at a disadvantage.

"Well, Mia Palinski, I didn't expect to meet you
again."

"I didn't expect to meet you the first time," she said
before thinking better of it. She was a natural peace-
maker and hated confrontations. Plus, her mother had
drilled politeness into her from a young age, warning
her she never knew when she'd come across a potential talent scout or rich stepfather. "Sorry. This is all
so unexpected and I'm not usually so flustered like

this—not that you would know. We don't really know each other at all."

"As I recall, we never did officially introduce ourselves. I'm Garrett McCormick." He held out his right hand, his other still gripping her file.

"Mia Palinski," she said, sticking out her own to shake his. Yep, there was no forgetting those hands. He had on silver knotted cuff links this time and she wondered what it was about this guy that made him want to dress to the nines, even at work. "Wait. I thought your name was GP."

"How'd you know my nickname?"

"I could hear...uh...your father call you that when you were talking to him on the phone in the bar."

His eyes grew darker, from hazel to a cloudy deep brown, and she mentally kicked herself for bringing up a touchy subject.

"Well, only he calls me GP anymore. It's short for Garrett Patrick. But if he'd had his way, he would've just named me Junior."

"You don't really look like a Junior," she said, not sure she wanted to bring up the subject of overbearing parents again. Although, it was safer to talk about that than the big pregnant elephant in the exam room.

"I've tried my whole life not to feel like a Junior, either." That was pretty telling. And so was the fact that Mia's small hand was still wrapped possessively in his larger one. She snatched it back before wrapping both of her arms around her midsection.

The motion startled him and must've brought his attention back to the present. "So I've never really done this before," he said, still holding her file.

"You mean you're not really an orthopedic surgeon?"

"Of course I am." He gestured to the framed diplomas and awards he'd yet to permanently hang on the walls. So he'd gone to the Naval Academy at Annapolis, followed by med school at Dartmouth. Pretty impressive—if they weren't forgeries. But even someone as suspicious as Mia had to doubt that anyone would go so far as to fake a medical career in the military and then open a board-certified surgical practice. "I meant I've never had a relationship with one of my patients."

"We didn't have a relationship." It was best for her to make sure he understood that what happened between them was a one-time deal and there would never ever be an encore. "And maybe it's not such a good idea for me to become one of your patients."

Mia looked down then took a step back and tripped over the stool, which banged into the metal exam table as she lost her balance and tumbled to the floor. Her bad knee thudded against the wheel of the stool and she gasped in pain.

Garrett was beside her in a heartbeat, straightening her leg and asking where it hurt. When she didn't answer, he said, "Looks like you're going to be my patient whether you want to or not. I think you should let me help you up onto the table so I can take a look and see if you did any damage."

Unless she wanted to sit on the floor indefinitely, she would have to allow him to assist her. But instead of pulling her up, he reached behind her back and under her legs and lifted her toward his chest.

When he stood, all the blood left her head and was replaced with a spinning dizziness. She didn't know if it was the nausea that had been plaguing her, the stress of the situation or feeling him so close to her again.

Either way, she tamped down her instinct to wrap her own arms around his neck and reached toward the exam table to steady herself as she maneuvered her body onto it and away from him.

He stepped back, eyeing her as though she should be seeing a psychiatrist, not a surgeon. He rubbed his finger across his forehead and she remembered the gesture from the hotel bar.

"Why didn't you tell me you were a doctor? Or that you were opening a practice in Sugar Falls?"

"The subject never came up." His lips were clamped tightly and Mia realized he was keeping something a secret... *Oh, no.*

"Oh, my gosh! Are you married?" Her eyes darted to his ring finger, but it was still bare—just as it had been that night. Of course, that didn't necessarily mean anything.

"What? No, I'm not married. Are you?"

"Of course not. I already told you I was a miss." She tried not to sound offended at the suggestion that she would cheat on her nonexistent spouse with a stranger in a hotel bar. But she'd considered the same thing about him.

He opened her file and glanced at it briefly, almost as if he didn't believe her verbal answer and was looking for written proof. She held her breath, knowing what information he was about to read and then saw him do a double take when his eyes got halfway down the page.

Right where the question about pregnancy was.

"Oh, my God." He looked at her still-flat stomach. "How far along are you?"

This was it. She could lie and say she was further along to try to get him to believe that the baby wasn't his. But since he was actually going to be working in Sugar Falls, he'd see her regularly and figure things out when her baby was born nine months after the night they spent in the hotel.

"I'm in my first trimester," she said, giving a generic but truthful response. "My first appointment with the OB/GYN is next Monday so I'll know for sure then." She stood up, wanting to end this conversation before it could even begin, but her leg buckled and she had to hold on to the edge of the table so she wouldn't fall to the ground.

"What's going on with your knee?" he asked, still looking at the papers in his hand. This time, he didn't make an effort to help her back up, which was fine because she was balancing okay on one limb and she didn't think she could handle having him pick her up or hold her close to him again.

She'd almost forgotten her entire reason for making this stupid appointment in the first place. Her damn knee was getting her into more problems lately.

"I had replacement surgery three years ago, and it just never felt like it healed right. Anyway, it's been bothering me more lately and I thought I should get it looked at before the ba…" The word froze in her mouth when he looked back up at her. "But seeing as how this is probably some sort of conflict of interest or something, I think I'll probably just see a specialist down in Boise."

"Do you go to Boise a lot?"

He was inches away from her and his eyes were staring deep into hers, questioning her, challenging her to explain an answer to something he wasn't coming out and asking directly.

The back of her good leg bumped into the exam table and she realized she was trying to get away from his intent gaze. "Why does Boise matter?"

"It doesn't matter," he said and looked back at her file. What exactly didn't matter to him? Her driving habits to the nearest big city? Or the night they shared there?

"Why don't you let me take a look at your knee?"

"I don't think that's such a good idea..." She pulled herself up straighter and looked at the closed door, wondering how quickly she could hop through it.

"Listen, Mia. You can let me do my job and examine your knee, or we can talk about your obstetrician's job and whether your due date is anywhere close to nine months after September third."

He remembered the exact night they'd been together. And he obviously wanted to discuss it, yet he was being a gentleman and giving her the opportunity to talk about her injury instead.

She scooted her rear onto the exam table as quickly as she could, having never felt so grateful to have a bum knee as she was then.

Mia Palinski.

The woman he hadn't been able to get out of his mind for the past two months was now sitting in his office, tugging her leather boots down over a pair of tight black leggings.

And she was pregnant.

He'd dreamed about her disrobing in front of him again, but not in his barely established medical practice. And definitely not with Cessy Walker hanging out on the other side of the door. Garrett was a consummate professional, which was the only way he was going to get through this increasingly awkward appointment.

He was dying to ask her a hundred questions, but Mia looked at him as though he were a drug-resistant strain of some unheard-of disease.

What was she playing at? Most women in her position would be salivating at the good fortune of successfully accomplishing the oldest trick in the gold digger's handbook—getting impregnated by a famously wealthy man. Or in his case, the man reality television had once dubbed the most eligible doctor in Southern California.

He was usually so careful about using protection for this exact reason, but he was fast realizing that his brain and his body simply didn't react the way he wanted them to when Mia was around. Which was why he needed to treat her like any other patient. Not only would playing the doctor role force him to keep his emotions in check, but it might also make her more willing to talk and let her guard down so he could figure out exactly what she was up to.

He didn't want to resort to using their barely established doctor–patient relationship to try to get personal information, but she was pregnant—possibly with his child—and he deserved to know the truth. If he could get through performing an emergency spinal cord surgery on board a naval hospital ship during hurricane-force winds, then he could get through a routine examination.

Actually, there really was nothing routine about this at all.

He slowly touched her knee, and even through her black tights he could still feel the heat radiating off her. He concentrated on staring directly at her leg and not letting his eyes stray to her beautiful face to see if his touch could still bring her pleasure the way it had that night in Boise.

She was his patient. He needed to treat her as such.

But she was holding her body with such tension; she was as stiff as one of his father's favorite surfboards. And just like a fiberglass board, she might snap in two if he didn't handle her smoothly.

How could he get her to relax when he was so damn dismayed himself?

Go through the motions of the exam. Keep it steady. You're the king of control, McCormick.

"Where did you have surgery?"

"I had it on my knee."

Was she serious? He chanced a look at her, but her eyelids were squeezed tightly closed. He was barely touching her, so he doubted she was in pain. Was she truly that uncomfortable in his presence?

"I know the surgery was on your knee. I meant, where was your surgeon located? I would like to get your records from him or her and get an idea of what exactly they did."

"Right. Of course. It was in Miami. Dr. Ron Prellis."

"I don't think I've heard of him."

"He specializes in sports injuries. The team doctor referred me to him because they were trying to keep the whole thing quiet."

"What team doctor?" She was on a sports team? And why would they want to keep it quiet? Mia Palinski seemed to have a lot of things she wanted to keep under the radar.

"For the NFL."

"As in football?" That didn't make any sense.

"Yes. I was on their cheerleading squad after college."

Crap.

When she'd told him that she was a dancer, his first thought had been stripper. But then she'd made it sound like she was a professional dancer. Professional jersey chaser was probably more like it. While he couldn't believe he hadn't made the initial connection, he kept his mouth shut and continued the exam.

He felt some definite swelling, but he doubted she would be willing to remove her tights so he could get a better look.

"I'd like to get an MRI on your knee, but just to be on the safe side, we should wait until after the first trimester. Are you currently taking anything for the pain?"

"I used to take ibuprofen before I found out about the baby. But I've been too scared to take anything since then."

He sat back on his stool and let out a breath. At least she was taking healthy precautions with his unborn child's life.

His child. Possibly. He was going to be a father.

"I take it you plan on keeping it, then?"

"My baby?" Her eyes grew even more icy with the question and she wrapped her arms around her midsection. "Of course I plan on keeping it!"

He'd noticed that she'd referred to the child as *hers*—not *theirs*. Did he get any say in this? Should he? She hadn't denied it that the baby was his, but if he could keep her talking, maybe she would give him confirmation. "Were you planning to tell me about it?"

She looked away quickly, but not before he'd seen the guilt flash in her eyes. She was probably planning to wait to tell him when the due date grew closer and there was nothing he could do but sign a hefty child support agreement.

"Even if I'd wanted to, I really didn't have any way of contacting you. Up until now, I didn't know your real name or how to get in touch with you."

Wait. Did she just say even if she'd wanted to? Implying that she had no intention of telling him about the baby? He braced his feet on the floor. If he could roll his stool back any farther from the exam table and her duplicitous mind, he would have.

"You know, if you would've stuck around that morning instead of sneaking off like a common criminal, I would have been more than happy to provide you with my name and contact information." He couldn't help the accusing tone of his voice.

He wanted to lash out at her and blame her for orchestrating this whole mess. But if he was being honest, he was more upset for letting her fool him in the first place.

She must have realized his exam was over because she sat up and reached for the boots she'd discarded before climbing up on the table. "I didn't sneak off."

"Well, you didn't wake me up to say goodbye and I certainly didn't find a note anywhere thanking me for the good time."

She reached for her boot on the floor and must've thought better of swinging it at his head because she shoved her foot into it instead.

"Did it ever occur to you that maybe I was embarrassed? Or that perhaps I wasn't well rehearsed in one-night-stand protocol because I've never done anything like that before?" She stood up and stomped her leg as she tried to get the zipper unstuck, then sucked in a tight breath.

"Hey, take it easy. No wonder your injury has been aggravated again."

"Look, I think it's in everyone's best interest if I find a different doctor. You don't need to worry about my knee anymore and you certainly don't need to concern yourself with my baby."

"Wait, Mia. Please." He moved in front of the door. He would never physically restrain a woman, but at this desperate moment, he wasn't above impeding her escape route. "We really need to talk about this."

"What's there to talk about?" she asked.

"Are you kidding me? I'd say there's a whole lot to talk about. First of all, you can barely walk—you're visibly in pain. Even without an MRI, you probably have a loosening of the device components. It sometimes happens a few years after surgery when the artificial replacement is faulty or doesn't graft properly to your bones. Which means you might eventually need a revision surgery. But I can understand if you want to go see another specialist. Second of all, you're carrying my child. I mean, it *is* mine, right?"

Her head whipped up as if he'd slapped her. "Of course it's yours."

"You can't blame me for asking," he said. "Up until an hour ago, I didn't even know your name, let alone your relationship history. You've had almost two months to get used to this whole pregnancy idea, so forgive me for being a little slow in wrapping my head around everything that's just happened."

She gave a barely perceptible nod, but her nostrils flared slightly, indicating she was still on edge with him. But at least she could acknowledge that he wasn't trying to be confrontational.

"I'm still trying to get used to it all myself. Like I said, running into a former one-night stand and having him find out I'm pregnant with his child isn't something I've had much practice at."

"Fair enough." Garrett heard the office phone ring and was reminded that they still had an audience out in the waiting room. "Look, maybe we should take some time to think this all through and then meet later. Somewhere in private and figure out where we are going to go from there."

Mia lifted herself up to her full five-foot-four frame and arched a perfectly sculpted black eyebrow. "How private? I think I made it pretty clear that I don't normally engage in…you know…what happened at the hotel in Boise. So I hope you're not expecting me to hop right back into your bed."

"First of all, I think it was *your* bed we were in." Although, as discombobulated as Garrett felt, he couldn't help but be intrigued by spending another night with her. *Don't go there, McCormick.* "And second of all, unless you allow me to give you a shot of cortisone for the pain, you'll be lucky if you can hop anywhere."

She sat back down and he opened up his cabinet, pulling out a clean syringe and small glass vial. He turned his back while she removed her black tights and, he assumed, shoved them into her purse. She closed her eyes, while he injected her knee with the pain reliever, then turned around again and busied himself in his cabinets as she pulled her boots back on—her legs remaining bare.

When it seemed that they'd both gotten their emotions under control, he finally said, "I just meant we could meet someplace that didn't have the town busy-body sitting right outside the door."

"I prefer the term 'town socialite,' Dr. McCormick," Cessy Walker shouted from a location that was much closer than the reception desk.

"Sugar Falls is a small place. It's pretty hard to go anywhere without seeing someone who doesn't already know your business." Then Mia raised her voice a few octaves. "Which is why I'll know exactly who to blame if any of this leaks out."

Garrett heard a sudden increase in volume over the computer's desktop speakers.

"Why don't we meet for dinner tonight?"

"I can't. After school, I teach two ballet classes and then I'll have rehearsals for the Christmas pageant until eight."

Garrett remembered the small sign on the pink Victorian building downtown. He'd passed by it several times when he'd been driving into town to check on the progress of his office remodel. "At the Snowflake Dance Academy?"

If women had hackles, Garrett would've sworn that he'd just seen hers rise. "If you didn't know anything about me, then how'd you know about my studio?"

And here he'd thought they were making progress. Maybe the cortisone wasn't as effective as he'd thought it would be. "It wasn't a difficult deduction, Mia. I know I haven't been here long, but that's the only dance place in town. At least, that I've seen."

She wrapped her cardigan sweater tighter around herself and let out a small breath. Jeez, did this woman think he was some kind of creepy stalker?

"Well, if you can't meet me tonight, then what about breakfast tomorrow at the Cowgirl Up Café?"

"Nope. The Quilting Club meets there on Wednesdays."

God forbid they bring the attention of the Quilting Club upon them. "Is there any place we can go where there won't be a swarm of townspeople?"

She bit her lip. "I guess we could meet at my place."

"Great. When?"

"On Saturday. My last class is at three. So any time after five should guarantee us some privacy. But come to my apartment above my studio. I know our situation will come out eventually, but the longer we keep things anonymous around town, the better."

Anonymous? That's how they'd gotten into this predicament in the first place. Yet, he was too much of a gentleman to point that out. "Okay, your apartment on Saturday. I'll meet you there at six, just to be safe."

Mia nodded and left the exam room, still limping, but at least she wasn't on crutches. The doctor in Garrett wished he could have finished his examination and made a better recommendation for her treatment. But the man in him was relieved to be alone for a second to get control of his thoughts. There was something about that woman that turned his brain to spaghetti, and he needed all his wits about him if he was going to take control of this situation.

He slumped down in his stool and rubbed his palm over his forehead. He couldn't believe it. He was going to be a father. This wasn't what he wanted, and it definitely hadn't happened the way he would have planned if he *had* wanted it. But he couldn't help but feel a small kernel of anticipation. Not at all the unknowns that lay ahead—he was too pragmatic to see this as an actual blessing—but at this chance for familial redemption. He always knew that when he became a dad, he would break the overbearing cycle of parenthood that he'd been subjected to.

Cooper had assured Garrett that once he moved to Sugar Falls and the locals embraced him as one of their own, he wouldn't have to worry about the potential celebrity ramifications that tended to follow his family name. After all, if his building contractor, who Garrett soon figured out was baseball legend Kane Chatterson, could hide out in this small, tight-knit community, Dr. Gerald McCormick's long-lost son should be able to fly under the radar, too.

But all it would take to blow his cover would be some tourist with a smartphone and a fondness for reality shows about plastic surgery makeovers spotting him in the quaint ski resort. But maybe that was what Mia was hoping for.

Suddenly, the Quilting Club and some low-level town gossip didn't seem so bad.

Chapter Five

Mia had been kicking herself the past couple of days for not clarifying that she'd actually meant she'd meet Garrett McCormick at her studio, not her apartment.

Of course, where the meeting took place was probably the least of her worries.

At least she now knew the name of her child's father. And so did her friends, who were aware that she'd be seeing him tonight. They'd convinced her that she was perfectly safe with the reputable doctor and that she would've looked paranoid and suspicious if she had called him and changed the location of their rendezvous.

Sheesh. She needed to stop thinking of it like that, of *him* like that. This was a formal discussion and she'd keep things as proper and as professional as she could. There would be no drinking, no sultry piano music, no dim lighting. In fact, she'd been debating all afternoon whether or not she should take a quick shower before he showed up or whether she should play it casual and stay in her work clothes.

At five-thirty, she suddenly decided that she wanted to at least look physically put together, because her spinning emotions had her feeling like a mental wreck on the inside. As she stood in her bathroom blow-drying her long dark hair, she considered everything she'd been able to find out about him so far.

She'd done an internet search on him the moment she'd gotten back from his office. She'd already known he'd been in the navy and was licensed to practice medicine, but not much else. The name was common enough to land several hits and she'd even been directed to a website for some reality shows on Med TV about rich plastic surgeons in Southern California, but that Dr. McCormick was in his sixties. She'd found a couple of articles published by Garrett McCormick in a medical journal. Other than recent developments in robotically assisted surgeries, she hadn't been able to narrow anything down. At least there weren't any glaring articles about serial killers or other criminals with that same name.

Of course, Mia knew all too well that narcissistic spoiled jerks, especially ones such as Nick Galveston, with wealthy families, usually kept their sociopathic personalities well hidden. Even though Garrett's office was sparsely furnished, underneath that white lab coat he'd worn, his clothes reeked of fine taste and fortune.

A firm knock sounded at her front door and she took one last look in her bathroom mirror. *Please don't let my baby's father be anything like Nick Galveston.*

Her soft-soled flats didn't make much noise as she

crossed her small living room to let him inside, but honestly, she couldn't hear much over the pounding of her heart. She almost lost her nerve when she looked through the small peephole and saw his hazel eyes and freshly shaved jawline.

Why did he have to be so handsome?

She took a deep breath, just as she used to do before a big performance, steeled her spine and swung the door open. But she must've been standing a little too close because she yanked the doorknob right into her hip bone.

"Ow," she said, trying not to double over as she rubbed the spot just below the waistband of her jeans.

"Are you okay?" he asked, coming quickly to her side. But she wasn't comfortable with his attention focused anywhere near the location of her injury so she sucked up the pain and pretended she couldn't feel the throbbing ache or the sting in her pride.

"Yes, I'm fine. I just misjudged how far I was from the door. Come on in."

Her apartment was a small one-bedroom and, up until this moment, she'd never felt cramped by the lack of space in the tiny entryway.

She gestured him toward the white-and-blue sofa upholstered with a soft paisley print, and tried not to worry about how he might perceive her eclectic decorating skills. Most of her furniture and accents were funky pieces she'd picked up at nearby antiques stores and came in a multitude of shades of blue and painted oak. She'd moved around so much as a child, she'd always been drawn to furnishings that were old and had a deep history. But she also had an artistic streak that extended beyond dancing and she liked the abstract hodgepodge of it all—the uniqueness that was reflective of her personal style.

"I feel silly showing up to your house empty-handed like this," Garrett said, before taking a seat. "But, I wasn't sure what to bring. It didn't really seem like the occasion for flowers, and, well, you probably aren't drinking much champagne these days."

She probably shouldn't have been drinking champagne two months ago, either. But Mia kept that thought to herself. "Please, don't worry about it. Speaking of beverages, can I get you something?"

"What do you have?"

That was a good question. In her angst over having him over to her house, she hadn't thought about what she would do with him once he got there. She didn't entertain people other than her friends and she hadn't been to the market all week so her inventory wasn't exactly up to par.

"I have water. And ginger ale."

"I'll take the ginger ale."

She grabbed the liter bottle and two glasses and carried it over to the small round coffee table she'd painstakingly sanded and painted the color of a pale robin's egg. She should've planned for a better seating option because she couldn't very well sit down on the sofa next to him. That'd be way too intimate. She didn't have any chairs besides the ones pushed into the dining room table and it would look suspicious if she hauled one of those over here. She spied the white tufted ottoman and decided that was better than nothing.

Mia tried to casually move the overstuffed footstool out of the way by using her left calf, but her attempt at nonchalance was rewarded by a sharp pain in her Achilles tendon when its clawed wooden foot tripped her up.

She sucked in a whispered curse as she plopped ungracefully onto her impromptu seat. "Are you sure you're okay?" Garrett asked.

"Yep," she said, although it came out more like, "Whepppp."

He rubbed his forehead as though he was pondering whether or not to believe her. He must've opted for the politest choice because he didn't say anything else.

Instead, he shrugged out of what looked to be a cashmere coat and laid it over the back of her couch before pouring them both a drink. He was dressed in a soft gray sweater, definitely just as pricey as the starched custom-looking button-up shirt she'd seen him in before. But this time, there wasn't a cuff link in sight.

Relieved to have something to do with herself, she reached for her ginger ale and gulped it so quickly, she inhaled tiny carbonated bubbles into her nose. She let out a small sneeze before he had even raised his own glass.

"Are you coming down with a cold?" Garrett leaned toward her and put his cool and smooth hand to her forehead.

Mia jerked away as if he'd burned her and almost toppled off her backless seat.

"Whoa." He relocated his hand to her shoulders as if he could help steady her. Why was he always touching her? "Are you okay?"

She scooted toward the center of the ottoman, causing his fingers to fall away. "I'm fine."

"If you say so."

"Sorry, I'm usually much more graceful than this."

Which was true. She was a dancer, after all. But after tripping in his office and now tonight, she had to conclude that there must be some sort of hormonal imbalance wreaking havoc with her body because she was all kinds of thrown off by his nearness.

"I think it's safe to say we're both a little out of sorts." He smiled at her, probably in an attempt to be reassuring, but it didn't quite reach his eyes. It was probably the same smile he gave to wounded soldiers when he had to tell them they needed major orthopedic surgery—which was pretty apropos considering she felt as if her future was being amputated.

"Speaking of hands, uh, I mean..." She trailed off since they hadn't been speaking of anything to do with his hands. Instead, she reached into the little wooden treasure chest on the coffee table and pulled out a small gold circle. "One of these fell out in the elevator, uh, that night."

His brows lifted and his eyes grew darker when he ran his finger over the onyx stone. "Thank you for returning this to me. I'd wondered where I lost it."

Her face had to be the most unflattering shade of red. "I found it when I was leaving the morning after and was kind of in a rush to get out of there." Her stomach, which had been acting queasy all week, was threatening to take center stage if she didn't calm down and relax. "Anyway, I thought you might want it back."

He angled his torso and slipped it into his hip pocket, thankfully not mentioning the last time he'd shoved it away. "I never should have left them on the bar in the first place. I was being stubborn and perhaps a little bitter toward my father when I pulled them out. I was glad when you reminded me to take them and then, well, one thing led to another and I got a little careless afterward. I kicked myself for it after the fact, but it was one of many recriminations I carried from that night."

Recriminations indeed. At least she now knew he'd regretted their lovemaking.

It should make what she was about to say a lot easier. She'd rehearsed exactly what she was going to tell Garrett several times these past three days, but now, with him sitting in what used to be her cozy and safe living room, her mind had just exited stage right.

She could hear the retro clock on the kitchen wall ticking in a steady cadence and felt each awkward notch of the second hand push them further into an uncomfortable-silence territory.

"Have you had dinner yet?" he asked.

"Uh, no. Why? Are you hungry?"

"Actually, I am. I skipped lunch today because the MRI techs, who were supposed to set up my equipment yesterday, didn't show up until this afternoon. So I've been at the office all day."

"I would offer to fix something to eat, but I haven't been to Duncan's Market since, well, since I saw you last and I've been trying to avoid too many public places until…" She trailed off, her excuses sounding lame to her own ears.

"Oh, I didn't expect you to cook for me. I just thought maybe we could go grab a bite to eat. Maybe it would help lighten the mood if we had something else to do besides talk about…you know. But, if you're worried about being seen in public with me, I could pick up something to go and bring it back here."

"I'm not afraid to be seen in public with you." Okay, that was only partially true. She might not be afraid, but she definitely didn't want her personal business broadcast all over town just yet. And having a meal in public with him was tantamount to a front-page article in the *Sugar Falls Advocate*. "But getting takeout sounds good."

Great. If she couldn't even have dinner with the man, then how was she going to raise a baby with him?

"There's that Italian restaurant about a block from here. What's it called? Patrelli's? I hear they have excellent lasagna and these amazing garlic knots. Why don't I call in an order?"

The thought of garlic made Mia's stomach do another cartwheel and she quickly clapped her hand over her mouth. But it was just a false alarm. She took a small sip of her drink, hoping it would be enough to quell her nausea and her sketchy nerves.

Unfortunately, Garrett was instantly alert. "What's wrong?"

Of all the random men she could've accidentally gotten pregnant by during a one-night stand, why did she have to choose a doctor who was trained to be attuned to even the slightest physical discomfort? She almost giggled at the absurd thought, but didn't want to risk choking on her beverage. It wasn't as if she'd known he was a doctor at the time.

"Sorry." She waved him off with her hand. "I'm just getting a little firsthand experience with the wonderful world of morning sickness. Unfortunately, it's been taking place in the evenings and usually centers on all things smelling of garlic."

"I could pick up something else?"

"No," Mia said, a bit too loudly perhaps. "I can just

order a salad or something. And maybe some plain bread."

Ever since seeing Garrett again, all she'd been able to stomach were peanut butter sandwiches. Of course, that wasn't much different from what Mia usually wanted to eat. Her friends constantly ribbed her about her peanut butter obsession, but when one grew up with a mother who thought anything with more calories than a celery stick would cause her young daughter to balloon into a whale overnight, one tended to indulge in the foods she missed out on during childhood.

In fact, her mom used to keep a postcard of a large cartoon hippo ballet dancing in a tutu taped to their refrigerator door. At first, eight-year-old Mia had thought the image was humorous, but Rhonda Palinski had intended it to be a deterrent for anything her daughter might be tempted to put in her mouth that could jeopardize her dancing career. That picture moved each time with them and had graced several kitchens before Mia went to college and found it on top of her leotards in her suitcase with a note attached suggesting she affix the dancing hippo to her dorm room fridge. She'd torn it up and thrown it away before her ballet shoes had even been unpacked.

As if the unpleasant memory conjured up the woman herself, the apartment telephone rang and Mia's posture became even more erect. Only one person ever called her landline.

"Do you need to answer that?" Garrett asked.

"Nope. It's probably just a wrong number or a telemarketer. Most people who need to get ahold of me call my cell phone." That was true. She'd had the home line installed only when she'd first moved to Sugar Falls.

She'd still been traumatized after the Nick incident and her peace of mind dictated she have several means of access to call 9-1-1.

When the answering machine clicked on, she prayed that this time, it truly was just a telemarketer. But the second she heard the raspy smoker's voice, she should've known she wouldn't be so lucky.

"Mia, baby, it's Mom. I've been trying to call your cell phone all week but you haven't been answering. I just wanted to make sure we're still on for our Thanksgiving plans… Hello? Hello? What in the…"

The message continued to record as Rhonda Palinski pushed a series of buttons on her end of the line then abruptly disconnected. Several seconds later, the phone rang again.

"You know what?" Mia jumped up suddenly, knowing that her persistent mother would just keep calling and leaving messages until Mia answered. "Why don't we just walk over to Patrelli's and place our order?"

Maybe if she put on a thick scarf and hat, she wouldn't be as recognizable walking with a good-looking man down Snowflake Boulevard. The phone began ringing again. Even if she was recognized, it was less risky than staying in her apartment with him like a sitting duck, waiting to see what her mother said next on her machine. She was relieved to see that Garrett was now rising and following her lead, even if the amused expression on his face suggested he was enjoying her awkward discomfort. She'd made it to the wrought iron coat rack by the door and was just finished bundling up before the outgoing greeting started all over.

"Baby, it's Mom again. Your machine cut me off. Anyway…" Mia rushed Garrett outside and slammed her door behind them, effectively cutting off Rhonda's voice.

"So does your mom know about the baby and everything?" he asked as they made their way down the wooden staircase attached to the back of her building.

"Not yet. I need to tell her, but I've been putting it off. I guess I've been putting a lot of things off."

"Speaking of that…" He turned toward her and, sensing the direction of his thoughts, she wondered if maybe they should go back upstairs and have this conversation. "I still can't believe you were just going to have my baby and not even tell me."

Nope. It looked as if they were going to do this right here, in the dimly lit alley behind the Snowflake Dance Academy. "Garrett, I thought we went over this in your office. How could I tell you when I didn't even know you or where to find you?"

He buttoned up his coat, but his hazel eyes didn't look away from her. "You're right. There's no sense in looking back at the past. What's important is that we figure out what we're going to do from here on out."

"What *we're* going to do?"

"You can't seriously expect me to not want to be a part of my child's life."

"Actually, I didn't really know what to expect. It was never my intention to get pregnant that night in Boise, and I'm guessing raising a child with a complete stranger wasn't what you had in mind, either. So I completely understand if you want to pretend none of this ever happened and walk away. I'm more than capable of handling this on my own. No strings attached. You're off the hook." She shoved her hands in her pockets, but not because it was cold. She just didn't want him to see her crossing her fingers.

"Walk away? From my own child? Nope. That's most assuredly not going to happen. So back to what *we*—meaning you and I together—are going to do. I've been doing a little bit of online research about co-parenting and shared custody. If we do things right and put the baby first, there's no reason why we can't work together to raise a well-adjusted and happy kid."

"You want to co-parent?" She had never even heard of the term before. Mia's own father had bailed the minute he'd found out his mistress was pregnant. Actually, he didn't bail so much as he'd simply gone home to his wife and his real children. Maybe Dan Perez had co-parented with the mother of his legal offspring, but he certainly hadn't done so with Rhonda Palinski. "What does that entail?"

"Well, we would share custody. You get the baby half of the time and I get him or her the other half, and we make decisions together about what school they'll go to and who has to pick them up from sports class and that kind of thing. I mean, we live in the same city now, so it shouldn't be that difficult to coordinate our work schedules and pass off back and forth to each other."

Share her child? Was he delusional? Did he actually think she'd leave her precious son or daughter with some guy she barely knew? He made it sound so simple. Yet they were talking about an innocent human being. Not a basketball.

"But we don't know each other. What if you're a completely unsuitable father?"

"Me? I'd make a terrific father. I'm well educated,

I have a stable job and income, and I've been around kids before."

"What kids?" She remembered him mentioning that he had a strained relationship with his own dad and wondered if that extended to the rest of his family.

"I did a couple of rounds in the pediatric unit when I was doing my residency. And I found one of my old textbooks on childhood development when I was unpacking some boxes in my office." Even in this alley with the orangish glow of the light poles, her face must've reflected all the skepticism she felt because he squared his shoulders defensively and asked, "What about you? What if *you're* a completely unsuitable mother?"

"Garrett, I'm a dance teacher." Mia started walking, but not to get away. She needed to move around in order to redirect her normally nonexistent temper. "I work with children all day, every day of the week."

"Fair enough." He kept pace beside her as they turned the corner of the building and made their way along the main sidewalk. "But what if you end up being like one of those spiteful women who becomes bitter and vindictive and uses our child to punish me?"

Mia had never been prone to violence, but she had also never had her morals or her potential parenting skills called into question by a virtual stranger. She stopped and pulled her hand out of her coat pocket to point her finger at him. "I would never use another person, let alone my own child, to punish anyone. But even if I were the type who *was* like that, we don't have an invested emotional history so it's not like I'm some bitter ex. We didn't exactly have the kind of relationship where one would establish those kinds of feelings toward each other."

He rubbed his forehead, then reached out and took her hand in his own. What was up with him and this whole touching thing? It must be something they taught in medical school because Mia surely wasn't used to so much constant physical contact.

She also wasn't used to the heat that shot from her fingers, up her arm and deep into her chest. So then why was she so mesmerized by it?

Uh-oh. She was feeling that weird bubbly champagne thing again. If she'd had any control over her brain, she would've yanked her hand back. But he was using his thumb to stroke her palm, and the last thing she wanted to do was make a scene now that they were on the main street through town—or to lose his comforting warmth. So she kept walking, letting him hold her hand as if they were a couple of lovers on a leisurely evening stroll.

"Listen, Mia. We barely know each other at all. We certainly don't know what kind of parents we'll be, let alone how we'll get along in a couple of years. But I hope that we can both agree that deep down, we want what's best for our child."

She glanced at him as she nodded in agreement, and his lips split into a full grin. This time, his expression matched his eyes. Now, *this* was a reassuring smile.

"So we've got a couple of months before Pipsqueak gets here to learn everything we possibly can about each other and how to successfully co-parent."

There he went with that co-parenting mumbo jumbo again. But he was right in the fact that they would have to learn about each other and how to manage being in each other's lives for the next eighteen-plus years at least.

"Okay, co-parenting rule number one." She felt her

frown lift and her guard ease just a smidge. "We are not naming this child Pipsqueak."

They reached Patrelli's, and Garrett smiled as he pulled open the heavy oak door leading to the crowded Italian restaurant. Looking into his eyes again, Mia remembered why she'd let this man lead her back to a hotel room. Or maybe she'd been the one doing the leading. Either way, if she wasn't careful, the whole world would see just how eager she was to have him smile like that at her again.

At least on a Saturday night, Patrelli's was mostly filled with tourists since most of the locals knew to avoid the busier places on the weekends.

"Mia, what a surprise!" Mrs. Patrelli, the matronly woman who owned the restaurant with her husband, greeted them as they walked inside. "We're packed tonight, but we might have a booth opening up in a few minutes. I'll move you to the top of the list."

"Oh, no, Mrs. Patrelli. Please don't do that. We just wanted to put in an order to go."

The fortyish-year-old plump woman with short, dark curly hair looked at her and Garrett skeptically before pulling a pad of paper out of her black apron and taking their order. Hopefully, Mr. Patrelli wouldn't take too long in the kitchen because the normally pleasing smells of marinara sauce and yeasty dough were already playing havoc with Mia's sensitive stomach.

"I'll bring you both some Chianti while you wait."

"Actually—" Mia put a hand to her tummy "—I'm not really feeling up for any tonight. Could you just bring me a ginger ale instead?"

"But you and your friends always have wine when you eat here. You love the house Chianti. There's only

one reason a passionate woman like you wouldn't drink
wine and that's if she's…" Mrs. Patrelli paused as she
studied Mia carefully before turning her appraising eye
to Garrett. She looked back and forth at them several
times and Mia could see the moment the Italian woman
made the connection. "I'll go get your ginger ale."

"Great." Mia slumped into an empty seat by the hostess stand as Mrs. Patrelli bustled off to the kitchen.
"She totally knows."

"Knows what? About you being pregnant?" Garrett
sat beside her, his arm immediately going around her
as if to comfort her. "How can you tell?"

"Mrs. Patrelli has seven kids. I'm sure she's pretty
astute about things like that."

"Is it bad if she knows? I mean, it's not like everyone won't find out eventually, Mia."

"I know. I guess I'm still just trying to get used to
the fact that we're having a baby."

His expression softened. "We. I like the sound of—"

"Oh, my gosh, GP!" a beautiful blonde shrieked as
she walked by carrying a toddler covered in pizza sauce
and still eating half a slice. "I barely recognized you
without the tailored suit and stiff collar. How in the
world have you been?"

It took Garrett several moments to identify the
woman who had just intruded on one of the most important conversations of his life. With her nose job and
cheek implants, Cammie Longacre looked less like the
girl he'd known in high school and exactly like every
other debutante-turned-housewife he'd grown up de-
testing.

He could feel Mia trying to scoot her chair away,

but Garrett's arm around her shoulder was frozen—as if the shock that had been lying dormant in his body the past couple of days had just formed a glacier inside him. He could see Cammie's lips moving, and he even caught the words "senior class," "your dad" and "thought you'd disappeared off the face of the planet." But he couldn't make himself respond.

At least, not until the former yearbook editor for Newport Hills Prep Academy sat down next to him and leaned in closely before snapping a picture of them together on her smartphone.

"They're not going to believe it," Cammie said before looking over to Mia. "And I just couldn't help overhear you guys are pregnant! How exciting."

Realizing his former classmate must have overheard Mia's admission, he went into auto-pilot and switched over to damage control mode.

"What are you doing here, Cammie?" he asked, then wanted to kick himself for sounding so defensive.

"My husband and I brought the kids up to kick off the ski season." Just then, a man who looked as if he was still president of his college fraternity walked over with two laughing children under each of his arms. "Chip wanted to do Telluride again this year, but let's face it. All the good spots in Colorado and Jackson Hole are becoming so commercial lately. A friend of a friend recommended Sugar Falls and we decided to try out something new."

"Us, too," Garrett said capitalizing on her line of thinking. If he could convince this woman who'd led the campaign to vote him Most Likely to Model For Brooks Brothers that he was simply on vacation, then word about his permanent whereabouts would be less likely to leak out. He squeezed Mia in closer next to him, hoping she would play along. "We just love hitting the slopes, but there isn't any good snowboarding where we live in...Miami."

He'd blurted out the first city that had come to his mind, which was what he had been researching after Mia had sat in his office and told him that she'd used to be a professional NFL cheerleader.

"I should have known you were living on the coast somewhere. And snowboarding, too! You've finally turned into a beach boy, GP. Just like your dad." Her youngest child let out an unhappy wail before throwing his half-gnawed pizza crust to the floor. Being compared to his father left Garrett feeling like that piece of chewed-up bread lying on the ground. "Well, that's our cue to get going. Maybe we'll see you guys at the Snow Creek Lodge this weekend. We can catch up and I'll fill you in on what's happened to everyone since graduation."

"Sounds good." Garrett waved to the departing family, forcing a smile when what he wanted to do was crawl behind the hostess stand.

He waited until Cammie and her brood were well out the door before chancing a look at Mia.

She held her jaw firmly clenched, her eyes staring at the faded poster of Venice affixed to the wall across from them. Someone as naturally beautiful as Mia couldn't possibly be jealous of a woman like Cammie, could she? Or maybe she was embarrassed that he hadn't introduced her to his old classmate. Either way, he needed to get back into her good graces. "Look, I know what I just said to that woman might've sounded crazy, but trust me. It was for the best."

"Why would you let her think we were together? Or suggest we were living in Miami?"

Was that what had Mia so on edge? The fact that someone might actually believe they were a couple?

"Actually, I believe she overheard *you* practically announcing to the restaurant that we were having a baby." There went his defensive tone again. Perhaps Mia had set this all up.

"But Miami? I'd really prefer people didn't connect me with that place."

He almost laughed at her impractical concern. Anyone with a computer could figure out where Mia used to live. It really couldn't be that big of a deal. Clearly, she didn't understand the potential risk of having someone from his hometown recognize him.

Or maybe she understood it too well.

"Listen, when she snapped that picture, it caught me by surprise. The last thing I want is for her to broadcast on social media where I'm currently living. Florida was the first thing that popped into my mind since the other day you'd mentioned that you'd lived there."

"Why wouldn't you want anyone to know you've moved to Idaho?"

Was she serious? Maybe she was hoping for the camera crews to show up and for their unorthodox relationship to be broadcast to every major tabloid in America, but Garrett would be damned if he'd let the paparazzi find out about his child. "Let's just say that I value my privacy."

Something that looked like understanding flashed in Mia's pale blue eyes, but it was so unexpected, Garrett wasn't sure he'd interpreted it correctly. He hoped she did understand because this was one child-rearing issue that wasn't up for negotiation. The sooner she realized that in order to make this co-parenting thing work she would need to keep their relationship out of the press, the better.

He was relieved when she nodded and said, "I'm glad we're on the same page."

She brushed her long dark hair away from her face and he thought back to her not wanting to be seen together in public. Maybe she had something to hide, too. He wondered whether she'd be willing to sign some sort of confidentiality agreement—especially if he tossed in a decent amount of money as an added incentive to keep quiet.

God, that sounded so cheap and tawdry. As if he was trying to buy her off in order to keep his child a secret. What kind of man did something like that?

A desperate one.

"So, for now, we're just keeping this whole baby thing between the two of us?" he asked.

"Well, us and Mrs. Patrelli," she said, one corner of her lip lifting slightly. He liked seeing her smile and realized that during their brief encounters, he hadn't seen it too often. "And probably Cessy Walker. Oh, and my two best friends."

"What?"

"I had to tell them about you when Maxine called the hotel room the morning after and you answered the phone." So that *had* been someone looking for her and more than likely hell-bent on calling security to protect her. "They were also with me when I took the pregnancy test. But that was before I knew you were going to be living here and would want to be…uh…involved."

Okay, he could handle a couple of locals knowing

about them. After all, he'd figured he'd have to deal with as much when she'd limped out of his office the other day. He nodded and realized his arm was still resting along the back of her chair. If he moved it just an inch, he'd be able to feel her shoulders pressed firmly against him again.

"And Kylie and Max might've told their husbands. Which means your buddy, Chief Cooper, probably knows, as well as Dr. Gregson. Didn't you work with him when you were stationed at Shadowview?"

"I didn't know you were best friends with their wives." Yep. Word was going to get around Sugar Falls awfully quickly. "Anyone else?"

She opened her pretty pink lips to answer but was interrupted by the theme song from *Jaws*. She looked at the screen before pressing a button to silence the ringer. "Not yet, but I can tell you who isn't going to be happy when I *do* finally tell her," she said, flashing the screen at him. "My mother."

"Maybe you should take that."

"I'll call her tomorrow. Look, my tummy isn't doing all that great and I'm not really feeling up for dinner anymore."

"Oh. Okay. Should I cancel our order?"

"No. You take it to your place. Where is your place, by the way?"

"I've got a room at Betty Lou's Bed-and-Breakfast. But eventually, I'd like to find something here in town. Maybe one of those old Victorian homes to remodel."

"That sounds pretty permanent." He looked at her sideways. That was the point, wasn't it? She stood and he picked up his coat. "Where are you going?"

"To walk you home." Did she really think he'd be so ungentlemanly as to let her find her own way home?

"It's only a couple of blocks. I walk it all the time."

"So then you won't mind if I walk it with you."

"But what about your lasagna?"

"What about it? I'll come back for it."

He held open the door for her and they walked quietly down the street lined with gas lanterns and a heavier-than-normal amount of foot traffic, probably due to the weekend tourist crowd. If she wasn't feeling well, he didn't want to make her talk, even though there was still so much to say.

When they were almost to her building, he could no longer stand the silence between them. "So when do you see the obstetrician?"

"My first appointment is Monday afternoon. Why?"

He had a feeling the shy and reserved Mia wasn't going to like what he was about to say. But this was his future, too, and he wasn't going to take a backseat for any part of the process. "Should we take your car or mine?"

Chapter Six

Mia couldn't believe she was actually allowing Garrett to accompany her to such an important and intimate doctor's appointment.

But lately her emotions had been zooming up and down on the rickety roller-coaster tracks that were her nerves. So on Saturday night, when Garrett had asked in such a way that gave her no wiggle room for extracting herself gracefully, her already foggy brain couldn't come up with a good reason to deny him the simple request.

Besides, this child was his, too. As much as she'd wanted to keep the experience to herself, to keep the whole child to herself, she couldn't in good conscience do something so selfish—to either Garrett or to her unborn baby. Unless, of course, he proved himself to be untrustworthy or a bad father. In which case, she would pack up her son or daughter, along with the rest of her life, so quickly that nobody—not even her mother—would ever find them.

She kept her Prius at a steady and safe pace, which was more than she could say for her pulse rate, as she drove down the mountain highway toward Boise. Garrett sat quietly in the seat beside her, his fingers intertwined tightly together. They'd barely exchanged more than some simple pleasantries when they'd met in the back alley behind her dance studio after lunch. But that was for the best since Mia wasn't very good at making small talk.

"I could have driven us, you know," he said again for at least the third time.

"Yes, you mentioned that. Thank you for offering, but I feel more comfortable in my own car." *And in control.*

He fiddled with his seat belt before returning his hands to their original position. If Mia hadn't seen him so confident in several other situations, she would think that he was just as nervous as she was.

She saw the black cuff links, the ones with his initials secured at his wrists. "I see you're wearing your father's gift."

He clasped his hands together and held them in his lap. "I am. I was pretty angry at him that night I first met you. And you'll probably see me angry at him again in the future. But I decided to channel his words about remembering where I came from into something less bitter. Or maybe I'm a sentimental moron. I really don't know. Anyway, do you mind if I change the radio station?"

Mia frowned. But not because the guy didn't totally hate his father. That was actually a good thing. She was annoyed because this was her favorite CD, the one she'd once planned to use for her audition to the MFA program at Hollins University in Virginia. She'd just saved up enough money for the first year of tuition when she'd had to undergo reconstructive surgery on her knee. Nothing had been the same since then. "Do you have something against Mozart?"

"It's just so slow and tedious. It's making me really antsy and tense."

"Really? It's supposed to be soothing. I read an article that said babies can hear everything in utero, so I try to pick classic pieces for him or her to listen to whenever possible."

"The Rolling Stones are a classic." He shoved his sunglasses higher on his nose. At least he didn't just reach for the knob and change the station. Which was something that some of the entitled guys her mother had encouraged her to date in college would have done.

She glanced at the blue shirt that clung to his chiseled torso, his tailored khaki pants and his expensive loafers. Garrett dressed like the trust fund preppy types Rhonda Palinski insisted her daughter latch on to for financial security. But he'd also been in the military—and underneath those expensive clothes, she knew he had the well-muscled physique to prove it—so he didn't walk around town acting as if he owned everything in it, including her.

Plus, the fact that he'd been so standoffish with that woman who'd recognized him at Patrelli's was another thing she hadn't expected. At first, Mia had thought that Garrett's chilly response was due to his embarrassment of being seen with her. But when he wouldn't release her hands, as though he were holding on to her as he would a lifeboat in a stormy ocean, she realized that something else about Cammie Perfect Teeth had Garrett spooked.

Mia wouldn't characterize Garrett as being rebellious, but she'd definitely recognized the look in his eyes as the other woman had talked endlessly about the people they'd known in high school and running into his father. It was a look she'd seen reflected in her own mirror too often, such as right before she'd defied her mother by getting her nose pierced after college. But his hazel eyes had also held a fierce determination, like a cornered animal not willing to give himself or his starched collars up.

So who was after Garrett McCormick, MD, and why?

But before she could solve that mystery, she needed to get through her first obstetrician appointment.

She pulled into a parking spot in front of the three-story medical office building near Boise State University, but didn't dare look at the well-dressed gentleman sitting beside her. Maybe she could just try to pretend he wasn't there. She took a couple of deep but subtle breaths. Mozart hadn't been the least bit helpful thus far.

"You ready for this?" he asked, not looking entirely ready himself.

"No," she said. Yet, she opened her car door, determined to swallow her own uncertainties and discomfort for the health of her unborn child. They walked silently across the full parking lot. He was probably just as lost in his own thoughts as she was.

He held open the large glass doors for her and then found the suite number on the directory near the elevator. She could tell he was equally anxious, but at least he was being solicitous.

Almost too solicitous. When they walked up to the receptionist, it was Garrett's voice that announced them. "Mia Palinski to see Dr. Wang."

The lady behind the desk was wearing scrubs printed with storks and handed her several forms to complete. But before Mia could take the clipboard, Garrett said, "Here, let me help with that. I'm a doctor. And the dad. Not *her* dad. The baby's dad."

The woman laughed, as if she dealt with nervous expectant fathers every day. Which she probably did. Next, she handed Mia an empty plastic cup and pointed to the restroom before saying, "Can't help with this one, Dr. Dad."

"Honestly," Garrett whispered as they walked toward the chairs in the waiting room, "I can't really help with the forms, either. Besides what I memorized from my own medical charts, I still don't know much about you. I guess I just wanted to feel useful."

Mia's spine tingled, but not out of apprehension. He'd memorized her medical history? Not that she could blame him. She would look through any records she could to find out as much information about him as possible. In fact, she'd talked to her best friends' husbands at length yesterday, quizzing them on everything they knew about Garrett.

Kylie's husband, Drew Gregson, was a psychologist at Shadowview Military Hospital and assured Mia that her baby's father was a well-respected doctor who treated his nurses and staff well and had a reputation for being professional.

Cooper could also vouch for the man's military record and skills as a surgeon, but she could tell the police chief knew more than what he was admitting. When it came to a personal background check, all he would tell her was that Garrett had a clean criminal record and was a trustworthy guy.

Drew was trained to notice abnormal behavior and Cooper was a good judge of character. They were two of the few men Mia trusted implicitly, which was what had ultimately swayed her decision to allow Garrett to be a part of her pregnancy.

But after she'd left her urine sample and changed into a plain cotton gown, Mia had to wonder if the small confines of the obstetrician's office, with all the pictures of women's reproductive organs on display, was the best place for her and Garrett to get better acquainted.

He offered to take Mia's blood pressure, but the nurse pointed to the chair in the corner and told him that he could either sit out of the way or out in the waiting room.

"Well, she could certainly work on her bedside manner," Garrett said when the medical assistant left them alone to await the doctor.

"I thought she was sweet and more than capable. Besides, you're not her patient so she probably doesn't care too much about your bedside requirements."

Garrett crossed his arms and, as if by silent agreement, they looked everywhere around the room except at each other.

At least he didn't show too much interest in the posters or the life-size model of a uterus. Instead, he kept checking out the medical equipment and even commented on the newness of the ultrasound machine.

Dr. Wang, an older woman with a short, messy ponytail and bifocals, finally entered and relieved some of the tension. "Congratulations, you two. The urine sample was positive, so let's take some measurements and figure out when exactly this baby will be arriving."

Garrett must have taken that as his cue to leave his seat of exile and hover around Mia as the doctor performed her exam.

"Aren't you the curious one," Dr. Wang said, lifting her wiry eyebrows high above the rim of her glasses.

"I'm in orthopedics," he said. They spoke briefly about medical school, the people they both knew at Shadowview Military Hospital and the differences between joint replacements and fetal development.

Mia wanted to wave her arm and call out, *Hello! I'm the one with the baby inside me*, but she was so accustomed to not trying to draw attention to herself that she remained still and quiet, trying to absorb the fact that she was truly and officially pregnant. It was one thing to see a couple of lines on a plastic stick. It was quite another to lie back in a sterile room with two doctors conversing about due dates and trimesters and fundal height measurements.

Somehow, everything was so real yet so surreal at the same time. Mia felt as if she was the cute and cuddly kitten in the poster tacked to the ceiling, looking down at the nervous and excited woman lying on the exam table.

Whoa. A fleeting moment of déjà vu replayed in her mind as she remembered having this same out-of-body experience when she'd entered the mirrored hotel elevator with Garrett and watched him pull her into his arms.

It was as though she knew this was her. But at the same time, it couldn't possibly be her.

"What's that?" Garrett asked when Dr. Wang pulled a small instrument out of her lab coat pocket.

"This is a fetal Doppler," the obstetrician said. "We're going to try to hear your child's heartbeat."

Mia tensed when the doctor opened the hospital gown and exposed her abdomen. She lifted her arm up so it lay across her face, hopefully hiding the blush spreading on her cheeks. Garrett had seen her much more intimately than this, plus, he was in complete medical professional mode and would hardly observe her body as anything other than for its basic anatomical purpose.

"Are you okay?" He rubbed her forearm, causing her to move it away from her face and make eye contact with him.

"Yep," Mia replied, her jaw stiff. "It's just cold."

When the quick-paced whooshing noise filled the small room, Garrett's hand slid along her arm, until it was locked tightly around her fingers above her head. Instead of looking at the doctor, he looked at Mia. His hazel eyes had turned dark green and slightly misty. "Is that it?"

She felt her own eyes grow damp and couldn't stop her fingers from squeezing back. "I think so."

That was *her* baby moving inside *her* body—dancing to its own pulse and synchronizing its heartbeat with hers. Her throat grew tight and she felt the wetness of a happy tear trickle toward her ear. She pulled Garrett's hand tighter, moving it to just below her chin. She was so relieved he was there and that she wasn't experiencing this wonderful moment alone. She'd never heard such a beautiful sound in her life. Not even Mozart could top this.

Garrett's other palm moved toward her bare stomach

and it felt like the most natural thing in the world when his thumb traced a circle around the small monitor.

"Can you believe it?" His grin was full of pride and awe, but it was also contagious. "That's our Pipsqueak. Can we see him on an ultrasound?"

His eager voice reminded her of a kid who'd just been given a brand-new toy and was already tearing into the packaging trying to get it out. For a skilled surgeon, he certainly wasn't exhibiting an ounce of impulse control at that moment.

"We can." Dr. Wang pulled the bigger machine over. "But as of now, I'm estimating you to be at ten weeks. So we won't know just yet whether your Pipsqueak is a boy or a girl for another few weeks."

"I can't wait," he said, then removed his hand only when the doctor pushed it away to squirt a cold lubricant on Mia's belly.

"Being a parent takes lots of patience," the obstetrician said. "Making it through the next several months will be your first taste of that."

I can't wait. The words he'd uttered without thinking ricocheted inside his head all the way back to Sugar Falls. Along with the fact that what he'd said was true.

He didn't know how to be a father or how to co-parent, for that matter. And he assuredly didn't know this woman who was carrying his child. But when he'd heard the thrilling wish-washing sound of his baby's heartbeat, he knew with a deep certainty that he'd never been so excited for anything in his life—not even for that plane ride that had taken him from his family home to his future dorm room at Annapolis.

And just like joining the navy, Garrett knew this

journey of fatherhood would have its ups and downs and that in no way would it be an easy road. But for some reason, he was no longer looking at the situation the way a third-year resident dreaded getting deployed to a combat zone.

"Why are you smiling?" Mia asked as she steered her little hybrid car onto the interstate.

"I can't stop."

"I know. Me, neither. Earlier in the exam room, I was thinking that this whole experience is so surreal."

"Exactly. It's just so crazy, you know? I should be scared to death of what the future holds. But I'm not. It's a weird sensation for me because usually I like order, I like rules. It's why I joined the navy."

"I thought you joined the navy to get away from your father."

"Well, partly. But I could've gone anywhere to get away from him. The navy was both a physical and an emotional escape for me. Growing up in my family was like being on an eighteen-year concert tour with Jimmy Buffet. I became a surgeon because I'm good at remaining steady when there's chaos all around me."

"What about your mom? You've never mentioned her."

He looked at Mia, something about the emotional experience they'd just shared making him decide to open up a little. "She died of breast cancer."

"That must've been very sad."

"I was two when it happened so I really don't remember much about her."

"I'm sorry," Mia said, but Garrett didn't want to end their day talking about something depressing. He fingered his cuff links, the ones that now had a little more sentimental meaning to them than they had that night he'd lost one.

"So that ultrasound was pretty amazing, huh? Pip-squeak looked pretty healthy in there."

She smiled at him. "I'm happy you're excited and, for what's it's worth, I'm glad we're off to a good start with this whole co-parenting thing."

"Me, too."

They'd had a relaxing drive back from Boise, neither one of them talking much, but neither one of them on edge, either. Something had happened in that doctor's office that had allowed them to accept the fact that they were embarking on a special journey together, and that they were going to be partners in whatever happened from here on out.

Sure, Mia still hadn't given him any indication that she was willing to let him see too much of who she was, but at least she hadn't insisted on playing that "sooth-ing" classical music on the way home. In fact, Garrett had been surprised to discover she actually had a couple of classic rock stations preprogrammed on her car radio.

They were listening to Crosby, Stills, Nash & Young when Mia parked the small vehicle in an assigned spot behind the building housing the Snowflake Dance Academy. He thought about her warmly decorated apartment above it and hoped she'd welcome him back there again before the baby was born. At some point, they would need to get to a familiar place where they would feel comfortable in each other's presence. Yet after the miracle he'd just been a part of, he didn't want to rush anything that would force them together.

But he didn't want to go back to his empty and lonely room at the bed-and-breakfast, either.

"Thank you again for letting me go with you to the first appointment."

"Honestly, I was a little surprised that you'd want to."

"Why would that surprise you?" Did she think he planned to be some sort of deadbeat dad?

"I just figured with you being a man of science and a doctor and all that, it wouldn't be too thrilling for you."

"I probably would've thought that myself a few months ago. But it's different being the one on the other side of the curtain, so to speak. When I'm the doctor, it's all about business and caring for the patient and being the one in charge. Plus, I only have a basic fundamental understanding of childbirth from medical school since I've never been too interested in that field before. I guess it's more exciting when it's your own child— your own future—at stake."

"I can understand that." She nodded toward the freshly painted Victorian building that housed her studio. "When I watch my students perform their routines in a recital, it just feels like a job well done. But then I get a glimpse of their parents sitting in the audience, holding up their cameras and leaping up to applaud when it's over, and I think about how much more invested they are than me."

A tiny knock sounded at the driver's side window and she turned her head to smile at a little girl wearing a heavy pink coat over her pink tights.

"Hi, Madison," Mia said as she exited the car.

"Hey, Miss Mia." The six-year-old pulled a finger out of her left nostril then smiled, revealing two missing teeth. "I've been practicing my kick ball chains all week and my mom brought me over early so I could show you before the other students get here."

"I can't wait to see them. We have about fifteen more minutes until class starts so give me a couple seconds to get inside and then I'll watch." Mia pulled a bobby pin out of her own sweater pocket and used it to straighten the girl's lopsided bun. He'd seen her in work mode for only thirty seconds, but she seemed pretty invested in her students so far. She turned to Garrett. "Tap class starts at five, so I better get going."

She put her hand out, but must have thought better of the formal action after the intimate afternoon they'd just shared because she pulled it back and then drew the edges of her cardigan tighter around her waist instead.

They weren't quite at the hugging-goodbye phase, but he'd like to think they'd at least gotten past the hand-shaking stage. As Dr. Wang had suggested, he would try to be patient over the next seven months. Too bad he wasn't ready to go back to the B and B just yet. "Actually, do you mind if I come inside for a second and use your restroom?"

Okay, so maybe that was just an excuse to linger and gain more of a glimpse into her world. But who could blame him? He *should* see the environment where his child would be raised part-time. She'd had the opportunity to see him at work, so why shouldn't he be afforded the same?

"Sure," she said, shrugging her shoulders. He followed her inside to where another instructor was conducting some sort of hip-hop dance class.

So she had employees—legitimate ones, not just a socialite sitting behind a reception desk in a start-up orthopedic practice—working for her. Business must not have been too bad.

As soon as their feet hit the parquet floor, Mia's steps

picked up speed and she lifted her hand in a halfhearted wave toward several parents sitting on folding chairs in an alcove off to the side of the main dance floor. But she didn't stop to make small talk, or to otherwise introduce him to anyone. Either she was hoping nobody would pick up on the fact that his truck had been parked in front of her studio all afternoon and, therefore, surmise that they had been together. Or she thought he must really need to use the bathroom.

While he was washing his hands, the bass pounding through a mounted wall speaker down the hall came to an abrupt halt. He checked his watch and assumed the hip-hop class had just finished. Maybe if he took his time in here, he'd get the opportunity to watch her in action teaching a class.

But a loud knock on the door, followed by a young voice yelling, "Mommy, I really gotta go and I don't wanna be late for Miss Mia," threw a wrench in his stall tactics.

Garrett walked slowly out of the unisex restroom, tempted to stop by the wide-open doorway of what must've been Mia's office. Maybe he could slip in there and take a look around, find out some more information about her.

Oh, come on. What was he thinking? When had he become such a spy? He'd never had to dig up information on women before. Of course, he had never been that interested in another woman before.

Whoa. He needed to back up. Obviously, he wasn't interested in Mia as a *woman* woman. He was merely interested in her as the person carrying his child.

Be patient. He reminded himself of Dr. Wang's

words yet again. He would find out what he needed in due time.

He passed her office, for now, and hung back against the wall behind some folded-up floor mats. She had thrown her hair up into a knot on top of her head and was dressed in the same leggings she'd worn to the obstetrician's office. But she'd removed her outer sweater and his eyes were drawn to the scoop neck of her leotard. Her throat and upper chest were on full display and his mind took him back to their magical night. He remembered the feel of her collarbone beneath his lips as he'd trailed kisses along its silky-smooth ridges and the way her skin had tasted when her body had arched up into his arms and she'd pulled his head down lower.

A sudden burst from the speaker right above his ear brought him back to the present. Mia had put on some jazzy swing music and was now watching the little girl from the parking lot tap her little heart out. After she applauded the girl's solo performance, she called out, "Okay, my dancing butterflies. Let's get started."

Several other six-year-olds click-clacked their way out onto the floor and Mia led them through a series of toe shuffling, heel tapping and arm spinning.

He watched her try to stifle a giggle when one little girl spun too much and landed on her rear end. He also watched her soothe that same little girl when her two younger brothers, who were sitting and observing from the sidelines, roared with laughter during a second fall.

He wondered if Mia even knew he was still there. That he was watching her. He hoped not because right that second, she was more at ease than he'd ever seen her—even that night in Boise. She was clearly in her element and hadn't been lying when she'd said she was used to being around children.

When she started a conga line of sorts, the dancers followed her as she wove back and forth along the wooden floor. But the few stragglers at the tail end got separated and when the last butterfly ran to catch up with her classmates, she slipped in her metal-plated shoe and Garrett watched her go down awkwardly on her right ankle.

He was by the girl's side before Mia had even turned around—getting there before the poor child's mother, whose scream stopped the entire class and put an end to the conga line. The little one was crying and Garrett could tell by the odd angle of her foot that this was more than a sprain. He immediately went into emergency mode. His first job was to stabilize the patient. Someone else could deal with the flustered parents and everyone who crowded around to see what had happened.

"Honey," he said to the girl, but loud enough for the distraught mom to hear. "My name is Dr. McCormick and I want to help you. What's your name?"

"Madison," she said through trembling lips. Her mom stroked her hair as she knelt on the other side.

"Okay, Madison, I'm going to put my hands on your leg and check to see how strong your dancing legs are." Madison nodded but didn't make an effort to wipe away the fat teardrops spilling down her rosy cheeks.

Mia leaned over him and said, "What can I do to help?"

He pulled his keys out of his pocket and handed them to her. "I have a small bag in the backseat of my truck with some splints and a first aid kit in it. Can you get it for me? Also, we're going to need an ice pack." Then, so he wouldn't alarm his young patient, he said, "Wow, you've got some pretty sturdy bones and trust me, I've seen a lot of bones. That's the kind of doctor I am."

"Okay, class," Mia said. "Dr. McCormick is going to take good care of Madison, so let's call it a wrap and finish early tonight. I'll see all you butterflies next Monday."

Several parents herded their children toward the exit and Garrett was glad Mia was helping to draw their attention away. He didn't need the other students, who looked to be still shaken up from the injury of one of their own, to make his patient any more anxious.

"Do you have a skel'ton at your doctor office?" Madison sniffed her nose.

"I do, but it's not a real one."

"My friend Chelsea had a skel'ton at her Halloween party and I was the only girl who wasn't afraid to touch it."

"You know, that sounds very brave. In fact, I think you're being pretty brave right now."

He gently removed the patent leather shoe from her foot, trying to be mindful of the swelling that had already started.

"Owie, owie, ow!" Madison yelped, but she didn't release any more tears. She was a tough one, all right.

"Mom," he said, looking at the mother, who was still trembling. "Is her pediatrician close by?"

"Uh…" Madison's mother looked lost, as if she couldn't understand what he was asking. He repeated the question. "Not really. She's in Boise, but we've seen Dr. Suarez before for emergencies."

Garrett had met the older town doctor who had one foot out the retirement door and most likely wouldn't be able to do much more than stabilize the little girl until she could be seen by a specialist anyway.

Mia returned with his medical bag, which she placed on the floor beside him. "I'll be right back with an ice pack."

"Thanks," Garrett told her before turning back to the concerned mom. "I'm an orthopedic surgeon, so this is my forte. My office is only about five minutes away from here and with your permission, we can at least take an x-ray so little Madison won't have to sit around doctors' waiting rooms for the next few days."

The woman ran a plump hand through already frazzled hair. "My husband is out of town for business right now and there is no way I can take off work this week to take her to a bunch of appointments. Do you think it's bad?"

"Until we get to my office and do the x-ray, I can't be one hundred percent sure. Judging from the swelling and what I can feel, it's most likely a clean break. She'll need a cast just to help the bones stay in place while they heal, which we can take care of tonight."

"Like a real cast?" Madison looked hopeful. Why was it that children thought having their bodies restrained in plaster was an adventure? "One that my friends can sign and stuff?"

Garrett smiled at her. "Yup. But first, I want to take some pictures of your leg to see if you even need it. And if you do, I'll make you the most beautiful cast your friends will ever lay eyes on. How does that sound?"

She nodded enthusiastically and wiped her still-damp face.

Mia handed him the ice pack before walking toward a group of lingering parents and children who seemed reluctant to leave without ensuring their classmate was in good hands.

Thank God Mia was there to handle the onlookers so that he could focus on his patient. He spoke with Madison's mom about driving the girl over to his office as he put a temporary splint on her ankle and then wrapped it to keep it in place.

When he was done, he lifted the six-year-old and carried her out to her mother's older minivan and got her strapped in before getting into his own truck to lead the way to his office.

It wasn't until he pulled away from the curb that he realized he hadn't even said goodbye to Mia.

Chapter Seven

Mia was worried Garrett's office would be locked by the time she'd finished her last class of the evening. But when she pulled her Prius into the dark parking lot, she saw his truck and Mrs. Rosellino's van parked in front of the building and made her way inside.

She'd sprained her wrist once in junior high and she remembered her own mother fluttering around the gymnastic mats and yelling for someone to call an ambulance. It might have been the first time her mother had actually been more concerned with her daughter's injury and subsequent pain than the fact that Mia would be missing out on practice. That whole week her mom had babied her, making her grilled cheese sandwiches and buying two gallons of chocolate peanut butter ice cream so they could pig out on the sofa and watch *Dirty Dancing*, *Grease* and old Fred Astaire and Ginger Rogers movies.

After that, it was back to celery sticks and rice cakes and two-hours-a-day dance workouts. But for that one week, Mia herself, not her talent or her career or her future, had been Rhonda Palinski's main concern. She'd seen the same caring transformation with Mrs. Rosellino tonight. So maybe there was something more to these stage moms than she'd been giving them credit for all along.

She hadn't even realized that Garrett was still at her studio when little Madison had slipped and done a number on her ankle. It wasn't until after he'd carried the injured little girl out to her mom's car that it had dawned on her that he must've stayed to watch her class.

Why would he have done that? Really, why would he have done any of the things he'd done today? Such as, why had he gone with her to her doctor's appointment and then asked the doctor for his own printed set of ultrasound pictures—which he'd folded carefully and slipped inside his leather wallet with a designer logo on the front. Aside from his fashion sense, the man wasn't fitting any of the rich-playboy stereotypes she'd had him pegged for. What else would he do to surprise her?

Even though the front door had been open, the reception area was dark and empty. She saw lights on in the back and made her way toward the exam rooms.

She tried not to think of the last time she'd been in this hallway or the panic that had gripped her when she'd realized that Garrett was going to find out about the baby. She also didn't want to think about the way he'd smiled at her when they'd heard that same baby's heartbeat earlier today. Or the way he'd opened up more about himself during that car ride.

So much had changed in less than a week… How much more would change over the next seven months?

"Miss Mia!" Madison squealed when she got to the doorway of the same exam room she'd been standing in when Garrett had made that fateful discovery.

"Hi, sweetie," she said to the little girl. "I would have come earlier, but I had to teach my yoga class. I knew you'd be in excellent hands with Dr. McCormick, though."

He looked up from the bright pink fiberglass material he was carefully wrapping around Madison's foot. She could see the surprise in his hazel eyes, but he was probably too professional to comment on her unexpected arrival.

"Dr. McCormick says that I'm his first patient ever to get to have a pretty pink cast. I can't wait to show it to my friends at school tomorrow." Madison's excitement was short-lived when she frowned and added, "But he says I can't do any more tap dancing until my leg gets better."

"Maybe you can come to class and be in charge of the music? Or help me pass out the props? I'd love to still be able to see you, and I know the other girls will be pretty impressed with that fancy pink work of art you've got there."

Madison turned a pleading gaze to Garrett. "Can I, Doctor?"

Garrett finished his task, then stood up from his stool and said, "I think being a dance teacher's assistant would be a perfect job. As long as you promise to always use your crutches and get right back to tapping as soon as the cast comes off."

"I promise," the girl vowed and Mia gave her a high five.

"I had crutches like these once," Mia said before helping the little girl off the table.

As Garrett provided Mrs. Rosellino with a list of instructions, Mia helped Madison practice on the new crutches and tried not to think about the year she'd spent using the blasted things. It had been the most painful and demoralizing time in her life.

But for a six-year-old with a bright pink cast, it must seem like a wonderful adventure.

"Thank you so much, Dr. McCormick." Mrs. Rosellino followed her hopping daughter toward the front door. "We were so lucky you were there when it happened."

Please don't ask what he was doing there in the first place, Mia silently begged the woman, even though a little while ago she'd been wondering the exact same thing.

But this was Sugar Falls and, of course, any little detail outside the norm was cause for speculation and gossip. She and Garrett were still getting used to this whole co-parenting thing and their new unorthodox relationship. Mia didn't need the added bonus of unwanted opinions and assumptions to get in the way of their goal.

Wait. Did they even have a goal, besides raising a healthy, well-adjusted child? They hadn't really defined their own roles yet and Mia was hoping that once they decided to do so, it wouldn't be with an audience.

"Why were you there, anyway?" Mrs. Rosellino asked.

Ugh! There it was. Mia knew the question was coming, but had hoped for a lucky break—just this once.

"We had just come from the obstetric..."

"He was using the bathroom," Mia interrupted loudly. Maybe too loudly because the woman slowed her pace to turn back and tilt her head, looking side to side at each of them.

"I know!" Mia tried to make her pleasant surprise sound believable. "It's pretty, random, huh? I guess we were lucky that Dr. McCormick was in the right place at the right time."

Madison's mom probably didn't buy that dumb explanation any more than Mrs. Patrelli would have. But instead of asking more questions, she started walking again toward the door.

Garrett caught Mia's eye before giving her a wink and adding, "I seem to have a knack for being at the right place at the right time lately."

Mia's feet locked into place and she couldn't have commanded her body to move if she'd wanted to. Had he seriously just winked at her? Sure, Mrs. Rosellino hadn't seen him do it, but only a fool wouldn't have caught the implication in Garrett's tone.

Or the reminder that he *did* seem to have a habit of walking into her life just when she least expected it. And each time he did, the man turned her whole world upside down.

"I'll see you next week, Madison." Garrett touched the girl's lopsided bun as she maneuvered herself through the door. "Make sure you tell your mom if your leg starts hurting or if you think something is wrong with your cast so she can bring you back sooner."

"I will," the girl said as she hobbled toward the parking lot. "Thanks, Doctor."

Mia finally got her shocked muscles moving but had

to pause again when she realized that the way Garrett was holding the door blocked her from exiting unless she slid her body against him to pass through.

Her brain was telling her to follow the Rosellinos to the parking lot—not only to diminish the appearance of suspicious activity, but to prevent her from having to be alone with the man who had a tendency of showing up everywhere she didn't want him to be. It had been an emotional day—really, it had been an emotional *week*—and she didn't think her nerves could afford even the simplest polite conversation.

But her tired and taut body was telling her that if she so much as chanced the slightest contact with the hero doctor, she would wind up melting like smooth and creamy peanut butter left out too long in the sun.

For the thousandth time she asked herself why he had to be so good-looking. And so strong and capable. She had never needed a man before, and she had no intention of becoming susceptible to one now, when her emotions and hormones were spinning in a fast and reckless pirouette—one she knew she could maintain for only so long until she spun out of control.

"So, thanks again for taking care of Madison," Mia said, deciding she had no choice but to wait until he moved out of the way enough to let her pass.

"No problem. I'm glad I found that pink fiberglass wrap in my supply closet." His face turned toward her, but his body stayed firmly planted in front of the door.

"So you're still not unpacked?" She saw a breeze ruffle his brown hair, causing it to stray away from his perfectly combed part.

Sheesh, wasn't the man cold? The November night

air was coming in through the open door and Mia had been in such a hurry to drive over here after her yoga class, she hadn't even bothered putting her sweater back on.

"Nope. I really hadn't anticipated having many patients these first couple of weeks while I was getting situated." He looked down at her camisole, and Mia felt her nipples grow tight, but not because of the chilly temperature. "But for some reason, I keep having beautiful dancers show up at my office."

Mia wrapped her arms around her torso despite the fact that his gaze had just launched a sudden influx of heat to her bloodstream.

"Well, technically, the last dancer didn't show up here." Because at this exact moment, with the way he was looking at her, she wasn't sure she wanted to know why he had been at her studio.

"If we're going to be technical, I should probably also clarify that the first dancer is the only one whose beauty has completely affected me. In fact, it's wreaked havoc on my normally sound code of ethics."

He let the door close, which brought him close enough to her that she had to lift her face up to his. She watched his eyes trail down her neck and stop at the spot where her collarbone dipped into a small V. *Stop this, Mia. Now's your chance to walk away before this conversation gets dangerous.* But she didn't stop. Instead, she asked, "Why your ethics?"

He stepped closer, yet her body defied her brain once again and she didn't step back.

"Because for the first time in my life, I am deeply tempted to kiss one of my patients."

Her breath caught in her throat. "But I thought we established that it would be best if I saw a different surgeon about my knee. So, I'm not really your patient anymore."

"Thank God," he said before lowering his head toward hers.

She gasped when his lips touched hers, and opened her mouth to draw in air, but instead drew in more of him. Her arms followed an instinct of their own and soon Mia was plastered against him like a hot pink cast, matching each thrust of his tongue.

It was as if her mind had gone on vacation, leaving no instructions or provisions for her body—a body that had clearly remembered his kiss and was suddenly desperate to make up for lost time.

He never should have kissed her again.

As part of his rigorous naval training, he'd had to skydive out of a plane traveling at high altitude. All it had taken was one simple jump—more of a step off the cargo door ledge, really—and he'd been spiraling down in a free fall, feeling the air rush out of his lungs. He'd known that kissing Mia again would have that same effect on him. Unfortunately, this time he hadn't had the foresight to pack a parachute.

And as much as he liked order and organization, who could plan anything when confronted with this kind of temptation? One minute she'd been standing there, her skimpy camisole showing off her perfect body, and the next minute he had her wrapped up in his arms, claiming her mouth as if it was his own personal oxygen mask.

Mia moaned, but Garrett's brain wasn't so high up in the clouds that he mistook it for one of pleasure. He pulled back quickly. "Did I hurt you?"

"Just your height," she said before leaning down and rubbing her knee. He drew in his brows and she added, "I haven't been on my tiptoes that long since my last ballet audition several years ago. I guess the pressure was too much for my injury."

"Oh," he said. "I forgot you were wearing heels last time…" He let his voice trail off, not sure it was wise for either of them to be reminded of what had happened the last time they'd shared such a passionate kiss.

"I should probably be going," Mia said, her arms doing that wraparound protective-stance thing she tended to do any time he got within a couple of feet of her. Her eye tic was back, as well. Did she honestly think he was going to hurt her?

"Right. It's been a pretty emotional day for you. For *both* of us."

"Yes!" She seized upon his lame excuse a little too quickly and he wondered if he would have preferred that she deny it. That she correct him and say she wanted to kiss him because she'd been aching for him these past couple of days—hell, these past couple of months—just as badly as he had been for her.

But Garrett didn't do awkward conversations. Not with his family and definitely not with the women he normally dated. Which, he should point out, he and Mia certainly were not doing.

Still, it would just be more comfortable all around if she left now and they pretended this little lapse in lust had never happened. So he waited until she opened the door—he should've been gentleman enough to open it for her, but he couldn't trust himself to let her walk by him—and allowed the cold breeze that rushed in to cool his emotions and his libido, before he spoke. "Okay, so take care. I guess I'll see you around town."

Her response was an over-the-shoulder wave that she threw out while darting across the parking lot before quickly getting into her car. Hmm. Her knee clearly didn't seem to be bothering her anymore. Or maybe she just wanted to get away from him that badly.

After watching her drive away safely, he turned and sat down heavily in one of the chairs in the waiting area. Mia Palinski was truly unlike any other woman he'd ever met. On one hand, it was refreshing considering he'd spent the past ten years avoiding women like Cammie Longacre—women who would just want him because of his family's money and his father's notoriety. But on the other hand, it was also quite perplexing because he just didn't know what to make of her. He hoped that she was a solid, trustworthy person who had his and his child's best interests at heart. If not, eighteen years was a long time to have to engage with someone who was only looking out for number one.

On Thursday night, Garrett found himself sitting in Cooper's living room, getting ready to play poker with Mia's best friends' husbands and some other men he'd met since he'd moved here. Actually, he'd known both Cooper and Drew Gregson from the Shadowview Military Hospital—way before he'd even learned Mia's name, let alone that they were married to her friends.

So it wasn't as if he could be accused of trying to

infiltrate her ranks in an effort to spy on her. But, hey, if the guys wanted to provide a little background intelligence on her during their weekly poker game, Garrett wouldn't stop them.

Besides, the only thing he'd been able to find out about Mia on his own so far was an article on the internet about her being attacked by some sort of stalker back when she'd been a professional cheerleader. But it was weird that there wasn't more information on what exactly had transpired or who the attacker was. There were no court documents, no police reports, no media statements. At least none that his limited research capabilities could find.

Someone must have paid good money to keep that incident under wraps because in Garrett's former world of reality television, the spotlight would have shown brightly on something like that, and there would have been no end to the bad press.

Being attacked would explain why Mia was so jumpy, but it only left him with more questions. It also made him think that someone with some deep pockets had helped that situation go away—which usually translated into a cash settlement of some sort.

Mia certainly wasn't flashy or living a glamorous lifestyle, but maybe she'd blown her monetary award already and was patiently awaiting her next meal ticket to arrive. And arrive he had. Hell, Garrett had practically been delivered to her on a room service cart.

The shuffling of cards brought him back to the present.

"So the buy-in is a dozen chocolate-chips and six maple-pecans." Cooper made the announcement while looking around at the men who were pulling cookies from Maxine's famous bakery out of cellophane wrappers and stacking them neatly on the green baize-covered table.

Luke Gregson, Drew's twin brother, walked in the door with his own set of identical sons and said, "We got to the bakery right before closing, but by the time these two hungry monkeys got their little hands on the bag, all I have left are some cranberry-orange ones and those pumpkin-nutmeg things left over from last week."

The eight-year-old boys still had their mouths full and gave Luke a chocolaty hug before running off to Cooper's stepson's room to play with Hunter. The former navy SEAL looked as if he certainly had his hands full. And judging by the tired look on the man's face, Garrett was sure glad Mia's obstetrician had heard only one heartbeat.

The men were on their second hand when Kane Chatterson, Kylie's brother, who'd done the renovation of the old lumber mill for Garrett, came in through the door carrying a white sack from Domino's Deli.

"I hear congratulations are in order," Kane said as he passed out sub sandwiches. Garrett looked around the room to see who the former baseball pitcher was talking to, but all eyes were on him. Realizing what they were talking about, Garrett was surprised that he didn't feel any need to hide it. In fact, he was glad the secret was finally out.

"Word travels fast." Garrett took a sip from his bottle of beer, wondering who had spilled the beans.

"That it does," their host and the police chief said. Cooper knew about Garrett's family because, well, he was Cooper and tended to find out anything he wanted. Hopefully, he also knew what would happen if the rest of the world found out. But his next comment allayed some fears. "At least you can rest assured that it will end at the city limits signs. This town protects its own."

"Maybe." Kane shrugged, not looking entirely convinced. Garrett had confided in him about his identity as well, once he realized that the man was also performing his own disappearing act to avoid the limelight. "Time will tell."

"So everyone in Sugar Falls knows? I wonder how Mia will react to that." Garrett casually moved his sandwich to the side and ate a snickerdoodle—the poker cookie with the highest value and the closest proximity—hoping nobody noticed his subtle attempt to fish for information.

"I heard it from Donatella Patrelli, who just hired me to add a bathroom on to her house," Kane said.

Alex Russell, who owned the sporting goods store, folded before adding his own two cents. "I heard it from Jake Marconi's dad, who stopped by the store to pick up the new basketball team uniforms. He told me Mia was at his gas station filling up the other day. I guess she went inside to pay and when the person in line ahead of her opened up the beef jerky dispenser, she threw up right in front of the snack cake display. Said his wife knew then and there she was in the family way."

"The twins told me about it." Luke reached inside the deli bag and pulled out a container of hot peppers. "They found out at school from some little girls in Mia's tap dance class."

Drew laughed. "Word on the street is that you were

quite the hero at her studio the other night. One of the kids broke her ankle and Dr. McCormick was hiding in the wings and sprung into action."

"I wasn't hiding in the wings."

"Then what were you doing at a dance class for six-year-olds?" Cooper asked.

"I was using the restroom. So how long has Mia been a dance teacher?"

"Really? The Snowflake Dance Academy was the only business in town where you could find a place to go?" Nope, Cooper wasn't going to make things easy for him.

And here, Garrett thought *he'd* be the one getting answers tonight. Man, he should've known better than to become friends with a former MP who'd been trained to interrogate terrorists.

"Okay, so I had gone with Mia to the baby's first doctor's appointment in Boise on Monday and I used the bathroom when we got back from the long drive."

"How was it?" Luke asked.

"Her bathroom? It was fine."

"Not the bathroom, Doc. The first appointment. When Samantha was pregnant with the twins, I was on deployment and couldn't go to ours. But she'd recorded the whole thing and I must've watched that ultrasound video five hundred times."

"I'll never forget ours, either," Drew said, even though his was probably just several months ago. "The only thing keeping me from passing out when the doctor told us Kylie was having two girls was hearing my father-in-law whooping and hollering on the other side of the door. Kane, your old man has the loudest voice on the planet."

"At least he was happy. You should hear him when one of his pitchers gives up a walk." Kane finished his beer, then looked at Garrett. "Anyway, I just wanted to say congrats. I came to play cards, not to listen to the Daddy Train toot its own horn all night."

It was true. Garrett was entering an exclusive club for fathers, and the ones sitting here with him were as proud as could be. And he was now among their ranks. He remembered the thrill that had shot through him earlier this week when he'd heard his baby's heartbeat. He'd also remembered Mia's mad dash across the parking lot later that night when she was trying to get away from him after he'd kissed her.

"Well, Kane, we *could* talk about how the high school varsity team still needs a pitching coach this spring." Alex looked at the quiet baseball player, who shook his head once before going back to the refrigerator for another round of beers. "What about you, Doc?"

"What about me?" Garrett asked. "I'm not a pitching coach."

"No, but the high school also needs an athletic trainer. They have a couple of students volunteering now, but if you wanted to take on the team doctor role, you could oversee things. It's only on Friday nights for the football games right now, but eventually they'll need someone to help out with the other sports."

He thought about his office, which was practically unpacked and ready to go as soon as he got some new patients. Mia certainly wasn't blowing up his phone wanting to spend time with him, and this poker night constituted the extent of his social life. It wasn't as if Garrett had much else going on right now. Besides, the more time he spent with people who knew Mia, the more information he could find out about her.

"Sure. Why not?"

Chapter Eight

Mia didn't go to all the local football games, but she helped the varsity cheerleaders choreograph their bigger performances and had come with Maxine and Kylie to watch the halftime show tonight.

This was her last weekend of freedom before her mom showed up on Monday for a weeklong visit. She didn't know how she was going to get through Thanksgiving if her mom found out about the pregnancy before then. And knowing Rhonda Palinski's nose for drama, the woman would surely find out. Especially if she spent at least five minutes in town, where everyone else seemed to have already clued in.

As Mia walked with her friends toward the stands, the small marching band blasted out a loud rendition of the Sugar Falls High School fight song. She turned toward the field and saw a man dressed in track pants and an SFHS Huskies hooded sweatshirt bent in front of one of the players, unwrapping tape from the teenager's wrist. A bubbling blast of energy shot through her veins and Mia recognized the feeling—the sensation she got only when Garrett McCormick was close by.

That couldn't be…

"Watch where you're stepping, little mama," Kylie said when Mia stumbled over the first row of bleachers. She forced her head straight and concentrated on watching what she was doing, rather than looking behind her to see what her body already knew.

He might not be dressed in one of his fancy button-down shirts with his perfectly creased slacks, but there was no doubt of exactly who it was.

What was he doing there? It was bad enough that several of her students' parents had congratulated her this week on her pregnancy, and even worse, that most of them asked her directly if the father of her child was also the handsome new doctor in town. But did he have to flaunt it to everyone by showing up at the same events she did? No wonder the flames of gossip had been fanned into a citywide forest fire. They'd barely been seen together, but all it had taken were a few slips and a handful of sightings for suspicions to become facts.

"Nachos?" Maxine lifted a yellow goop-filled paper boat up under Mia's nose, causing her to gag.

"No, thanks. That processed cheese smells horrible." So did the popcorn Hunter was eating, as well as the hot dog Kylie was stuffing in her mouth.

"I was like that several weeks ago," her pregnant friend said around bites. "Couldn't stand the smell of anything. I think I lost ten pounds my first trimester.

Then I hit twenty weeks and lately it seems like I can't *stop* eating."

But Mia couldn't blame the sudden queasiness in her tummy on pregnancy-related nausea alone. She'd eaten anything she'd wanted to just fine since she saw Garrett on Monday evening. Well, almost anything. There *had* been that unfortunate beef jerky incident at the Gas N' Mart earlier this week. Otherwise, it was only when he was around that her stomach did backflips.

She narrowed her eyes. "What's Garrett doing down there on the sidelines?"

Kylie licked the mustard off her fingers. "Drew told me he agreed to help out as the team doctor and athletic trainer of sorts."

"Why? Is he trying to drum up business or something?"

"Wow. That doesn't sound like our sweet, even-tempered Mia," Maxine said, a tortilla chip paused on its way to her mouth. "What's got you in such a snit over Dr. Dreamboat?"

"Really?" Mia lifted her brows. "Is *that* the nickname we're going with?"

"Well, Dr. Handsome got taken when Kylie married Drew, so we wouldn't want to get the two men confused. Anyway, spill it. Why are you so on edge around him?"

"Besides the fact that I barely know the man but now have to 'co-parent' with him since I got knocked up after a one-night stand?"

"Hey, Mom." Maxine's eleven-year-old son leaned in to be heard over the loud trombones below. "What's a one-night stand?"

The blonde cookie baker pulled some cash out of her purse and shoved it at Hunter. "Here, sweetie, go to the snack bar and buy Aunt Mia a Sprite. And a king-size package of peanut butter cups."

"We shouldn't give her those until she tells us what's going on between her and Dr. Love Muffin," Kylie suggested.

Mia shuddered under her down-filled coat. "Suddenly, Dr. Dreamboat doesn't sound so bad. Okay, you two, I'll tell you but you have to swear not to say a word to your husbands." Her two friends held up their forefingers in a number one and touched the tips together. It was a gesture from their cheerleading days they always used to secure a solemn promise.

Mia told them about Garrett's reaction to hearing the heartbeat and how his excitement only intensified her already overwrought emotions. Then she filled them in on how she'd gone to his office that same night to check in on Madison Rosellino, which resulted in them sharing that passionate kiss.

"Boy, when we dared you to live a little, you sure took the ball and ran with it," Maxine smiled.

"Don't remind me of that text," Mia said. "If I wasn't a more responsible adult, I'd totally blame you both for this situation."

"So what did you do when he kissed you?" Kylie wanted to know.

"I kissed him back."

Kylie rolled her eyes. "Duh. Obviously. Then what?"

"Then we stopped kissing and I ran off."

Maxine dropped her shoulders and actually looked crestfallen. "Oh, Mia, you can't keep running forever."

A loud whistle signaled the end of the first quarter and Mia knew she would need to make her way down to the field soon to help get the cheerleaders ready for their halftime routine.

"I know that. Especially now that I'll have a little one who needs more stability than what my own mother gave me. But it would be so much easier if I didn't have to deal with its father."

"Would it?" Maxine asked. "I raised Hunter pretty much by myself until Cooper came along. Believe me, single motherhood is just as unglamorous as it sounds."

Her friend was right. She'd seen Max struggle financially and emotionally when she'd been raising her son on her own. And Lord knew Rhonda Palinski hadn't provided an award-winning example of single parenting. But Mia was used to being alone. She'd learned early on from her absentee father that men didn't stick around long. Therefore, she'd always been resolute in her determination to never rely on one for anything.

At least she *had* been until Garrett had taken her hand, first on Snowflake Boulevard and then on Monday in the obstetrician's office. When she was with him, it was so easy to get lost in the belief that everything was going to be okay, that he was strong enough and capable enough for both of them.

Which was why she was now trying to avoid the guy like her mother avoided carbs. He might make her body crave more, but nothing good could come of overindulging in too much bread—or too much Dr. Dreamboat.

Halfway through the second quarter, Mia made her way down to the field and was standing on the dirt track talking to the young cheerleading coach when Garrett spotted her. They hadn't talked all week and she was still embarrassed about the way she'd let herself come unglued in his arms.

She'd heard of doctors, specifically surgeons, having a God complex, thinking they could do no wrong. She didn't necessarily get that vibe from Garrett, but he'd admitted he liked control and order. Not to mention, there was definitely something about the way he carried himself that led her to believe that he was used to getting what he wanted. And clearly, his actions thus far demonstrated that he did not want her as anything more than a vessel to carry his child.

On Monday night, she'd expected him to run after her, or show up either at her studio or her apartment to try to win her over. That's what persistent men did when they learned she was unobtainable. Especially spoiled rich guys like Nick who weren't used to anyone telling them no. The jury was still out on whether Garrett was spoiled, but she could tell by the way he dressed and the new four-wheel-drive platinum-edition truck he drove that her baby's father was definitely living off more than what most naval officers brought home in their paychecks.

Judging by the fact that Garrett hadn't pushed her further that night or sought her out since, she had to assume that he was equally embarrassed by what had happened in the doorway of his office and no longer had any romantic interest in her at all.

But as he turned and walked toward her, seemingly heedless of the empty paper cups and the gravel crunching under his top-of-the-line cross-trainers, Mia realized that he was looking at her as if *she* was the very thing he wanted. Just like the tiny dirt pebbles lining the track, Mia's heart threatened to crumble with his every step. If she let him get too close, she might not be able to put those fragments back in pace.

"Hey," was all he said when he finally stood in front of her.

"Hey," she responded. "So, you're the new team doctor?"

"I'm just kind of helping out for now."

"How's it going?"

"Well, our defensive tackle was a little wobbly there during the first quarter because he'd heard a rumor that some girl he likes might be asking him out. But he threw up in the trash can behind the bleachers and I think everyone's in good shape now. What are you doing on the field?"

"I helped do some of the cheerleaders' choreography—" Before Mia could finish, four teenaged girls in matching cheer uniforms and bouncing ponytails interrupted them.

"Excuse me, Miss Palinski." The cocaptain spoke for the group. "Sophie wanted to know if at the end of our routine, we could all hold up these signs we made asking JoJo Patrelli to go to Sadie Hawkins with her?"

"Is JoJo Patrelli the defensive tackle?" Garrett whispered and Mia nodded.

"That should be fine, as long as you wait and do it *after* the final basket toss. I don't want any of you getting hurt during the stunts. Right, Dr. McCormick?"

The man looked completely confused about why the teenaged girls burst into a fit of giggles when he smiled at them. Did he not realize that a couple of the adolescents and many of the grown women in town would probably have lovesick crushes on the handsome single doctor?

"So." He rubbed his forehead as he spoke with the

cheerleaders. "You're holding up signs to ask a boy to go to a dance with you? Is this a thing now?"

"Come on, Garrett." Mia stood up straighter. "Why shouldn't girls be able to ask out a guy? We're all about gender equality here in Sugar Falls. Besides, it's for Sadie Hawkins. It's a tradition."

"No, I know what Sadie Hawkins is. I meant, is it normal to ask someone out in such a public way?"

"Oh, totally," Sophie said and the girls all agreed and launched into some of the most memorable invitations. And bless Garrett's patient heart for listening to them go on and on.

There were thirty seconds left on the clock when one of the girls turned to her and said, "So are you going to chaperone Sadie Hawkins this year, Miss Palinski?"

"Yeah, who are you going to invite this time?" another girl asked as she wiggled her head toward the new team doctor.

Garrett's eyebrows went into high alert and he crossed his arms across his sweatshirt. "Yes, Miss Palinski, who *are* you going to invite to Sadie Hawkins this year?" All the girls giggled again at his obvious ploy.

Cornered by cheerleaders? Her own kind turning against her? She'd have to think twice before giving this squad her best moves again. "I, uh, wasn't going to go this year because of my bad knee, Dr. McCormick. But if I was going to ask someone, I'd probably ask Mr. Cromartie again."

"And who exactly is Mr. Cromartie?" She saw him clench his jaw and narrow his eyes as he looked at the crowd in the stands. The girls giggled even more and she wondered if Garrett had any idea how jealous he appeared at that moment.

Mia pointed out the eighty-year-old coffee-skinned man with a thatch of bushy white hair and a long conductor stick. "See that gentleman leading the marching band out of the stands and toward the track? He knows his way around music and the dance floor."

"Hmm," was all Garrett said, but he did allow his shoulders to drop.

"Don't worry, Dr. McCormick," Sophie said. "I'm sure you could find another woman to ask you to Sadie Hawkins if you want to go."

The referee signaled for halftime and the girls took off running to gather their pompoms and their signs.

Mia and Garrett were left on the side of the track alone. She tried not to smile at the idea that he might have been a little peeved that she would go out on a date with another man. She wanted to ask what it meant, but she didn't want to embarrass him. Or hear him deny it.

Say something, her brain commanded. But a whiff of his musky citrus cologne mingled with the night air and she found herself staring at the light pulse thrumming along his neck. "So, I scheduled another ultrasound for next month."

If she hadn't been standing in front of a crowd of a hundred or so people, she would've slapped her palm to her forehead. She was such an idiot. Couldn't she have come up with a better conversation starter than that? In fact, why did she even need to speak with him in the first place? She should've run off with the cheerleaders.

"Oh, good." His hazel eyes lightened and his lips softened. "Let me know the date and I'll clear my calendar."

Great, now she was stuck going to another doctor's

appointment with him. How did she completely lose all sense of subtlety every time she talked to the guy?

Ever since she'd been a teenager, she had trained herself to be skilled at avoiding men and their advances—not that Garrett was making any real advances toward her—so that she could focus on her career. It had started when her mother refused to allow her to date in high school because time spent with boys was time not spent practicing. Then, when she'd gone to college, she'd gone out with a few guys, but they always seemed to want her to be their personal cheerleader just as she was finally learning to be more independent, so it was just easier to keep them at a distance. She used to be savvy enough to speak casually with the opposite sex and not lead men on or otherwise invite them into her life.

Maybe this self-imposed exile she'd been under since she'd moved to Sugar Falls had caused her to completely fall out of practice.

The band launched into a drum line performance and Mia watched the football teams hustle off the field. But Garrett still stood in front of her, as though he didn't see sweaty jocks in full pads running right past them. She took a deep breath. "So, is that your cue?"

"What? Oh. Yes. I better follow them to the locker room and make sure nobody has any sprains or concussions."

"Yeah, and I need to get the cheerleaders set up for their routine."

If they were business associates, this would be the part where they shook hands. If they were lovers, now would be when they kissed. But they were neither of these things. Plus, they were standing on a high school football field in full view of the crowded bleachers.

The wind picked up and blew a strand of dark hair

into her eyes. Garrett reached out and pushed it back behind her ear. Then he rubbed his thumb along her cheek. She remembered from her high school science class that physics dictated bubbles were supposed to rise up. But the ones tingling inside her made their way clear down to the core of her womanhood. Those hands were surely going to be the death of her.

"Okay, so I'll see you around," she said then did an eight count as she forced her legs to walk slowly away from him.

It was almost the same thing he'd said to her when she'd left his office on Monday, and she hated the way it sounded tonight as much as she'd had then. The implication was that they had no need or desire to speak to each other except in passing. The truth of the matter was that she was afraid of everything she wanted to say to him—like the fact that no man had ever been able to make her feel as if she was on the edge of a cliff, about to free-fall into the unknown.

But at least this time she hadn't run from him. That was progress.

The following Tuesday, Garrett was craving a hot home-cooked meal. Since his arrival in Sugar Falls, he'd been living on stale muffins and the whole grain cereal offered at Betty Lou's B and B, which was turning out to be more of a bed place and less of a breakfast place. While eating like that was fine when he was on deployments or too busy in surgery to make it to the mess hall, he was now a full-fledged resident of the Potato State and intended to partake in some skillet-cooked home fries. Plus, he'd heard the Chamber of Commerce met at the Cowgirl Up Café on Tuesdays and now that his practice was almost up and running, it was time to establish himself as a permanent part of the business community.

Plus, he hadn't seen Mia since the football game on Friday and knew her mom was supposed to be arriving any day, if she hadn't already. Garrett was curious to find out if Mia had told her mother about the baby, and there was no better place to accidentally run into her than downtown Sugar Falls.

He entered the restaurant, which was housed in its own gingerbread-shaped cottage across the street from Mia's dance school. He should have known by the purple exterior of the building that the inside would be just as eclectic.

Apparently, a rodeo queen with a penchant for do-it-yourself crafts had gotten some great deals on every horse riding–themed picture from each flea market west of the Mississippi, and then thrown them up on pink-and-white-striped walls. Stirrups and bridles had been spray painted in glitter and tacked up alongside the equestrian art. The long and winding rope spelling out "Cowgirl Up" behind the counter seating area was an interesting touch.

He doubted Cammie Longacre or any of her interior design friends would have thought to use old cowboy boots planted with cacti as centerpieces on all the wooden tables of varying sizes, shapes and years of origin.

But he was a business owner and he was here to meet with the Chamber of Commerce, not to research decorating tips for his sparse office.

"So we finally get to meet the infamous new doctor in town," an older waitress wearing a zebra-print apron said. The woman had dyed red hair teased clear up to heaven and a tight lime-colored V-neck shirt plunging clear down to—well, the opposite of heaven.

If he hadn't left his sunglasses in the truck, he would've pulled them down until his eyes could grow accustomed to the bright and vivacious surroundings. But he could hear a grill sizzling, and the smell of bacon and maple syrup told him that there was a reason this place was packed with locals clamoring for a delicious hot breakfast.

Many of the customers' faces turned to look at him and Garrett's heart dropped, thinking they'd found out exactly why his name was semifamous. But the waitress's coral-painted lips smiled to reveal a slightly crooked tooth and she held out her hand to him. "I'm Freckles and I own this place."

"Nice to meet you, Miss Freckles, but you'll have to fill me in on how I earned the title of infamous."

"Oh, darlin', it's just Freckles. And everyone in town has been talking about how you finally got our sweet little Mia to come out of her shell."

Come out of her shell? Even a remote mountain town like Sugar Falls had internet access. Didn't they know that their sweet little Mia had been an NFL cheerleader? She'd most likely danced on a Jumbotron in front of over seventy thousand screaming fans, as well as on the living room television sets of millions of people watching the games from home. That didn't seem too shell-worthy to him.

At least Mia had proved to be pretty sweet. So far.

Just then, the subject of their conversation walked in the door.

"Speak of the devil," Freckles said then sashayed behind the counter to get a coffeepot.

Great. Now Mia would think he was gossiping about her around town. Which was exactly what he would have done if she hadn't shown up and interrupted the question he'd been about to ask the café owner.

"Hey," he said, sounding like the same idiot he'd been when he saw her a couple of nights ago at the football game.

"Hey," she responded, but didn't really smile. Her eyes scanned the room as she pulled off her jacket, probably hoping they didn't have any witnesses to yet another awkward and unexpected meeting.

Of course, by now everyone was most likely aware of the fact that she was carrying his child. As far as he knew, nobody had made any sort of huge announcement from the gazebo in Sugar Park, the grassy square in the center of downtown. But these people weren't stupid. They'd eagerly picked up the clues about one of their beloved townspeople's delicate condition and word had spread down Snowflake Boulevard like an avalanche.

She was wearing another one of her soft wraparound sweaters over tights and a tank top and he wondered how the men in this city didn't go wild seeing her walk around in her dance clothes.

Garrett rubbed his forehead before firmly shoving his hands in his pockets. He needed to put those things away before they were tempted to reach out and touch her again. "So, did your mom make it to town yet?"

She looked toward the several tables that had been pushed together. "Yes. She arrived last night and I'm already about to move in with Maxine and Cooper for the rest of the week."

"Did you tell her yet?"

"Tell her what?"

"About the baby?" His voice dropped to a whisper. "About me?"

"Not yet, thank goodness. But I don't know how much longer I can keep it a secret."

"Why would you want to?"

She took a step back and looked at him as though he'd just asked her why she would want to drive on the right side of the road.

He should clarify what he meant, but Maxine was waving them over to where the rest of the Chamber of Commerce members were sitting. There were two empty chairs between her and Kylie, who had offered her CPA services to Garrett right after the football game. Although, he had to wonder if Kylie was actually interested in helping him file his taxes, or whether she was hoping to get a glimpse into his personal financial records on behalf of her best friend.

Everyone sat down and Garrett noticed most of the businesspeople left the seat closest to Mia open. They all seemed friendly enough toward her so he had to deduce that they weren't treating her as a pariah so much as allowing him the option to sit next to her.

He was going to have to work extra hard at keeping his mouth closed so he wouldn't stick his foot in it during the breakfast meeting.

"Let's get started." Cliff Johnston, the mayor, called the meeting to order. "Weather reports show that the ski season is starting early this year and with the holiday weekend about to start, we need to get a game plan locked down for how we're going to handle an increase in tourists."

A jingle interrupted and drew everyone's attention. Kane Chatterson pulled open the door to the café and was about to walk inside when something outside on the street caught his eye. Garrett watched the man pull his cowboy hat lower, turn right around and walk quickly down the road.

That was odd. Was everyone in this town avoiding someone? If so, then maybe they should think twice about eating at one of the busiest local restaurants.

But less than a minute later, Garrett saw what Kane was fleeing from. A sixty-year-old man wearing a loud Hawaiian print shirt and flip-flops in forty-degree weather would normally stand out on his own. But when that man also had a shaggy gray ponytail topped off with a red Angels ball cap and held open the door for a guy carrying an oversize video camera with a boom mike attached, it was hard not to take notice.

"Oh, no," Garrett muttered, wanting to duck under the table.

"What's the matter?" Mia whispered before glancing toward the door. When she spotted the camera, a shocked look shot across her face.

Why? Hadn't she set this up?

Whether she had or not, there was really nowhere for him to hide. He would have to weather this situation with the leading members of the Sugar Falls business community by his side, being allowed full access to the spectacle that was about to be unleashed.

"GP," the man said as he opened his arms up wide— to create the most dramatic display possible, naturally. "I've been looking all over this backwoods town for you."

"Dad, what are you doing here?" Garrett stood up, hoping to direct the focus away from the table—and from Mia—and the curious stares aimed at them. "And why in the world would you bring a camera crew with you?"

"One of your old friends from high school swung by the office the other day and said she'd found out that you were having a baby. I wouldn't have believed it myself until she showed me her social media page with a picture she'd posted of you with your arm around this pretty young thing here." His father turned to Mia and held out his hand. "Hi, I'm Dr. Gerald McCormick. I'm GP's dad and the soon-to-be grandpa." He shook his head ruefully. "Wow, that word really made me sound old. Anyway, I agreed to give the network an exclusive interview with my reclusive son and the touching journey of his transition from rebellious teenager to elite navy surgeon and father. It's going to be an award-winning piece and if we're lucky, we might be able to talk them into a spin-off. Nice cuffs, by the way."

Garrett looked down at the monogrammed cuff links and shook his head, trying to let go of the rage building inside him.

"Oh, my gosh." Mia's face went pale and instead of shaking Garrett's dad's hand, she gripped the armrest of her wooden chair tighter, her eyes glued to the huge video camera. That was one reaction he wasn't used to seeing women exhibit when they suddenly had the lens turned on them.

"Dad, I told you way back when I was eighteen that I wanted to be as far away from your reality shows as possible. Nothing's changed. Why do you think I moved out here?"

But before his dad could answer, Garrett heard Freckles' loud, countrified accent.

"My stars! If it isn't Dr. McCormick from that plastic

surgery show on TV. I woulda recognized that lucky red cap anywhere. I'm Freckles and I own the Cowgirl Up Café. I gotta tell you, I'm a big, big fan. I never miss an episode of the new season. It would be a real pleasure to serve you in my restaurant." She set her coffeepot down on an empty table and reached out to shake his father's still-outstretched hand. Which made Garrett all the more surprised when the waitress said, "But I'm going to have to ask you to leave your camera outside."

"Thank you for the compliment, ma'am," Gerald McCormick said and tilted his head humbly. Garrett knew that look. His dad may look like a beach bum, but he was a determined man who could—and had—talked a woman into signing a prenuptial agreement mere minutes before she walked down the aisle. The older, sassy waitress didn't stand a chance. "My crew and I will just be a second and then we'll be out of your way."

This was his father's usual way of minimizing the video presence, trying to get everyone to act natural and forget the cameras were even there. As if Garrett could ever forget.

A man Garrett had seen tying his horse to the hitching post in front of the restaurant stood up. Garrett hadn't been formally introduced to the old coot, but he knew Scooter and his old mare were permanent fixtures around town. "I think you misunderstood Miss Freckles, Doctor. She said that your man here would need to wait outside. See, us backwoods types don't take too kindly to cameras filming us here in Sugar Falls."

"But I'm not filming *you*." His dad's teeth smiled brighter than the puka shell necklace around his neck. Uh-oh. This wasn't going the way his father must have anticipated, and Garrett couldn't help but relish in the man's sudden shift of power. "I'm filming my son."

"Seems to me like the young doc here doesn't really want to be filmed," Freckles said. "And seeing as how he's now one of us—what was it, backwoods types?—I think it's best if you gentlemen skedaddle on outside. But let me know if you want to order some biscuits and gravy or one of my famous maple-glazed cinnamon rolls and I'll be happy to box it up for you."

Garrett glanced at Mia, who now had her face completely turned away from the camera and was slowly lifting an open menu higher in front of her.

Enough was enough. He needed to get his father out of here. But before he could tell his old man to hit the road, several more business owners rose from their chairs without much fanfare and slowly found their way in front of his and Mia's seats until they'd fanned out around them, forming a human barrier of sorts.

Garrett blinked several times. Never in his life had he seen anyone—besides himself, that is—stand up to famed television producer Gerald McCormick. Yet these small-town strangers were pulling rank around not just Mia, but Garrett, as well.

It was a nice gesture, but honestly, Garrett didn't need anyone to fight his battles for him. He scooted his chair out from the table, but before he could walk toward the chaos, he felt a sharp tug on his starched oxford shirt sleeve.

"It's best not to make a big scene and draw more attention in this direction," Maxine whispered. "Besides, they've got this under control."

It was true. Nobody uttered a single rude or threatening word. In fact, they were being just as cordial as one would expect small-town folk to be. A woman Garrett recognized from the local market asked for an autograph, distracting his old man even further. "Make it out to Marcia Duncan, please."

"Is this thing still running?" Jonesy, a cowboy who was usually seen riding his horse around town with Scooter, stood directly in front of the camera, thereby ensuring any footage contained only the image of his dusty, sweat-stained Boise State cap. "You know I was Special Forces back in 'Nam. They should do a reality television show about us vets."

"Special Forces? You don't say." Garrett could now only hear his dad's voice, which had taken on a note of frustration, but couldn't see much around the growing group of protective townspeople. He didn't dare look at Mia to see how she was reacting.

"Yep," Jonesy continued. "Learned a lot of life skills back in the corps. Did you know they taught me over a hundred ways to kill a man?" Okay, so maybe that was a bit threatening. But the cameraman lowered his equipment and shook his head toward his boss. "Anyway, just wanted to come on over to meet you and say I'm really looking forward to watching your show next season."

When the offending camera was finally switched off, the crowd opened up a little and Garrett was able to move closer to his dad. "Listen, son, I'll be in town a few more days. I'm staying at the Snow Creek Lodge if you want to give me a call."

"I'll talk to you later, Dad. But not with cameras nearby."

"I'll take whatever I can get. But just to give you a little warning—my producers weren't the only ones that got wind of you resurfacing and the pregnancy rumors. Besides me, nobody knew you were actually living in Idaho. Yet. All I'm asking is that you talk to me before the rest of the media figure things out and you have news vans parked up and down this charming little main street."

Garrett knew he'd had good reason to be suspect of Cammie Longacre when she'd spotted him with Mia in Patrelli's. This had the potential to be a media debacle of epic proportions. But before he could think of his next step, the horseshoe-shaped wind chime tinkled above the door and a fifty-something-year-old woman with bleach-streaked hair and a rhinestone-studded denim jacket walked in. She yanked her dark glasses off her overly made-up face so quickly, they got stuck in one of her giant fuchsia hoop earrings.

"Oh, my!" the newcomer said, still trying to get untangled. "Nobody told me they were filming in Sugar Falls."

"Mom?" Mia suddenly spoke up. "What are you doing over here?"

Chapter Nine

Seeing the cameras had been shock enough for Mia, but hearing her mother's forced cheerful voice was more than even she could bear. How many embarrassing introductions was she expected to endure in one morning?

Or puzzles, for that matter. From what she'd been able to piece together in the past five minutes, the father of her baby's father was some sort of reality television mogul with a sense of fashion that was best described as *surftastic*. When the man called his son rebellious, Mia had to cover her mouth to keep from bursting out in nervous laughter. Gerald McCormick could easily be referring to his son's preppy appearance, but most likely he was discouraged that Garrett didn't share the same media objectives.

In fact, judging by his reaction just a few moments ago, Garrett seemed to be just as freaked out about being caught on camera as she was. Sure, he had Hollywood good looks and she'd correctly assumed that he came from money. But she knew firsthand that people didn't relocate their lives from Hollywood to a town so small that horses took up parking spaces.

Instead of answering her question, her mother was chatting up the famous plastic surgeon and Mia's stomach dropped. Rhonda Palinski had always kept her acrylic manicured finger on the pulse of the entertainment industry and clearly recognized Garrett's dad.

Mia's posture was so stiff, her solid oak chair felt like a sagging life raft. Why hadn't she stayed home this morning and told her mom about the baby?

Now that the woman was here in the flesh, it wouldn't be long before she figured out that not only was she going to be a grandmother, she was going to be a grandmother to a baby with a famous pedigree that obviously came with its own publicity.

This was a nightmare and Mia needed to wake up—and get the heck out of there. And by there, she didn't just mean the Cowgirl Up Café. She meant the town of Sugar Falls. It'd been easy enough to run before. She looked at the distance from her seat to the kitchen.

"Simmer down, Mia," Maxine whispered. "Don't get spooked and do something you'll regret."

How could her best friend be so calm?

"That's your mom?" Garrett had the audacity to ask, as if today's version of "Surprise Your Offspring at the Chamber of Commerce Meeting" was reserved for him alone.

"Yep. Looks like it's turning into one big unhappy family reunion around here," Mia said under her breath. Her eyelid began to shudder and she couldn't stop her

foot from tapping on the tacky turquoise paisley carpet. Oh, no. The nervous twitching was spreading to
her other extremities.

Her mother, most likely sensing she was about to
miss her prey, finally looked her way.

"Mia, the dance studio was closed when I went by
so I knew I'd find you here." Rhonda looked down at
the barely touched bagel smeared with peanut butter.
"Eating, of course."

*Don't think about the dancing hippo. Think about
sure-footed bunnies hopping their way to freedom.*
"Mom, I left a note telling you I'd be back after my
meeting."

"I know. But when I saw the news vans, I was worried sick." Funny, her mom didn't look too sick. Or too
worried. "I thought maybe Nick had gotten out of prison
and come after you again."

"Who's Nick?" Garrett asked at the same time
Rhonda Palinski stepped around Scooter, the kindly
old man who'd quickly jumped up to protect both her
and Garrett's privacy. "So, what's going on with all the
cameras?" she asked.

That figured. Her mom was so worried that instead
of rushing across the street to check on her only child,
she'd gone straight toward the celebrity limelight, her
large knock-off designer tote bag bumping into the nervous twenty-year-old kid holding the video recorder at
his side.

A loud crash sounded when the expensive-looking
equipment dropped onto a table. Several cowboy boot–
shaped water glasses exploded on the ground, sending
ice and shards of glass every which way. When the last

dish clattered to the floor, the only sound in the room was her mother's familiar, "Oopsie."

How the clumsiest woman in the world could have given birth to a daughter whom dance teachers had praised as "graceful" and "fluid" and "mastery in motion" was beyond Mia. Then again, she herself hadn't been too poised lately. Maybe that branch hadn't fallen too far from the genetic tree after all.

"Is she drunk?" Garrett asked.

"No. She's always been a bit accident prone. And extremely dramatic." Mia leaned toward Kylie, figuring she had precious few moments during the crash's aftermath to sneak out while everyone's attention was diverted. "Listen, I really need to get out of here."

"Done," Kylie said as she slipped her keys into Mia's hand.

"No good." Freckles, who had made no move to assist cleaning up the spill, spoke out of the corner of her heavily painted lips. "Your and Maxine's place will be the first place they look. Doc, you and Mia meet me in the kitchen. On the rack by the back door, I've got a spare set of keys to Cessy Walker's lake house. She's in Vegas this week for that Barry Manilow show and I'm supposed to be house-sitting. Nobody will look for you two there."

"Thanks," Garrett said as he edged his seat back and reached for Mia's hand.

Wait. What? Did he seriously expect her to take off with him? She was trying to get away from the guy and this crazy cast of characters he'd just drop-kicked into her life. Well, not Rhonda. That one wasn't his fault. She would have to shoulder the blame for that particular character.

"I'm not going with you," Mia said quietly, but firmly. She glanced between the scene her mother was causing by gushing all over Garrett's famous father, and the remaining customers still shuffling around their table, just waiting to pounce again if there was a problem.

"I'm guessing you didn't drive yourself across the street, so unless you want to risk having *Med TV's* executive producer and your, uh, mom—" a bright flash shot through the restaurant and Dr. McCormick Sr. was now squinting his eyes closed as her mother tried to snap a selfie with him "—follow you back to the dance studio, you might want to think about sneaking out the back door with me."

"If you don't wanna go with the doc here," Scooter said, his dirty Stetson in his tan, weathered hand, "then you're more than welcome to ride Blossom on back to my cabin. She's a real sweet filly. After we distract these folks a bit more, I can hop on the back of Klondike with Jonesy and meet you out there."

Jonesy nodded then shifted a wad of tobacco from one cheek to the other.

Mia weighed her options, but she needed to act fast. Since she'd never ridden a horse, escaping out the back door with Garrett seemed like the lesser of two evils. At least for the time being. She'd have one of her friends come get her as soon as the coast was clear.

"Thanks, Scooter, but I think it's in Blossom's best interest if I go with Dr. McCormick." The older man widened his eyes and Mia clarified, "Junior. Doctor McCormick *Jr.* But we will definitely take you up on that offer of distraction."

The two cowboy buddies turned back toward her

mother and Garrett's father. "Forget vets. You know what you should do a television program on?" Scooter asked way too loudly, but succeeded in getting everyone's attention. "Rodeo cowboys!"

Jonesy sniffed then added, "Let me tell you about the time..."

Mia didn't wait to hear the story. She silently counted to three then said, "Let's go, Junior."

He stood up and pulled her behind him as several townspeople drew closer together to form a blocking wall that they passed behind on their way to the kitchen.

"You know, I hate being called that," Garrett whispered as they slipped by the short-order cook flipping pancakes as if he hadn't noticed that all hell was breaking loose in the dining room.

Mia didn't respond, but neither did she let go of his hand. Apparently, this was another crazy mess they'd have to wade through together. She watched Garrett grab the keys hanging on the small rack by the back door. He glanced out into the alley before ushering her outside.

The frigid air penetrated her cotton sweater and tights and Mia was reminded she'd left her heavier coat inside. And her purse.

As far as escape attempts went, this one was certainly the least and worst planned. Sheesh, even when she'd snuck out of the hotel room in Boise, leaving Garrett sleeping in the big king-size bed, she'd had the good sense and the forethought to take her belongings with her.

They walked between two Victorian structures, and when they'd made their way around the front corner of the building, he paused and she pressed up against his back so she could peek out onto the street, as well. There was an empty white van parked next to the hitching post where Blossom and Klondike stood drinking water out of a tin trough. She spied her mother's red convertible Camaro across the street—the one that still had Florida vanity plates reading DNCEMOM. Otherwise, there wasn't much traffic on Snowflake Boulevard. Yet.

Had his father really said that there would be more news vans coming soon? The ingrained instinct to hide overwhelmed her. It felt as if she'd left her stomach behind in the alley as they ran to his fancy truck and he held the door open.

She waved him away, but he practically stood at attention, waiting for her to get situated inside the fully loaded cab. Good manners were nice and all, but they needed to hurry.

"Do you know how to get to Cessy Walker's house?" Garrett asked when he finally climbed in and started the engine.

"Flip a U-turn and head north toward Sweetwater Bend." Mia's seat belt had barely snapped into place when he gunned the big truck across the double yellow lines. She looked behind her, making sure nobody else had exited the café. She could see him checking out his rearview mirror, but her own nerves told her to keep a lookout, as well. By the time they turned off the main highway, Mia had a permanent crick in her neck and an ache in her knee.

"I think we made it." He let out a breath, but didn't decelerate or otherwise look relieved.

And why would he? Just because they'd temporarily escaped the eye of the storm didn't mean they wouldn't be affected by the aftermath. When she'd lived in Florida, she'd learned that devastation caused by hurricanes lasted long after the harsh gale winds blew through.

And now they would be stuck doing damage control together.

She pointed out the turn to Cessy's gated community. With shelter in sight, Mia finally asked, "Why didn't you tell me your dad was some famous television producer?"

"Are you kidding?" He punched in the code written on the tag attached to the house keys, then looked at her incredulously as they waited for the ornate gate to swing open. "How did you *not* know that?"

"Why in the world would I even suspect that?" Even as she asked the question, several comments he'd made in the past came back to her and things began to click in place.

"Didn't you at least look me up on the internet? I looked *you* up."

He'd researched her? Had he found out about Nick? She didn't want to know. "I did a little bit of research. I even saw a link to your dad, but I guess I was too blind to see the connection. Or maybe my brain just didn't want to see what was right in front of it all along."

He drove through the gate then waited for it to close behind him, one side of his mouth quirked up in disbelief. "Why would you not want to see that? That's usually the first thing that draws women to me."

"Constant media attention and an absolute lack of privacy actually *draw* women to you?"

"Isn't that what drew you?"

She could feel her brow furrowing as she shook her head. "Your sad eyes, your boyish smile and the way your strong hands circled around that crystal glass of single malt scotch were what drew me to you. But trust me, it didn't matter how sexy you were or how my body responded to you. If I would've known who you were, I would've bolted in the opposite direction so fast I'd still be running."

He didn't respond for several seconds. He just stared at her, his hazel eyes trying to read her face as though he was debating whether or not to believe what she'd just said. Either that or he was debating whether or not to kiss her again.

And God help her if he opted for the latter because even after the hellish morning they'd just had and her claims to the contrary, she really didn't think she could run too far from him. Or those lips.

"If that's the case, then you are the exact opposite of pretty much every single woman I've known my entire life."

"Oh, come on, Garrett. I find that extremely difficult to believe. Sure, there may be some women out there who would love that type of public life—my mom, for one—but most rational ladies I know wouldn't want anything to do with that kind of constant exposure."

He took his hand-tooled wingtip off the brake and resumed driving toward Cessy's house. But every few hundred yards, he would look over at her, as though the tooth fairy had just fluttered into his truck with him and he couldn't quite accept the realness of the situation.

She pointed to a large craftsman-style home with a huge wraparound deck that looked out over Lake Rush. "That's it up ahead."

His four-wheel-drive tires crunched along the U-shaped gravel driveway. "Do you think there's room to park my truck in the garage so it can be out of sight?"

"Probably." She took the keys out of the cup holder in the center console. "I'll go in and open the garage. I might have to move Cessy's car and park it out front."

"Wait," he said, reaching out and wrapping his fingers around her upper arm. "Are you really willing to hide out here with me? I mean, how do I know that you're not going to be calling the paparazzi the moment we get inside and blabbing out our location?"

She stiffened her back, trying not to be insulted by his question. None of his behavior this morning had been the reaction she'd expected from him when she'd first spotted his famous dad and the cameraman today.

The second she'd heard his father say "GP," her first thought was that Garrett had lied to her. She'd been right and he was some spoiled rich guy used to getting what he wanted. Her second thought was that he'd gone just as pale as she had, if not more. Then he'd told his notorious father to get out.

At first, she'd assumed that he didn't want it found out that he'd gone slumming with some has-been cheerleader and was now expecting an illegitimate child. But she'd quickly seen that his disgust was directed at the camera and his anger aimed at the older guy dressed like some big kahuna. Several comments he'd made in the past were finally adding up.

"First of all, my only other choice would be back at my apartment with my mother. Second of all, why is it so hard for you to believe that I want nothing to do with any of that forced notoriety, Garrett? From what I saw back at the café, you weren't too thrilled to be in front of those cameras, either. So if that's the case, clearly it would stand to reason that there are other people in the world who aren't any different from you—people who would detest the intrusion just as much as you do. I'm not even sure why you hate it, but let me assure you that some of us have a lot more than just our privacy to lose."

His eyes narrowed. "Is this the part where you decide to tell me about whoever the hell this Nick guy is?"

He still didn't know whether he was buying it. But he had to admit she'd looked downright petrified at the thought of having her whereabouts disclosed on television. Then, when her mom had walked in and made that comment, Garrett recalled that article he'd read on the internet. The one about her stalker.

If they were going to lay all their cards out on the table, now would be the time. He held her gaze, willing her not to clam up now.

"Okay. I'll tell you about Nick. But let's get inside the house first. I'm freezing."

He looked down at her skimpy attire and mentally kicked himself for shutting off the truck and its heater. "Fair enough."

She jumped out and ran up the front porch steps. Damn, he would never get tired of watching her body in motion. She sashayed through the large redwood door and slammed it closed behind her.

The garage door slowly lifted and he saw the taillights of Cessy Walker's red coupe back out into the driveway. Once Mia had it parked along the side of the house, Garrett pulled his truck inside. He had to park at an angle to make the extralong bed fit, and he cursed himself for purchasing such a useless vehicle.

Sure, when he'd bought it, he'd just come home from

a two-year assignment in Afghanistan and he'd been missing some of the luxuries he'd grown accustomed to stateside. Being stationed just outside Boise, it hadn't seemed like that much of a splurge at the time since he'd needed something for the rugged mountain landscape, but with the hint of the luxury he preferred.

His whole life he'd tried to do everything the exact opposite of his old man. When he'd started junior high, his dad took him back to school shopping at Tommy Bahama. So when it was time to go to high school, Garrett begged to attend an elite prep academy with uniforms so he could wear a coat and tie. His dad drove an old VW bus, so Garrett bought a used Buick for his first car. But blood ran thicker than premium unleaded and extra starch, and he wondered if he would ever be able to escape his connection to his family.

And now that he had his own child on the way, he wondered how he would feel if his son or daughter turned out to be the opposite of him. Deep down, he knew he would still love him or her and would never give up on his offspring.

He looked at his cuff links, then unfastened them and dropped them in the center console before rolling up his shirtsleeves. There were a lot of ways he was exactly like his father, and persistence was one of them. Garrett's clothes and the car he drove didn't make him who he was. But how could he prove that to Mia?

Mia reentered the garage and held open the mudroom door for him. He jumped out of the truck and followed her inside. They bypassed the kitchen and entered a living room three times the size of the Cowgirl Up Café.

Speaking of going overboard on luxury, Cessy Walker's decorating bill had probably eaten up a large chunk of her monthly alimony payments. Vaulted wood-planked ceilings with exposed beams arched high above his head and huge unadorned windows faced the crisp blue lake outside.

Her overstuffed sofa was covered in a soft taupe-colored suede while chairs and throw pillows in matching beige tones filled up the living room. Several pottery vases were lined up along a glass-topped coffee table that had the same square footage of his sleeping quarters on board the *USS Bowler*. The vases were probably more expensive than the rest of the furnishings in this entire room. But they were ugly as sin. Hopefully, Ms. Walker wouldn't bring up any more suggestions for decorating his office.

Mia walked over to the thermostat and pushed some buttons before finally giving up. "I can't figure this stupid thing out. It's too high-tech for me."

"Maybe I should make a fire," he said, nodding toward the wide hearth made entirely out of river rock.

"That would help. I'll check the kitchen to see what the food supply is like. I hope we don't have to stay here too long because if I know Cessy, there's probably only expired carrot juice and a fifth of vodka in the fridge. If we're lucky, we might find some frozen diet meals and a bag of Snickers miniatures in the freezer."

Mia left the room and he walked toward the fireplace, noticing there wasn't a log to be seen. He looked around the room again and then stuck his head behind the screen before realizing it was a gas line with a hidden light switch to turn it on. He flipped the toggle and a roaring fire shot to life.

That was easy.

His cell phone vibrated in his pocket and his first

thought was that his dad had probably just come to the conclusion that he had vanished and was already on the hunt.

But when he looked at the screen, he saw Cooper's number pop up instead. "Hello?"

"Hey, Doc," his friend said. "It looks like you've been found out. Maxine told me about your old man showing up at the café. She said you and Mia hightailed it over to Cessy's place to ride out the storm."

"I was right about the provisions," Mia said, walking back into the room holding a spoon and a small container of peanut butter. "But at least she had this in her pantry. Oops, sorry," she whispered when she saw him on the phone.

"It's Cooper," he mouthed and watched her settle in on the floor in front of the fire. She took off her shearling-lined boots, then winced before lying on her back and stretching one leg up into the air. She pointed a toe before bringing her shin all the way to her forehead. Man, she was flexible. He'd remembered that from when they'd made love that night in the hotel room. He watched her, mesmerized as she put that leg down and raised the other one up for the same stretch.

"Did you hear me, Doc?"

"I'm sorry. What was that you were saying?" Garrett turned his back so he could concentrate on the call.

"I asked how persistent your father was. As in, how long do you think you're going to have to hide out before he gives up and takes his camera crew home?"

"I don't think it should take more than a couple of days."

"A couple of days?" Mia yelped from the floor. Garrett looked back at her to nod, but she was now sitting up with her legs in an open position, her torso leaning forward and her back arched.

Aw, hell. How was he going to last a couple of hours alone in this house with her, let alone days?

He walked toward the back deck and opened a sliding glass door, needing to cool off.

Cooper continued. "Well, Mia left her purse and cell phone at the Cowgirl Up. The ladies think that if she plans to be there for a few nights, she might want a change of clothes. Kylie's going to hit Duncan's Market and grab some groceries for you guys and Max is going to pack her an overnight bag. They'll meet up and bring some stuff over later. What about you?"

"What about me?"

"Do you want me to swing by your condo and grab some gear for you, too? I mean, Cessy has a pretty extensive wardrobe and I know you're a sucker for the designer clothing. But I don't think you two wear quite the same size."

"Oh, yeah. I guess I probably will need some clothes. Thanks, man."

"No problem. So how's Mia doing?"

"I think her knee is a little bit sore."

"I wasn't talking about her knee, Dr. McCormick. I meant, how is she doing considering the big blowup at the café earlier?"

How the heck was he supposed to know? She'd seemed flustered at first, but then she'd gotten a little attitude in the car when she'd insisted that not all women were after his money or his notoriety. Actually, he'd liked seeing her square her shoulders and challenge him. But at this second, he really just didn't know what to think.

He looked back toward the fireplace. Mia had removed her sweater and was lying on her back, her arms extended above her head and her feet out in a wide V.

"I'm not entirely sure. She looks pretty fantastic, if you ask me." A heat rose up Garrett's cheeks as he realized he'd just confessed exactly what he'd been thinking. "I mean she's...uh...stretching right now and... Aw, hell. You might want to tell Maxine and Kylie to just hurry up."

Garrett pulled the phone away from his ear so that Cooper's sudden burst of laughter wouldn't pierce his eardrums, then discontinued the call when he realized his buddy's loud guffawing wasn't going to stop anytime soon.

He returned his cell phone to his pocket before rubbing his forehead. "Your friends are going to be here any minute with some clothes and groceries and stuff." His voice sounded unusually scratchy to his own ears.

Mia sat up and he suffered a moment of guilt for bending the truth. Really, nobody would be here for probably a couple of hours, but he needed to tell himself otherwise so he didn't put either one of them in a compromising position.

"Then we might as well relax while we wait for them."

Relaxing and letting down his guard was the *last* thing he wanted to do. "Why don't you tell me about Nick?"

There. Hearing about a former lover would dim any man's desire.

Her blue eyes grew darker, and her lips turned down slightly. But she nodded and stood up. "Okay."

Her bare feet padded over to the sectional sofa. He

waited until she was settled in one corner and then sat on the opposite side of her, wanting—needing—to keep his distance.

She ran a hand through her long dark hair, then deftly wrapped it into a loose knot on top of her head—as if she were preparing to get down to business. "Nick Galveston was a guy I met when I was cheering in Miami."

"Nick Galveston? Where do I know that name?"

"He was the punter for the team I cheered for a few years ago." Aha. She'd been involved with a professional athlete. Maybe he'd had her pegged right, after all. But he sat silently, keeping his forming opinions to himself. "I'd never really met him, but he called me out of the blue one day. Said he'd seen me during one of the halftime routines and had bribed someone in the admin office to get my personal number."

He nodded, but she wasn't looking at him anyway. She stared straight ahead at the fire, seemingly lost in her recollections. "I told him that there was a strict rule against players and cheerleaders fraternizing off the field. And honestly, even if there wasn't, he certainly wasn't someone I would normally date anyway."

"And what kind of guys do you normally date?"

"Lately?" Her head whipped back toward him and he saw the flash of sadness in her eyes before it was replaced with an air of defiance. "Not *any* kind of guys. Actually, back then, I didn't date much, either. I was focused on my career."

"Your cheerleading career?"

She looked at him as if he was a bunion on her foot. "No. On my dance career. I was planning to attend Florida State to get my master's, but my mom had been pressuring me to audition for an NFL team and I needed to earn some money to cover my first year's tuition. Anyway, even if I *had* been in the market to date, it surely wouldn't have been with some spoiled, rich playboy who'd paid someone money to break the rules just to obtain my number."

"So, you have a thing against rich guys?"

"Not because they're rich." She looked down at his shoes before quickly refocusing her gaze on the vaulted ceiling. "I don't like them because of their sense of entitlement."

Why did he have the feeling that she was lumping him into this same category?

Whoa. He needed to check himself. Mia'd been on the cusp of opening up and he'd put her on the defensive. While she was cute when she got riled, he needed to stop acting like a jealous lover and more like a compassionate listener. "So this dirtbag… I mean, this Nick guy was pretty entitled?"

"That's okay. You can call him a dirtbag. Lord knows Kylie and Maxine have called him way worse. I have, too." She put her elbows on her knees and propped her chin in her hands, her resignation obvious. She took a deep breath before continuing. "But he was even more creepy than entitled."

She leaned forward to reach for the jar of peanut butter on the coffee table and sucked in a breath, grabbing her knee instead.

"Are you okay?" He was by her side in an instant.

"I think so. I'm pretty sure I just tweaked my leg when we were running to your truck earlier. I was stretching it out, but it's still pretty tender."

"Here, let me see," he said, then sat next to her and

pulled her leg onto his lap. He kneaded the muscles around her knee, not wanting to put too much pressure on her tendons. "Feel better?"

She nodded then leaned toward the container on the glass table again, but Garrett was quicker and handed it to her, along with the spoon she'd brought from the kitchen.

"Thanks." She lifted the edge of her mouth shyly, but Garrett could tell the smile wasn't heartfelt. He had a feeling telling this story was harder on her than he'd anticipated.

"Maybe we should talk about this later. It's kind of been an emotional morning and…"

"No." She held up her spoon to interrupt him. "You need to know and I'm supposed to be able to talk about it and put it in my past."

She unscrewed the lid of the container. "I'm also supposed to watch the extra calories during the first trimester, but since I tend to use food as a coping mechanism, well, I figured I might just need a spoonful of PB reinforcement."

He watched as she took a bite, mentally steeling herself for the conversation, and decided she was much tougher than she looked. He could sit here all day, watching the emotions cross her face. But when he heard her take in a resigned breath, he knew he wouldn't have to.

"Anyway," she continued, "the first couple of times he called, I was polite, but told him no. After that, he had roses delivered to me at one of our rehearsals. I was mortified and my choreography coach was wondering who had sent them. So, not wanting to get in trouble, I refused the bouquet and sent the deliveryman on his way. When I got out to my car the next night after practice, there were torn flowers and stems all over my car."

"That *is* creepy."

She bit her lip and nodded. He kept massaging her knee, more for support than pain relief now. "Things just progressed from there. All season long, he called me and drove by the practice field and the studios where we had our rehearsals. I changed my number, but then he started escalating. He got bolder, coming over to talk to me during the games while I was on the sidelines. During the last game of the season, he missed an easy kick, causing a fumble and the team lost. He ran over to me afterward, screaming that I had distracted him and that because I was all he could think about, he hadn't been able to focus."

Garrett could feel her leg tensing and knew her whole body was reliving the fear and stress of the verbal attack. He wanted to relax her and remind her that she was safe now. But he also needed to keep her talking. Not only because he needed to hear the rest—but because he sensed she finally needed to let it out.

"Where was security during all this? Where were the managers and coaches? Did everyone see this happen?"

"The station had cut to commercial break already and, did I mention that it was Nick Galveston?" She took a bigger bite of peanut butter, as though she was using the food to wash the jerk's name off her tongue.

"Yeah, you said that. He's some self-absorbed football player. Big deal. They... Oh, wait. You mean he was Neville Galveston's son?"

"You guessed it." She pointed the cleaned-off spoon at him. "His father's a big deal in the Florida business world and was a big sponsor at the time. Since the season was over and I was planning on going back to school for my MFA anyway, I didn't make a big deal of it. Plus, his coach assured me that he would be going to mandated counseling."

She shook her head. "Looking back, I wish I would have at least filed a formal complaint."

"So Nick was your stalker? He was the guy who attacked you?" Her neck angled back in surprise, as if she thought she'd been able to keep this awful episode completely hidden before now. "See, I looked you up online, too. But I could only find one article and it was pretty brief. Sorry for interrupting. Go on."

She took a deep breath. "A couple weeks later, I came home to my apartment. It was dark and I hadn't seen or heard from the guy in a while and thought I was safe enough. But out of nowhere, here comes Nick. And he glares at me with such hate in his eyes. Crazy hate." He felt her whole body shiver. "I'd never seen anybody look like that at another human being before. I couldn't move, couldn't blink. I didn't even see the golf club he was holding. He told me that if I wasn't going to be his little dancer, then he'd make sure I never danced again. That's when he swung at me and smashed my kneecap."

"That son of a…" Garrett wished he had access to a nine iron and a dark room with the bastard trapped inside it. But he could still feel the tenseness in her leg and he realized he'd stopped massaging and was gripping her tighter. "Sorry."

But she didn't seem to hear him, so lost was she in her terrifying memory. "I screamed and one of the neighbors ran out, but not before he hit me several more times. One was to the back of my head. I was in a coma

for a week." A tear trickled down her proud, high cheek-
bone and she shook her head, as if she could shake loose
the pain she'd been holding inside. "After I woke up, I
found out about my knee and I knew it was all over. My
dancing career, my whole life. Everything."

Neither one said a word for a few seconds and he
could tell the dam holding back the rest of her tears
was threatening to come loose.

"They caught him, though, right?" he asked, trying
to divert her.

"They did. It helped that I lived at a complex with
video surveillance in the parking lot so the cops had everything on record. They charged him with attempted
murder and he pled down to assault with a deadly
weapon. He's serving time and his dad paid off the
right people and everything was kept hush-hush."

Mia shuddered, then used the edge of her knitted
sleeve to wipe her face. Garrett had to exhale and count
to ten to get his anger in check. He could only imagine the toll that kind of event had taken on her. Years
had gone by and he could still see the way it had im-
pacted her.

It really explained why she was so skittish and looked
at him sideways any time he walked in the room. He
used to wonder if she was pretending to be coy, but there
was no way to act out this kind of anguish.

He was a healer and not at all prone to violence. But
he had never wanted to hurt anyone the way he wanted
to hurt the man who had crushed Mia's leg. Her dreams.
Her trust...

"It's okay. He can't hurt you anymore. I've got you
now," he said and pulled her into his arms. Her body
shook as she finally let out a small sob, but she al-

lowed Garrett to hold her as the dam inside her finally broke, to let him absorb all the hurt she'd been hiding for way too long.

Chapter Ten

Mia hadn't told the story to more than a handful of people, including the police officer who'd taken the initial report, and her best friends when she'd first moved to Sugar Falls.

She had expected to cry her way through it as she usually did, especially considering the hormonal imbalance she'd been experiencing lately. But she'd never allowed herself to be this vulnerable before. Especially not in a man's strong embrace. When she finally had her tears under control, she wiped her face and scooted away from Garrett, but her knee was still awkwardly draped across his lap.

Yet for some reason, she didn't feel as embarrassed as she had before. Although she'd gone through an awful lot of peanut butter and her tears had left a damp spot on the shoulder of Garrett's shirt where she'd been crying, Mia felt emotionally drained, but also surprisingly stronger.

Talking about Nick with Garrett was like getting a root canal. Now that she'd gotten to the core of her problem and eased some of the ache, her nerves were still throbbing, but more out of a sense of relief.

"So everything worked out in the end, then?" Garrett asked. His hands had dropped back to her leg, but this time, they were a bit higher on her thigh.

"I never thought of it that way before." She angled her head. "But I guess if it hadn't been for that incident, I wouldn't be sitting with you at a mansion on Lake Rush right now. At the time, I was in such a dark and scary place. Not only from being stalked and attacked, but also from the surgery that had taken longer than expected and the fact that my knee had never healed quite right. Kylie and Maxine thought I should get a second opinion, that I shouldn't rely on the team doctors whose best interest was their franchise and keeping things out of the news. But afterward, I just wanted to get as far away from it all as I could."

"So that's why you moved to Sugar Falls?"

"Yep. My best friends were already established here and there was no way I was going to move back in with my mom. Ballet had always been my goal, not living in some small remote town in Idaho, teaching dance classes to little kids." She shook her head ruefully. "Spending day after day explaining to parents that it's okay if their child isn't the best one on the stage as long as they were having fun was never my dream. But dreams have a way of changing."

He nodded and took the empty jar of peanut butter from her, setting it down on the table in front of

them. Her leg was still across his lap, and the movement caused him to shift in a way that brought his free
hand farther up her thigh. "But at least you no longer
have to worry about that bastard following you around."

Mia shivered. "Actually, last year I had a feeling
someone was. I've never really been able to shake that
sense of unease, and then I got a letter from the parole
board advising me that Nick might get an early release
due to budget cuts and the fact that he was a first time
offender. Cooper called in some favors from a buddy
with the Florida Department of Corrections and when
they searched his cell, they found a bunch of recent
pictures of me and the dance studio and my apartment.
The jerk had hired a private investigator to look me up."

Garrett's hands stilled and when she finally chanced
a peek at him, she realized his jaw was unusually rigid.
She'd seen him look at his father in frustration, but she'd
never seen him look so intently furious. For a moment,
she wondered what kind of anger he was capable of.

She reached out and rubbed his arm. "Hey, don't be
so upset. The parole board found out and denied him.
Plus, they're watching him more closely now."

"I just hate what he did to you. What he put you
through. No human being should have to go through
that."

"I know. I used to run around afraid of my own
shadow. I still do sometimes. But now that I have a little one to think about, I can't keep living my life in fear.
I have to be strong for both of us."

Saying it out loud made it ring even more true.

He looked at her face, then at her hand on his biceps. She felt his muscles flex ever so slightly, and her

thumb slipped into the ridge along his muscle. Underneath those starched custom-made shirts, Garrett McCormick was solid as a rock.

She glanced down at his fingers, which were still on her thigh, commanding herself not to move, even as the rest of her was bubbling up inside, wanting to feel more of him.

The morning had been intense, to say the least, and now she'd just let down this huge emotional wall in front of him. If she truly knew what was good for her, she'd jump off this sofa and never look back.

"So you're not afraid anymore?" His voice was deeper and she knew he was equally aware of their proximity—both physical and emotional.

"Of you? No. Two months ago—heck, even two weeks ago—I would've been terrified to be in the same room with a strange man. But ever since I met you in that hotel bar, my entire body feels at peace around you. Even when my brain is trying to tell it to stay on high alert. And now, for some strange reason that I can't explain, being with you gives me this sense of empowerment. It's made me realize that I'm tired of running. Tired of being afraid."

It was the truth. She could have told this story to anyone, but it was Garrett who made her feel safe. It was Garrett whom she'd chosen to open her heart to. And if she was being one hundred percent honest, it was Garrett whom she loved.

She felt the weight of her hair slip loose, so she reached up to unclip it from its makeshift knot, allowing it to tumble down her back. And like the heavy raven locks, her stored-up self-consciousness followed suit and she relished the freedom.

She brought her hand up to his smoothly shaved cheek and watched his nostrils flare slightly when she traced her fingers along his jaw, behind his ear and toward the back of his scalp.

His close-cropped hair prickled at her fingers like spiky little speed bumps, warning her to proceed with caution.

Screw that. She was done with caution. *No more living in the dark*, she vowed, right before pulling his head down to hers.

When her lips touched his, she was no longer tentative or ashamed. She was eager and reckless and on a mission to make up for lost time. There had been so much she'd given up and so much more she'd never allowed herself to experience. But not anymore.

Just as she'd done in that hotel bar on the night she'd met him, she set her inhibitions free and exploded in his arms. His hand traveled up to her ribs, and her skin couldn't contain her any more than a glass bottle could contain the bubbling champagne released by its cork.

His mouth wasn't enough. She needed to feel him, needed to get closer.

She brought her other leg up and maneuvered herself into a plié before straddling his lap. Her lips caught his groan and heat shot through her core when she felt his zipper pressed against her thin cotton leggings. He grabbed her hips and pulled her tighter against his arousal until she was the one moaning.

She threw back her head as he kissed his way down her neck and along her collarbone. When he pulled down the spaghetti straps of her sports tank, she released him long enough to yank the entire thing over her head, not wanting to keep him or his incredible hands away from her aching breasts any longer.

He rewarded her by drawing one tight nipple into his hot mouth, before kissing his way over to the other one and loving it equally.

"Garrett, you make me feel so good." He paused and she opened her eyes, wondering what she'd said wrong.

"I couldn't remember if I'd even told you my name that night we met. But afterward, all I could think about was making love to you and hearing you scream it out."

She put her palm to his face, cupping his cheek, and whispered it again. "Garrett."

"That sounds even better," he said before slipping his hands inside her waistband.

She reached for the buttons on his shirt, but when the first one proved too difficult for her restless fingers, she yanked through the rest. The sound of tearing fabric didn't cause her to slow down as she pushed the material off his shoulders and ran her hands over the well-formed pectoral muscles of his chest.

Bringing her lips back to his, she moved with him when he leaned forward to shove his shirt off. The light hair on his chest tickled her breasts and when she arched up, he used her leverage as an opportunity to push her black leggings down to her thighs.

Twenty-five years of dance enabled her to maneuver her limbs effortlessly as he removed the rest of her clothing while she remained firmly in place on his lap.

Now that she'd decided to take control of her life, she wasn't about to waste a second.

Raising her body slightly, she allowed him to kiss the sensitive area just above her rib cage while he unbuckled his pants. But before he could take the time to remove them, she came back down until the tip of his erection was situated directly below her.

She paused, relishing this small act of power. She was in charge now.

Briefly, she thought of the dark fear that had ruled her life for too long. And she remembered the dark hotel room where they'd once made love. Then she pulled her face back, taking in the bright light streaming in from the vast wall of windows. She needed to see him, needed to watch him.

When she finally allowed herself to slide down over his hard shaft, it felt as if she was claiming him, claiming her life.

"Aw, Mia. My sweet Mia," he whispered.

He'd been right. Hearing her name cherished by his lips was something she hadn't realized she'd missed out on the last time.

She moved slowly at first, letting her body become accustomed to him once again. She watched his lids grow heavy, heard his breathing become more shallow and rapid. He held her waist firmly, but didn't try to manage her movements.

"I don't know how much more I can take." His voice was ragged and his hands trailed down along her backside until they fully cupped her bottom. Mia took him deeper and quicker, her eyes never leaving his face.

It was like focusing on the brightest spotlight in the theater as she danced in sync—her pirouettes becoming faster and faster until she didn't think she could hold her spin any longer. When he gripped her tighter and her muscles contracted around him, she finally let go as though she was floating off the stage and twirling through the air without a cable.

Garrett held Mia to him until they both got their breathing under control. But the woman who had been so graceful just a few moments ago, defying the laws of physics with her balancing and flexibility, was slowly toppling over like an untied satin ribbon on a well-used ballet shoe.

And he was falling with her.

As they drifted to their sides and nestled into the cushions, he pulled a brown throw blanket off the back of the sofa and wrapped it around them. She had straightened her legs, but he could feel her breasts pressed firmly to his chest, her stomach softly resting against his.

His child was growing there.

As a medical professional he knew what they'd done hadn't endangered their baby. But he wondered what kind of father didn't even bother to fully remove his khakis before so thoroughly ravishing the mother.

Actually, it felt more as if *he'd* been the one ravished. Mia had seemed intent on taking the lead and for once in Garrett's life, he'd allowed himself to sit back and let someone else take control. He was learning that as much as he'd fought to establish his independence from his father and take charge of his own future, he couldn't micromanage every single detail.

He would have to start getting used to relinquishing power some of the time, especially to Mia, who had just proved herself to be more than capable of leading him to paradise.

He kissed her forehead and her sigh was the last thing he heard before drifting off into a blissful sleep.

Which was better than what woke him.

"Okay, you two, company's here," Maxine's voice called from the closed-off kitchen before two sets of distinctly male laughter echoed through the room.

"Oh, no." Mia pulled the blanket over her head. "I forgot they were coming over."

So had Garrett. Which wasn't like him. Enough of this reckless leisure. He needed to get himself back in charge.

But not until they got dressed. He gave her one last kiss and sat up, watching her walk around the room gathering their clothes as she tried to keep the blanket wrapped around her.

"Here." She tossed a wrinkled wad of cloth at him before pulling on her top and leggings. He put his arms through the sleeves, not taking his eyes off her. Watching her wiggle into the tight, stretchy fabric was almost as pleasurable as watching her remove it.

She looked at his shirt, which was hanging open, its buttons probably scattered somewhere in the sofa cushions or along the hardwood floors. She gasped then blushed. "I'm so sorry I ripped it like that."

He grinned. "I'm not."

She glanced around the room. "Did we miss anything?"

He stood up, revealing the fact that he was still wearing his pants and that they hadn't wasted time when it came to disrobing. He chuckled when her blush got even deeper.

He attempted to tuck his shirt in so he would at least look presentable and then thought, why bother? Surely the couples politely hiding out in the kitchen already knew what they'd been doing in here.

"They're going to know," Mia said, their thoughts on the same page.

He looked pointedly at her still-flat belly. "I don't think it's much of a surprise to anyone that we've made love." She returned his appraising look and he couldn't help but add, "Your top thingy is on inside out."

She slapped her hand to her chest, then quickly threw her sweater on over the whole ensemble.

He chuckled at her embarrassment, and then to his surprise, she joined him. They were looking at each other, giggling, and Mia finally walked up to him and tried to straighten his shirt so the button holes at least lined up. But when he felt her fingers on his bare skin, he couldn't help but pull her in for another deep kiss.

"It's been five minutes," Cooper called out from the kitchen. "We're coming in whether you're dressed or not."

Kylie was the first to emerge through the door. "I've had to pee since we turned in the gate," she yelled before doing some sort of running waddle toward the bathroom.

Maxine rolled in a suitcase behind her and Mia walked over to her friend, her posture erect and her chin high—as if they had absolutely nothing to be ashamed of. And really, they didn't, seeing as how they were two grown, consenting adults. But he still felt a small thrill of pride that she wasn't humiliated to be caught in such a flagrant situation with him.

"Sorry to intrude like this," Drew said, ever the diplomatic psychologist. "We did bring steaks, though, as a sort of peace offering."

"Actually, we brought half of Duncan's Market with us," Cooper said, gesturing his thumb toward the kitchen. "We weren't sure how determined your parents were going to be so we wanted to make sure you two were well stocked to ride out the storm."

Kylie came out of the bathroom just then. "Thank goodness. I'm starved."

"You're always hungry," Maxine said.

"That's because I'm eating for three. Why don't I whip something up?"

"No," several voices, including Mia's, shouted. Apparently, the redheaded CPA was not known for her prowess in the kitchen.

"Cooper knows how to work Cessy's grill, so why don't the guys go outside to barbecue the steaks, and us ladies will take charge making the side dishes?"

Garrett didn't like Maxine's suggestion only because he could see a light dusting of snow on the deck already and knew it would be freezing outside. But he wanted to give Mia her space and figured she would probably like some time alone with her girlfriends—hopefully, not to talk about him.

Thirty minutes later, they were sitting around Ms. Walker's dining room table, which looked as if it could seat the entire marching band from Sugar Falls High School, along with their instruments. Even the teak-and-bamboo-filled mansion in his father's house didn't have anything this ostentatious.

Speaking of his father, Cooper brought up the Botoxed elephant in the room. "So what's the plan for getting Dr. McCormick and his television show out of town?"

"Maybe you can just arrest anyone walking down

the street with a video camera," Kylie suggested before spearing a piece of filet mignon.

"As much as I'd like to, I can't. It's a public area. Plus, the chamber of commerce isn't opposed to some free publicity. But the mayor did say that if things get too crazy in town, it could diminish our reputation as a... what were his words... 'A tranquil and idyllic vacation destination.' So suffice it to say, it's in everyone's best interest if we get them to leave as soon as possible."

"Does that include my mom?" Mia asked. "She doesn't have a camera, but I'm sure she would be the first one lined up to offer an exclusive interview."

"Your mom didn't seem that bad," Garrett said. "A little clumsy, maybe, but relatively harmless."

"Clearly, you don't know my mother. What she lacks in grace, she more than makes up for in tenacity."

Maxine passed the bowl of mushroom risotto to him. "If you think *my* ex-mother-in-law is persistent, Ms. Palinski could run circles around Cessy Walker and be on the phone with every talent agent in Hollywood while she was doing it. No offense, Mia."

"Trust me, none taken. It's true, Garrett." She looked at him briefly before piling her plate full of spinach salad. At least her appetite was back. "My mom's biggest goal in life was to make a name for her only daughter by any means necessary. She can be a hammerhead shark when she makes up her mind about something."

"So what's the goal for you two?" Drew asked. "Once we figure out what we want to achieve, then we can formulate a plan to make that happen."

Garrett knew Kylie's husband was great at his job treating soldiers with PTSD, and this was one of the first rational ideas he'd heard all day.

"My short-term goal is to stay out of the news and off my father's television show," he said. "I'd been doing pretty well at it, too, until one of my schoolmates publicized my personal life. My long-term goal is to get my medical practice up and running and live a relatively quiet and peaceful life up here in Sugar Falls."

Everyone but Mia laughed as if this was the funniest idea they'd ever heard. "What?"

"You're about to have a child," Drew said. "I don't think your life is ever going to be quiet or peaceful again."

Not that Garrett had been around too many kids, but surely it wouldn't be all that bad. So far, Mia and he seemed to be on the same page with this co-parenting thing. Although, after this afternoon on the living room sofa, Garrett wasn't exactly sure that he wanted to keep his distance from her too much. It wasn't as if he believed in marriage or happily ever after, but they were getting along really well so far and if what they'd done a couple of hours ago was a perk of parenthood, then he'd be a happy father, indeed.

"Mia." Cooper reached for a piece of hot French bread and slathered it generously with butter. "What about you?"

She shrugged. "I just want to have a happy and well-adjusted baby. I want my knee to get better, or at least as better as it's going to be. I want to teach dance without my mother constantly telling me I'm settling. And I want to make sure that Nick Galveston never gets out of prison or finds out where I am."

And there it was. The reason why she could never truly be with Garrett.

If he was in her life, he could guarantee every single

one of those things *except* Nick finding her again. Or her mother issues. Everyone had to deal with wacky parents, so she was on her own with that. But if his famous father and the media's obsession with exposing his whereabouts brought Mia or their child into danger, he would never forgive himself.

Chapter Eleven

"Okay, so here's what I suggest," Kylie said after dinner as she brought out a tray full of Maxine's cookies with ice cream sandwiched inside.

Garrett didn't take one as she passed the tray. He hadn't been able to eat much at dinner. But now that he'd resigned himself to the fact that he and Mia couldn't ever be together, his appetite was completely gone.

She continued. "My brother, Kane, had to pull a disappearing act back when he was leaving Chicago so the press wouldn't constantly hound him about whether or not he would be able to play baseball again. He told everyone he was going to Scottsdale, Arizona, for surgery and some R and R."

"But I'd prefer not to go anywhere," Garrett said. He'd been on the move since he'd been eighteen. He was finally at a point where he wanted to put down roots.

Where he wanted to stop running. "I'm trying to get my orthopedic clinic up and operating and I can't do that from Scottsdale, or anywhere else."

Mia pulled her cookie apart and started on the ice cream first. "I have dance classes scheduled and the Christmas pageant I'm working on. I mean, I could probably get you ladies and a couple of my other teachers to cover for me, but I can't just leave all my students hanging indefinitely."

"No, that's not what I'm saying," Kylie said as she took two ice cream sandwiches off the tray before passing it on to her husband. "I meant you *tell* everyone you're going somewhere and leave a fake trail of bread crumbs for them to follow. They take off to look for you and when it's all clear, you two resurface and go back to living your ordinary lives."

"Like a red herring!" Drew took only one dessert, unlike his wife.

But then they'd still be living with the threat of being discovered again. Garrett thought of Kane and the way the famous baseball pitcher had ducked out of the Cowgirl Up Café when he'd seen the cameraman coming. The whole point was to *stop* hiding out.

"We'll tell them that you eloped," Cooper suggested and Garrett almost choked on his ice cream.

"Nobody will believe that I've run off to get married. Even my dad knows me better than that." He didn't see Mia set her uneaten cookie on her plate or look down at the napkin in her lap.

"Not if we make them believe it," Kylie said. "I can sell anything. First, you guys call them and tell them that with all the pressure, you decided to just run off to Aruba or Bali or somewhere for a babymoon."

"What in the heck is a babymoon?" Cooper asked.

"It's when the expectant parents go on vacation as a sort of last hurrah before the baby gets here. Drew and I are going back to Reno for ours. It's a totally romantic thing to do."

Several voices chirped into the conversation to discuss the fake destination for their fake plan—a plan Garrett thought was absurd at best.

"Reno was the most romantic place they could come up with?" he whispered to Mia.

"That's where they got married," Mia whispered back. "But they were both drunk and didn't remember it, so they're going to go back and renew their vows."

He glanced over at the unlikely couple—a straight-laced, bespectacled psychologist and a sassy redhead with a penchant for high heels. Maybe it wasn't the most orthodox of marriages, but it seemed to work for them. Besides Cooper and Maxine, Garrett had never seen a couple more in love with each other than Drew and Kylie.

The psychologist stroked a loving hand over his wife's extended stomach. Seeing the glow of pregnancy reminded Garrett of where he and Mia were going to be in just a few months. And even though they'd just made love and he was feeling closer than ever to her, the fact remained that there were still so many unknowns. Plus, she was somewhat, in a sense, hiding out from that Nick guy, and Garrett's father was on a full-blown crusade to expose both him and Mia to the world. Or at least, to his adoring viewers.

The couples continued to discuss the types of clues they would leak to the press, and the plan was sounding more asinine by the second. Gerald McCormick may look like an old, sun-weathered surfer, but he was a smart and savvy man. He would be waylaid for only so long before he and his television crews ended up right back in Sugar Falls. And as long as that possibility was an issue, Mia would never truly be safe.

"Listen, guys." Garrett held up his hands, quieting the dramatic crowd. "My not being completely up-front with my father about my feelings is what got us into this mess. I'm not going to lie to him or spend my life hiding out. I'll get in touch with him tomorrow and speak with him one-on-one."

Even as Garrett said the words, he knew there was no guarantee that any conversation he'd have with his dad would have any long-lasting effect. He needed to provide Mia with a bit of security, no matter how temporary it might be, but that didn't mean everything would be lollipops and rainbows after that. As much as he wanted to, he wouldn't be able to protect her privacy forever.

And he couldn't bring himself to be the person who was constantly putting her in jeopardy of being exposed to the press or the reason why she needed to live like a hermit. She'd eventually resent him and he'd end up hating himself.

Nope. It could never work out between them.

Once he explained things to his father and they got rid of the immediate threat, then Garrett would need to figure out a way to let her go—for her own safety.

"Hi, Mom," Mia said into her cell phone after her friends and their husbands left.

"Don't you 'hi, Mom' me." Rhonda wasted no time. "The entire Sugar Falls Chamber of Commerce knew my baby girl was pregnant before I did. And then you just left me there with that big shot producer trying to figure out what was going on and how we could put a positive spin on it."

"I'm sorry I took off like that and didn't tell you myself. It's just that things with Garrett and the baby have been so sudden and unexpected and I was trying to get everything in order before I shared the news with you."

"Who's Garrett?" Sheesh, was her mom serious?

"*Garrett*, Mom. You know the man from the café?" *The man who is the father to your unborn grandchild?*

Okay, so she left out that part at the end, but it was a fact Mia *couldn't* afford to forget. She watched the subject of their conversation as he stood at the kitchen sink, doing dishes and looking more sexy than domestic.

"Oh, you mean GP? Dr. McCormick's son?"

"Uh, yes, he *is* Dr. McCormick's son. But his name is Garrett and he's also a doctor."

"Well, I don't care what you want to call him, Mia. He's loaded and his dad has a lot of connections in Hollywood. If you play your cards right, you could land some sort of dance school reality show. Even if you can't dance yourself, you might be able to make something of your career."

The old Mia would've winced at the careless remark. But the new and improved and empowered Mia was going to speak up for herself.

"Mom, I like my career just fine. You know that I don't care about that show business stuff."

"Well, you *should* care. Do you have any idea how many jobs I lost hauling you around to audition after audition? How many know-it-all dance teachers I had to kiss up to in order to get you enrolled in their classes?

And for what? To have you bust up your knee and get knocked up? I did not sacrifice my entire life for you to sit around and play Holly Homemaker out in the Idaho wilderness." Mia listened to the familiar rant, one hand nestled over her own baby, as if she could cover its ears from the harsh and unfair reprimand. She'd never asked her mother to make those choices. "But at least this time, you landed yourself a good catch. You're finally making some lemonade out of those damn lemons you've been hauling around."

"You're right, Mom. I've always made the best of things, even when you coerced me into everything you wanted me to do. And I'm making a lot more than lemonade this time. I'm going to be an amazing parent and I am very excited about this baby."

There was a long silence on the other end of the line and Mia had to wonder if her mother even heard what she'd just said. She could see the woman pinching the bridge of her nose, trying to think of a different way to get what she wanted. "Gah, I can't believe I'm going to be a grandmother already. You're going to lose your figure, you know."

"Probably."

"Well, at least your father-in-law will be able to do a tummy tuck and boob lift afterward. Wait. You and GP *are* getting married, right?"

She doubted it. But she didn't want to bring up his comment at the dinner table while she was trying to convince her mom that she had her life under control.

"It's Garrett, Mom, and we haven't gotten that far."

"Are you taking your prenatal vitamins?"

The maternal question tugged at Mia's heart and she

was reminded that her mother really did love her, in her own selfish way. "Yes, Mom."

She could hear her mother sigh on the other end of the line. "I worry about you, you know? I've always wanted what's best for you."

"I know that." She really did. The problem was that Rhonda Palinski wanted what *she* thought was best for her daughter and wasn't willing to listen to anyone else's opinion on the matter. Mia squeezed her eyes closed. She was not going to get emotional right now. Not here. "But you have to trust me that this is what's best for me and for your grandchild."

"I know. And I do trust you, even if I never stop worrying about you. As a parent, you'll learn that it's hard to just switch off the caring button when your own baby grows up. Speaking of which, do you know whether we're having a boy or a girl yet?"

"Not yet."

"M'kay, but don't forget that a lot more boys have been getting into dance now. So don't worry if it's not a girl. We can still work with him and make sure he gets a good background in ballet and tap, but we might have to enroll him in gymnastics pretty early on. Thank goodness GP's family can probably afford private lessons."

"You know, that's a great idea. If you see Garrett's dad before he leaves town, make sure you run that idea past him."

One of Garrett's brows shot up and she wondered if he could hear the other side of the conversation. Sheesh, she hoped not. She swallowed a pang of guilt for purposely unleashing her persistent but well-meaning mother on her child's grandfather. But really, if they were both going to interfere in their grandchild's life, then Rhonda and Gerald would have to duke it out between themselves first. At least it would keep them occupied and off her back.

"Anyway, Mom, I'm not coming back to the apartment tonight. I'm going to be staying with a friend." She chanced a look at Garrett to see if he had any reaction to her mentioning her plan to spend the night with him, but he was scrubbing a pan with the same concentration he probably used in the operating room. "Maybe we can meet up tomorrow and catch up?"

"Of course. Bye, baby girl," her mom said, then disconnected.

Mia let out a breath and set down the phone. Talking to her mom was like getting her eyebrows plucked—painful, but thankfully necessary only every few weeks.

Plus, some positive things had come out of their conversation, so it hadn't been a complete failure. She'd stood up to her mom and reminded her that Mia was now calling the shots in her own life. Nobody else.

Now, if she could only figure out what to do with her baby's dad.

Garrett had clearly said he wasn't the type to run off and get married. Sure, they could co-parent all they wanted to, but where did they draw the emotional line? After what she'd experienced on the sofa earlier, Mia didn't think she would be happy with such a casual relationship. Either they were a couple or they weren't. As much as her behavior lately suggested otherwise, she wasn't a woman who would allow herself to be used at a man's whim.

They didn't need to make any decision tonight, but she would have to bite the bullet soon and tell Garrett that their child would eventually need stability. Whether they provided that individually or together was a choice they would both need to be comfortable living with. Once that choice was made, though, she wouldn't be jumping back and forth between roles.

It could wait until after he talked to his father and they hashed out their issues. She picked up a dish towel and started drying dishes so she would be forced to stop staring at him and wondering what he was thinking.

She wanted to know whether he was doing any of this for her because he thought that was what she wanted. She'd already had to face her world—the town of Sugar Falls and her mother—with the announcement of her pregnancy and the paternity of her child. But he had yet to face his world, which would be much more judgmental and unforgiving.

She wanted to tell him that things in his life would be so much better once he explained his feelings to his dad. But Mia was just barely learning how to take control of her own life. How could she try to tell him how to control his? Then she would be no better than her mother or Dr. McCormick Sr.

But just as her friends had once dared her to come out of her shell, maybe Garrett just needed a push in the right direction.

It wasn't that Garrett was nervous about talking to his father. He just doubted the effectiveness of their conversation. He'd overheard most of Mia's phone call with her mom and was proud of how well she'd handled herself and how she'd stood up to the woman. But putting Rhonda Palinski in check was probably an afternoon frolic in the kiddie pool. Dealing with Gerald

McCormick was like being dunked into deep, shark-infested waters.

Garrett watched Mia as she put dishes away and wondered if she doubted him as much as he doubted himself.

She'd been quiet as she'd helped him clean up the kitchen, and Garrett was trying not to draw attention to how useless he felt.

Normally, he was a proactive man—someone who got stuff done. People entrusted their lives to him. Hell, he had been an officer in one of the most elite branches of the military. Sitting back and waiting until the camera crews left town so that he could confront his father made him feel like a coward.

Even if it did mean guaranteeing the privacy of the woman he loved.

He stroked his forehead. It was true. He loved her. He didn't know how that had happened or when he'd let his heart even consider the possibility. But this gut-twisting agony and the decision he knew he had to ultimately make was definitely because of love.

Watching his father bring wife after wife into their lives had done nothing to cement the concept of matrimony in Garrett's young mind. In fact, before his twelfth birthday, he had sworn off the idea of marriage altogether. He told himself it was a sham, that it was for suckers, or that it had a failure rate to rival any property division percentage his former stepmothers had ended up relinquishing. If his beach-loving, ultrasuccessful father couldn't make it work, then how could he?

But Garrett wasn't a failure and he sure as heck wasn't his father. He knew that he could make a marriage with Mia work. But the unfortunate irony of the situation was that now that he'd finally realized it, he would never be able to make it happen.

After the kitchen was back in order, Mia walked around the house making sure the outer doors were secured and bolted. He wondered how often she'd followed this same procedure in an effort to ensure her safety. All Garrett had to do was avoid some cameras if he didn't want to be seen. But a few photos or some video footage never truly endangered him. What did it feel like to live in a state of fear such that her very life depended on whether or not she locked a door?

Maybe there wasn't much of a threat with her attacker now in prison. Still, he couldn't marry her and risk exposing her and their child to unwanted attention, but he also couldn't live without her.

He was so angry at his selfish father for putting them in this situation and he was just as pissed at himself for not telling his old man where exactly he could stick his reality show and its ratings sooner.

When he'd been surprised at the restaurant earlier, he'd reverted to his standard operating procedure. It had always been easier to just take off and leave. But what worked back when he was a teenager no longer felt like an effective solution now that he had so much more to lose.

Mia yawned as she made her way toward the stairs. "I'm exhausted," she said, reaching for her suitcase.

"Here, let me carry that up for you." Garrett jumped out of his chair. He needed to feel somewhat useful. "Any idea what the sleeping arrangements are like upstairs?"

"I, uh, well." A pink blush spread up Mia's neck and blossomed over her cheeks. She hadn't been ashamed earlier when she'd taken charge of their lovemaking on the sofa. Tonight, a lot of questions had arisen in his mind about which direction their relationship should be headed in. And he was willing to bet she'd been thinking about some of the same issues.

In his heart, he knew they would have to end things eventually. But maybe for just one more night, the magic could last a little bit longer. He wrapped an arm around her and pulled her toward him before kissing her deeply. When he felt her respond, he knew she'd come to the same conclusion as him.

"There's a guest room at the end of the hall," she said breathlessly.

It was all he needed to hear. He lifted her into his arms and had to remind himself to go slowly. To savor every detail of tonight. Because when this was all over, he would have to let her go.

He carried her past both the master suite and one that was decorated as if a slew of adolescent boys stayed over frequently. By the time they made it to the guest room, Garrett wasn't concerned about who normally slept where in this house or whether there were even sheets on the bed.

And by the time they finished making love and fell asleep in each other's arms, Garrett wasn't concerned about anything beyond the people inside this lake house.

But the sun streaming in through the windows was a cruel reminder of everything in his life he hadn't concerned himself with before now. His cell phone vibrated and he saw a text message pop up on the screen from Cooper.

Just saw your pops walk into the Cowgirl Up Café. He was driving a nondescript sedan with plates registered to a rental company. I called the Snow Creek Lodge and confirmed that his crew checked out earlier this morning. So my guess is he'll be on his way out of town after breakfast. I'll keep you posted.

Garrett should be thrilled. He should be elated that he finally had the chance to confront his father without anyone video recording what he needed to say. But what about the next time his old man came to town? And knowing his dad, there would be a next time.

"Morning," Mia said, stretching like a cat in the sunlight. Man, that woman could sure move her body into the most alluring positions. But her smile fell and she asked, "What's wrong?"

He answered by handing his cell phone to her so she could read the text.

She sat up, her beautiful shoulders poised perfectly straight. "But this is good news, right?"

"Is it?"

"Didn't you want the chance to talk to him alone?"

"I honestly don't know what I want."

She pulled the thousand-thread-count sheet higher under her arms. "Do you want me?"

This was it. This was his opportunity to tell her that he didn't. His opportunity to let her go. To keep her safe.

She didn't deserve to be lied to, but she also didn't deserve to keep living in fear. This was a woman who'd done everything in her power to protect herself. So why couldn't he make the decision to do whatever he had in his power and do the same?

"You know what? You don't need to answer that." She stood up, letting the sheet fall to the floor as she walked toward the door.

It was on the tip of his tongue to tell her exactly how much he wanted her. But maybe it was better this way. Why give her false hope?

He resisted the urge to rush after her, to stop her from reaching the suitcase she'd left downstairs. He'd already dealt with having her sneak out of his life once, and this time she wasn't sneaking.

Damn it.

He stared in anger at the black screen mounted to the wall.

Television and his father's stupid shows had shaped his life, but he couldn't allow it to shape Mia's. She deserved to live her dreams, even if it completely ruined his.

He walked to the hallway, but when he heard the zipper of her suitcase, followed by the sound of little plastic wheels rolling along the hardwood floor, he froze.

She was leaving. And he had to let her go. For her own safety and peace of mind. Outside, the engine of Cessy's Lexus shot to life. Garrett didn't know if it was the powerful engine or all the frustration he felt toward his father that was causing the roaring in his ears.

Mia might be gone, but it was still up to Garrett to keep his old man from making things worse.

Chapter Twelve

Mia wasn't one hundred percent sure that taking Cessy Walker's car had been the best idea. She couldn't even operate the CD player, let alone figure out how to turn off the squawking GPS, which was directing her away from Sugar Falls and toward the shopping mall in Boise.

Yet she'd had no other choice.

Hearing Garrett's deafening silence after she asked him if he wanted her had been worse than taking a golf club to the knee. But seeing the aching look in his hazel eyes had been a crippling blow to her heart.

She knew his answer. And she knew how to fix this. She hoped.

Mia ignored the blinking triangle on the screen and drove straight to the Cowgirl Up Café.

As much as she wasn't looking forward to the upcoming confrontation, she didn't want to cower and she didn't want to be protected.

She made a right turn onto Snowflake Boulevard and took a deep breath just as Barry Manilow belted out about being ready to take a chance again.

Her brain flashed back to that stupid text her friends had sent her when she'd been sitting in that bar in Boise.

Even though she'd had no intention of accepting their dare, that one spark of confidence had changed the entire course of her life.

And now some crooning love ballad stuck on Cessy Walker's car radio was daring her to put her love on the line.

Garrett better not be pissed that she was about to fight his battle for him. But seeing the way he'd looked at her back in the bedroom, she knew he'd go to battle for her if the situation was reversed.

Now all she could hope was that the stubborn man would come to his senses and follow after her.

The downtown city street was a bit more busy than usual and she'd had to drive around the block twice before she'd become impatient and created her own parking spot.

By the time she walked across Sugar Park, a spot opened up right in front of the restaurant.

Garrett's truck pulled in at an angle and Mia was relieved the cavalry had arrived. Or else he'd come to stop her.

"What are you doing here?" Garrett said after doing a double take of her walking toward him.

She stood up straighter, hoping her initial instinct had been right. "When I asked you if you wanted me, your eyes gave me your answer. I'm pretty familiar with the I'm-doing-this-for-your-own-good look. So I decided to rescue you before you made the mistake of attempting to rescue me."

At his confused expression, she went on. "I planned to catch your father before he left town."

"You were coming to see my father?" Garrett asked, walking toward her.

She tried not to think about the fact that they were having what should be a private conversation in a very public location. But that seemed to be a habit between the two of them.

"Yes. I figured you'd end up confronting him and decided that maybe I could talk to him beforehand and convince him to hear you out this time."

"I don't know if that would be enough, Mia. I've been over it several times in my head and I'm not sure anything could convince him that I don't want my life—our life—to be on TV."

"Is that why you were so miserable last night?"

"You moaned my name out loud several times. I hardly think I was miserable."

She blushed, hoping the two horses tethered out front were the only ones who'd heard him. "I meant is that why you were in such a quiet mood in the kitchen after dinner?"

"Partly. I was angry because I shouldn't even have to explain all of this to my dad in the first place. But I was also sad because I knew that anything I did would be temporary anyway because it's not like I can be with you permanently."

Her legs grew shaky and her throat threatened to close up. But she wouldn't cower anymore. Hell, she'd already driven Cessy's prized Lexus into town and parked it illegally in front of City Hall. Mia was invested at this point and wasn't going to back down.

"Why not?" Was there something she didn't know about preventing them from staying together? Had she misread the protective look in his eyes?

"Because of my father."

"He doesn't want you to be with me?"

"He probably doesn't care either way as long as ratings go up. And him going after those ratings is the problem."

She still didn't understand his line of reasoning. She knew he was strong and that he'd rebelled against his father plenty of times—albeit, his idea of a proper rebellion was up for discussion. So now what was different?

"Do you want to be with me, Garrett?"

"Of course I do. I've been half in love with you since that night we first met in Boise. The other half of me followed suit the minute you limped into my office."

Her heart did a little kick ball change at him finally saying it out loud. "Then what does Gerald McCormick have to do with whether or not we're together?"

"Mia, don't you see? If you marry me, you'll never be fully safe from the limelight. You worked so hard and sacrificed so much to get away from Nick, that all it would take would be one camera to start all that drama back up again."

"Maybe. You're right that I got away. And if I have to, I'll get out of it again. But not by escaping. If it comes to it, I'll face things head-on." He didn't look persuaded. "Listen, Garrett, yesterday, after I told you about my past, something powerful came over me. You know what that was? It was the realization that nobody but me was in control of my life. My mom, God bless her misguided heart, tried to shape me into the person she wanted me to be and then that whole thing with Nick crushed my spirits and I went into hiding. But from the second I met you and opened myself up, not only in that hotel room, but also in the doctor's office when we heard the heartbeat and then yesterday when we ended up at the lake house, I knew that I no longer wanted to stay in that world where I was scared, little Mia."

"But what about the baby? How do we keep it safe?"

"How does anyone keep their child safe? There're going to be accidents and there're going to be mistakes. We protect our child as much as we can and we love it unconditionally. But we also need to allow him or her to experience things. Last night, my mom reminded me of how much she'd sacrificed for me. But I never asked her to do any of that. In fact, it was an overwhelming responsibility she'd burdened me with at such a young age. Her happiness was always dependent upon how well I'd done at a rehearsal or performance. I would never put that kind of pressure on our child. So while I don't condone the whole television producer lifestyle, we can't keep our baby in a bubble forever."

He looked down the street toward the park in the center of town, where two young children were climbing on a slide. "I always hated having my childhood exposed to the whole world due to the life decisions of my father. You're right. Forcing our child to live some secret existence based upon our choices would be no different. But what if I can't keep you two out of the public eye?"

She stepped closer to him and wrapped her arms around his waist. "See those kids playing in the park without a care in the world? I want this baby to have the freedom to do whatever it wants. And I also want you and I to be able to have the freedom we need, too. So I figured I could go inside the café to talk to your dad and explain things to him…"

"Whoa. If anyone's going to explain things to my old man, it's going to be me. Lord knows I've tried to make him see things from my point of view for the past twenty years. But, like you said, it's not just about me anymore. My whole life I've been talking big, but my actions have been to say my piece and then take off to avoid any further conflict. It's the only way I knew how to take control of my world. But I don't want to just talk anymore. I need to stand my ground on this one and make sure he listens to what I have to say."

"If you tell me that part about falling in love with me again, I'll listen to *anything* you have to say."

He pulled her closer and when his mouth claimed hers, she felt his resolve and his promise that they were going to stand together on this and claim a life neither one of them had thought possible.

Garrett held Mia's hand tightly as they walked into the Cowgirl Up, the jingling horseshoe wind chime not slowing him down.

He saw his father sitting all alone at a turquoise up-holstered booth in the back corner of the restaurant. But before he could march over there, his friend greeted him.

"Figured this is where you'd end up," Cooper said from his seat at the counter beside Mia's two best friends. The man had an uncanny knack for knowing what people were going to do before they even did it. Hell, it seemed everyone in Sugar Falls, especially Mia, knew his mind. "I knew you would be by first thing this morning. We can't all keep running forever."

Garrett remembered when Cooper was recovering from a major career-ending surgery. He'd had nowhere to go, then found a home in Sugar Falls. It was a good reminder that some people came from more broken homes than he had. Gerald McCormick wasn't abusive or absent. He was just a pain.

"I think I've known that for a while now, but it's still nice to see we've got someone in our corner."

"You've got a lot of someones in your corner." Garrett looked at Kylie, who was speaking around a mouthful of cheesy hash browns. "Drew assumed the same thing and that you'd show up here. He had a group therapy session this morning, but he asked me to come and take notes."

"I'm just here for the fried chicken and waffles," Maxine said, then shoved something drenched in syrup into her mouth. "And for the fireworks."

"Thanks, guys," Mia said and squeezed Garrett's hand. Not that he needed the reassurance, but it felt good to have her by his side. To know what he was fighting for.

He took a deep breath and squared his shoulders as they approached his father's table. Lights, camera, action. It was showtime.

"Dad," he said. "We need to talk."

"GP." His father wiped his mouth on a paper napkin, then indicated the bench seat across from him. "I hoped you'd come find me once the cameras left. At least this time you didn't have to fly halfway across the globe to make your point."

Garrett allowed Mia to go first and slide in. He hoped she wouldn't think less of him if he lost his cool.

"That's the length I was willing to take if it meant keeping as far away from your show as possible."

"You and your new friends made that pretty clear yesterday, son."

"But I should have explained why. My whole life, it was easier to just avoid you and avoid the argument. But now I need to make you see that it's a lot more than just me trying to steer clear of the cameras." He looked at Mia. "Do you mind if I tell him?"

Garrett waited for her to nod her assent before telling his father about Nick Galveston and the potential danger Mia could face. Gerald McCormick listened and even asked about her knee and the possibility of having another surgery to fix the lingering damage. The man might be a showman and a fast-talking, famous television producer, but he was still a doctor first.

"You know, I'm just thinking out loud here, and I'd have to run this by the network, but maybe we can do a segment on this jackass Nick. Domestic violence can ruin a lot of people's lives and if we do a documentary on these kinds of lowlifes and expose them, we can help other women out there who may be victims."

"I think that would be a wonderful idea," Mia said. "But not for me. It's taken me a long time to move on with my life, and I wouldn't want to have to relive it all over again. Especially on television."

His father tilted his head to the side as if he understood what they were saying, but couldn't figure out why they would feel that way.

"Look, Dad, I know you love being on TV. It's your

life and I get that. But what you've never been able to understand is that it's not for me."

"Oh, son, I knew you *thought* it wasn't for you, but I figured you'd eventually shake off this whole nomadic lifestyle and see the opportunities that I'd worked so hard to provide for you. Growing up, you and I, well, we never really had anything in common. You were so studious, so damn formal. You saw the world in black-and-white and looked down your nose at me every time I couldn't make a marriage work."

"I wasn't trying to look down my nose at you." Garrett felt somewhat chastised. He'd never stopped to think that his father had also felt the strain of his failed relationships.

"I know you didn't try to, but you were such a serious little boy. A lot like your Grandpa McCormick, you know. He always thought I was too flighty. He used to tell me there was more to life than being a hippie surfer. I could've gone pro on the long boarding circuit but instead I became a surgeon and it still wasn't enough for him. So, I decided, why not show him that I could have a successful career and that I could have fun doing it? When you went to med school, I thought, 'Maybe GP and I have more in common than either of us realized. Maybe he's going to follow in his old man's footsteps.' I mean, after all, if you hated me so much, why would you have become a surgeon, too? I guess I just thought if I gave you enough time, you'd come around."

"I'm thirty-six years old, Dad, and I can assure you that I'm not going to come around. At least not as far as reality television goes. Please understand that I never hated you. I hated the constant shows and the paparazzi. And I really couldn't stand that one producer you had a few years back—the pushy dude who tried to sneak into the base hospital."

"Yeah, I'm sorry about that. I never authorized that one. I hope you know that I would never risk getting you in trouble or putting you—either of you—in danger."

Garrett released the breath he hadn't realized he'd been holding. "I hoped as much. I love you and I know that deep down you wanted what you thought was best for me. But just like you're not Grandpa McCormick, I'm not *you* and I can't live my life in front of the cameras. It makes me feel like a spectacle in a three-ring circus."

"I'm not going to apologize for my career." His dad took a sip of coffee. "I enjoy what I do and I enjoy how I live. But I am sorry if I ever made you feel like you couldn't be what you wanted because of me. When your grandpa tried to pigeonhole me into joining the family practice, I promised myself I would never do to my children what he was doing to me. When I gave you those cuff links, it was like a peace offering telling you that if you came back into my life, you could wear whatever the hell old-fashioned clothes you wanted to."

Garrett thought about the gift, what the gesture must've meant to his father, and how he'd almost left that black case on some hotel bar in Boise. But Mia had saved the cuff links—twice. And she'd saved him from himself.

"I appreciate that, Dad." Garrett put his arm around Mia. "We made the same promise for our child not too long ago."

She met his eyes and they shared a silent reminder of the fresh bond they'd recently forged.

"I hope you two will be able to keep that promise. I

wish I would have, back when you were younger," his dad said before rubbing his eyes. "I also hope that you'll give a vain old man a chance to know his grandchild."

"Of course we would." Mia smiled. "And when this baby grows up, if he or she wants to be on one of your shows, then we'll cross that bridge when we get to it."

His dad let out a small chuckle. "That's more than fair. Listen, son, I've always wanted the world for you. When you joined the navy, I was as proud as a father could be. I know that my world isn't what you wanted back then. And now I understand that it most likely never will be. I don't get it, but I guess my own father never really got my decisions, either. Maybe, though, if you change your mind, just consider the possibility of doing a guest appearance?"

"Nope."

"How about we broadcast the wedding? Maybe if this stalker dude knows Mia's married, it will help keep him off her back. If not, I'll call Neville Galveston my damn self and threaten to expose his crazy son to the world. I didn't spend years cultivating my media connections for nothing."

Garrett looked at Mia. "Actually, that's not necessarily a bad idea. But not filming. Just pictures. You can choose which wedding photos we release to the press."

"Slow down." Mia lifted her hand. "I hate to point out the obvious here, but you haven't even asked me to marry you yet. Who says I'd even be willing?"

He hadn't thought about the possibility that she might say no. Or might not want to get married. Of course she would be reluctant to enter into a serious relationship with someone after what she went through.

But he would give her the choice.

He looked at the crowd of diners and how everyone—especially their friends—had somehow moved their tables and chairs so they were all closer to the rear corner of the restaurant where he and Mia had confronted his father.

Hell, he'd spent the last half of his life trying to avoid being a spectacle and now he was on center stage. Well, if he was going to make a scene, then he'd make it a huge one. After all, he was Gerald McCormick's son. Showmanship was in his blood.

He scooted off the edge of the bench and dropped to his right knee. He picked up Mia's hand and spoke loud enough for the whole café to hear. "I love you, Mia Palinski. Not only can I not live without you, I wouldn't want to. I know that I'm not perfect and that a life with me might not be what you've dreamed about. But I promise that if you marry me, I will try my hardest to be perfectly right for you and to make some new dreams come true."

"That's not a proper proposal," his dad said, shaking his head. Seriously? Here Garrett was, exposing his heart for the first time—in a public forum, no less—and he was getting criticized? "Nope. There was hardly any flair, and to be honest, it was a little lacking in production value. A woman like Mia is an artist. She needs a grand gesture. Something significant that she'll remember for the rest of her life."

"Well, this is my first proposal." Garrett looked at his father in disbelief. "You've done what, six of them so far?"

"At least give her a ring."

"I don't have a ring," Garrett said, patting his pockets and looking around at the crowd behind him.

Freckles tried to pull a behemoth monstrosity of pink and purple stones clustered into the shape of a peace symbol from her finger. "Y'all can have this one. My third husband gave it to me, but we were just common-law married and he left me for some hippie gal living on a commune outside of Billings."

Mia was shaking her head at him, and he didn't know if she was turning him down altogether or just object-ing to the peace ring. She was sucking in her cheeks, as if she was trying to suppress a giggle, and her eye wasn't doing that nervous blinking thing so he hoped she wasn't saying no to him.

"Here, kiddo," his dad said, sliding a platinum band off his pinky. Except during filmed surgeries, he'd never seen his father without it. "This was the ring your mom gave me when we got married. She was a good woman, and I never was able to find another one to take her place."

The metal was warm in Garrett's hand, and even though he couldn't recall any memories of his mother or her love toward his father, it somehow felt perfect. He held it up between his thumb and forefinger. "Will you marry me, Mia?"

She smiled and the sparkle in her blue eyes lit up the restaurant. "I love you more than I could have ever thought possible. I didn't think I had any more dreams left inside me. But being with you has been exciting beyond my wildest imagination. I *will* marry you, GP, Garrett, Dr. McCormick or whatever your name is." He grinned as he placed the ring on her finger. "And just for the record, that was the best proposal I could've hoped for and, hopefully, the last one you'll ever make."

She moved across the seat, and when she threw her

arms around his neck as he knelt in front of her, he kissed her for all the world to see.

Then he lowered his head and kissed her abdomen, thinking of his child growing there. Several cheers pierced the air, and Maxine and Kylie were the first to rush over to Mia and offer their congratulations.

Garrett rose to his feet and was the recipient of numerous handshakes and backslaps. But behind him, he heard Freckles talking to his father.

"I'm sure glad you two were able to work everything out. But just remember that if you ever decide to start filming them again, I'll be on the horn with Mia's momma so fast, you'll have the clumsiest broad from Florida knocking into your set before you can even say 'roll tape.'"

"I'll take that under advisement. Now, Miss Freckles, have you ever considered being on TV? You've got a personality that our viewers would eat up."

"Sure, darlin', as long as it's not one of your plastic surgery shows. After all, you can't fix what ain't broke." Several shouts of laughter floated through the restaurant and Garrett couldn't help but join in.

"What about the other news vans that might find out you're here?" Cooper asked.

"Don't worry about those guys," Gerald McCormick said. "I'll put out a press release saying you guys ran off to Bali or something. Send them all on a wild-goose chase."

"Hey." Kylie wiped her mouth. "That was my idea!"

Garrett pulled Mia in close to his side and planted soft kisses along her jawline until he reached her ear.

"Actually, I was thinking about that babymoon we haven't gotten to yet," he whispered and felt her shiver in his arms. "I know we'll probably need to figure out where we're going to live together eventually, but I was thinking that since Cessy Walker's house is still available for the next couple of days…"

He raised his eyebrows and asked, "What do you think?"

The woman who was about to become his wife and the mother to his child smiled brighter than any star over the Hollywood Hills, but it wasn't for the cameras or for the crowds. It was only for him. "I think that you can't fix what ain't broke."

Epilogue

It was Thursday night and Mia sat with Maxine and Kylie at their usual spot in Patrelli's. Well, technically, Kylie had to sit in a chair outside their booth because the tall redhead was almost full term and her stomach wouldn't fit between the high-back seat and the table unless she was angled sideways.

Now that Mia was in her second trimester, her morning sickness was long gone and she was craving Italian food as if it was going out of style. In fact, as soon as the waitress showed up, she planned to order a double batch of garlic knots.

Her phone buzzed and Mia looked down at the screen, trying not to blush at the text message Garrett had just sent her.

"So, what should we throw first, Mia?" Maxine asked, thankfully interrupting the direction of her thoughts. "Your baby shower or your bachelorette party?"

"I vote for the baby shower first," Kylie said. "The bachelorette party needs to wait until after I have the twins. I barely remember Maxine's and I'm not going to miss another one."

"I doubt there will be time for a bachelorette party. Now that Garrett's practice is up and running, we wanted to get married before I became too big to waddle down the aisle," Mia said, then looked at her very pregnant friend. "Not that you waddle, Kylie."

"You can say it. I own my waddle. Man, I can't wait for these two little girls to finally get here. Even if it *does* mean I'll have my hands too full for any more wild and crazy nights."

Mia smiled, looking forward to it, too. "Anyway, we were just thinking of doing a small, quiet wedding at the courthouse."

Both of the ladies gasped and then craned their heads around the restaurant as though they hoped Mia hadn't been overheard.

"What are you two worried about?" she asked. "My mom's back in Florida and Garrett's dad started filming a new season in California. I doubt they can hear me."

"That's not who I'm worried about," Maxine said. "If I were you, I'd be really careful not to let Cessy Walker hear you talking about quiet weddings at the courthouse."

Kylie nodded. "That woman doesn't believe in small or quiet anything."

Mia let out a small chuckle. "I know. Garrett says she's still showing up at his office once a week and trying to play receptionist. Maybe I should take some pity on him and give her some wedding-planning duties to keep her out of his hair."

Both of her friends looked at her as if she'd just announced her plans to walk down the aisle naked. Although, after the text message Garrett sent her a few minutes ago, she knew her husband-to-be was anxious to get her naked as soon as she got home tonight.

But before she could think about what she and Garrett would be doing later on that night, Mrs. Patrelli made her way to their table carrying two waters and a glass of cabernet for Maxine. But Maxine held up her hand. "Actually, Mrs. Patrelli, I'll just have a ginger ale tonight."

"But you always have wine with..." The restaurant owner trailed off and glanced at Kylie's protruding belly and Mia's slight rounded bump then back at Maxine. Kylie let out a loud squeal and Mia clapped her hands when they realized the reason their best friend wasn't drinking.

"Well, I guess I'll just save this for after all you ladies have your babies." Mrs. Patrelli returned the stem glass to her tray, even though the woman looked as if she was about to drink it herself. "Let me assure you, when the three of you get to the toddler years, you're gonna need it."

The women laughed and Mia thought about how far they'd come since first meeting in college. They'd gone from cheerleaders, to single career women, to a trio of devoted friends. They'd embarked on many journeys together, but none of them had warmed her heart as much as this one. They'd all found love and, judging by the next stage of life awaiting them, there was so much more to come.

But those adventures were still a little ways off. For now, Mia was looking forward to tonight's gossip session, and then going home to cozy up to her husband-to-be.

* * * * *